fumble

X's and O's
Book Four

allie lasky

prologue

. . .

Mackenzie

I CAN'T SLEEP. It's not the alcohol buzzing in my veins. It's something else.

Adrenaline.

I make a cup of hot chocolate using some of my brother's super secret stash of marshmallows. They're not so secret. All of the guys know about them.

Tonight I went to a college party. I drank a beer and flirted with cute guys. I didn't go as far as touching them, not with my brother watching over me like a hawk.

Maybe coming here next year won't be so bad. As much as I would prefer to go to Princeton, Newton is in my blood. My parents met here. They fell in love here. We grew up coming to Newton football games and tennis matches.

At the same time, I want to forge my own path. I want to figure out what my own destiny is, not the life someone else has chosen for me.

And I have to admit, I'm a little worried what it will be like with my big brother watching over me all the time. Or will we never see each other? Both scenarios terrify me. Miles and I get along pretty well, but I don't need an overprotective shadow watching my every move. Especially not someone who's the size he is, as strong as he is, and who recently went through a code of conduct hearing for punching out some douchebag.

No, Miles and I will need some distance next year.

I take my hot chocolate and move to sit in the armchair by the fireplace. It looks cozy. Wes, another one of the defensive tackles, was planted in it earlier. He didn't go to the party with us. I don't think he gets out much at all. Miles acted like the world was ending when he opened his mouth to say two words.

As much as I wasn't interested in any of the college guys at the party, I can admit I was intrigued by the hulking football player who sat in the corner all night long with a mug of tea and a thick mystery novel. It wasn't the same book he was reading earlier at dinner. He disappeared into his room not long after we got home from the party.

There was a rhythmic thumping coming from Miles's room that told me exactly what my brother and his girlfriend were up to. Wes had mumbled something under his breath as he disappeared into his room. I was left alone on the couch to sleep—or not sleep, as the case may be.

Now, a light clicks on in the hall, and I hold my breath. Shit. Was I too loud in the kitchen? The last thing I want is to wake up the whole house when I'm only a temporary guest.

After a few moments, a door creaks open, and Wes pads into the hallway. He's wearing grey sweatpants and a black shirt that stretches tight across his broad frame. His feet are covered in dingy white socks.

"Did I wake you up?"

He jumps, whirling in my direction. His dark blond hair is sticking up every which way. It makes him look younger than his twenty-one years. He rubs blearily at his eyes, blinking in the harsh light of the hallway.

"Wes?"

He grunts.

"Did I wake you?"

He shakes his head. Limping his way into the kitchen, he wordlessly fills the kettle and sags against the kitchen counter, the fluorescent light illuminating his broad form.

"You okay?"

He grunts again.

The inside of his arm is bruised blue and yellow, no doubt leftover from that amazing sack he made on Boston College's quarterback. It had the entire stadium on their feet cheering. He took a hard tackle in the third quarter. He stayed down for an eternity before getting up and walking off the field under his own power. He was back in the fourth quarter like nothing even happened.

The kettle whistles. Wes turns off the stove and pours the water into his mug. He wraps his hand around the ceramic and sighs.

I take another sip of my lukewarm cocoa. The fire is dying down. Sparse embers still trying to stay alive keep it hovering just above death.

Wes pads into the living room. He towers above me, six foot five inches and two hundred and eighty-five pounds of pure muscle and strength.

"You're in my spot," he says, his voice a low, hoarse growl.

I jump. Hot chocolate sloshes over the side of my mug, and I curse. I lick the liquid off my hand—and freeze.

He's staring at my hand, his eyes wide. He swallows, and I'm momentarily mesmerized by the bob of his throat.

"I can move," I offer awkwardly.

He shakes his head. He collapses into the chair beside mine with a groan.

"What are you doing up? Couldn't sleep?"

He grunts again.

"I can't sleep," I admit. "Too excited."

Tomorrow, I'm going to a women's basketball game. It's

not my first; I've been coming to Newton games all my life. This is a pre-season match up, an intra-squad meet where the team plays against itself. Next year, it will be me out there. Next year, I'll be suiting up for Coach Carson and the silver, blue, and black.

But for now, I'm just an observer. Anonymous.

Wes sips his tea and doesn't speak. I don't think he speaks much in general. I kind of like that about him. When he does talk, his words carry meaning.

Through the years, he's been steady and silent, hovering in the shadows of my brother's life. He's usually reading, and one time, he recommended a book for me to read. It was *not* a good book, and I chewed him out the next time I saw him— and all he did was smile, and recommend another book to read.

I hope we can be friends next year, when I'm here at Newton full-time.

We sit in quiet silence, broken up only by the crackle of the dwindling fire. He's restful company. He doesn't push me to talk, doesn't try to make me into someone that I'm not. He simply lets me be.

It's nearly an hour later when he moves, heaving himself out of his chair. He holds out a hand for my empty mug, and I let him take it. His calloused fingertips brush mine, and I jump again.

He's staring at me, his mouth dropping open. Immediately, my focus is drawn to his full, plush lips. His tongue comes out to wet his lips, pink and glistening. I can't. stop. staring.

It must be the alcohol making my brain fuzzy. That has to be it. I drank my one beer over the course of an hour and a half. I don't normally drink. I'm not a teetotaler, but with my lack of experience, it doesn't take much to get me tipsy.

And right now, it feels like the whole world is tilting on its axis. Everything is shifting twelve degrees to the left.

Wes stares at me. I stare at him. We're trapped in a battle of wills. Neither of us want to be the first to look away. Neither of us *can* look away.

The fire crackles and pops, and we both startle. He gulps and takes a quick stutter step back.

"Goodnight," he says, his voice rich and thick. He clears his throat. "Have a good sleep."

Spoiler alert: I don't sleep a wink.

one

. . .

Wes

I'VE NEVER BEEN a man of many words. Even before everything happened, I was never particularly talkative. Since then, everything is different. Other people might have issues with it, but it doesn't bother me. I'm perfectly capable of getting my point across. I reserve my words for when they matter.

It's a Saturday night, two weeks into the new semester. The end of my senior year is fast approaching. My football career is officially over. I almost don't know what to do with myself. So I do the same thing I do every night, weeknight or weekend: sit in my chair in the living room with my book and a cup of tea, while typically a varying cast of my roommates plays video games or watches TV in the same room, and ignore the world.

It's rare that I have the house to myself. Miles is accompanying his girlfriend, Sam, to a frat party. Tucker is with his girlfriend, Mason, at a track team party. Barrett and his girlfriend, Diana, are visiting her parents this weekend in Amherst. Amir and Greg are out—they didn't tell me where they were going, and I didn't ask.

Rain pelts the flimsy windows, hovering between liquid

ice and sleet. There's no way I'm stepping foot outside in this downpour, even if I had someplace to go. I don't. I don't go to parties. I don't drink.

I go to class, I do my homework, and I read my books. Until recently, I had football practice and games cluttering up my schedule, but now that I've completed my final collegiate season of eligibility, there's a gaping hole in my day to day that was previously taken up by team and solo workouts, scrimmages, tape review, weight lifting sessions, and physical therapy. Now, I just have the occasional workout on my own or with my roommates, and weekly physical therapy. That will probably continue for the rest of my life. My body is fucked, my back disintegrating from a bad break a few years ago. I'm resigned to it. I kind of have to be; I'm a physical therapy major.

There's a knock on the door. Briefly I consider answering it. It's nearly midnight. Nothing good happens in Athlete's Village after midnight. I'm not expecting a pizza. There's no cars allowed in A.V. after dark. I'm not expecting anyone. None of my roommates are home.

I turn the page in my book.

There's another knock, followed by the doorbell. It rings twice in quick succession.

Sighing, I mark my place with a bookmark and heave myself to my feet. My lower back twinges in protest. Everything hurts these days. It's a different hurt than the everyday pain of playing football. It's the ache of disuse, the ache of inactivity.

More pounding on the door. Whoever this is, their intensity is really making me not want to deal with them. Grumbling to myself in the sanctity of my own head, I trudge to the entry and unlock the door. I pause two beats and then wrench it open.

Mackenzie Cavanaugh is standing on the doorstep, her fist raised as if to pound on the door some more. She looks like a drowned rat: her dark blonde hair hangs in limp strands nearly to her elbows, her wool coat is soaked a darker, angrier grey than usual, and her leggings and boots are soaked through. Makeup is creased in dark semi-circles beneath her eyes.

She's absolutely fucking gorgeous.

She blinks at me. "Hey, Wes."

I grunt.

"Is Miles here?"

"Out."

"Oh." Her face falls. "Um…" She hugs her arms around her chest.

I take a half-step back, and she flinches. She glances down at her feet.

Clearing my throat, I step aside and look expectantly at her. She tilts her head.

"I thought you said my brother wasn't here?"

"He's not."

"I don't want to impose."

I can't hide my snort of derision. She is never an imposition. She's absolutely fucking perfect. But I know there's nothing I can say to make her believe it. I know there's nothing I can do to show her how amazing she is and how much I truly value her friendship.

We are friends, right? Sometimes I don't even know.

Leaving the door wide open, I head back to my chair by the fireplace.

It takes a few seconds. Maybe half a minute. And then she lets herself in, locks the door behind her, and hangs up her coat. I pick up my book.

She perches tentatively on the edge of the couch. She's hugging her backpack to her chest, looking lost.

She must be freezing.

Heaving myself to my feet once more, silently I head down the hall to my room. I did laundry this afternoon; it's still in a pile on my bed. Fishing out a clean towel, I return to the living room, where she has released her death grip on her backpack. She still doesn't look very comfortable.

Mackenzie swallows. "What's that?"

I thrust the towel in her direction. She frowns.

Clear my throat. Offer her the towel again.

She takes it, her brow furrowed.

"I don't have anything to—my bag is soaked," she says.

It's my turn to frown.

"I'll borrow some of Miles's clothes."

My grunt of displeasure erupts out of me before I can control it. She blinks at me, confused.

So I return to my room and find the smallest pair of sweatpants I own—a pair I haven't worn in years—and a Newton Football shirt. It has my name and number on it.

She looks up at me, her lipstick-free lips pursed, as I approach with my clothes in my hand. Silently, I offer them in her direction. I would give my left nut to see her wrapped up in my clothes.

A shy, tentative smile spreads across her small mouth.

"Thanks, Wes," she says softly.

Jerking my head, I retake my seat and open my book.

She waits a few beats before she unwinds, heading to the bathroom down the hall.

The water turns on. Exhaling slowly, I shake out the jitters in my hands and return to my room. There's a spare pillow in my closet and an extra thick blanket I keep around for these occasions. We don't get many visitors on our couch these days. Four of my roommates are shacking up with girlfriends, and Greg is more likely to invite girls into his bed than have them sleep on our uncomfortable couch.

Mackenzie is more than Miles's sister. She has the roommate from hell and an incompetent RA. It's no wonder she would rather spend two or five nights a week on our lumpy sofa than share a room with a woman who violates her perfectly healthy boundaries and has sex with her boyfriend without regard for her roommate being present in the room.

The only real surprise is what she's doing here so late. Most of the time, she arrives closer to eight. We typically sit and read while a movie plays in the background. She's easy company. She might be my best friend. I certainly like her more than I do her brother these days.

Of course, she doesn't know that.

About ten minutes later, Mackenzie opens the bathroom door. Her dark blonde hair hangs in a wet sheet down her back. She's swallowed whole by my t-shirt. As much as I hate myself for it, my cock jerks to life at the sight of her wearing my name and number.

"Thanks," she says, clasping her hands in front of her, cracking each of her knuckles one by one.

I clear my throat. "Any time."

Her face softens at the sight of the pillow and blankets set out for her.

"You didn't have to—thank you."

Nodding, I close my book and struggle to my feet.

"Good night."

"Oh."

I blink at her in confusion. Why does she sound so disappointed? I'm leaving her alone to rest and relax. I can read in my room just as easily as in here.

"You don't have to go to bed yet. Not if you don't want to," she says. "I don't want to chase you out."

"You're not."

"You can keep reading."

Studying her for a minute, I make my decision. It doesn't take much deliberation. Set the book down on the end table. Grab my empty mug. Lumber into the kitchen. Busy myself with the familiar motions of preparing tea. On autopilot, I grab a second mug from the cabinet and prepare some of the pre-packaged hot chocolate we keep here just for her. I even steal some mini marshmallows from her brother's completely obvious "secret" stash.

Mackenzie is sitting on the couch with her legs covered by my blanket, a battered novel in her hand. She looks up as I walk into the room. A soft smile flitters over her face at the sight of two mugs in my hands.

"You're the best," she says, and my heart skips a beat.

Handing off her hot chocolate, I retake my seat and pick up my own book.

This is as comfortable and familiar as breathing. I don't think Mackenzie realizes how much I enjoy the time we spend together. We're both occupied with our own books, our own beverages, but I like the reassuring familiarity of her company. We don't need to talk. We simply co-exist.

two

. . .

Mackenzie

WESLEY ALEXANDER BRADFORD is one of the most interesting men I've ever met. He's the definition of stoic; nothing fazes him. In the four and a half years I've known him, he's probably said fifty words—total.

The only time I've ever seen him without a book in his hands is when he's on the football field. Sometimes, I even see him reading as he walks through campus. He reads through meals. He reads through movies. The only time he ever puts down his book is for Wheel of Fortune and Jeopardy, which he watches religiously every night.

He has always treated me with nothing but kindness and respect. I'm his teammate's sister. I've been hanging around in the periphery for the last few years. I'm sure he still sees me as the dorky brace face who didn't know how to brush her hair. Sometimes I still feel like that girl, sixteen and awkward in my own skin. Hell, I'm nineteen now and still awkward in my own skin. I don't know that it will ever go away.

We sit on the couch in comfortable silence. I drink my hot chocolate. He drinks his tea. We read our books. The fire crackles innocently in front of us. There are worse ways to spend a Saturday night.

This is not how I imagined college would be. I never thought I'd be getting ready for bed when my roommate would come in with her boyfriend, stone-cold sober, and start undressing. Less than ten seconds later, he's nailing her from behind over her desk. It's not like this happens once in the middle of the night. It's at least three or four times a week.

Yeah, I got out of there in a hurry.

I wish I could say it was an infrequent occurrence. I wish I could say my roommate wasn't a raging bitch with no regard for healthy boundaries. I don't care if she fucks her boyfriend in our room. I just don't want to be present when it happens.

As much as I enjoy my time with Wes, I don't want to camp out on his couch every night. I shouldn't have to vacate my room every night. At least next year I'll have my own room in a house in Athlete's Village, with a door that locks, instead of being stuck in a freshman dorm in the student athlete's wing.

But I won't have Miles here. I won't have Wes. All but two of the guys are graduating. Yeah, my teammates are great, they've welcomed me with open arms, but I've known these guys for three or four years, ever since they started at Newton and joined the team with Miles. The other players are as much my family as my brother is. They've stayed at my parents' house, and showed up to my swim meets and my sister's cheerleading competitions. They crashed my eighteenth birthday party. They let me visit them when I was a lonely high school kid hanging out with the cool college kids.

Nobody has ever said boo to me for crashing on their couch a few times a week. Greg has offered to beat up my roommate's boyfriend. Tucker threatened to report Claire to her team's coach. Amir graciously allows me to keep my toothbrush, some shampoo, and a box of tampons in the downstairs bathroom he shares with Wes.

I visit said bathroom to brush my teeth, take out my contacts, and get ready for bed. My clothes might be dry by now, but Wes's shirt smells like him, so I'm not in any hurry to change. I adjust my borrowed pillow at the far edge of the couch and spread the blanket over the cushions.

Wes looks at me seriously over the top of his book. He chews on his lip as he stares at me. After a moment, he clears his throat and gets to his feet. He takes his mug and picks mine up off the coffee table.

"Oh. I can…"

He shakes his head. It's not unkind. I get the feeling he likes doting on me. Deep down inside, he's a caretaker. He's itching for someone to take care of.

He's always been a quiet guy. He doesn't go out to parties. From what I've pieced together, he doesn't date. He doesn't have any friends outside of the football team or his roommates, his fellow linebackers. He is the very definition of antisocial.

He's also one of the kindest people I've ever met. He goes out of his way to make me feel comfortable on the all too frequent nights I spend on his couch. He makes me hot cocoa and brings me blankets. He doesn't press me to talk about how frustrated I am with my roommate situation. He simply lets me exist. And sometimes that's all I need. A space to be myself, a space to relax and decompress, without analyzing and talking the situation to death.

I don't know what I'm going to do next year when he's gone. I don't like to think about it. His graduation is looming over us and soon he will be moving on to bigger and better things. I know that's par for the course: people graduate from college, move away, find jobs, and forget all about their friends still in school. I've already lost contact with half of my high school friends. I don't expect the exceptionally non-verbose Wes will want to keep in touch. I'll be lucky if we stay friends on social media.

He's made this difficult year bearable. We've spent way too many Friday and Saturday nights in this room, reading and hanging out while the rest of his roommates filter in and out, partying or hooking up or playing video games. I relish my alone time. Living with someone that doesn't know how to respect that is exhausting. Having someone who understands me so well… I'm really going to miss him, and I don't know how to tell him that.

Wes pads into the room. He opens his mouth, like he's about to say something, before he sighs and shakes his head.

"Goodnight," I offer lamely, getting into my makeshift bed.

The corner of his mouth quirks up. "Night."

Laying back, I stare up at the ceiling and contemplate the mess that is my life.

I'm a freshman in college, a student athlete at a relatively decent university with a relatively decent basketball program —and I spend most of my weekends sleeping on my big brother's couch. I'm a nineteen-year-old virgin. I've never gone as far as second base with a guy, and it's unlikely that's about to change any time soon. The only friends I've made are my teammates, and even then, it's the perfunctory type of friendship that comes along with forced proximity. My roommate is a raging bitch even when she isn't getting laid while I'm in the room. I have almost nothing in common with the people in my classes.

So I escape into the welcome embrace of fiction. I don't read nearly as much as Wes does—I don't think there is anyone on the planet who reads as much as he does—but I know how to enjoy a good book or two a day. I usually have a few in my backpack and another half dozen downloaded onto my e-reader. I never want to be without a book, and I never know what I'll be in the mood for, so I like to have multiple options at my fingertips at all times.

Briefly, I debate turning on the light and reading some

more. My tired eyes drift over to the clock beneath the TV. It's close to three AM. The guys who are coming home tonight have already come home—which is none. Miles is probably staying with Sam. Tucker is most likely at Mason's. Barrett and Diana went to her parents' house for the weekend. Amir had a date with Jill—looks like that's going well. And Greg… Well, he's gorgeous and he's never exactly hurting for female company, so it's not unusual that he found somewhere else to sleep tonight.

Which leaves me alone in the house with Wes, who might be my favorite of the six guys to hang out with. He's kind and charming and doesn't treat me like Miles's little sister, but as a person in my own right. He sits with me as we read. He doesn't give me useless advice like talking to our incompetent RA or complaining to my coach. He gives me the space I need to breathe.

It doesn't hurt that he's not exactly hard on the eyes. He's tall and broad, the perfect build for a defensive tackle, with dark blond hair I want to run my fingers through and hazel eyes that brighten to green when he's in a good mood— which, frankly, isn't often. His smile is kind and reserved for only those he knows well.

Okay, so maybe I have a little bit of a crush. Who wouldn't? He's gorgeous, and he's actually a decent person, which is so rare to find these days. He's my friend. He might even be my best friend here. But that's all he can ever be.

three

. . .

Wes

I'M GOING to fail this class. It's week two, our third class meeting, and I'm already certain I'm going to fail. Again. For the third time.

But if I drop the class, I can't graduate on time. If I drop the class, my plans for grad school next year go up in smoke.

Who needs to learn how to speak in public anyways? I'm perfectly capable of speaking. I just don't want to.

The salt in the wound is that I'm a fifth year senior taking an entry level class full of freshmen. These children were in high school last year. I've spent the last four and a half years getting battered and bruised by full-grown men on the football field, all while being broadcast for a national audience's laughs and jeers. When I was their age, I'd already been through both of my parents' funerals and the sale of my childhood home along with most of my worldly possessions.

What makes it even worse is that the beautiful, perfect Mackenzie Cavanaugh is in this class. I don't know if she noticed me in the last two class meetings. I sit in the very last row, all the way on the end, and hide as low as possible in my seat—which isn't very much, considering I'm 6'5" and close to three hundred pounds. I'm too big to sit in the front of the classroom—the short people always complain—and I don't exactly want to be seen in this room right now.

My sister thinks I need this class. She thinks it will be good for me. Just because Sarah actually enjoys public speaking—she enjoys all talking, she never shuts up—she thinks, magically, I will enjoy it too. It doesn't work like that. She won't listen to me, though. At least we live on opposite coasts. I don't have to deal with her too often. Aside from our "still alive" texts every morning, we don't talk much. When she does call me, once every other week or so, she does most of the talking for me.

Mackenzie is sitting in the third row, four seats over from the aisle. Her dark blonde hair is pulled into a tight ponytail and she's wearing her glasses today, dark purple frames that turn her brown eyes a warm honey color. She hates wearing her glasses. I wonder why she's wearing them.

The professor is talking, but I can't focus on what she's saying. All of my attention is centered on my roommate's sister at the front of the room. My friend.

Halfway through class, Mackenzie knocks her notebook off her desk. She leans down to pick it up and her eyes meet mine from across the room. She blinks twice, and then she breaks into a bright smile.

I look down at my desk.

The rest of the hour ticks by impossibly slowly. Every few minutes, Mackenzie turns around and tries to catch my attention. I grit my teeth and avoid her eyes. No, no, no. It's bad enough that I'm stuck in this class with a bunch of freshmen babies. It's impossibly worse that she's going to see me stutter and suffer my way through five separate speeches over the next fifteen weeks.

The second that class is dismissed, I race out of there. I don't think I've ever run this fast in my entire life.

Of course, not for nothing, Mackenzie is a Division I athlete in the prime of her career. She's quick on my heels, dogging me out of the Communications wing, down the hall, and across the quad.

"Wes!"

Gritting my teeth, I put my head down and motor faster.

"Wes!"

There's an inconveniently placed bench that is right in my path. I try to hurdle it and instead find myself spilled ass over teakettle, staring up at the foggy January sky.

Mackenzie looms over me. She's frowning, concerned.

"You okay?"

With a grunt, I force myself to a sitting position. She offers me her hand. Briefly, I consider taking it.

No, I can't risk it. If I take her hand, I will never want to let her go.

"I didn't realize you were in that class," she says, crossing her arms over her chest. "Why didn't you say anything?"

Struggle to my feet. Pick up my backpack. Avoid her gaze.

"We can study together," she says, and involuntarily, I make a noise in the back of my throat. My mind immediately flashes to long nights in the library, sitting opposite each other at the too-small tables, our heads down over our respective books. We're both tall, too tall—our feet would touch under the table, our knees would knock together. She would look up at me with her heart in her eyes, and my whole world would fall apart.

So, no, I didn't say anything when I saw her in that classroom for the first time. I don't take her hand now. I have to pretend like my roommate's sister is invisible half the time, so I don't ruin the fragile detente we've managed and kiss her senseless.

"I'm heading to the ASC for lunch," she says, tightening the straps of her backpack. "Want to join me?"

Yes. No. Yes. No.

The longer I stand there, not saying anything, the more her face falls.

"Oh, okay. Maybe another time," she says. She sniffs and looks at a point over my left shoulder.

I turn on my heel and start in the direction of the Athletic Student Center, where the student athlete dining hall is housed, along with other resources like study rooms, workout equipment, and lounge areas. If I have to be on campus and I'm not in the library or in class, more than likely I'm at the ASC.

She scurries to follow me, matching me stride for stride. I slow down a bit so she doesn't have to jog to keep up with me.

I reach the doors first, so I open them for her. She gives me a smile that makes my heart skip a beat.

Swiping our ID cards, we each grab trays and make our way through the cafeteria lines. It's a cold, blustery January day. Filling a bowl with shepherd's pie and a plate with salad, we head towards the linebackers' usual table, all the way in the back of the dining hall. I like to sit on the end. Mackenzie typically sits across from me.

For the first time, I hesitate. Do I take out my book, like I do at literally every meal? Will she think I'm ignoring her? We've never gone to lunch, just the two of us.

The decision is made for me when Mackenzie reaches into her bag and pulls out her current novel. It's a different book than the one she was reading on Saturday night. This one has a soft purple cover with a shirtless man wielding a sword on the front.

So I pull out my own book and crack it open. I'm about halfway through. More than likely, I'll finish it before bedtime tonight.

We sit in easy silence, reading our books, eating our meals. I can't seem to concentrate. The words swim on the page in front of my eyes. She's sitting right. there. I can smell the green apple and pear blossom of her shampoo, the same one she keeps in our bathroom. She's wearing a light layer of makeup, just enough to make her eyelashes darker beneath her glasses frames. Her mouth is a soft pink color.

I can't. stop. staring.

She makes a noise and meets my eyes. Her eyebrows furrow. "What's up?"

I shake my head to clear my mind.

Mackenzie shrugs, unfazed, and takes another bite of her lunch before returning her attention to her book. I make a mental note of the title, so I can look it up when I go to the library later. Although maybe this is one I should reserve for my e-reader… I'm man enough to read a book with a shirtless man on the cover. I don't know that I want her to know I try to read every book she does.

We sit in quiet silence for the better part of half an hour. It's easy being with her, peaceful. The itch in my soul is soothed when I'm in her presence.

Our completely non-romantic lunch is interrupted by her brother and my teammate and roommate, Miles. He frowns at the sight of us sitting together.

"Hey." He tugs on her ponytail.

Mackenzie looks up from her book. She grins. "Hey, Mi. Where's Sam?"

"On her way. She needed to talk to her TA." He takes the seat beside her and digs into his lunch.

"I have practice in a few hours, but I was thinking of going to the bookstore after," she says. I look up at her. "Do you want to come with me?"

She isn't looking at me. The invitation isn't for me. My stomach turns. Of course, she doesn't want to spend time with me.

Miles considers. "Regular bookstore or student bookstore?"

"Either. Both. I just want that new book smell."

"Yeah, we can go around five," he finally decides. "I'll meet you at the gym after you're done with practice."

Her smile is aimed at her brother, but it still makes my heart stop. "Great!"

My skin starts to itch. I have to get out of here. I can't do this. I can't sit here and—

I push back my chair, and her honey brown eyes focus on me. "You're leaving?"

Briefly I incline my head. My bowl is empty. She still has half of her lunch to go.

"Library," I manage. There's a lump in my throat I can't clear.

Her face clears. "Have fun," she says warmly. "Pick out good books."

And so, I escape.

four

. . .

Mackenzie

I THOUGHT BEING a three-sport athlete was tough. It's nothing compared to being an athlete in one sport at a Division I program. I've never worked out this hard in my life. We're three-quarters of the way through the regular season, and I still feel like I can barely keep up.

Dareesa, one of my fellow freshmen, gives me a tired smile and chugs from her water bottle. She lives two doors down from me with Lauren, who's out for the rest of the year with a sprained knee sustained in the third game of the season. They're nice enough, I guess. We get along. But they have very clearly formed a friendship from playing together and living together and being in the same major and doing everything together, and I'm very clearly not part of their little circle. Somehow, they were lucky enough to get paired together, and I got… Claire.

My entire body aches. All I want to do is go home and crash into my bed. Tonight we have a nutrition seminar at the ASC. We have to go to at least two seminars every month, and although topics typically vary, the nutrition ones tend to be slightly more interesting than the ones on conditioning, study habits, sexual intimacy, or substance abuse. Or so Miles has told me.

He leaves me alone. He's not the overprotective rage monster hovering over my shoulder I was afraid he would be.

It helps that I have gone on literally one date since I stepped foot on campus, and that one didn't work out so well. My romantic life is as pitiful as my social life. Most Saturday afternoons, we have a game, plus another on Sunday mid-afternoon, so I can't go out and get wasted on the weekends, even if I were interested in drinking. The few frat parties I've gone to with Sam, Miles's girlfriend, have been… lackluster. Mason's track parties are far more interesting, but again, I can't get drunk the night before a game, and it's no fun to be the only sober wallflower at a party, so after the first few weeks of the school year, I backed off.

Most weekends, I hang out with Wes. We read or sometimes watch a movie and we just—exist in the same physical area.

There haven't been many guys to show an interest in me. I get it: I'm nearly six feet tall and in incredible shape, if I do say so myself, and I know better than to waste my time on a scrub who would rather smoke pot than crack open a book. I'm not pretending I'm some bombshell; I just know my worth. I don't want to lose my virginity to a loser. When it happens, if it happens, I want it to be with someone who cares for me, who treats me the way I deserve to be treated.

Not that I'm in any hurry. As much as I want to have sex, I don't want to be pressured into it. I do just fine on my own the nights my roommate doesn't interrupt me. (I've learned to schedule solo sessions for nights when she has golf tournaments out of town, or has clearly confirmed she's staying at her boyfriend's for the night, which is totally normal when living with a roommate, or so I've heard.)

It would be different if there were any guys I was interested in. For ten years, I was a three sport athlete, and now that I only have one sport to worry about, I need to focus on school. College is entirely voluntary: if I don't want to be here, I don't have to be, and they don't have to keep me on the team. I need to remain in competition shape and contribute every game, pull my weight in workouts, and keep my grades up. I have too much on my mind to worry about boys and getting laid and going drinking. There's nothing wrong with that lifestyle; it's just not for me.

Coach calls the end of practice, and Dareesa and I hit the locker rooms along with the rest of the team. We shower and change in record time. We're all in a hurry to get to the dining hall. Tonight's menu is a curry smorgasbord, featuring Japanese, Thai, Indian, and British curries.

We book it across campus to the Athletic Student Center, where the best dining hall is kept hidden from most of the students. There's a good group: me, Dareesa, and Lauren, the freshmen; Rebekah and Amber, the two sophomores; and Pia, Jacki, Miri, and Ericka, the juniors. The seniors are always welcome to join us, of course, and sometimes they do. Tonight, Jaz has a study group, Tara has a date with her girl-friend, and Natalya tweaked her ankle at practice, so she's not interested in running around with us. The rest of the team is doing their own thing, which I wholeheartedly support. I like to be on my own a lot, too.

But sometimes it's nice to have my girls around me. Even though we're not best friends, at the end of the day, we're all part of the same team, and we spend upwards of forty hours a week together. That forms a bond, whether we like it or not. Over the next three seasons, they'll become my family. I hope.

I've never been that girl that had a lot of close friends. Sure, I've had teammates. I've had friendly interactions with people in my classes. But that lifelong best friend, that person I can call at three o'clock in the morning to help me hide a dead body? Yeah, I've never had that. I've always been too busy; as soon as I was done with one sport, I started up another. I've never had free time. I've never relaxed. It's always been go, go, go. Now that my schedule is opening up a bit more, I almost don't know what to do with myself.

So I read. Books are a familiar friend. They don't demand anything of me. They're there whenever I need them. There are so many genres to choose from: I'm never bored.

Miles, Wes, and the rest of the guys are at their usual table at the back of the dining hall. My brother nods to me as I pass by. Wes looks up from his book and his eyes lock on mine.

My throat goes dry.

After an impossibly long moment, he clears his throat and returns his attention to his book.

Dareesa nudges me with her elbow. "You okay?"

I blink back to the task at hand—dinner. My stomach rumbles on cue. We both crack smiles.

"Yeah, I'm fine," I tell her. "Just hungry."

five

. . .

Mackenzie

AFTER A LAZY DINNER—TOPPED off with a super healthy sundae from the frozen yogurt machine—the girls and I troop into the conference room where tonight's seminar will be held. It's reservation only, with about a hundred chairs set out in orderly rows. I hope we don't have to break out into smaller groups and do team building exercises. I am so not in the mood to be peppy and cheerful tonight. That's not me. I can pretend with the best of them for a short while—a *very* short amount of time.

There are a few people that I recognize. A trio of guys from the swim team—they live on my floor, a few dorms down. Two girls from the tennis team—I worked out with them over summer. They're not my friends, more acquaintances than anything else. We both play for the same school and same athletic department, just on different teams. Some guys from the football team—freshmen, I think, or maybe sophomores. Not my brother's friends.

Wes files into the conference room, a book tucked under his arm. Our eyes meet from across the room, and I wave.

Pia, the junior power forward, raises her eyebrows. "You know him?"

"Yeah, that's Wes Bradford." I wave at him again.

"I know. How do you know him?"

"He's my friend," I say, because that's the easiest explanation. "He's on the football team and lives with my brother."

Wes nods at me before scanning the room. His eyes return to mine, his lips pressed together tightly.

He's uncomfortable. He doesn't want to be here. He likes to go straight home after dinner and watch Wheel of Fortune and Jeopardy. It doesn't matter that he can record the episodes and watch them later. He doesn't like when his routine is messed up. He is the very definition of a creature of habit. If I didn't know him so well, I'd think it was neurodivergence, but I know with him it's anxiety-driven.

"Scoot down," I tell Dareesa.

She looks from me to Wes with interest before she budges over. Slowly, the rest of the girls are cajoled into moving down a seat.

Wes makes a beeline for us. He stands in the aisle, and I smile broadly, projecting a confidence I don't actually feel.

"Do you want to sit with us?"

He clears his throat. His eyes are wide, panicked, as they meet mine.

He hates every single second of this.

"You don't have to," I add quickly. "No pressure."

Gingerly, he falls onto the chair beside me and slouches in the seat, like he's afraid he's going to be called upon to make a presentation here. His broad shoulders brush against mine, and he twitches away from the contact. As much as every fiber of my being wants to be offended, rationally I know better.

Wes doesn't like physical contact. The first time we met him, my mom tried to give him a huge hug, and my brother had to cut in and explain why his 6'5", 300 pound teammate was about to cry. He can tackle fully grown men on the football field, but he can't tolerate the kind touch of a hug or a pat on the back. It's been this way as long as Miles has known him.

"Did you have a good dinner?" I ask.

He nods, not looking at me. His attention is on the podium at the front of the room. The knuckles wrapped around his novel—a fantasy series I told him about a few weeks ago—are white with exertion.

"Do you have any plans for the week?"

Wes shakes his head, though his death grip on his book lessens ever so slightly.

"We have a game this Friday, if you want something to do," I say casually. His shoulders lift. "My parents are coming in, and Miles and Sam will be there. I think Tucker and Barrett might be going, too."

He makes a questioning noise.

"I'm not sure about Amir and Greg, but if the rest of the guys are there, they'll probably show up, too."

Somehow my socially inept brother found a group of football players equally as socially awkward as he is. I like the guys, they're like giant teddy bears, and I especially like that they all make a point to try to come to my games. Women's basketball doesn't have a very large cheering section as it is. I haven't made any friends outside of my brother's roommates and their girlfriends. I go to all of their home games and most of the regionally local away games. At least two or three of the guys have been at all of my home games this season. When one of the guys shows an interest, the others are usually quick to follow. They all go to Sam's softball games, Mason's track and field meets, Diana's soccer games, and Jill's field hockey games.

"Tip off is at one if you feel like coming."

Wes clears his throat and shifts in his seat. His eyes dart to mine and he dips his head before he focuses his attention on the front of the room. I think that's a yes. I think that means he's in.

Wes smells good, spicy and warm like cinnamon and cloves. The familiarity of his scent lulls me into relaxation. When he loans me blankets, they smell like him, too. It's so incredibly comforting, I don't know how I fall asleep on nights I'm not wrapped up in them.

My roommate Claire is gone for the next three nights on a golf trip. Finally I'll get a chance to relax in my own dorm without being bombarded by the sight of her fucking her boyfriend in every position possible. I'm not judging her for having sex—that's totally cool. What's not okay is her doing it in front of me, when I've told her multiple times it makes me uncomfortable that they start going at it while I'm in the room.

I might end up at the football house tonight anyways. After spending so much time there the last few months, it's almost like my second home. And none of the guys have ever said anything about all the hours I'm over there. Amir treats me like his kid sister. Greg pulls my pigtails and asks me to set him up with my teammates. Tucker and Barrett act like I'm just one of the guys. And Wes…

I don't even know. Sometimes I think we're almost friends. We're both introverted homebodies who would rather spend our Saturday nights reading than out at a frat party. Other times it's like he can barely stand to be in the same room as me. I like the guy. He's nice, he's interesting, and he treats me with respect. We have common interests. By all accounts, we should be friends. I'm not sure what's holding him back except his own insecurities.

In theory, I should be paying attention to this seminar. It sounded interesting on the promotional email. But all of my attention is focused on the man beside me, the enigma caught in a maelstrom of mystery and wrapped in a cloak of intrigue. He's worse than an onion. As soon as I think I've finally unraveled him, I find another translucent layer to discover, and so the search for the true person continues.

Wes is staring inscrutably at the speaker at the podium. He can't actually be interested in absorption of complex carbohydrates and how they relate to athletic performance. His grip on his book hasn't loosened—he doesn't want to be here. His jaw is clenched. I'm well aware I'm staring at him now. He isn't looking at me. It's not that he's avoiding looking at me, I don't think—it's that he's so thoroughly focused on the presentation. It's his coping mechanism: block everything out, focus on one thing, until all of the rest falls away.

Just once, I want to be the thing he focuses on. What I would give to be the center of his attention, to feel his warm green eyes pinned to me.

six

. . .

Wes

MY SISTER CALLS me on my walk back to the house. She's always had impeccable timing. I=It's like she has some creepy sixth sense that tells her how much I do *not* want to talk to her, so she decides to call, knowing I'll pick up. Ignoring her call isn't an option. I don't need her calling my coach again because she didn't hear from me for 48 hours and thought I was dead.

Yes, I'm aware I shouldn't cater to her anxiety. Truth be told, it's reassuring to hear from her, too. The loss of our parents at such a young age forced us closer, and even though we've lived on opposite sides of the country for the last four and a half years, we try to see each other in person at least once or twice a year. My tentative plan is to spend my spring break with her. Whether we're at her place in Seattle or in a different city, I don't care. I don't want to sit in the football house for a week all by myself with nothing to do but go stir crazy. I'm not about to fly down to Miami and pickle my liver on the beach. I just don't want to be alone.

I've been alone way too much.

"How was your day?" Sarah asks, her voice a familiar buzzing in the back of my head.

"Fine."

I can practically hear her roll her eyes. "Okay, fine. Tell me three things you did."

This routine is as natural to us as breathing. We always share three things that happened in our day.

"Finished my book."

"Wes."

Normally, that doesn't count as a "thing" in our list of things we've done, because I read so often. This time, though…

"It was a good book," I tell her. "I'll send you the title."

"Okay, so what else? You're not at home?"

"Athletic department seminar."

She makes a noise of commiseration. "Could be worse. Could be with your academic department."

I frown. "I like my department."

"Okay, okay. So what's your third thing?"

"New PB on deadlifts."

"Wow! Good job, Wes!"

My sister's audible pride makes me puff up my chest. I like that she cares about me and what I'm up to. She shows an interest. She doesn't need to baby me. She genuinely cares what I'm interested in, and even though she probably doesn't even know what muscle group a deadlift works, it makes me happy that she takes as much pride in my accomplishments as I do.

I clear my throat to change the subject. "Three things."

She sighs. "I got an A on my torts paper. I stress cleaned my bathroom at two o'clock in the morning and found a necklace I thought I'd lost. And… I have a date this Friday."

I stop in my tracks. "A date?"

"He's in my corporate strategy class," Sarah says, a bit haltingly. "We're going to dinner."

A low rumbling noise emanates from deep within my chest.

"I know, I know," she says quickly. "He's nothing like Derek."

I crack my knuckles. I'm two seconds away from booking a flight out there to interrogate the guy.

"You don't need to fly out here," she says, reading my mind. "It'll be fine."

"Won't."

"It will," she says firmly. "I've known him since we started law school. He's a decent dude. I'm not about to fall in love. I'm just trying to get laid."

"Sarah."

My sister laughs. "I'm allowed to have a sex life, Wesley."

She's allowed to do whatever the fuck she wants. But there's a line, and this is crossing it. I want to know absolutely nothing about my sister's bedroom activities.

She changes tacks. "When are you going to go out on a date?"

"I'm not."

"You don't have to do anything you don't want to do," she says gently. "But isn't it time you put yourself out there?"

"You know why I can't."

Sarah sighs. "That won't happen again."

"It will."

"I'm not going to die if you have sex with someone. The universe doesn't work that way."

I'm not about to take that bet.

"Mom and Dad were going to—"

"I don't want to talk about it."

"Wes…"

"I'm hanging up. I'm almost home."

"Okay, okay. Text me tomorrow," she orders, the same way she does every time we talk. "I love you."

"Love you, too," I mutter as I trudge up the stairs to the house. Greg, standing on the porch with some girl I don't recognize, looks at me with raised eyebrows.

Shoving my phone into my pocket, I maneuver past them into the house. I've missed both Wheel of Fortune and Jeopardy. Yeah, I've recorded them to watch later, but it's not the same as watching live. I don't have the energy to watch them right now.

Once I'm in my bed, protected by the heavy layers of my blankets, I let my mind drift to the other thing of note that happened today. I didn't feel like telling Sarah about it. She'd make a big deal out of nothing. I sat side by side with Mackenzie for an hour and a half and didn't melt down over it. We sat shoulder to shoulder and survived the most boring seminar in the history of the planet. She didn't flinch away from me. She didn't complain about sitting with me—she *invited* me to sit with her. In front of her friends! She didn't care about being seen associating with me.

Yeah, I might not want to talk to my sister about it, but it's a pretty fucking amazing accomplishment for today.

———

I'm not opposed to spending time with my roommates. I would just prefer it be at our house or in a group than in a situation where alcohol is provided, with as few extraneous people as possible. Crowds make me nervous. Being the focus of attention makes me crawl out of my skin. This isn't new; I've been like this since I was a kid.

The fact is, I'm a reclusive, anti-social freak who doesn't like people. That said, when the people in our lives have events, we show up... all of us, or as many as our schedules allow. So depending on the season, my week fills up with Sam's softball games, Mason's track and field meets, and Diana's soccer games... and, this year, Mackenzie's basketball games. She's Miles's sister. Of course we're going to go to her games. She's one of us.

The fact that I think she is the most gorgeous girl on

campus is entirely irrelevant. The fact that I read a book during all of the sporting events except for basketball doesn't mean anything. I don't even like basketball. It's easily my least favorite sport, right up there with cricket and lacrosse. The sound of shoes squeaking on the hardwood floors makes me cringe. It's worse than nails on a chalkboard for me.

And still, I go to every home women's basketball game. I've only missed two this season—one, I had an appointment with my academic advisor I couldn't rearrange, and the other I was battling a nasty stomach bug. Nobody wanted me around that day, and I don't blame them.

It's not even awkward spending time with her parents. Steve and Nancy have accepted all of the guys in the house unconditionally. We've gone over to their place in Charlestown for Sunday afternoon barbecues in nice weather and the big Cavanaugh holiday party every December. They invite us out to dinner after every football game and every basketball game.

I never take them up on it, or course. That's family time. I would never want to encroach upon that. It's all too precious and all too fleeting. Mackenzie and Miles don't realize how good they have it. I hope they never take it for granted. I don't. Not anymore.

The arena is sparsely populated. Women's basketball isn't the most popular on the best of days, and even less so when the game is in the middle of a Friday afternoon snowstorm. Most of the people in the crowd are friends or family of the athletes. The few students in the stands are the die hard fans, the ones who show up to every single game, rain or shine.

Mackenzie is warming up on the sidelines with her team-mates. She's wearing the regular navy blue Wolfpack jersey and shiny sweatpants. Her long blonde hair is tied back in a tight braid, framing her face. She has a tiny wolf's paw stick-on tattoo pasted on the back of her neck. Her hot pink sports bra plays peekaboo beneath the sleeves of her jersey.

My heart thumps loudly in my chest. I'm sure half the arena can hear it. She's totally in the zone, focused on her stretches. She doesn't know that any of us exist. Her sole focus is on preparing for her game.

I stumble.

Amir, standing below me on the stadium stairs, turns and gives me a look. I grunt, and he rolls his eyes, shuffling into our row. I take my seat beside him, Greg on my left, and automatically pull out my book.

I don't want to read. Opening my book would mean getting absorbed by the story, and I don't want to do anything that pulls my attention away from Mackenzie right now.

In the row ahead of us are Miles, his parents, and his youngest sister. Ashley is sixteen or seventeen, and a competitive cheerleader. She's… fine. I have no issues with her. A bit talkative. She's happy enough to talk at me without me needing to respond, so we're fine. I don't spend much time with her.

My eyes flicker down to the court again. Mackenzie is standing on the sidelines with her teammates and laughing. The dark-skinned woman beside her was sitting with her the night of the nutrition seminar a few days ago. I think she's a freshman, too. As they chat, she leans down and takes off her sweatpants, revealing her long, toned legs—and the shorts she's wearing.

This is sick. I'm disgusting, lusting over my friend's barely legal sister. Sure, I'm only three and a half years older, but I've done a lot of growing up in the last three and a half years. She turned nineteen six weeks ago. She lives half an hour from her childhood home and sees her parents at least once a week, if not more often. She doesn't know loss—she still has all four grandparents, and three great-grandparents. I wouldn't wish it on her. I don't want her to have to experience it.

But I have. And whether I want to admit it or not, it's changed me.

Amir is focused on the game. Greg is more interested in his bag of snacks. He pulls out a pile of turkey sandwiches and passes them down the row, to where Tucker and Mason are sitting with some of her track teammates.

As much as he would deny it, Greg is the caretaker of the group. He always carries the snacks. He initiates the snack duty roster. He nags us into cleaning the house in between visits from the professional cleaner. He makes sure to check in with each of us at least once a week. He cares.

I'm not used to having someone care about me. I'm not sure how I feel about it.

My eyes drift over towards Mackenzie again. They're huddled in a circle, listening to the coach give a peppy prep talk. She's not paying us any attention, her entire focus on the game ahead of her. I want her to look up, to notice us. To notice me. The elephant sitting on my chest roars.

I am so totally fucked.

seven

. . .

Mackenzie

AFTER THE GAME—A 76 to 65 win over Vermont—the girls and I shower and change before heading out to meet up with my family. They're all assembled in the lobby of the arena.

My dad opens his arms, and I run to him, letting him wrap me in a hug like I'm still a little girl.

Standing a few feet away are Wes, Amir, Greg, Tucker, and Mason. Wes meets my eyes over my dad's shoulder, and his mouth drops open. He shakes his head and presses his lips firmly together, looking away.

Inexplicably, I feel a sense of loss. It ricochets deep within my chest. Involuntarily, I make a noise and my dad holds me tighter.

"Great game, Mack," my mom says. "Ready for dinner?"

Taking a step back, I smooth down my sweatshirt. "Yeah. I'm starving."

Dad tugs on my braid. "I bet. Twelve baskets. You did great, Mack."

Their praise washes over me like a warm glow on a late summer's day. I indulge in it for a few seconds before reality brings me crashing back down to earth.

"Would you boys like to join us?" Mom asks the guys, the same way she does every week.

Tucker smiles broadly. "We'd love to, but I have a hot date tonight," he says, throwing his arm around Mason's shoulders. She beams up at him, utterly besotted. He presses a kiss to the top of her head and snuggles her closer.

"Maybe next time," Amir says, exchanging a glance with Greg.

Wes meets my eye again. He clears his throat loudly.

"Wes, honey?" Mom starts towards him and then retreats, as if suddenly remembering his issues with physical touch.

His grimace is awkward and pained. "Thank you," he says. "I wouldn't want to intrude."

The same thing he says every time they invite him.

"You're more than welcome," Dad insists.

Wes stands his ground. He shakes his head and takes a half step backwards.

"I'll catch you all back at the house," Miles says, addressing his roommates.

My nuclear family and Sam all pile into Mom's SUV, and she drives us across town to the Grotto, the chintzy family-owned Italian place that's been on the outskirts of the college since my parents were students here. After all of Miles's football games, we went to the pub; when it was time for them to start coming to my games, I put my foot down, and we picked a new place to go every week. I'm sure once Ashley starts here, she'll pick her own restaurant to go to every week.

Like usual, we have our pick of the tables in this place. Like usual, we order family style, a few shared entrees and plenty of salad and breadsticks. With four student athletes and two older, retired athletes who still work out a few times a week, there are plenty of hungry forks ready to dig in.

"Do you have anything fun planned for your weekend?" Dad asks.

I don't think he's going to like my answer.

"Homework, yoga, and maybe a trip to the library."

Alone. I'm *always* alone.

Mom sighs. "I wish…"

Dad glares at her. "Nancy."

"I know, I know." She sighs. "I just want what's best for you, Mack."

"Yeah, me too." I force a laugh.

It's not my fault I have basically no friends. It's not my fault I don't have a bustling social network like my sister or five years of teammates to rely on like my brother. I've never been particularly social, and that's not about to change just because I'm in college now. I like to work out, I like to read, and that's pretty much it. Hell, my Saturday nights sitting on the couch reading with Wes are as close as I get to a social life these days, and that's fine by me.

Wes.

I wish I could read him. I wish I knew what he was thinking. Most of the time, he communicates in grunts and shrugs, and yeah, he gets his point across, but it's not the same as sitting down and having a conversation. I want to know what makes him tick. I want to know what's going on behind those dark green eyes. I want to lick—

Wow, okay. That took a sharp turn into left field.

Wes is my friend, or as close to a friend as either of us have. That's all we are. That's all we can ever be. Even if he was the type of guy to date—and he's not, the guys have assured me countless times—Miles has made it clear that his friends and teammates are off limits. And Wes is his roommate. Yeah, that's definitely a boundary I can't cross, not in this lifetime.

Besides, five months from now, he'll be gone. Who knows where he'll go after graduation. I don't know what his plans are—we definitely aren't privy to that sort of information about each other. I have three more years of college ahead of me. I don't need to get bogged down by a guy who is about to eclipse me, leave me in the dust, and forget I ever existed while he's out living his best life.

"There's a party at Delta tonight," Sam offers, referring to her sorority's brother fraternity. "I can introduce you to some—"

I make a face. "No, thanks. I think I'm good on parties."

"Mack, honey…" Mom cuts off.

"It's fine. I'm fine," I tell her firmly.

It's not fine. I'm not fine.

But I don't know how to change this. I don't know how to make friends. My teammates are fine. We get along well enough. My classmates are fine. I haven't met anyone I want to spend time with outside of a study session. My roommate is a raging bitch.

I'm so fucking lonely, and at the same time, I've never been less alone. I'm constantly surrounded by people. I can't even crawl into my bed and hide away from the world, because now I share a room with the roommate from hell.

The only place I've been able to find solace lately is in my books. Fiction or nonfiction, sometimes all I want is to escape to a reality that's different from my own.

On the outside, my life is pretty damn great. I'm a Division I athlete at an amazing school with a great program. My teammates have welcomed me with open arms. My family is warm and supportive, there for me at every turn. They come to all of my home games, and even some of the away games. My brother invited me to dinner with him and his friends a few times a week.

But I haven't made any friends. Not real ones. I have acquaintances. I have people I know. I don't have any real friends.

I'm surrounded by people, but I've never felt so alone.

eight

· · ·

Wes

THERE'S a knock on the door at nine thirty-two. I run a hand through my hair and tug at the hem of my t-shirt. My heart thuds dully in the back of my ears.

Mackenzie is standing on our doorstep. There's no rain this time. She's wearing the same outfit she wore after her game, her hair now loose from the tight braid. Soft waves frame her face.

"Hey, Wes," she says, and my stomach lurches at the way my name sounds on her tongue. She looks up at me with her big brown eyes, and her teeth sink into her lower lip. "Is it cool if I hang out here for a bit? I'm not ready to go home yet."

Yes. YES. Come in and hang out with me. Stay forever.

Clearing my throat, I take a step back and usher her into the small foyer. She steps close to me as I close the door.

There are so many things I want to say to her. Good game, you played well. You look gorgeous tonight. I think I might be in love with you.

Instead, I retake my seat in my favorite armchair and pick up my book. It's a fluffy contemporary romance a few people in one of my online book clubs recommended, and so far, they weren't wrong. I haven't read many books set in New Zealand. It's a simple, happy story, and sometimes that's what I need. It doesn't always need to be a dark, gritty, intellectual mystery. Sometimes I want something to make me happy—and, yes, sometimes I want a little bit of sex in my books. It's not like I'm getting laid in real life any time soon. I'm well aware of my baggage, and I'm nowhere near ready to face it.

Even though I know I can never fall in love with someone in real life, sometimes I like to read about a nice couple falling for each other. It helps make that empty ache inside of me feel a little less hollow. Other times, it only serves to make me all too aware of how lonely I am.

"What'cha reading?" Mackenzie settles on the couch, her long legs folded on the cushions so she can fit sideways.

Lifting the book, I show her the cover.

"Oh, I've heard good things about that one. How do you like it?"

I consider.

"I liked the second book better than the third," she continues. "The first is still my favorite."

I clear my throat. "The first is the best. Third is okay."

She beams at me, and my stomach flips.

"I hear she's releasing the fourth book in May. I'm looking forward to it," she says, pulling out her own book.

Her face is pale, wan. I want to ask her what's wrong. How did dinner go? What has her so upset?

"Thanks for letting me hang out," she says, tucking a strand of hair behind her ear. She bites her lip and looks up at me. "I really needed it tonight."

"Any time."

I mean it. She's always welcome here. She can sleep on our couch every night if she wants. Hell, I'll give up my bed for the rest of eternity—she can sleep in my room, and I'll crash on the couch. Sure, it might break my back, but I'd gladly do it for her.

She cracks half a smile. "Thanks, Wes."

Her fingers run over the spine of her book. She doesn't open it. She looks at me, like she wants to say something. She opens her mouth. Closes it. Looks away.

Setting aside my book, I make my way to my feet.

"You're leaving?" She almost sounds... disappointed?

Grunting a noncommittal answer, I head towards the kitchen. With practiced movements I fill the kettle, turn it on, and retrieve two mugs from the cabinet. Hers, I fill with hot chocolate powder. To mine, I add a strawberry ginger tea bag.

"Did I chase you—?" Mackenzie stops in the doorway to the small galley kitchen. She swallows. "You're making tea?"

"Hot chocolate."

"You don't like hot chocolate," she says slowly.

No, but she does. It's her favorite thing to drink at night. Coffee keeps her up, even decaf, and it will be a cold day in hell before she willingly drinks a cup of tea. Warm milk upsets her stomach—she's not fully dairy-free, only mildly lactose intolerant, but milk is a no go for her.

That she knows I don't like hot chocolate, though... My heart thumps loudly, straining to break free from my chest cavity.

The kettle whistles, and I turn away from her, adding water to each of our mugs in turn. From the cabinet, I steal more of Miles's stash of mini marshmallows and add a generous handful to her mug.

She looks up at me, her face bright. "Thanks, Wes," she says softly.

Nodding in acknowledgement, I hand over her mug. Her fingertips brush mine as she takes the mug.

Sparks crackle along my spine. Goosebumps prickle on my skin.

Yeah, I'm so fucked. I've never wanted another person the way I want Mackenzie Anne Cavanaugh.

Mackenzie wraps both hands around her mug and leans against the doorframe. I'm trapped. I couldn't leave the kitchen even if I wanted to.

"What do you have planned for the weekend?"

I shrug.

"Tomorrow I'm going to try to play tennis," she says.

"I like tennis," I say, like an idiot.

Her eyes snap up to mine, wide and full of hope. "You do?"

I mean, I'm not good. I haven't played in years. When I was eight or nine, I did a two week summer camp where we played tennis all morning and swam all afternoon. I gave it up a few years later, when I started getting more invested in football.

"Do you…" She stops, chews the inside of her cheek.

I wait.

"Would you want to play tennis with me? Tomorrow?"

Yes. YES. Absolutely.

I clear my throat. "Three o'clock?"

Mackenzie beams at me, and I swear I lift three feet off the ground. "That sounds perfect."

I grin stupidly at her.

We're making plans. We're going to spend time together, outside the confines of this house or the dining hall or—

She's willingly spending time with me! She wants to hang out with me! The prettiest girl on campus isn't just giving me the time of day—she's choosing to spend her precious free time with me.

After a few moments, she turns and takes her hot chocolate back to the living room. By the time I've gathered my wits together, she's laying on the couch again, her book on her lap, staring at the waning fire.

She must be cold.

Dropping off my tea, I pad over to my room and grab the spare blanket, the one I always reserve for her. I drape it over the end of the couch.

She looks to me, her face bright. "Thanks, Wes."

She doesn't need to keep thanking me. It's only basic human decency.

Mackenzie spreads the blanket over her legs, pulling it up over her torso, so she's fully enveloped in my blanket. After an impossibly long moment, she sighs and opens her book.

I want to know what made her sigh. I want to know why she's so disinterested in her book. Is it just not an engrossing story? Or is there more going on?

But that's not for me to know. It's not my place.

Slowly, I crack open my own book. The words swim on the page. I can't seem to make sense of them.

I have no idea how long I stare at the same page. Some time later, I hear a soft sigh and the thud of a book dropping to the floor.

Mackenzie is fast asleep. Her fist clutches the blanket tightly to her chest. Her neck is bent at what has to be the most uncomfortable angle ever.

I shouldn't touch her. I should leave her alone. But I don't want her to wake up sore. This couch is already uncomfortable enough as it is, and she's way too tall for that to be a healthy sleeping position. I can't in good conscience leave her like this.

Gingerly, I slide my arm beneath her back. She stirs, and I hold my breath. She sighs, and I adjust her positioning to something that won't kill her neck. The blanket has slipped down, so I pull it up over her shoulders.

She looks so peaceful.

Before I can second guess myself, I lean down and press a soft kiss to her forehead. Just this once.

nine

. . .

Mackenzie

I WAKE up disoriented on the worst couch in the existence of man. My neck doesn't hurt as much as it usually does. My back doesn't feel like I slept on a thousand pokey springs. Actually... I feel pretty good.

It has to be a dream. There is no earthly way that Wes Bradford tucked me in last night and kissed me on the forehead.

Though my vision is surprisingly clear, my eyes are dry. It takes a few blinks to realize I fell asleep wearing my contacts. It definitely wasn't my intention to stay the night here. All I wanted was to hang out for a few hours...

It's early, about an hour earlier than I usually get up the morning after a game. I feel oddly refreshed. Well rested. Which is insane, because this couch is objectively terrible, and I've never had a decent night's sleep staying on it.

Taking care of my morning ablutions, I feel so much more human. I open the bathroom door and come face to face with Wes.

He's gorgeous.

His fine blond hair is sticking up every which direction. His sleepy hazel-green eyes go wide at the sight of me. One of his big, strong hands comes up to scratch at the stubble on his cheek.

"Good morning," I manage.

He grunts, dipping his head. He tugs at the hem of his shirt. It's a plain white cotton tee, faded and dingy. The fabric stretches over his strong shoulders and broad belly. My eyes continue their leisurely perusal of his body. The front of his grey sweatpants are tented by—oh good lord, is that—

Wes coughs.

My eyes snap up to his. He's staring at me, eyes wide, a little alarmed. His cheeks tint pink.

I start forward, and he takes a quick step back. A pang of hurt ricochets through me at how quickly he moved away. He tugs at his shirt again.

The only thing to do is pretend I don't notice the giant morning erection in the room.

Twisting my shoulders, I ease out of the bathroom and return to the couch. It doesn't take long to fold the blanket, pack my backpack, and slip on my shoes.

I'm putting on my coat by the time Wes is exiting the bathroom. He looks over in my direction and makes a confused noise.

"I'm going to head out," I say unnecessarily.

His forehead wrinkles.

"Need to change and take care of a few things." I bite my lip. Do I… can we… I take a deep breath and throw back my shoulders. "Are we still on for tennis this afternoon?"

His hazel-green eyes are glued to mine as he nods.

"Great. I'll meet you at the east court."

"Sounds good." His voice is deep and rumbly, even more so than usual.

Something deep inside me clenches.

"Thanks for letting me crash last night."

He snorts and shakes his head.

"What?"

He turns around, clearly intent on returning to his room.

"Come on. What was that about?"

He sighs.

"Wes."

He faces me again. His eyes seek mine out, anxious and needy.

"You are welcome here," he says slowly. "Always."

There's a lump in my throat I can't clear.

I want to call out for him. I want to reach for him.

But I know he won't answer the questions I want to ask. Even if I was able to verbalize them, there is no way he would entertain the thought.

No, I need to move on. This crush is only going to crush me.

Reluctantly, I start the trek across Athlete's Village to the student housing complex. The dorms are on the dividing line between the northwest corner of campus and the sprawling Athlete's Village complex. My room is nestled on the fifth floor of the "special" housing for student athletes. The only special thing about it is that all of the residents are involved in athletics. They try to pair up people from the same teams. Since there are three freshmen this year on the basketball team, I get to be the lucky odd one out. Even if I liked golf before I met Claire, and I didn't, her behavior has put me off the sport entirely.

My roommate is laying in her bed when I crack open the door to our room. She props herself up onto her elbows and then sighs.

"Oh. You're back."

"Not for long."

"Well, make it quick, then."

Rolling my eyes, I toss my backpack onto my neatly made bed and begin the near daily task of preparing my bag for a day (or two) away from home. A fresh change of clothes. Two novels. A handful of snacks. I change into an outfit more suited for yoga and pack something for tennis later.

The walk to the ASC is even more lonely than usual. This early in the morning, the campus is nearly empty. There are maybe fifteen people in the dining hall. Filling a plate, my eyes drift automatically to the table at the back of the room, where the linebackers usually gather. It's empty now.

It wouldn't feel right sitting there without my brother. Without Wes.

With a sigh, I head to a small table for two in the middle of the room. There's just enough room for me, my tray, and my book. Putting on my headphones, I crack open my novel and proceed to block out the world.

I lose track of how long I sit there. Maybe twenty minutes. Maybe two hours. I get about a third of the way through my book. I finish my breakfast. My morning coffee is stone cold and gross. Blinking my eyes a few times, I stretch my arms out and knock into a plastic tray.

"Oh, I'm sor—"

Turning, I spot Wes standing in front of me, his hands laden with a tray. He clears his throat.

"Hey."

He looks at the seat opposite me, then back to me.

"What?"

Wes starts forward and then stops. He swallows. Takes a deep breath.

"This seat taken?"

I don't get why everyone is so surprised when he talks. He's not an idiot—he's just not verbose. I've never had any difficulty understanding him.

My stomach flips. "It's all yours."

He nods curtly, and I move my dirty dishes out of the way so he can sit down. He has an egg white omelette and oatmeal on his tray, plus a little dish of berries. Raspberries and blueberries. No strawberries. I don't know if he's not a fan or if he knows I'm allergic. There are two steaming mugs of dark liquid, one with a tea bag bobbing on the surface.

Without a word, he sets one of the mugs in front of me. Coffee, with enough creamer to match the light tan shade of my skin in summer. Just the way I like it.

"Thank you," I tell him, wrapping my hand around the cup.

He grunts, cracking open his book.

Okay, then.

I wait a beat and then I open my book again.

A strange sense of calm washes over me. Even if all we're doing here is sitting here silently and reading our respective books, it's nice to have someone to share it with. I'm not alone.

Slowly he eats his breakfast, his attention diverted as his eyes zoom across the page and, occasionally, up to mine. I drink my coffee and let the stress roll off my shoulders.

We sit there for the better part of two hours. Maybe three. I don't want to leave. I don't want this to end.

Wes reaches the end of his book. Closing the novel, he sighs and runs his hand through his hair.

"How was it?" I nod toward the book.

He purses his lips, considering. "Not my favorite."

"I understand that. Would you recommend it?"

He chews on the inside of his cheek for a moment before he slowly shakes his head.

"I'll take it off my to-read list, then."

ten

· · ·

Mackenzie

AS MUCH AS I don't want to, eventually I have to get a move on. "I'll see you at three?"

He nods slowly.

"Great. See you then," I tell him, slinging my bag over my shoulder. I move to pick up my tray and suddenly he's in motion, grabbing my dirty dishes and his onto his tray, so all I have on mine is my empty coffee cup. After a moment, he plucks it off the tray and sets it onto his.

"I can get my own dishes," I remind him, and he snorts, shaking his head. "Wes, I'm not helpless."

"Didn't say you were." Turning on his heel, he strides away towards the tray return.

Lamely, I follow him with my empty tray. Dropping it off in the proper receptacle, I adjust my backpack and head for the lobby. My muscles are tense, and after spending so much time sitting in the uncomfortable dining hall chair, my back is starting to protest, too.

Upstairs, the studio is empty. Kicking off my shoes, I plug in my headphones and run through a guided yoga session. I miss my lazy Sunday mornings going to yoga with my mom and my sister. Even though I get to see them all the time, it's not the same as going out and doing activities with them, week in and week out.

I'm not homesick, not exactly. I see my family every week, and I talk to them at least three times in between. My brother and I have lunch or dinner maybe twice a week. My parents would drive me home any weekend I wanted.

But it's not the same. I'm half an hour in traffic away from home, and I'm basically in a whole other universe. I'm less than ten miles from the house I grew up in, and I might as well live across the country.

By the time I make it to the tennis courts on the periphery of campus, my muscles are warm and stretched. The courts are empty on this blustery late January afternoon. A little bit of cold weather can't scare me. Even though the indoor tennis courts are nice enough, there's nothing like being outside and feeling the fresh air whip my lungs in a punishing assault with every swing. I knew what I was doing when I gave up swimming and tennis to be a full-time basketball player at a Division I school. But I didn't know how much I would miss it.

At 2:59, the gate creaks open. Wes pokes his head through and then sighs with what looks like relief from a distance, entering the court fully. He's wearing a Newton Football windbreaker over a dark hoodie and athletic pants. In his hand is a tennis racquet—good, I forgot to ask if he had one. Depositing his backpack in the corner, he meets me in the middle of the court.

"Hey. You made it."

He inclines his head. His eyes scrub over me in a warm shower of intrigue. My whole body lights on fire. I'm not wearing anything special, just regular leggings and a long-sleeved shirt. My lightweight athletic sweatshirt covers the rest of me. It's a decidedly unsexy outfit. I didn't come here to be sexy. I came here to work out.

Perspiration dots his temples. His cheeks are a dull pink.

He's already warm—good. Wes swings his arms a few times, warming up the rest of his muscles. He has a lot of muscles. He's one of the strongest defensemen on the team. They're sure going to miss his presence on the field next year.

I'm going to miss him, too. He's made this year, my first year, bearable.

We've never hung out before. We've never purposefully spent time together. It's one thing for us to read silently in the same room on a Saturday night. It's an entirely different animal to decide to do an activity together.

My muscles are loose and limber from my earlier yoga session. Withdrawing a new tube of tennis balls from my bag, I bounce one over to him and shove the other two into my pocket. I forgot how much I missed the scent of brand new tennis balls.

With a brisk nod, he heads to the other side of the court. He hits the ball with his racquet a few times, testing the bounce. It's satisfyingly responsive.

When I'm ready, Wes serves the ball. His swing isn't bad. He's definitely going easy on me.

Not for long.

It doesn't take much effort for me to return the ball. We trade back and forth for three, four, five volleys. He's quick on his feet, quicker than I expected for someone of his size. My brother is the same height as him and within ten pounds of muscle, and he's not nearly as fast. Swinging hard, I manage to hit the ball just out of his reach. It bounces behind him and then lamely a few times onto the court.

Breathing hard, he strips off his windbreaker, leaving him in his hoodie and athletic pants. It's chilly, yes, but not nearly as cold as it was last week. Moving around, working hard, it's barely noticeable.

It's my turn to serve. Lofting the ball into the air, I plant my feet and swing. The ball sails over the net and lands neatly on the strings of his racquet. He returns the ball in my direction. It's an easy shot that I meet with little effort. We go back and forth, back and forth, until I manage a shot that lands just shy of his reach.

Wes bends down to pick up the ball. His eyes are bright as he stares at me from the across the court. Yeah, he's learned his lesson. He's not going to take it easy on me anymore.

We play for—an hour? Maybe longer? I'm easily beating him four to one, and he doesn't even seem to care. Not that he's apathetic—that's not it. More that his ego isn't bruised by a woman—a younger woman—beating him. Not just beating him. I'm wiping the court with him.

We take a water break. I expect him to tap out, but after a quick rest, he picks up his racquet again and takes his place in the back court. Okay, let's do this.

My muscles are pleasantly sore, the kind of bone-deep ache that comes with a good day's work. My blood hums in my veins. I'm flying high on a cloud of adrenaline. My body feels weightless. I can do anything.

Wes readies his stance. When I'm ready, I serve the ball, and away we go. Back and forth, back and forth. I lose myself in the familiar rhythm of it. Chasing around the court. Tracking the flight in mid-air. The satisfying thwack of the ball on my racquet. We play for at least another hour, until we're both breathing hard and exhausted. My sweatshirt is discarded, the simple long-sleeved shirt beneath it dripping. There's a sticky film coating my skin.

After three hours of exercise today, I'm done. My head hums with the tired satisfaction of a good workout. We meet in the middle of the court. I down half my water.

He's soaked with sweat. Without much ado, he strips off his sweatshirt. As he does, his baggy t-shirt rises up a few inches. A thick expanse of his hairy belly is exposed. There's a solid inch of his supportive undergear visible above the waistband of his athletic pants.

Wes goes pink. But instead of pulling down his shirt like I expect him to, like he usually does, he pulls it off entirely.

He's big, bigger than I expected. There is so much skin on display. I don't know how to look away. His chest is broad, covered in a healthy smattering of hair. It extends down over his thick belly, disappearing into the waistband of his shorts. His skin is pink. He's not just damp—he's soaked with sweat.

He's not looking at me. Digging into his backpack, he pulls out a small towel. After a quick rubdown, he tugs on a fresh shirt and a new hoodie. A stick of deodorant appears in his hand. He applies it liberally. His unique scent of cinnamon and cloves swirls around me.

I can't look away.

Wes clears his throat. I force my eyes up to his.

"Hungry?"

I force out a relieved breath. "Yeah, always."

He jerks his head towards the gate. Gathering the balls and my racquet into my bag, I let him lead me out of the court. Two of the other courts are in use—I can hear the tell-tale thwack of balls ricocheting off the court, and the grunts of the people running after them.

"I forgot how much I missed this," I tell Wes.

He turns to look at me, making an inquisitive noise.

"Tennis. Being out on the courts. I love basketball, don't get me wrong, but tennis was such a big part of my life for so long. It's still weird that I'm not juggling three sports at the same time. I like this free time thing, but I miss it."

He mumbles something I don't quite catch. I look expectantly at him.

"Play again," he says, shoving his hands into his pockets.

"You would want to play tennis again? With me?"

He nods.

It's like there's an elephant sitting on my chest. I can't quite get enough air into my lungs.

He wants to do this again!

Instead of heading towards campus like I expect, he turns in the direction of town.

"Where are you going?"

Of course, he doesn't answer me. He zips up his jacket against the wind whipping around us. His thick shoulders are braced.

"Wes?"

He turns to look at me. His mouth is set in a determined line. He's not grimacing, not quite. It's not like I'm holding him against his will—going to grab something to eat was his idea.

"You don't want to?"

I shake my head. "I do. I just want to know where we're going."

He lets out a heavy breath. Relief smooths his features.

"Avila's," he finally says.

The build-your-own burrito place. Okay, that works for me. I like burritos. I like spending time with him even more. I'd probably follow him to the ends of the earth if he asked. Even if he didn't ask, I'd still probably follow him like a lovesick puppy.

Adjusting my backpack over my shoulder, I smile at him and nod in the direction of town. "Okay, then. Let's go."

eleven

. . .

Wes

THE GUY behind the counter looks up and grins at me. "Hey, Bradford. The usual?"

I have no fucking clue who this guy is.

So I nod, and he starts making a burrito. I guess I'll eat it. I'm not that picky.

Mackenzie stares at me with wide eyes. She probably thinks I'm some big shot on campus now, some hotshot football player. It's so laughable, it couldn't be farther from the truth.

What the hell am I saying? Of course she knows it's not true. She's met me; she knows me better than almost anyone here.

The guy behind the counter dumps fillings into the tortilla. It's all stuff I like, so I don't complain.

Behind me, Mackenzie orders her own food. She doesn't deliberate over the menu: she's precise and deliberate, in this and everything else she does, and I like that about her.

"Just the burrito?" The cashier asks, bored. "Do you want a drink?"

I nod, and he hands over a cup.

"Anything else?"

Clearing my throat, I jerk my head towards Mackenzie. "Two?"

Nodding, I hand over my card. In return, he gives me the tray with two burritos and two drink cups.

Her mouth drops open when she sees me stuffing the receipt into my pocket. "Wes, did you—I can—"

I don't indulge her with a reply. Tray in hand, I start off towards the drink fountain. She has no other choice but to follow me if she wants her food.

"Wes, I'm perfectly capable of—"

Rolling my eyes, I fill a cup with raspberry lemonade—no ice, add a lemon wedge—and the other with iced tea—extra ice. She grabs two straws and a bunch of napkins. It's my turn to follow her to a secluded table at the back of the eating area.

She must not want everyone realizing that we're here together.

Setting the cup down in front of her, her eyes go wide as she lifts it to take a drink. She gives it an experimental shake.

"No ice?"

Deliberately, I shake my head.

"Wes…"

I take a sip of my iced tea and pretend like I have absolutely no clue what's going on.

"Thank you," she says quietly, settling into her seat. "You got it perfect."

I know I did.

She can't stand ice in her drinks unless it's a frozen slushy —blue only, never red. She prefers coffee over tea, and hot chocolate over coffee, but she has to start her day with caffeine or she gets headaches. She hates juice. Every Sunday she has a berry smoothie from the fresh pressed juice place in town—no strawberries, because she doesn't want to break out in hives. Even though she'll drink Gatorade during a game, she absolutely hates it—she wants water first and foremost.

Every once in a while, she'll drink soda—only from a bottle, not from the fountain machine.

But her secret weakness? Raspberry lemonade, with an extra lemon wedge squeezed in. The dining hall doesn't serve it, nor can it be found anywhere on campus, so she only gets to have it on special occasions, and as a freshman in the middle of her first season, she doesn't have much opportunity to go off campus.

"Thanks for lunch," she says, but her eyes belie her frustration. She doesn't like to be coddled.

She doesn't have a job. She relies on her parents for pocket money and on student loans to cover the fees her scholarship doesn't cover. She wasn't lucky enough to get a full ride; the school only pays for two thirds of her expenses, which is a lot better than zero percent.

Every month I get a reasonable distribution from my parents' estate, which is a fancy word for their life insurance payout and the interest from selling their house after they died. The vast majority is invested where I can't touch it until I turn thirty, and Sarah lets me have a small stipend so I don't have to take out loans for basic living expenses.

It's not much, but it's mine to do with as I like. I can buy what I want at the grocery store without having to clip coupons. If I want to buy some books, I have that flexibility. My expenses are minimal: food, some toiletries, maybe a video game every now and then. Most of my wardrobe is apparel the school has given me over the last five years. Most of my meals are on campus in the dining hall, though every Sunday I treat myself to breakfast at the diner.

I'm a simple man. All I need are a steady supply of books, a well-stocked supply of snacks, and a never-ending supply of tea.

So, yes, I'm going to treat the broke college student I have a monstrous crush on to lunch. I might even suggest getting dessert. I'd do pretty much anything for her short of proposing marriage. I know neither of us is ready for that, and I don't want the potential of what could be soured by inevitability.

"Next time," I manage, the words getting caught in my chest. "You can get it next time."

If she still wants to be seen with me in public after this…

The burrito is better than I expected for having absolutely no input into what went into it. Whoever that guy was, whatever he thinks my usual is, I'm going to have to order it again.

Mackenzie is quiet, concentrating on her food. It's weird not having our books separating us. I kind of like it. I like sitting with her, I like spending time with her, and it's even better without each of us being absorbed in our little worlds.

I wonder what she's thinking. I want to know what is causing that little frown line in her forehead. I want to know what turned her happy mood into contemplative. I want to know—

But I can't ask. I don't know how. And even if I did, I don't know that she would answer.

She clears her throat and I lift my eyes to meet hers. "Have you started on your speech yet?"

Started? Yes. It's written. Am I prepared to stand in front of twenty-five people—to stand in front of *her*—and talk for two and a half minutes?

No. Not at all.

"We can get together later and work on them," she suggests. "I have all these ideas, but when I sit down in front of the computer to actually write them, they all disappear. I'm stuck. I have nothing."

I know how that goes. I'm a relatively intelligent person, I make good grades and can apply my knowledge to real life situations, but the second my eyes fall on her, my brain turns to mush.

So I nod, and her whole face lights up.

"Great. Tomorrow? We can meet at the library."

Oh. Oh shit. The two of us, alone in the library? It's like my every fantasy and every nightmare come to life. We'll be sitting at a too-small table for two. Our heads bent together over our respective notes. Our feet would brush against each other. I would…

Mackenzie frowns. "Or… not. We can meet somewhere else. I just thought… it's quiet."

I clear my throat. "Library's fine."

Her smile is tremulous. "Great," she says, though the positivity injected into her voice doesn't match the crestfallen look on her face. "That's perfect."

"Eleven?"

I can still go to the diner for breakfast, my usual Sunday morning ritual. It's not too early or too late. After we work on the speeches, I can conceivably suggest we grab lunch, thereby casually extending our time together without looking like I'm desperate to spend every waking moment with her.

Yeah, this can work.

She nods. She ducks her head to take another bite of her burrito, her hair slipping into her face. I want to brush it away, to tuck it behind her ear like they do in all those cheesy 90's movies.

But life isn't a movie.

Also, I'm pretty fucking sure she's hiding something from me. She's not happy. Whatever she thinks she read on my face told her more than my words ever could.

I love you. I love you. I love you.

It appears our telepathic mind link isn't working, because she isn't getting the memo.

twelve

. . .

Mackenzie

I HAVE no idea what happened yesterday afternoon. One minute we were fine, eating our burritos and having a good (albeit quiet) time, and the next, everything is awful. He couldn't flee away from me fast enough.

So I made up some excuse about needing to run some errands while I was in town, and he didn't offer to come with me. We went our separate ways. I walked through town for the better part of an hour before I made the walk back to my dorm. Claire was out—for once—so I crawled into bed and stared at the wall for a little while, trying to figure out where it all went wrong.

We were having such a good time. It was going so well. And then it all fell to pieces, and I have no earthly idea how or why.

And, because I clearly love to torture myself, we're going to spend more time together today.

Public speaking doesn't bother me. I've played on enough sports teams with enough people, I can put on a front and be personable for a few minutes. I just think about how my little sister would act and mimic her, and everything is fine.

This is a simple introductory speech, two and a half

minutes, no research required. All I have to do is tell a group of people everything pertinent about me and my life. So why is my mind blank?

Everything I come up with sounds so lame and pathetic. I'm a nineteen year old freshman, a middle child, and mediocre in pretty much everything I do. Sure, I got a scholarship to a Division I school... but I wasn't good enough for a full ride like my brother, and I've made literally zero friends in the six months I've been on campus. I like to workout and I like to read, which isn't exactly a social hobby. I've never had a boyfriend—there has never been enough time, and there hasn't been anyone who has caught my interest enough for me to try anything more than a few fumbling kisses at tennis camp a year and a half ago.

And now I have to stand up in front of Wes, my professor, and twenty something other people and tell them what a pathetic loser I am. As if it isn't bad enough I crash on my big brother's sofa a few nights a week because I can't bear to sleep in my dorm room bed. Now everyone will know I have no social life, no hobbies, and basically nothing going for me.

At least Claire didn't come home last night. I don't think I'd survive having to live through her fucking her boyfriend while I'm in the room again right now.

It's rainy, a steady drizzle. My hair and clothes are covered in a fine layer of mist from the quick walk from my dorm to the ASC. I do a quick workout—a stretching session, half an hour on the spin bike, some core work, and a leisurely three mile jog—before showering and heading downstairs to the dining hall. Sunday brunch is always sparsely attended, and today is no different. The athletes who are there seem to be hungover or exhausted—if they're not preparing for a game today.

There's a group of wrestlers at the football players' usual table. I guess they didn't get the memo that the table is reserved. Amir is having breakfast with Jill and her field hockey friends—he is so totally smitten, it's adorable. Greg is sitting at a table for two with his headphones on and a scowl across his face—yeah, I'm not about to interrupt him.

Settling into a table by the window, I tuck into my breakfast. It's not nearly as fun eating by myself as it was sharing breakfast with Wes yesterday. I wonder if I can subtly ask him to do it again. If I come right out and ask him, he'd probably say no. It's not trickery I'm after, more... persuasion.

He's already at the library by the time I get there. I'm not late; if anything, I'm five minutes early. I feel bad for making him wait. At the same time, it's a little gratifying that not only did he show up early, he seems to want to be here. Which is a change from how upset he looked yesterday at the idea of meeting up today.

Still... he's here. He picked a small table for four in the middle of the room, so we're surrounded by other tables—should anyone decide they want to study at eleven o'clock on a Sunday morning, which is not likely.

He looks up as I approach. A look I can't identify crosses over his face before he blanks it away. He stands when I get close, nodding towards the empty chair across from him.

"Hey. Have you been waiting long?"

He shakes his head.

"Cool. Sorry I'm late."

Wes frowns. "Not late."

I don't fight him on it. Taking a seat across from him, I pull out my communications textbook and a spiral notebook. Although I've jotted down a rough outline of how this speech is supposed to go, I don't know how to flesh it out. I don't like to talk about myself—I have nothing to talk about.

"How far are you?"

He sighs, running a hand through his sandy blond hair. He opens his laptop and opens a file before turning the computer around.

My life is in flux, his speech begins. *After seventeen years involved in the sport, as of six weeks ago, I am officially retired from football. Although I've applied to a half dozen grad schools, I don't know where or if I'll be accepted. I don't know what will happen three months from now, much less three years or a few decades from now.*

My eyes meet his. He's chewing the inside of his cheek, his face pink.

"Wow, Wes. That's really good."

He grunts something and moves to take the computer back. I scroll down on the document.

I grew up in suburbia outside of Detroit. My older sister is in law school. Our parents are dead. I don't like to talk about myself. The end.

Well, it could use some work. A little massage of phrasing, a little fleshing out the structural bones...

But it's not bad.

"It's more than I have," I admit, and he raises his eyebrows. "I know. I realize the speech is in two days. Usually I'm a lot more prepared. This one is just... hard. I don't like to talk about myself, either."

He leans forward, almost like he's about to divulge a secret. He opens his mouth.

"I don't know who I am. The only way I know how to describe myself is by sports, and that seems like a copout. I'm more than a basketball player. I'm more than an athlete. But I don't know how I want to identify myself."

Wes frowns.

"Who am I? How do I even start to—" I sigh. "I don't know. This is harder than I expected."

Without a word, he takes back his laptop. He clicks some keys before his fingers start flying in a furious flurry.

My heart rate ticks up to dangerous levels. I'm glad whatever I said gave him some sort of inspiration, but I would prefer he could help me instead of writing his own speech.

He chews the inside of his cheek. His typing slows. After a

minute, he clears his throat and turns the laptop around again. His massive shoulders straighten.

Mackenzie Anne Cavanaugh: The Chameleon.

I didn't even realize he knew my middle name.

I am invisible, he wrote. *Sometimes I like that. Sometimes I hate it.*

My stomach flips. How did he…

I am a classic middle child, always trying to please others and forgetting about my own thoughts, fears, and worries. My wants are the least important ones in the equation. I've spent so many years trying to make everyone around me happy, I've forgotten how to put myself first. Even though I'm living away from home, I spend a lot of time with my family. My parents are supportive and attend all of my games, my sister is my biggest cheerleader, and my brother is okay, I guess.

I stifle a snort and raise my eyes to meet his. Wes scratches at the dark blond stubble covering his cheek.

"Miles is more than okay," I tell him, and he hides a smile in his hand.

His eyes are bright, happy. He's pleased.

My favorite hobbies are sports and reading, which don't always go together, but they make me happy. I like to curl up with a good book and a cup of hot chocolate and listen to the rain fall. I'll watch pretty much any sport on TV except horse racing or NASCAR—or rather, I'll watch them and complain the whole time.

I laugh out loud. Yeah, he's got me pegged.

Wes nods towards the computer. "It works?"

"It's accurate," I admit, and he frowns at my hesitation. "I can't use it."

"You can."

"You wrote it. Not me. It's your speech about me."

He shakes his head. "Doesn't work that way."

"It's cheating. You're the one who wrote it."

"I helped," he insists. "You have to stand up there. That's all you."

"Wes…"

"Change it. Put it in your own words. I'm not offended."

"It's perfect," I tell him, because it is. In a few short minutes, he's described me more accurately than anyone else I know possibly could. Definitely far better than I ever could.

His cheeks tint pink and he looks away.

"You're a great writer."

He mumbles something I can't quite make out.

I want to return the favor, to help him as much as he's helped me. I don't know that I know him nearly as well. He keeps everything so close.

"You like to read," I tell him, and he laughs, conceding the point. "If there are words, you'll read them, but your favorite genre is mysteries. You like to keep your brain engaged and puzzling through the clues. You don't like murder, gore, or gratuitous violence."

Eyes bright, he nods, typing something on his computer.

"You crave order. You don't like when your routines are changed, and especially so when it's because of something outside of your control. If you have enough time to prepare, you can adapt to pretty much any situation. You hate surprises."

His guard comes up. He draws his bottom lip between his teeth, his eyes focused on a point just over my left shoulder.

"You need alone time to reset and recharge. You like living in the house with all the guys, but you like when they go out and leave you alone, too." His eyes dart back to mine, surprised. "I'm sorry I keep interrupting your nights by yourself."

"You're not." He's gravely serious. He leans forward, his eyes intent on mine. "Come over anytime."

"I know. And I probably will," I admit, and Wes cracks a smile. "It doesn't change the fact that you need that time to yourself."

He opens his mouth, stops, closes it again. He chews the inside of his cheek.

After what feels like the longest minute in the history of forever, he takes a deep breath.

"I like when you're there," he finally says. "I like spending time with you."

My heart starts pounding a thousand beats a minute.

"Wes..."

He clears his throat. "We should work."

"I like spending time with you, too," I tell him.

He grimaces. He doesn't believe me. He thinks I'm just repeating his own words back at him, plying him with platitudes, instead of opening up to him.

"I do. I had a lot of fun playing tennis. I like reading with you. I like when we have breakfast or lunch together. You're..." I sigh. I have to admit it. "You're my best friend here."

His eyes snap up to mine. "Friends?"

Would I kill to be more? Yes. Absolutely, yes.

But it's been made clear to me time and time again that Wes doesn't date, doesn't sleep around, doesn't get involved romantically with anyone. And Miles has made it very clear that his teammates are off limits for me to be involved with.

So friends it is, and friends it will be. It's better than nothing. At least this way, I still get to have him in my life.

I force a laugh. "Do you think I'd spend every Saturday night on your couch if I didn't like hanging out with you?"

He mumbles something, scratching at his stubbly cheek.

"Yeah, we're friends," I tell him. "Unless... you don't want to be?"

"I do," he says, his gravelly voice full of conviction. "Friends."

thirteen

. . .

Wes

IT WAS TUCKER'S IDEA. I have to blame him. It's because of his boneheaded idea that I'm even at this stupid event. How is a self-defense class going to help me? I'm 6'5" and nearly three hundred pounds. I don't need to defend myself—people look at me and run away in fright. They think I'm far more scary than I actually am.

Sure, I've gotten into some fights over the years. I'm only human. By and large, I'm not the type of person who raises a hand in anger.

Yeah, I can throw a punch. I'm not afraid to stand up for people who need it. I've flown to the other side of the country to beat up the guy who broke my big sister's heart.

Physical violence doesn't solve problems: it only creates more of them. It's the last resort, the final choice. By physical size and strength, I have most guys outmatched. It's not fair to them. Their ineffectual little fists are no match for me. I've spent the last five years tackling fully grown men on the football field. Even though I'm now "retired," I haven't lost my ability to bench press two hundred fifty pounds.

I'm the type of guy people see following them on the street and run away from. I'm not offended—I know that purely by looking at me, I appear like I could fuck some shit up. They don't know me. They don't know that I would rather read a book than do pretty much anything else, ever, and I'm the biggest baby that ever was. Unless you're a bookstore or maybe a library, I'm of no threat to you.

At the same time, I recognize that not everyone is afforded that luxury. Most of my friends—well, really, all of the people I associate with—are athletes, but that doesn't mean they're my same size and shape. I'm more than a foot taller than Sam, and outweigh lithe track star Mason by more than a hundred and fifty pounds. Diana has strong legs—she has to, she's a soccer player—and almost no upper body strength. I don't really know Jill well enough yet to know how she could improve her physical strength.

It's only natural that this turned into a massive double-triple-quadruple date. Half of our group activities these days do. The couples all pair off: Miles with Sam, Tucker and Mason, Barrett and Diana, and now Amir and Jill. Even Greg has found a "date" for this evening, some girl from the water polo team.

As usual, that leaves me as the odd man out. I don't know any girls I could invite to be my buddy at a self defense class, and even if I did, I wouldn't know how to initiate that conversation.

I stand awkwardly with the rest of the group. Everyone else in the room is partnered off. I'm going to have to get paired up with a stranger—or worse, work out by myself.

A chill runs up my spine and the hair on the back of my neck stands on end. I turn to see Mackenzie approaching, followed by two of her fellow basketball teammates.

Like usual, she is absolutely fucking gorgeous.

She's wearing skintight fire engine red leggings and a matching sports bra that is doing dangerous things to my heart rate. Her plain black t-shirt fully covers her skin while leaving almost nothing to the imagination. And I have a very,

very vivid imagination where Mackenzie Cavanaugh is concerned.

Miles reaches out and shoves her gently. "Hey, Mack."

She grins at her brother, refusing to be swayed. "Thanks for inviting me. This sounds like fun."

Barrett frowns, counting out the group. "Do you have a partner?"

"No. Do I need one?"

"You can pair up with Wes," Amir jumps in, the traitor. "He doesn't have a buddy, either."

They planned this. They orchestrated this. I glare lasers at them. Tucker has the gall to smirk at me.

Mackenzie gives me a brilliant smile. My blood pressure soars. "Sounds good."

There's a lump in my throat the size of Michigan. There's an anvil sitting on my chest. I can't breathe, can't think.

We're going to learn self defense together. We're going to need to interact and communicate. We have to—

The instructor at the front of the room cuts the music, and attention turns to him.

"Welcome to the first night of the rest of your life," he says, and murmurs break out. "We're not trying to turn you into some ultimate street fighter. Our job is to show you how to be prepared in any situation, how to throw a punch, and how to block."

This will be a piece of cake. I don't like fighting, but I can hold my own.

Against my will, my eyes turn to my surprise partner. She grins up at me.

"I did three years of karate and two of tae kwon do," Mackenzie says, tightening her ponytail. "Oh, and a bit of Krav Maga."

"I think I might be in love."

She freezes, her head cocked. Did I say that out loud?

"Fuck."

She gives a shrill little giggle. Still nervous.

I stammer, trying to get the words out. I'm not apologizing for feeling what I'm feeling. I'm apologizing for springing it on her, in the most inopportune time, with no way to let her know it's one hundred and ten percent genuine.

But she plays it off as a joke, so I have to, too.

We start with some light stretching, getting our muscles warm. My eyes keep drifting over to her form in the mirror. She's tall, lean and stacked with muscle from a lifetime of playing three competitive sports year round. She catches my eye in the mirror and grins.

The music blasts at a decibel slightly below deafening. I should be focusing on getting my body warm, on preparing myself to relearn how to throw a punch. I'm not a fighter. I'm not afraid to throw down. It's just that usually I don't see the point. Aside from friendly (or not so friendly) tussles with the kids in my neighborhood growing up, I've never been in a "real" fight where I've had to defend—usually, it's me starting and ending things. Nobody has ever provoked me enough or made me angry enough to lose my shit through physical violence. My skin is thick—every bit of me is thick. My weight and muscles act as a protective forcefield against unkind words. And there are a lot of those. I don't talk much. People tend to think, because of that and my size, I must be an idiot.

That's okay. I know the truth.

But instead of working on myself, my eyes keep drifting to Mackenzie beside me. Her face is pink with exertion. She's absolutely gorgeous, with dark blonde hair, rich brown eyes, and a smile that absolutely devastates me. Her features are classically pretty. Sometimes she wears makeup, sometimes she goes around fresh faced. I like both equally as much. Really, I just like *her*.

The instructor walks around, correcting our grip. I keep

turning my wrist. Mackenzie reaches out to me and then stops, hesitant.

I don't like to be touched. I never have. She knows this. Everyone knows this.

Yet at the same time, I yearn for her touch, for her smooth skin to be on mine in any possible way. I nod and she approaches closer, her long fingers closing around my wrist.

Sparks shoot down my arm and coalesce into a ball of fury in my gut. My heart hammers a thousand beats a minute. She's touching me. She's *touching* me. She's touching *me*.

Gently, she turns my wrist in her grasp. Her other hand supports under my fist.

"Like this," she murmurs, moving my arm back and forth.

I should feel panicky. I should feel anxious. My skin should crawl at the feeling of another person's skin touching mine.

Instead, I feel… at peace. Something deep within me clicks into place, spreading peace and serotonin through my bloodstream. This feels kind of good. No. It feels *right*. I want her to touch me. I want her to keep touching me, for ever and ever.

"You okay?" she murmurs quietly. Her rich brown eyes search mine for an answer I'm not sure she wants.

I've never been better.

fourteen

. . .

Mackenzie

MY ROOMMATE IS A TOTAL BITCH. She decides that it's a great time to lock me out of our shared dorm after I've grabbed my bathrobe and shower caddy and hit the bathroom at the end of the hall. So now I'm the one who looks like a lunatic and gets dirty looks for banging on our door at six o'clock in the morning, wearing a bathrobe, shower shoes, and not much else.

It takes seventeen continuous minutes of knocking on the door and calling her name before she graciously consents to let me in. It might be the quickest I've ever gotten dressed. My hair is in a soaking wet bun, my clothes don't match, but I get the fuck out of there as fast as I possibly can.

It's early, much too early for me to want to be awake, so I hit the dining hall for some emergency caffeination. I have a quiz in my British Literature class and my introductory speech for Public Communication. Tonight, I have to work on a ten-page paper about the Industrial Revolution. All of this on top of practice, team dinner, and a team-building event after.

But for now, I'm going to sit here with my coffee and just breathe: one minute at a time, one breath at a time.

Tucker and Barrett are already at their usual table. Tuck lifts a hand in greeting. I nod back and he points to the empty seat at the end of the table. My spot. Laughing, I start in the direction of a little table at the other end of the dining hall. I don't even get to set my tray down before Tucker and Barrett descend upon me.

"What are you doing?" Barrett says rhetorically.

"Eating breakfast?"

"There's a perfectly good seat for you at our table," Tucker reminds me.

I frown.

"Come on, Mack. You don't want to hang out with us?" Barrett pouts.

"I'm not a football player, and I'm not dating one." *A fact of which I am uncomfortably aware.* "I don't belong there."

"You're part of the family," Tucker says seriously. "You don't have to spend time with us if you really don't want to, but you are always welcome at our table and at our house. You're one of us."

My eyes are suspiciously wet. After being banished this morning, the easy declaration thaws the ice around my heart.

"Come on," Barrett says kindly, wrapping his arm around my shoulders. Tucker takes my tray, and I curl into Barrett's warmth. He gently maneuvers me in the direction of their table, guiding me to the seat at the far end of the table. "There you go. Now you're with us, but you can have some space if you need it."

My usual spot. Across from Wes and next to Sam, my brother's girlfriend, who has welcomed me into her social circle with open arms. Whether we like it or not, pretty much everyone has assigned seating here. All of these guys are creatures of habit. They thrive on routine.

None of the other guys are here now, though, so there's an empty seat acting as a buffer between me and Barrett. I'm with them, but I'm allowed my own bubble to breathe.

"Where is everyone?"

"Getting a lift in," Tucker says. "Seven o'clock weights don't end just because the season is over."

"And you didn't join them?"

"Got a late start," he says with a sheepish grin. "I'll work something in this afternoon."

Barrett laughs. "I'm retired now. I don't need to work out before dawn. I'll save my gym time for the middle of the day like normal people."

It feels a little weird pulling out my book. Usually that's such a Wes thing to do. We sit at the end of the table and read. Right now, Tucker is on his phone. Barrett has his laptop out. They're both busy with their own things. So I crack open my latest novel and escape for a little while.

I'm distracted by a tray setting down in front of me, nudging into mine. The scent of cinnamon and cloves surrounds me. Without looking up, I know it's Wes.

Sure enough, there he is. His cheeks are tinted pink from exertion and his sandy blond hair is damp, fresh from the shower.

"Good morning."

He meets my eye and nods. That's about all I expect from him, especially this early in the morning.

My attention returns to my book. Less than a minute later, I'm interrupted by a gentle tug to my tray.

Wes sets a cup on my tray. Coffee. Exactly how I like it. Because he knows exactly how I like it.

"Good morning," he mumbles, ducking his head.

My heart blooms deep within my chest.

"Did you have a good workout?"

He nods slowly. "How's your book?"

It's a heavily fictionalized take on Nazi hunters in Argentina during the reign of Juan and Evita Peron. Revisionist history with a thick splash of romanticism. In actuality, they weren't nearly as successful at eradicating abusers in positions of power. Add in a completely unnecessary romantic subplot and it's a pretty decent story.

"Good. I like it so far. I'll let you borrow it when I'm done."

His shy, pleased smile makes my stomach flip.

I clear my throat. "Are you ready for your speech today?"

His face falls. Bit by bit, his expression shutters, locking away all emotion until he's a blank slate, unreadable as stone.

"It won't be that bad."

He gives me a dark look and lifts his tea.

"You've got this. You're going to ace it."

He scoffs.

"Whatever you do, don't imagine the room in their underwear. Trust me. It doesn't work."

Wes's face goes pink. He coughs and looks away.

Greg laughs. "Oh, ho. What's this about underwear?"

My brother looks over at us with a scowl. Amir and Barrett are laughing.

"We have to give our speeches in class today," I explain. "Everyone always says to imagine the crowd in their underwear. But it doesn't help."

"Yeah, don't do that," Miles interjects. He glares at Wes, who has done absolutely nothing wrong except for being in the wrong place at the wrong time. "How about we don't talk about my little sister's unmentionables at the breakfast table?"

Wes chokes on his tea.

"Unmentionables?" I roll my eyes at my brother to keep from reaching across the table and throttling him. "What is this, 1952?"

Miles turns his glare to me. "Mack."

"I'm nineteen. What, are you going to chaperone me on my next date?"

He frowns. "You're going on a date?"

Fuck. Why did I have to start this fight?

Wes's stare is heavy on me, a yoke on my shoulders I can't escape from.

"No," I finally admit to my brother. "This is all hypothetical. It's bad enough you have your lackeys hounding me at all hours of the day. I can't even eat breakfast in peace without being surrounded by you idiots."

Tucker laughs and leans back in his seat. "You love us, Mackie."

I stick my tongue out at him.

"You're like our kid sister," Barrett adds in. "I only have my big brother and, frankly, he's kind of a dick. I've always wanted a sister. We can each share you. We can take turns."

Is that how Wes thinks of me? As his little sister? I'm afraid to even look at him. I don't want it to be true.

Slowly, reluctantly, I bring my eyes to meet his. He's watching me with an inscrutable expression on his face—not quite a scowl, not quite a frown. Definitely not a smile.

He's intense. I've always known that; it's never been a secret. Something about his intensity calls to me. I know he's been hurt. He's lived through unimaginable pain. Over the years, I've pieced little bits together, here and there. His parents died his senior year of high school. He got dropped from his first choice university at the last minute, and only made it into Newton by the skin of his teeth. His first game, freshman year, he broke two vertebrae in his back. It's been a long, challenging road, and now that football is over and done with, he has to learn how to be an adult without his family to lean on.

He'd never complain about it, though. It's simply his lot in life. He takes what's dealt to him and rises to the occasion. It doesn't mean he doesn't deserve better, though. I want more for him. I want *him* to want more.

fifteen

. . .

Mackenzie

ALTHOUGH I'M NOT EXACTLY a fan of public speaking, I get by all right when I have to do it. I just do my best and get it over with. So while I'm not exactly looking forward to giving my two and a half minute introductory speech to my class today, I'm not dreading it, either. This class is a requirement for a reason. I'm here to get in, get out, and get on with my day.

Wes, on the other hand…

He looks petrified.

He's fidgeting uncontrollably. Since our first meeting in class, I've been sitting in the back row with him, and usually he's as still as a statue for the ninety-minute class period. His only movement is his arm shifting as he takes copious notes.

Today, though…

We're called in alphabetical order by last name, so there's no quibbling over who gets to go first or last. There are four people ahead of him. They're… not terrible. Hopefully, they learn how to calm down and relax when speaking in public.

And then it's Wes's turn.

He's nervous. His face is pale, wan. Sweat beads at his

hairline. He takes a deep breath and shuffles his notes on the small lectern. Fidgets.

"Whenever you're ready," Professor Black says.

Wes opens his mouth. No words come out.

His eyes go wide with panic. They dart around the room, beady and unfocused.

You can do this. You've got this.

His eyes land on mine, and I hold the contact, nodding slowly. He can do this. He's got this.

He clears his throat. With his eyes trained on me, he takes a deep breath and squares his shoulders.

"My life is in flux," he says, and then pauses.

Go on. It's okay.

"I was a football player for—for seventeen years," he says, then lets out a weak chuckle. "I mean, look at me. Can't you tell? As of six weeks ago, I'm officially retired."

He's sweating now. His face is getting more pale by the second.

"I've applied to—to grad school for physical therapy, to a half dozen schools." He coughs. "I don't know where or if I'll be accepted. I don't know what will happen after graduation, or a year from now, or ten years from now."

That's okay, I tell him. *You don't have to figure it out right now. You have time.*

"To look at me, you might not expect it, but I love to read." There are a few nervous titters, and he goes red. His eyes dart in the direction of the noise before they return to me. I nod. He clears his throat again. "I like mysteries. They keep my—my brain engaged. I don't like murder, gore, or gratuitous violence. I've had enough of that in my life."

He clears his throat one more time. His eyes drift down to his notes and then back to me. He squares his shoulders.

That's it. It's just you and me in this room. Nobody else matters. It's just you and me.

"I'm originally from a small—a small suburb of Detroit

that nobody has ever heard of," he says. He shifts his weight. "My sister is in law school. My parents are—my parents are—"

He stops, stricken. His face contorts with pain.

You can do this.

Wes takes another deep breath. "My parents are dead."

The classroom erupts into quiet murmurs.

Professor Black clears her throat.

Wes falls silent. He looks down at his notes for the third time. Shuffles the papers.

"I can't—I can't—"

He looks directly at me.

"I can't do this."

And then he bolts from the classroom.

I glance at the professor. She's marking a note down on her clipboard.

Alphabetically, my turn comes next. Before I even know what is happening, I'm up and out of my seat, pushing open the heavy doors to the hallway. I don't even grab my backpack. All I know is, I have to get to him.

The hallway is eerily empty. The sterile walls feel like they're closing in on me. I race down the hall, head on a constant swivel for any sign of life.

There he is. He's standing at the top of the stairs, shaking. His whole body is trembling.

"Wes!"

His head snaps up. His eyes are wide, unfocused.

My pace slows. I don't want to scare him off.

"What…" He clears his throat. "What are you doing? You have your speech."

"I wanted to check on you."

"I'm fine," he lies, and I roll my eyes.

"Okay, if you say so."

"I am."

Slowly, deliberately, I take a step closer. He flinches.

"I know you don't like to be touched, but you look like you can use a hug right now." I swallow. "Can I give you a hug?"

The fight seeps out of his spine. He crumbles in on himself. "I... I..."

"If you don't want it, I don't want to make you more uncomfortable. I just thought it might help."

Am I doing this for mostly selfish reasons? Yes. Do I genuinely want to make him feel better? Also yes. The two don't have to be mutually exclusive.

Wes takes a deep breath. He lets go of the stair railing and steps towards me. He stops.

He doesn't know how to do this. I don't know the last time he had a hug.

With careful movements, I approach. My hands land on his upper arms.

He flinches. A pang of pain ricochets through me. He's so hurt. All I want to do is soothe his pain.

We're so close. I can't stop now.

Making eye contact, I slide my hands up his biceps to his strong shoulders. He lets out a heavy, blustery sigh. His breath ruffles against my hair.

More, more, more.

Our bodies come together, an innocent brush of my chest pressed to his. My hands move up to lock behind his neck. My head rests perfectly against his shoulder.

Slowly, haltingly, his arms come up around me. His chin rests against the top of my head.

We're so close. I can feel his chest rise with every breath, the hitch in his lungs as he works to regulate his breathing. He's still tense, panicked.

"It's okay. You're okay," I murmur quietly. His arms tighten around me.

sixteen

. . .

Wes

MACKENZIE CAVANAUGH IS TOUCHING ME. She is *hugging* me. I am holding her in my arms.

Holy. fucking. shit.

I don't ever want to let her go. I don't know if I can. Now that I know what this feels like, I don't know how I can ever live without this again.

I don't want this to end.

I can live with making a fool of myself in front of her and thirty other classmates. I can live with failing this class again, not graduating, and having to repeat the year. I can live with pretty much anything.

But I don't know that I can live without the feeling of her in my arms ever again.

She eases her head back and looks up at me. "Are you feeling better?"

Yes. No. I don't know.

She curls her body into mine, her arms tightening around me. I'm gratified by the feeling that she doesn't seem to want this to end just as much as I don't.

Shit. Wait.

"Your speech…"

"Don't worry about it," she tells me.

I frown.

"I'm where I'm supposed to be right now," she says, her forehead drawn with conviction. "I'll figure it out."

I can't be the reason she fails this class. I can't be the reason she destroys her GPA in her first year of college, the way I did mine.

"Mackenzie..."

As much as I want to take a step back and reassess, to convince her not to throw her life away for the likes of me, I want to be close to her even more.

She leans up and brushes her lips against mine. It's quick, fleeting—innocent.

This time I do step back. I feel the earth move without her body pressed so tightly to mine. The eighteen inches separating us feels like eighteen miles.

Her face falls. She swallows and looks away.

"Listen, I..."

What the hell am I doing? This is the woman I've been pining over for who knows how long, my best friend, the person who knows me best in this world.

And she hugged me! She *kissed* me!

I square my shoulders and step towards her. She can't blink away the hurt in her eyes fast enough.

Threading my fingers through her hair, gently I tip her head up and let my lips brush over hers. A soft kiss, an innocent brush of lips on lips, no pressure. Slowly, tentatively, she opens her mouth, and I deepen the kiss, letting my tongue sweep inside her mouth and taste her in earnest.

She melts. Slowly, she unwinds, her hands landing on my pecs and sliding up to wrap around my neck again. She smells like her green apple and pear blossom shampoo, and something sweet and homey. I can't get enough.

Easing back, I steal one last peck before I retreat.

"Go back to class," I tell her.

My voice is low and hoarse. She flinches.

I have to resist the urge to touch her again, and again, and again.

"Do your speech. I'll still be here."

Her chin comes up, defiant. I give in to the desire to stroke her cheek, to feel her soft skin. Just once.

"Don't fail because of me."

I couldn't live with myself if she did.

"You're not coming back to class?"

Not now. Maybe not ever.

But that's not her burden to bear.

———

It's a truth universally acknowledged that office hours are the best way to ingratiate oneself to one's professor, especially true when one has a meltdown of epic proportions and basically self-destructs in the middle of class.

So it's with my figurative hat in my hands that I approach Professor Blake's office at the start of her availability window. By the time I finished sulking and went back to the house, my backpack was magically deposited in my room—thank you, Mackenzie—and now, I have the paper copy of my speech in a clear plastic folder.

Professor Blake looks up as I stand in her doorway. She clears her throat. "Well, come in."

I sit gingerly in the wobbly chair opposite her desk. Clearly, it's not made for someone of my size.

"So, what's your excuse?" She sounds annoyed already.

"I'm not good at this," I tell her bluntly.

She raises her eyebrows.

I don't like to talk to people in general. Public speaking? Count me out.

"This is my third time attempting this class."

She sighs, taking off her reading glasses. "I did see that, yes."

"I need to pass this class."

With a shrewd look she studies me. "Leaving in the middle of your speech won't help with that."

"I know."

I don't fidget under her speculative stare. I square my shoulders and meet her eyes head on, as if she were an opponent on the football field and not a forty-something year old woman who stands maybe 5'3" and 120 pounds soaking wet.

Professor Blake sighs. "All right, then. Let's give it another go."

"When?"

"Now. You can have a few moments to prepare."

My hands aren't just damp—they're as slick as the Charles River. Sweat pools at the base of my spine. I can't do this. I can't do this. I can't do this.

I take a deep breath. Close my eyes. There's only one person here. I can talk to just one person. So what if she's my professor? It's only one on one. She's not going to care if I make a fool out of myself. All she's doing is judging me for a grade.

It's already so much easier to do this knowing that Mackenzie isn't in the room. Sure, the rest of the class being absent doesn't hurt, either. But somehow it was made all that much worse having to stand in front of her and bare my soul. At the same time, I don't think I would have been able to get nearly as far into the speech as I did without her there, grounding me.

This is no different than staring down an opponent on the football field. Professor Blake is nothing but an erstwhile tight end trying to get past me. I will not let her defeat me.

My legs are shaking, but I can't do this sitting down. I stand behind the chair and clutch the back, as if it's my own personal lectern. I glance down at my notes.

"My life is in flux," I start, and then I stop. I sigh. This speech is supposed to be about me. If I'm being truthful…

"I'm in love with my best friend's sister. This is a guy I live with, work out with, do everything together with. Because of him, she's been in my life for four and a half years now. She's my best friend's little sister."

Professor Blake's eyebrows go up, up, up.

"Only it's not fair to call her that, because she's one of my best friends in her own right. She's amazing. She's entirely off limits for a variety of reasons, not the least is that she's way too young for me—legal, she's overage, but still too young for me," I add hurriedly. "She kissed me today, and even though I'm over the moon, at the same time, I'm freaking the fuck out. I'm way too messed up to be able to have a healthy relationship with someone, anyone."

This is shit I've never talked about with anyone. Not my sister. Not the half dozen therapists I was sent to. These sick, twisted thoughts have been rattling around in my brain for way too many years.

I want help. I need help. But I don't know where to start.

"For years I denied that I was traumatized," I start, and then I stop again. I sigh. "I've never been diagnosed with PTSD. I wasn't abused as a child. I had a good childhood. Idyllic, even." I meet Professor Blake's eyes. "But something broke in me when my parents died. A stupid sixteen-year-old ran a red light at a busy intersection in town. A guy I went to school with, a guy who played on the JV football team. The idiot had the gall to come up to me and apologize to me on my first day back at school a week later. I broke his nose."

She takes in a quick breath.

"Yeah, that wasn't my finest moment." I give a dark chuckle. "It was easier to lock everything away, to hide behind my books. I don't talk a lot on a good day, but I've never had trouble being understood. I save my words for when they matter. I haven't been back to Dexter since we sold the house. I don't think I'll ever go back. There's nothing for me there."

Sighing, I shake my head. "I've applied to a half dozen grad schools. My top choice is Newton. The program here is amazing, and I already know some of the professors. I'd love to stay here. Realistically, I don't know if that's an option."

This is the first place that's felt like home in I don't know how long. I'm comfortable here. I've made a little community of friends that feel more like family. Brothers.

And then add Mackenzie into the mix…

"I don't know what's going to happen next for me. My life is in flux, and the uncertainty only serves to make my medicated anxiety worse," I admit. "So I'm doing the best I can. Taking it day by day. Some days are better than others."

I meet Professor Blake's eyes. "I'm doing the best I can."

She nods and scribbles something on her notepad. Maybe a grade? I can't make it out.

"Thank you for sharing," she says. She pauses. "I can't allow you to give your speech privately every time. This is a one-time exception."

"Understood."

I'll do better. I'll work on this. If I'm not talking about myself, it should be easier…

I hope.

seventeen

. . .

Mackenzie

WHAT THE HELL did I do? Did I just ruin the single best thing I have going for me? My own selfish need for Wes ended up hurting him more than it helped him. I took from someone who was hurting.

I don't know how he will ever forgive me. I don't know how I can ever forgive myself.

Dareesa can tell that something is up with me. The coaches can, too. I've dropped close to every other pass sent my way today, and when I do manage to get the ball in my hands, I can't make the basket. I'm a basketcase.

"We're totally getting drunk tonight," she tells me under her breath when we have a water break. "And you're going to spill whatever is going on with you."

I don't drink much. I don't like the taste of alcohol, and I don't like the feeling of my head going fuzzy. I can tolerate one or two drinks over the course of several hours. Anything more than that… Count me out.

Tonight, though? Yeah, I could use some mind bleach to erase this day from ever crossing my memory again.

"You're on."

She grins at me.

I'm not usually invited to these types of impromptu parties. Dareesa and Lauren are a tightly knit twosome. They're friendly, sure, but it's always been made clear that I'm not part of their friendship group. They have a bond that I can't touch. They live together, they're in the same major, they train together. They're basically attached at the hip. And instead of living with them, I get… Claire.

No, I'm not bitter at all.

After practice, we hit up the ASC dining hall for some food. There's an official team event tonight—we're watching a Disney princess movie in our pajamas at one of the basketball houses. If there's some unofficial underage drinking going on, well, I'm not about to spill the beans. I need all the carbs to prepare for this.

Against my will, my eyes travel across the cafeteria. Wes is conspicuously missing. Miles is sitting with Sam, staring into her eyes like a lovesick idiot. Amir and Greg, sitting with him, wave hello but don't attempt to corral me over there this time.

"What's up with that?" Lauren asks, nodding in their direction.

"What's up with what?"

"You and the football guys."

"My brother is on the team."

Dareesa laughs. "Yeah, and you sit with them more than you do with us."

I frown. I don't spend *that* much time over there… do I?

"My brother and I get along pretty well." Along with our normal dinners once or twice a week, it's easy to eat breakfast with them when nobody else is awake. My schedule doesn't always align with the rest of the team. When I see the girls, I drop by and say hi. Sometimes I join them. Sometimes Wes and I have lunch at the same time before our public speaking class.

Wes…

I sigh, taking my seat and looking over at his empty chair

again. I fucked everything up. I ruined what could have been the best friendship I ever had.

That kiss though... Fuck, that was a good kiss. My body temperature skyrockets fifteen degrees at the memory of his mouth on mine, his tongue stroking mine, his hard, strong body pressed against mine.

I want that. I want that again, and I want it now.

His chair is empty. Did I scare him away? I dropped off his backpack after class—I was able to give my speech a few minutes later, I think I did relatively well—when none of the guys were at the house. A coincidence. I wasn't purposefully trying to avoid running into anyone...

Motion out of the corner of my eye brings my head back up. Wes is setting his tray down at his table. He doesn't look over in my direction. Without talking to his roommates, he sits down, puts on his headphones, and opens his book, blocking out the world.

That's new. He doesn't usually tell everyone so blatantly to leave him alone. Normally he's a little more polite in ignoring everyone.

Miri laughs at something Pia said, and I shake my head, forcing my attention back to my teammates. Tonight is about the team, about girlfriends and team bonding. Tonight isn't about some guy who might have been my best friend until I betrayed his trust and took advantage of him for my own selfish desires.

We have a good group on the team this year. I feel included and part of the team. Even if none of them are going to be my best friends anytime soon, I enjoy spending time with them when we're together. As the season goes on, as we travel and spend more time together, I'm sure we'll get closer. These growing pains will soothe.

"...okay, Mack?" Rebekah says, and I startle back to attention.

"Huh?"

"We're going to head out in a minute," she says. "Unless you want to stay and ogle the football players some more."

Jaz and Ericka laugh. It doesn't feel like I'm in on the joke.

"No, I'm good, thanks," I say with a bright, fake smile, and the whole table laughs.

We begin to clear our trays. I chance a glance back in the direction of the football table.

Almost as if he feels my eyes on him, Wes looks up from his book. He meets my gaze head on and lifts his chin, his expression stony. His eyes narrow.

Guess he's still pissed, then. I don't blame him.

Sighing, I roll my eyes and look to my teammate. "So, we're getting drunk, right?"

She laughs and throws her arm around me. "Fuck yeah, we are."

Without much ado, we head to the upperclassmen basketball house. There are two houses, one across the street from Sam's softball house, and the other a few houses down from Diana's soccer house. We're a block and a half away from the football house: so close, and yet so far away.

Tonight, I'm not Miles's kid sister, who hangs around the guys because she has no life. Tonight, I'm not the bookworm who spends my evenings on the football players' couch because I can't bear to be in my dorm. Tonight, I'm not awkwardly third-wheeling it with four other couples because I have no friends of my own.

Tonight, I'm one of the girls, a member of the team. I have every right to be here. I'm not just an invited guest; I belong here. Next year, Dareesa, Lauren, and I will be out of the dorms and living in this house, or another one like it with our teammates.

Jaz picks out a movie and Tara and Natalya pour everyone drinks while we get changed into our pajamas. It's only eight o'clock, but there's no way we can drink alcohol and watch Beauty and the Beast if we're not wearing our PJs.

The red solo cup handed to me smells vile, like pure rubbing alcohol with an undercurrent of super sweet pineapple. It's filled nearly to the brim. I take a tentative sip: cloyingly sweet, but not bad. I can barely even taste the alcohol. I take another drink. Never mind: there it is.

The girls pile onto the couch and armchairs, six people on a sofa designed for two or three. I sit on the floor in front of the sofa with Pia and Rebekah, a soft chenille blanket thrown across our laps. Miri passes around an enormous bowl of popcorn.

Yeah, I can get used to this.

Curling up with my teammates, I sip my drink and watch the movie. Jacki pretends to swoon over Gaston, and Jaz and Amber smack her with a couch pillow. We all sing along with all of the songs. Secretly, I long for a library of my own to mimic the castle's.

During the wolf's chase, my phone vibrates with a text. I take a sip of my drink and pull my phone out of my pocket. The cup nearly drops from my hand at the name on my screen.

Wes.

This isn't the first time he's texted me. Three months ago, he sent me directions to a bookstore in a nearby town. Last summer, I texted him my parents' address, when he and the guys were coming over for a barbecue. A year ago, he sent me the name of a book I should read.

We should talk, he texted now.

I turn my phone off.

eighteen

. . .

Mackenzie

EVERYTHING HURTS. My head throbs in time with my heartbeat. My eyes are painfully dry. My mouth tastes disgusting.

I am never drinking again.

The armchair isn't nearly as uncomfortable to sleep on as I expected. Dareesa is in the other chair. Lauren has the couch; it was an easy concession to let the injured one take the most comfortable sleeping arrangement.

The basketball house isn't nearly as homey as the football house. Or maybe that's my own twisted perception. I've barely spent any time here—a few hours for team building events or a movie night, maybe. It's not my second home like the football house has become.

There are flowers on the coffee table and another bouquet on the dining room table. The place is decorated with colorful throw pillows, soft blankets, and a cozy rug. It's warm and welcoming. But it's not home.

The remnants of last night's party are strewn about the room. The place is thick with the musty smell of stale alcohol and sweat. We didn't get too crazy; it was a school night, after all, and we have practice at three o'clock this afternoon.

Lauren groans and slowly maneuvers into a sitting position. She doesn't look too hot. I can hear retching from a nearby bathroom, and Lauren gags, distinctly green around the gills.

It's early, at least an hour earlier than I need to be up today. My first class isn't until ten. As much as I want a shower, I want to go back to my dorm and deal with my roommate even less. Maybe I'll make use of the showers at the ASC locker rooms…

On a normal day, I would just pop over to Miles's house and use his shower. It's not exactly what I call clean, but it's convenient. Today, though… yeah, I don't think I should be naked at the football house. I don't think I should be at the football house, period.

Pia stumbles down the stairs. She's fully dressed, if a bit groggy. Her hair is still in last night's braid—which is not unusual, she frequently goes two or three days with the same messy braid in, even when she admits it looks terrible.

"Coffee," she groans, stretching her arms above her head.

Dareesa pops up, seemingly out of a deep sleep. "Coffee?"

Lauren laughs and tosses a throw pillow in her roommate's direction. "Get dressed, loser, we're getting coffee."

I make it to the bathroom first. A quick rinsing with a washcloth and I feel a little better. Changing into real clothes —well, leggings and a sports bra, which is as close to real clothes as it gets most days—I'm almost a whole new person.

My phone is still off. I'm a little afraid to turn it back on. Do I want Wes to have texted more? Or do I want him to have not said anything besides his quick message? I honestly don't know.

It's a damp, misty morning, not quite raining enough to need a hood or an umbrella, and just enough to make the road slippery and slick. Pia, Dareesa, Lauren, Rebekah, Jaz, and I make our way to the ASC and the dining hall. Our trays are quickly laden with coffee, fried eggs, bacon, and toast. Jaz reaches for the oatmeal spoon and gags. Yeah, she's not going there—nobody is. Not today.

It feels nice, being with the girls. Being one of the girls. I'm being included in the group activities. Sure, we're all hungover and desperate for coffee and grease, but we're all in this together.

"What do you have planned for your day?" Lauren asks me as we sit down.

"Class at ten. Nothing until then."

"Want to hit up a hot yoga class? They have one starting at eight."

Dareesa groans.

"I need to sweat out this alcohol from my pores before practice," Lauren protests.

I have another change of clothes in my bag—I always do. My current outfit is perfectly serviceable for an hour of yoga.

"Sure, sounds like fun," I agree.

Lauren smiles, pleased.

Almost against my will, my eyes drift in the direction of the football table at the back of the room. Wes is there by himself. He's reading a magazine today—that's new. It looks like it might be a scholarly journal, which is not surprising in the least. He doesn't have his headphones this morning. He sips his tea and reads, lost in his own little world.

My stomach rolls. Fuck. Maybe drinking last night was a bad idea. Yeah, I had a fun night. I let loose and enjoyed myself. My teammates and I had a blast, drunkenly shout-singing Disney songs until the wee hours of the morning.

But now it's broad daylight, and my problems haven't gone away. And on top of the awkwardness of whatever is going to happen with me and Wes, I have the monster of all headaches and an upset stomach.

I don't know what to say to him. I don't want to *talk*.

I want to kiss him again, and again, and again, and we both know that can never happen. He's not built for that. And even if he was interested in me—which he most definitely is *not*—my brother has made it clear time and again that his teammates are entirely off limits for me. And they *live* together.

It doesn't matter that I've had an enormous crush on Wes for at least three years. It's a boundary that my brother has set, and I have to respect it. Just like I know he's respected that my teammates are off limits to him, I can keep my entirely non-existent romantic life out of his locker room.

Besides, he's graduating in a few short months. Next year, the football players are fair game…

Not that there are any that interest me. For years now, the only guy who has interested me has been a 6'5", 300 something pound football player with sandy blond hair and a heart of gold, the man who is more interested in books than pretty much anything else in the world, who is about to graduate in three and a half way too short months.

The man who has become my best friend.

Wes is still absorbed in his journal. Barrett and Amir have joined him now, Diana and Jill in tow for a breakfast double date.

I want that. I want to be able to indulge in the comfort and familiarity of a relationship, of having someone I can depend on, and who lets me be there for them in return. I want the security of knowing I always have a person to talk to, someone to eat my meals with and walk through campus with and work out with. Someone who has the same interests as I do, or similar enough that they're interested in the things I care about.

I don't want just any guy. I want Wes. And he doesn't want me back.

nineteen

. . .

Wes

MACKENZIE IS AVOIDING ME. It's more than just not answering my text; she won't look at me. Every once in a while, I feel her eyes on me in the dining hall, but when I raise my head, miraculously she's facing the entirely opposite direction.

Sometimes I wish I wasn't in love with her. My life would be so much easier if I didn't have feelings for my best friend, my roommate's sister, a woman who is entirely off limits in so many ways.

But I do. And try as I might, I can't change that. Most of the time, I'm not even sure if I want to.

She doesn't join us for dinner on Wednesday night like she usually does. In our public communication class on Thursday, she sits at the front of the room, as far away from what have become "our" seats at the back of the room as physically possible. On Friday, she eats breakfast at a small table by herself, and I don't see her the rest of the day.

Saturday she has a game. I don't want to distract her—she has to get ready, she needs to focus. The mental preparation is just as important as the physical. I don't want to interfere with her performance.

We need to talk, to clear the air. Yes, she kissed me first… and then I kissed her again. She wasn't exactly protesting at the time. Every signal she sent leading up to it told me she wanted to. Her reaction in the aftermath is proof enough that I was wrong. She offered a finite amount of comfort, perfunctory and performative, and anything else I was reading into the situation was all in my head.

I won't overstep again.

Mackenzie isn't the type of girl to go for a fling. (Not that I have any interest in one of those, either.) She's the type of girl someone settles down with. It doesn't have to get serious right off the bat. But she's the type of girl to date steadily, to bring home to meet the family, to create a life with.

For the first time, I wish I were the type of guy who could handle a relationship. I'm not talking about sex; I want companionship. And physical attraction aside, Mackenzie and I genuinely get along—we're friends now, actual friends. There is nobody else on this campus who puts me at ease quite like she does. Whether we're actively doing something or simply sitting on the couch reading our separate novels, I never come away from an interaction with her wishing it was over. If anything, I want it to continue, and keep going on forever.

And, yeah, I'm incredibly attracted to her. I've spent the last year wishing I wasn't. Her body is like my every fantasy come to life. Her smile makes my stomach flip. And when she touches me, an innocent brush of her hand against mine or her foot glancing across my shoe, my heart races. I've spent way too many nights thinking of her while she sleeps only a scant few feet away on my couch.

But even if she weren't my best friend, even if she weren't way too young for me, even if she weren't my roommate's sister… I don't know that I'm cut out for a relationship. I want it, I crave it, but I'm not ready for that.

Trauma is a strange and funny thing. I wasn't with my

parents when their car crashed. I didn't get woken up in the middle of the night by the phone call like my sister. When the police came to the front door, I think I already knew something was wrong.

I've grieved. I've—well, not moved on, because it's not the type of thing one moves on from. I've accepted it. I'm at peace with the reality.

It still really fucking sucks sometimes, though.

The two relationships I had in high school were child's play. I crushed on a cute girl, we danced around each other for a few weeks, I asked her out, and then we were together. I was a top ranked football star, on the Michigan All-State list, a five star recruit, and scouted by the top ten programs in the country. I was a fucking catch. My first girlfriend and I parted amicably. Then I started dating someone else, and it was fine —for a little while. She broke up with me two weeks after my parents died because I was "too sad" all the time. Yeah, that stung.

I haven't dated since then. There hasn't been anyone to spark my interest. I'm fine on my own. My libido functions normally for a twenty-two year old man. I don't need anyone to take care of it; I'm perfectly capable. I have my right hand, and occasionally my left, to satisfy any physical urges. I have my roommates for companionship and my teammates for my community. I don't need a girlfriend in order to make friends.

Although it might be nice if my hypothetical girlfriend *was* my best friend. The person I spend the most time with, the person I am the most comfortable with. The person who makes my pulse throb and my stomach flip. The person who left class right before her own presentation because I was upset, who reached out to comfort me.

The person I took advantage of, and has been avoiding me ever since.

Yeah, I'm royally fucked here.

It's not like there's anyone I can talk to about this. Definitely not Miles—hell no. That is not a conversation I want to have with Mackenzie's brother, even though we've been friends and teammates for four and a half years. Barrett *might* understand—he's dating his longtime best friend, after pining for her for close to ten years—but he's still in that happy ever after la la land of a new relationship. Tucker wouldn't get it; he's been obsessed with Mason for years, and even when she dumped him and broke his heart, he still pined after her. Greg is perpetually single, and he seems to like it that way. And Amir would only laugh at me and say it's about time I'm admitting it. It's not like he hasn't already suspected it.

It's sick to objectify a young woman who has done nothing aside from offer me unconditional kindness. It's sick to pine after someone who so clearly is not interested in me, even after she rejected me.

I don't know where to go from here. If she hadn't hugged me, I never would have kissed her, and then we wouldn't be in this awkward limbo between friends and not speaking. Let's be clear: she's the one avoiding me. If she wants to talk to me, she knows where to find me.

I could go out of my way to reach out to her again. Her practice schedule is the same every week; I could hang out by the basketball gym and wait for her to be done. I could knock on her dorm room door. I could call her, or text her again, or send her an email explaining my version of what happened.

She doesn't want to hear from me. Her lack of response is telling enough. She doesn't want to talk to me, at least not right now. I have to respect that.

———

Of course, just because I'm respecting her boundaries, doesn't mean I'm going to stop supporting her. I show up to her basketball game Saturday afternoon like I do every home game. This time, the group isn't getting together; Mason has a track meet, so Tucker, Barrett, and Amir are supporting her, and Miles brought Greg to sit with his family.

I'm sure if I said something about going to the game, they would invite me to sit with them, too. I don't want to. Not that the Cavanaughs aren't lovely people; they are. They have welcomed me into their fold. I've gone to their house for summer barbecues and Thanksgiving dinner. They invite me to dinner every week, even though I turn them down every time. I feel comfortable with them, or as comfortable as I feel with anyone these days.

But it feels oddly inappropriate to sit with Nancy and Steve without the buffer of everyone else while I secretly lust over their daughter.

Instead of sitting in the plush arena seats with them, I get a free ticket to the student section. The bench seats are not nearly as comfortable—I'm pretty sure I'm sitting in what is supposed to be two seats—and the view is... well, it's not better. It's higher up. There are pockets of students around me, in the rows in front and to either side of me, but nobody sits too close, which is just the way I like it. I'm in my own little bubble.

Mackenzie is stretching on the sidelines. Blue athletic tape is wrapped around her knee. That's new. She doesn't normally have knee issues. She tends to have tightness in her shoulders or soreness in her elbows, leftover injuries from a lifetime of balancing swimming and tennis with basketball. She's never mentioned any problems with her knees.

She's focused on her preparations. She doesn't look up. Even if she did, I don't think she'd be able to see me. I'm too high up, not in my usual seats. Incognito.

I stifle a snort, and the person to my left looks over in annoyance. I ignore him.

If anything, I'm practically carrying a full-sized banner proclaiming my love for her. Yeah, it might be a secret, but it's pretty fucking evident. I haven't exactly succeeded at hiding it.

That kiss was proof enough. I saw a chance, and I took it. That it ruined everything is a whole other story. I want things to go back to the way they were. I want my best friend back.

All told, I'm a relatively simple man. I like to read. I like to work out. I like football. I like a good cup of tea. And I like Mackenzie.

It's hard for me to make friends. I keep to myself. Most of the guys I've worked out with and played on teams with over the years are more interested in a lifestyle that has never interested me, not for one minute. I don't want to drink. I don't party. I don't hook up. After we're done in the weight room or the training field, we don't have anything to say to one another.

This house, these roommates, it's the first time I've felt comfortable being myself in… years. I'm different than the *me* I used to be; this is the *me* I am now, and I'm happy with the way that's developed over the years. They accept me unconditionally for who I am. They don't care that I would rather read than hang out with them, that I tend to read through meals and video games and pretty much anything I possibly can. They still make a pointed effort to include me as much as possible. When I do choose to spend time with them without the buffer of a book, they treat me no differently than anyone else. I appreciate that. I appreciate them.

Mackenzie is sitting on the sidelines. She's frowning in concentration as she focuses on the game in front of her. As a freshman, she's not yet a starter; when she does get playing time, it's often in sheltered minutes, so she can shine her brightest and be as effective as possible.

She gets less than five minutes of playing time in the entire game. She's frustrated; it's written all over her face. Her knee isn't one hundred percent, either. She's not limping, not quite. There's a tenseness to her gait that's more than simply sitting on the bench most of the game.

On her way back to the locker room, she glances up at the crowd. She waves at her parents and siblings. There's a furrow between her brows. She scans through the arena, searching, searching.

As if by some miracle, her eyes land on me, and my chest gets tight. She gives me a small smile, ducking her head. The dark-skinned woman beside her nudges her and Mackenzie laughs. It's not mean. They're sharing a joke.

I'm glad she's making friends. It's one thing if someone doesn't want to spend time with other people; Mackenzie is the type of person who thrives being around other people. She's close to her family, and they're great, but she needs friends her own age, too. Peers. People who understand her, who know the types of things she's going through. Ideally, another athlete, someone who likes to read and play tennis and—

Fuck.

That's me. I'm describing myself.

twenty

. . .

Wes

THERE'S a knock on our door shortly after nine o'clock. The house is quiet—Miles and Greg are out at a party with Sam and her friends, Amir is out with Jill, Tucker is with Mason, and Barrett is with Diana. Nearly all of my friends have settled down into relationships. I'm the lone holdout.

My heart thumps at a thousand beats a minute. I know only one person who would knock on our door at this time of night. Most people are out having fun on Saturday evenings, getting wasted, and getting laid. That's not my idea of fun. And, I'm pretty sure, it's not hers, either.

Mackenzie is standing on our doorstep. As the door swings open, she exhales slowly and raises her eyes to meet mine. She's wearing light makeup, enough to highlight her big brown eyes and turn her lips a pale, pale pink. My attention hovers between her eyes, soulful and sad, and her mouth, with those perfectly kissable lips.

"Hey, Wes," she says quietly.

I grunt a greeting to hide my nervousness. It's been five excruciatingly long days without her in my life. I don't like feeling this way, like my heart has been ripped out of my chest and clawed to pieces by her silence. My heart muscle has been downgraded from filet mignon to lowly cubed steak, tenderized to bits and pieces.

"Can I..." She swallows. "Can I come in? We should talk."

It's all I've wanted all week. And now that it might actually be happening, I can't remember why I ever thought this would be a good idea. I don't want to talk. That means confirming this was all a mistake, that it can never happen again.

Taking a step back, I hold the door open for her to pass through. She slips off her coat, and I take it from her, hanging it on the hook holding mine.

She clears her throat. "How have you been?"

She doesn't actually want to know. She's just making small talk. Delaying the inevitable.

"I've, um, I've missed you this week," she says. Her teeth sink into the plush pillow of her lower lip. She looks up at me. "It's weird not talking to you."

I don't like it, either. It's like an itch deep within my soul that I can't scratch. Now that I know how great it feels to have her in my life, I don't think I can ever go back to the way it was before.

Exhaling slowly, I clench and unclench my hands. I meet her eyes. My stomach twists. "I'm sorry."

She blinks. "You're sorry? For what?"

"For... for..."

For taking advantage. For taking more than she was willing to give.

"I'm the one who should be apologizing," Mackenzie says.

She has done literally nothing wrong.

She flinches. "You were hurting and I—"

I flinch at the memory of my speech, of how much I humiliated myself, of how she had to witness my breakdown. She stops, frowning.

"Wes..."

My hands itch to touch her, to feel her soft skin again, her body pressed up next to mine.

I can't do this.

Sidestepping around her, I head towards the kitchen. On autopilot, I fill the kettle and pull down two mugs. She leans against the doorframe, arms crossed, watching me.

"Do you want to talk about it?"

No. Not at all. Not now, not ever.

She sighs. "I won't push you."

The most excruciating decision of my life is which tea to pick. Earl grey? Honey lavender? Spicy orange ginger? To distract myself, I busy myself with preparing her drink. A handful of mini marshmallows go into the bottom of her mug, topped off with some hot chocolate powder. The kettle whistles and I add water, stir, and top if off with some more marshmallows.

"So that's why it's so rich," she says slowly, and I glance over in her direction. "You put the marshmallows in the bottom and on top."

This way, they melt a little, and they thicken the drink while adding a creamy component.

I clear my throat. "My mom made it this way."

Her face softens. "Listen, about your parents…"

No. We're not doing this. Not now, not ever. My walls go up like a forcefield, surrounding me from any potential pain. I've had to deal with enough of it in my life. I won't anymore.

"I don't talk about that."

We can only delay for so long. I hand over her hot chocolate and her fingertips brush against mine. Her eyes are locked on mine.

"I think it was very brave of you to address it in your speech," she says, and I can help flinching at the memory. "It's an important part of who you are."

I wish it wasn't. I wish they were still alive. I wish I had died in that car crash instead of them.

I wish, I wish, I wish.

"I am sorry," she says, and I turn my head away. "You were hurting, and I made that worse."

My eyes snap back to hers. "Worse?"

I'm so confused.

She raises her chin, defiant, her eyes bright with nerves. "I hugged you for my own selfish reasons. I know you don't like physical touch. And then I…"

"I kissed you," I say slowly.

"Yeah, after I…"

I blink at her. "Mackenzie, I *kissed* you."

And she fled. And she went back to class. And she spent the better part of a week avoiding me.

"I apologize for making you uncomfortable."

Scoffing, I set my tea down on the counter and take her mug out of her hands.

"You didn't."

"I did. You were tense and—"

"If I didn't want it, I would have told you," I tell her slowly.

She doesn't get it.

"I kissed you," I repeat for the third time.

Her eyes are bright. Finally, it sinks in. She looks up at me from beneath her long, dark lashes.

"You wanted to kiss me?"

Only for forever.

I nod. She sniffs, ducking her head.

Moving closer, I stop when I'm directly in front of her. My finger on her chin forces her to lift her head. Her eyes are shiny.

"All the time," I tell her.

Right now. And now. And ten minutes from now. And a year from now.

She exhales a heavy sigh. "Wes…"

My thumb dances along her cheek. She leans her head into the contact.

"May I kiss you now?"

She nods, her teeth sinking into the pillow of her lower lip. Gently I brush my finger along her lip, prying it free from her grasp. She lets out a nervous giggle, and I can't hide my smile in time. I fucking adore this woman.

With deliberate movement, I cup her cheek in my hand. Slowly, I lower my head so my lips can brush against hers. Tentative. It's been a long time since I've done this. I almost don't remember how.

She sighs, melting against me. She raises her hands and then stops, unsure.

I pull back a little to meet her eyes. I don't know how to convey just how much she means to me.

"You can touch me any time," I tell her, and she swallows, hesitant. "I don't mind it when you touch me."

Her hand is pressed flat to my chest, over my heart. I'm sure she can feel it pounding a thousand beats a minute.

Mackenzie tilts her chin up, angling for another kiss. I'm happy to oblige her. My hand on her hip pulls her body flush against mine, supple curves against my bulky broad muscles. She lets out a quiet moan and tries to deepen the kiss.

She fists her hand in the fabric of my sweatshirt, gathering the fabric and tugging gently, pulling me closer, until we're as close as two bodies can be with clothes still separating us.

I soak in the moment, soft, sweet, innocent kisses. She doesn't hate me. She seems to want me to kiss her, if the way she's pressed right up against me is any indication.

On a sigh, she pulls back. She's breathing hard, her face flushed.

"Wes..."

I'm mesmerized by her. Her dark blonde hair is falling out of her ponytail. I wrap a tendril around my pinky finger, amazed at how soft it is. Her eyes soften.

"What does this mean?"

My heart is trapped in my throat. "I... I don't know."

I'm crazy about her. I want to be with her. But I'm not in the right frame of mind for a relationship. She deserves more than what I am capable of. And she deserves more than a fling.

Her face falls. "Oh. Um..."

I love you. I *love* you. I love *you*.

Curling my fingers, I brush my knuckle along her cheek. She sighs, and her eyes fall closed.

"I... you..."

My words freeze in my throat. How do I say this to her? This is all I've wanted for—I don't even know how long. And now that it could actually happen, I don't know how to make this work.

"I like you, Wes," Mackenzie says quietly. She slides her hand from my chest to my shoulder, down my arm, to curl her fingers around mine.

I marvel at the feeling of her palm pressed to mine, of her beautiful skin on mine. I can hardly focus on her words.

"I'm sorry I ran away. I know that hurt you," she says, and I take a deep, shuddering breath, meeting her eyes. "I won't do that again."

"I like you, too," I finally manage.

My chest feels tight and itchy. The world hasn't ended, and I have to laugh for ever thinking it might.

"So, where do we go from here?"

"The living room." That's as much as I can manage right now.

She blinks. "Okay."

The small galley kitchen's walls are closing in on us. I can't think, can't breathe. Tea in hand, I follow her to the slightly more open living area.

She settles on the sofa and curls her legs beneath her. Instead of sitting in my usual armchair, I take a seat beside her. With her eyebrows raised, she shifts to face me.

"You're my best friend here," she finally says. "I don't want to ruin what we have."

"We won't." Of that I'm sure. Slowly, deliberately, I reach for her hand. She lets me take it, lets me lace our fingers together. "I like you." My eyes are glued to hers. "But I can't be what you need."

She lets out a heavy sigh. "Why don't you let me worry about what I need."

I frown.

"I don't know how we do this," she admits. "I've never had a boyfriend. I've never... explored feelings for someone in the way I want to with you."

I want to be with her. I do. I want her smiles and her laughter and her thoughts and her book recommendations. I want to eat meals with her and walk with her through campus and be by her side. I want to be in her life. I want to be her partner, in this and everything else.

"I'm out of practice." It's been a long time since I've done this. I was a kid back then. I knew nothing.

Her smile is kind, shy. "So we'll figure this out together. We'll go slow."

I should take her on a date. She deserves a night out, an evening to feel special.

Clearing my throat, I trace my thumb over the back of her knuckles. "Mackenzie, would you like to go out with me? Next Friday?"

Her face falls. "We have an away—"

"Away game. Right. In Maine."

I didn't take that into consideration. She's gone the next two weekends for away games. There's no way I can go up to Maine or Connecticut to see her play.

"Tomorrow. Breakfast," I decide.

She nods, hesitant.
"Not the dining hall. Somewhere else."
Her expression brightens. "Yeah. I think I'd like that."
We can do this. We can make this work.

twenty-one

. . .

Mackenzie

MY HANDS ITCH TO touch him. "Can I…" I take a deep breath. "Can I kiss you again?"

Wes sets aside his tea, then takes my mug and sets it on the coffee table.

"Ground rules," he says, and my stomach sinks.

I paste on a cheerful smile, and he frowns. When I drop it, his expression relaxes, and he leans into me again. I don't think he realizes he's doing it.

"*You* can touch me. I don't like when other people touch me," he says slowly. He takes a deep breath, then lets out a measured exhale. "I like when you do."

I set my free hand on his forearm, covered by the fabric of his hoodie, and his whole face lights up.

"We take this slow," he continues. "I'm not ready… I can't… we have to…"

"We both need to be comfortable with this," I add, and he nods, relief evident in his features. "We're on the same page here."

He takes a deep breath. "No sex."

"Oh."

I hadn't considered that into the equation.

Eventually, yeah, I might want that. My pulse thuds dully at the idea of sex with Wes. Of getting naked. Of pleasuring him, and him pleasuring me. Learning each other's bodies, one excruciatingly devastating moment at a time.

His face falls. "I'm not ready—"

"I'm a virgin," I blurt. Heat rises to my cheeks. Clearing my throat, I meet his gaze head on. "I didn't mean to—I just —I'm not ready for that, either. I'm not saying never. Just not now."

"Not now," he agrees. His fingers tighten around mine. "I'm okay if we… experiment. We don't have to be celibate. But I'm not ready—I can't—I'm not there yet."

"Neither am I. I'm fine with… experimenting." My stomach swoops at the thought of touching him, of him touching me. "I don't have a lot of experience."

Basically none. A few awkward, fumbled kisses at summer camp. Some over the clothes groping at winter formal last year. There has never been a guy I've been interested in enough to pursue. For years, my sights have been set on sports and school, and now that I finally have enough mental bandwidth, I end up head over heels for the one guy I never thought I could have.

"We can't tell my brother."

His face goes pale. He nods emphatically.

"I'm not saying keep it a secret forever." I don't want to be some anonymous fuck he keeps on the side (with no actual fucking). "Just not yet."

"I don't know if I can… do this," he says. He swallows loudly. "But I'm going to try. I'm going to… talk more."

"You're doing great."

Wes gives me a sheepish smile. "It's easy to talk to you. Other people… I don't like it. Spending time with you makes me happy."

My heart pounds.

"We'll see each other as much as we can. I'll try to text

more," he says. If I thought he was short in person, his texts are even more curt. Although now I have to wonder if that was just a front to hide his feelings behind...

I have to laugh. "Did we just negotiate our entire relationship?"

He frowns. "Is that what this is? A... relationship?"

Hesitation quickens my heart rate. "I mean, I thought that's what you wanted."

"It is."

So why does his face say the exact opposite?

Wes clears his throat. "I don't... date. I don't hook up. I'm not interested in that lifestyle."

I hold my breath, unsure of where he's going with this.

"You... you are the only person that's ever made me wish I was."

Now I'm confused.

He tightens his grip on my fingers. "You're the only person I want to do this with. I'm not looking for anyone else. Spending time with you makes me happy."

A warm glow bursts within my chest. "I like spending time with you, too."

"I'll try to talk more. Try to... communicate," he says. He sighs, shakes his head. "I want to when I'm with you. I don't with other people."

Most of the time, he communicates with other people in grunts and monosyllables. I have noticed he seems to have no problem speaking when he's around me, albeit in short, hesitant sentences. Moreover, I never seem to have a problem understanding whatever he's trying to say. At least, it seems like we understand each other.

I clear my throat. "Right. Well. I should be heading home soon."

His face falls. "You're leaving?"

He hasn't asked me to stay. More than that, though, it feels oddly uncomfortable to sleep on this couch now that we are… whatever we are.

"It's getting late." As much as I want to stay and make out a little (or forever,) I know if we're going on this date tomorrow morning, I probably won't sleep all night thinking about it. I need some time to process this, to convince myself it's real. After all these years of hoping…

"You can stay." Wes draws his thumb over my knuckles again. I like this, the little, innocent touches, as much as I think I would enjoy more… exploratory touches. Naked touches. Okay, semi-naked touches.

But we're starting slow. Neither of us is ready to get fully naked. We're on the same page with that.

"I want you to stay," he says, more confident now. When his eyes meet mine, I see the hesitation there. He doesn't want to push me, either.

"We can make out for a bit before I have to go," I suggest, and his pleased smile is positively lethal. My stomach swoops.

With one firm tug, he pulls me into his strong chest. His arms wrap around me, holding me close. "This is okay?"

It's perfect.

I tilt my head up, expectant, and he delivers. His kiss is soft, sweet—hesitant. Sliding my hands over his strong biceps and around his firm shoulders, I indulge in his touch, innocent and sweet. His hand roams over my spine, caressing each vertebrae, and the other plays with my ponytail. Usually I hate whenever anyone touches my hair, even a hair stylist. It drives my nuts when my brother tugs on my hair, so of course he does it all the time.

I like when Wes plays with my hair. My entire body is alight with sensation in the best way possible.

We have the house to ourselves. It's Sam's birthday this week, so she and Miles are celebrating this weekend—which is more than I ever wanted to know about my brother's sex life, thank you very much. Greg invited me to a party, which I politely declined, as I do nearly every time he invites me. I'm not as antisocial as Wes is (nobody is,) but I'm kind of over the frat party scene. Diana and Mason assured me they were bringing their guys over to their respective places tonight—they're not the only ones to have noticed the weirdness with Wes this week —and would try to convince Jill to do the same with Amir.

Maneuvering on the couch, I angle myself against the cushions. Wes takes the hint I'm trying to give and hovers over me. With a slight tug, he's on top of me, every inch of his glorious body pressed to mine.

He lets out a groan that reverberates through me. My whole body sings with pleasure. He deepens the kiss and the first touch of his tongue to mine has me making noises, too.

"Wes?"

"Hm?" He pulls back just enough to get some breath, before he diverts his attention to my neck. I tilt my head back and give him room to work. My hands start to roam, mapping the contours of his muscles.

"I really like you."

He chuckles into my neck. "I really like you, too."

twenty-two

. . .

Mackenzie

WES MEETS me at the lobby of my dorm at nine o'clock sharp. He's dressed up in a collared shirt beneath his coat, and I suddenly feel self-conscious about my jeans, sweatshirt, and rain boots combo. His face lights up when he sees me. When his eyes scrub over my body, a rush of heat runs through me. Yeah, he isn't upset in the least.

He clears his throat and thrusts his hand out at me. It's only then that I see the collection of sunflowers in his hand, three long-stemmed flowers with a soft pink ribbon tied around them. My favorite color. I don't like harsh pink or hot pink; I prefer a blush, rosy pink. I didn't think he knew that. Beneath his silent and stoic ignoring the world exterior, Wes is a lot more perceptive than he lets on.

I don't know what to do with the flowers. Do I take them with us? Do I leave them in my dorm? I've never been given flowers by a guy before, only by family members after sporting events. Do I hug him? Kiss him? I mean, I want to kiss him all the time, and this is no exception. It feels like I need to thank him. Words alone won't be enough. He needs some sort of demonstrative action to show how much I like the flowers. What do I do?

Wes dips down and drops a soft kiss to my cheek. "Are you overthinking again?"

Yes. And I like that he knows that, that he can tell when I start to spiral.

He kisses my other cheek, like he can't get enough of me. I like that, too.

"Let's put the flowers up in your dorm, and then we can go to breakfast," he suggests.

With any other guy, I would take that as an attempt to get me upstairs and into bed. With Wes, though, I know he isn't trying to take my clothes off right now. He genuinely wants to wait for his own personal reasons, and they have nothing to do with the reasons I want to wait. It just so happens that our individual tendencies to be cautious and risk-averse complement each other.

I badge him past the security desk and we ride the elevator in quiet silence. It's peaceful being with him. I don't feel the need to talk to fill the space.

He's been to my dorm before. He helped me move in (along with all the rest of the guys), he brought me soup when I came down with a cold in October, and right before finals last semester he dropped off some books he thought I would like. Now I have to wonder if he was silently telling me he liked me all along.

It feels different now, though. Now I know he does like me. Now we're together, whatever that means. It's not just a friend dropping by my dorm; this is the guy I'm dating, the guy I hope to one day *experiment* with. Not yet. I'm not ready right now, and clearly neither is he. One day. Eventually. Maybe. Soon.

The door clicks open. My side of the room is... not quite pristine, but certainly more neat than Claire's. I like when things are put away, when everything has a place. Living with a roommate has its challenges, sure, but even without her... exhibitionist quirks, Claire and I wouldn't get along simply because of our different standards of cleanliness. My bed is made daily. My sheets are washed weekly without fail. My laundry is folded and put away the day I wash it. Even my library books are in tidy stacks. Everything has a place, and everything is in its place.

Wes's eyes are a little wide as he takes in my room. It's different now. He isn't just my older brother's teammate. He isn't just my friend. He's… whatever we are.

The soft pink comforter my sister and I picked out last summer feels babyish and immature now. I still have Ursa nestled against my pillows, the neon orange teddy bear I got when I was six months old and have slept with nearly every night since. My desk is cluttered with novels I keep meaning to return to the library. The bookshelf above my bed has even more books where most people keep knickknacks or framed pictures. The walls have a few photos of my family and past teams. It's plain compared to Claire's loud posters and wall to wall pictures.

He goes straight to the desk. He examines the titles before picking one out of the stack, thumbing through it. My cheeks heat up. It's not that I'm ashamed of reading erotica. It's not that I care if he knows—I've shared some pretty risqué romance and sci-fi titles with him in the past, so it's not like he has no clue what I like to read. Somehow it's different with him holding the physical book I read, seeing the same words I saw when I got myself off a few nights ago.

"I'll have to read this one," he says. His voice is lower, huskier than usual. Is he turned on from just a casual skim of the book? Or is it from being in my room? No, it can't be that. It *was* a pretty intense book… I might have read it twice. Okay, three times.

"I'd offer to let you borrow it, but it's a library book."

His eyes are dark. "We should go to the library."

I laugh. "Now?"

"No. After breakfast." His smile makes my stomach flip. "We can pick out books together."

That's… perfect. It's so perfectly us.

"It's a date," I say, a little self-consciously.

Wes grins. "Yeah, it is." He pushes the flowers in my direction again. "Do you have a cup?"

I have an old water bottle. The top leaks, so I can't throw it in my bag. It's a perfect receptacle to hold some pretty flowers from my new boyfriend, or whatever he is.

With the flowers situated, he holds his hand out to me. It takes me a second to realize he wants me to hold it. Wes pulls me to him and gives me a chaste, innocent kiss.

"Good morning," he says, his eyes bright.

"Good morning."

He kisses me again, quick, like he has to reassure himself I'm real.

"Ready for breakfast?"

"Yeah. You said we're not going to the dining hall?"

He clears his throat. "This is my Sunday tradition. I've never shared it with anyone before."

My stomach flips with anticipation.

He leads me to the elevator, where we make our way downstairs and out to the chilly grey morning. We have to separate to zip up our coats, but as soon as we're both done, he takes my hand again. I like this. I like tactile Wes, I like how eagerly he wants to touch me. For someone who has proclaimed to hate physical touch for the four and a half years I've known him, he sure isn't shy about touching me now.

We're walking towards town. After spending all my life coming to university sporting events and then the last few years visiting my brother every week, I'm more than familiar with the main drag of town and the scant few restaurants open at this time of day.

I'm not surprised when he leads me to the diner. He opens

the door for me, which is nice, and then his hand settles on my lower back, guiding me inside.

"We'll be right with you, honey," a waitress calls out with her back to us, clearing a table.

The diner is packed. There are barely any open tables. There is a cluster of people near the host's stand.

"Wesley, you're late," a woman says. An older waitress is standing in front of us, her hands on her hips. "Everything okay, baby?"

He nods.

Her eyes narrow in on me standing so close to him, his arm around me. "Two today, sugar?"

He nods again.

"Right this way." She grabs a menu and starts down the row, to the loud disapproval of the half dozen groups waiting.

She shows us to a booth at the back of the diner with a window view. We can see the entire street from here. Wes guides me into one side and then sits down across from me.

"I'll give you two a moment," the waitress says, unsuccessfully hiding her smile.

"So this is your Sunday tradition?"

"Every Sunday. I read and people watch." He clears his throat and looks away, his cheeks ever so slightly pink.

"That sounds perfect." It is exactly how I'd like to spend every Sunday, or even every day. I'm reliant on the student athlete dining hall for most of my meals. It's only when my parents visit that I usually eat off campus. My budget is stretched thin enough as it is. Luckily people watching is free.

He reaches across the table and takes my hand again. His thumb draws over my knuckles.

"I'm glad we're doing this," he says quietly.

"Me, too."

"I really like you," he says in the same voice.

I grin. "Me, too."

"Hey, Wesley," the waitress says with a friendly smile. She

deposits a teapot and cup for tea in front of him. "You have a friend with you this week?"

He nods.

"Your regular?"

He grunts. She doesn't seem to be offended. If anything, it seems like she can speak Wes, too.

"And what about you, hon?" Her warm eyes turn to me.

"The veggie scramble, please, and a glass of water."

She makes a note on her pad. "Anything else?"

"That's it, thank you."

"Of course, sugar. It'll be right out."

He busies himself with making his tea. It's a generic English breakfast, which I know isn't his favorite. When it's steeping, he takes my hand again.

"Do you have any plans for the rest of your day?"

"Hopefully getting some yoga or pilates in later this afternoon." I didn't play much last night, so my body isn't too sore. At the same time, I don't feel up for a heavy, intense workout today. Something light and low-impact will get my heart pumping without stressing my body too much.

Wes hums. "There's a pilates class I sometimes go to on Sunday afternoons."

"You? Pilates?"

I know some of the guys go—Tucker is really into it because of Mason, and Diana drags Barrett every chance she gets. I didn't think Wes was interested in that.

He nods. "Tucker and Barrett got me into it. It's part of my Sunday routine."

"What else is your routine? Aside from coming here?"

"Well, there's usually a walk to the library," he says, and I laugh, because that's so typically Wes. "Stock up on books, walk through town, sight see. Run errands. Do laundry. Read a little. Then pilates and sometimes a spin class. Dinner with the guys. Superhero movie to end the night."

Most Sunday dinners are strictly for the six guys. Girlfriends don't join them, at least not that I've seen. Miles has extended plenty of offers for me to have dinner with him or hang out at his house, but never on Sunday evenings. Sam, Mason, Diana, and Jill are always around, or the guys are off with them, but Sunday dinner is for the six of them.

I like that. I hope that next year, when I'm living in one of the basketball houses, our team gets along at least half as well as this house does.

My routine isn't nearly as set in stone as his. I'm still in the middle of basketball season, so every week looks different. Sometimes our games are on weeknights. Sometimes they're on weekends. Sometimes we're at home. Sometimes we're traveling.

"Do you like being retired? Do you miss football?"

He sighs. "I'm sure I will next fall. It will be weird not to spend all summer preparing."

"I still have to remind myself I'm not doing tennis or swimming anymore. I wake up at four o'clock for morning swim at least three times a week."

He cracks a smile. "We still have six o'clock lifts. At least now they're optional instead of mandatory."

The men's basketball team works out around that time every day. Our teams share a weight room, so our reserved lifting time is at three o'clock in the afternoon, followed immediately by practice on the courts. Football doesn't have to share their weight room with anyone else. Then again, they have close to a hundred guys who have to cycle in and out every day.

The waitress effortlessly carries a tray over. With practiced hands she delivers Wes's egg white omelette, grilled veggies, and baked beans. A healthier version of a full English, which I have reason to believe is his favorite given how often he eats it in the dining hall. A tray of toast follows soon after, then my breakfast.

"Anything else I can get you, baby?"

He looks to me. I have everything I need.

Wes shakes his head.

"All right. Enjoy, you two."

We're quiet for a few moments as we both tuck into our breakfast. The silence extends between us, an awkward elastic stretching the narrow space of the booth.

"This is weird. It's weird for you, too, right?"

He frowns. "How so?"

"You're not reading."

His laugh makes a few different tables look in our direction. "I can read if you want me to."

"No, no. I just… it's…"

"I brought a book," Wes points out, raising his brows. "And I know you have your e-reader with you."

Guilty as charged.

"How do you know?"

"Because you don't go anywhere without it," he says, which… true. "Also, you kept patting your bag on the walk over."

I like how well he knows me. Sure, we're going to learn more about each other, but we already have a solid foundation. We aren't going into this blind.

He pulls a book from his coat pocket. It's book seventeen of a mystery series he's been reading as long as I've known him, this latest released last month. I got about five books into the series before I had to quit. It wasn't the right fit for me. The main character is far too self-loathing for me to empathize with.

So I pull my e-reader out of my purse. He flicks through his book, trying to find his place. Wes is very anti-bookmark, for reasons I've never understood. He's also against dog-ears (which I agree with) and folding pages (also agreed). Although in my personal books, I like to annotate, and I will flag certain special pages with a post-it note. He won't. He doesn't like anything marring the otherwise pristine pages of his books.

We read and eat our breakfasts. It's just like every other meal we've shared in the dining hall, except even better.

My omelette is gone almost before I realize it. He's finishing up his breakfast, too. When he's done, he pushes his plate aside and reaches across the table for my hand. When he takes it, it's like my whole world slots into place.

Breakfast with Wes. Reading. Holding hands. Yeah, I can get used to this.

twenty-three

. . .

Mackenzie

EVENTUALLY, it's time for us to leave the diner. Wes pays —over my objection—and then takes my hand again.

I'm not afraid to be caught holding hands with him in public. I don't care if anyone knows. The only person who really can't find out is my brother—at least not until we figure out what we're doing. We've been together for about thirteen hours. Eventually, maybe, Miles can know. Not right now.

Besides, Miles never comes to town on Sundays. I probably won't see him all day. It's his day to sleep in and sleep with Sam, which, again, is enough about my brother's sex life. Sam is more than happy to share the details when she's had a few drinks. As much as I like hanging out with her, sometimes I need some brain bleach to deal with the things she tells me.

Wes clearly isn't in a hurry to get to the library. He grips my hand firmly as we walk leisurely through the town center. I've always loved Newton. Yeah, it's a college town, but I grew up coming here all the time. It's home now as much as Charlestown is some days. The university library is a special place to both of us. I like that it's now becoming a special place for us together.

Wes leads me to the elevator and up to the third floor, where the fiction is kept. I have to shove my hand into my pocket to keep from flinging my arms around him and kissing him senseless. He's being so sweet, so thoughtful—this is the most perfectly fitting first date I've ever been on.

Okay, so maybe it's the *only* first date I've ever been on. I've read enough that I know what to expect.

The mystery section is over to the left. That's his favorite genre. Instead, he heads in the direction of the romance stacks. That's where I normally find my books, and although I know he'll read pretty much anything he can get his hands on, I didn't think he was all that interested in the genre.

I tug gently on his hand and he looks at me. "Hm?"

"You don't like romance."

He cracks a smile. "I do."

"Since when have you read a romance novel?"

"Since you did."

My whole world shifts fourteen degrees to the left. "What?"

He swallows and looks away. I squeeze his hand and wait for him to look at me again.

"You read as much as I do."

"So how did you start reading romance?"

"Because you were. Because I wanted to know what you were reading." His cheeks are flushed, and it isn't just from the heater working overtime in here. "I wanted to know everything about you, Mackenzie. I didn't think this could ever happen. So I got as close to you as I could without crossing that line."

Well, I'm about to cross some lines now.

I drop his hand and his face falls. He squares his shoulders and lifts his chin.

And then I step to him, running my hands over his strong chest. He takes a deep, shuddering breath, his forehead falling forward to press against mine.

"I really like you, Mackenzie." His arms come up around me, settling low on my hips.

The first touch of my lips to his sends a spark of static electricity running down my spine. Short, sweet kisses. His grip tightens on my hips. Sliding my hand up to his neck, the scratchy stubble on his jaw, I kiss him more firmly. I don't really know what I'm doing. I've never really done this before —and certainly never in a *library*.

My blood sings with delight. This is so deliciously forbidden. If the librarians were to come across us, they would surely kick us out. There's a very strict no fraternization policy between the stacks.

Wes deepens the kiss, his tongue stroking into my mouth, and I can't help the little moan that slips out. He grins against my lips.

With his hands on my hips, he walks me backwards, deeper within the stacks. We're hidden from view. My back bumps against a shelf full of books, and he steps even closer, until his big, strong body is pressed all up against me. Either that's a cell phone in his pocket or he is certainly enjoying this —at least as much as I am.

I lose track of time. We make out for—maybe five minutes, maybe five hours. All I can think about is the feeling of his mouth pressed to mine, his delicious body pressed to mine. I never want this to end.

A sound a few feet away makes him jump back. We both look in the direction of the noise. There's nothing there.

Wes clears his throat and runs his hand through his hair. "I didn't bring you here for this."

His face is flushed, his lips swollen from my kisses. He tugs at the hem of his coat.

"You didn't?"

I can't quite catch my breath. It's like a part of me is missing now that I'm not touching him.

"No. I thought we could pick out some books." He

coughs. "You don't like mysteries very much. Historical fiction is fine when you're in the right mood. And I've read a few too many cyberpunk books this month, I need a break. So. Romance."

"And you're going to read it?"

He nods. "We both will. Not at the same time—on our own."

"Like a book club."

Wes laughs. "Or just sharing an experience together."

He offers me his hand again, and I take it. He tugs me towards him, pressing a kiss to the top of my head.

We walk through the stacks. I have some favorite authors, writers whose work I keep going back to time and again. Liz Hambleton. Emma Black. Ariana St. Claire. And Stella Nova. I'll read pretty much anything they write.

And then I see it. It's the sequel to a book I've read at least three times in the last three months, and more before that. There has always been a mile-long wait list for the sequel. I've never seen it out in the wild like this. Bookstores are always sold out.

There's only one copy.

"You read it first," Wes says. "Once you finish, I'll read it."

"Are you sure?"

"Yeah." He darts down and kisses my cheek. "I can wait for you. I always will."

twenty-four

. . .

Wes

THE WEEK PASSES by in the blink of an eye. Mackenzie joins us—me—for nearly every meal in the dining hall. Nobody is the least bit suspicious. We play footsie under the table and read our respective books and enjoy our limited time together.

On Monday, at lunch she hands over the book we selected; by Monday night, I've devoured it, and I'm about ready to devour her. Tuesday she sits beside me in class again. I might take every opportunity to touch her that I can. We hold hands while Professor Blake lectures. We meet on Wednesday afternoon in the library. We make out for a bit, hidden in the stacks, before we each pick out a new pile of books to read.

Thursday, we have breakfast together before class, along with two of my roommates and their girlfriends. I don't get to see her the rest of the day. She leaves later that afternoon for her game. It's only been a few hours. I miss her already.

She calls me shortly after nine o'clock. Greg and Tucker are playing video games on the couch, Miles watching and ready to play the next round. A rush runs through me, reminding me I'm dating my roommate's sister.

I answer the call right away. "Hey. Hang on one second."

All three guys look over with interest.

"Who's calling you?" Miles demands.

"My sister." *Your* sister.

Lies. Lies. Lies.

Locking myself in my room, I throw myself onto my bed and hug my pillow to my chest.

"Hey, baby."

Is that too much? Am I coming on too strong?

Mackenzie giggles on the other end. "Hey. How was your day?"

"Terrible."

She clucks. "What happened?"

"I didn't get to spend time with you."

She sighs. "Wes…"

Uh oh. The hairs on the back of my neck stand on end. "Yeah?"

"You always know just what to say."

My chest puffs up with pride.

"It must be all those romance novels you've been reading," she teases, and I laugh.

Shifting on the bed, I run my hand through my hair. "Yeah, it is."

"Really?" She's incredulous—that I'm admitting to it, or that it's true, I'm not sure.

"You think I go around trying out lines on every woman I meet?"

"So that was a line."

Shit.

"No. I meant—"

Mackenzie giggles. "I know what you meant. I know you don't go around chatting up random women."

I don't chat much to begin with. It's always been easy with her, though. Not quite effortless—I still have to put the work in. But certainly easier than with other people. I can count on one hand the number of people I'm comfortable with in this world. Aside from my sister and one cousin, they're all people I've met through school. My roommates. Two of my former coaches. James, the head librarian. Sam, Mason, Diana —the jury is still out on Jill, she and Amir haven't been dating long enough for me to really get to know her yet.

Even in the *before* time, I was never the most social guy. I had teammates, but I didn't exactly have a big group of friends. The few guys I talked to before have all disappeared into the woodwork over the years. I dated because that's what was expected of me, a top ranked football player expected to go places. Teenage hormones are a powerful drug.

I'm going nowhere, now, except grad school. Maybe. If I can get in. We'll see.

I need a backup plan. All of my friends are going in different directions this spring. Tucker and Mason are going to grad school—they're only applying to schools where they think they can both get in, since they're in the same program. Miles and Sam are graduating. She's working on getting a sports marketing internship in the city. He'll probably follow her. Boston is his home town. Barrett's family is from northeastern Massachusetts, and Diana's parents live on the other side of the state; they probably aren't going far from either of them.

Only Amir and Greg are sticking around for another year. They're not graduating quite yet, and they both still have another year of athletic eligibility. Sometimes I forget they're not seniors like the rest of us.

… and then there's Mackenzie. She's a freshman. In three and a half months, I'll be moving to I don't know where, and I'll have to leave her behind. I don't want to do that. As much as I was hesitant about my ability to sustain a relationship,

I'm just as worried about our future as I am about our present. I don't want to finally get a chance to be with her, only to have it all ripped away by our circumstances after I graduate.

Newton is my top choice grad school. It always has been, even before I started my undergrad here. Their sports therapy program is one of the best in the country. I was planning on starting out at Michigan before coming here for grad school. If I could manage to stay for both undergrad *and* grad school here… it would be all my dreams come true.

Well. Not *all* of my dreams. I have been having some quite… intense dreams the last few nights.

I've spent the last five years fucking my fist every night. I'm in no way ready to have sex anytime soon. I have too much shit to work out first. But some day, soon, maybe, potentially, it might be on the horizon.

And Mackenzie is like all my dreams come to life. She's all I've been able to think about for—years.

"How was your drive up?"

She sighs. "It was fine."

"The team still not gelling?"

It's hard being the new kid. It's even harder when everyone else seems to get along and you're sitting on the outside looking in.

"I'm rooming with Dareesa, which is kind of nice. Pia invited me to sit next to her, and then she slept the whole drive."

My heart sinks at her unhappiness. "I'm sorry, baby."

She's quiet for a few moments. "Say it again?"

"I'm sorry." I ache with the sadness in her voice.

"No. The…the other thing."

My stomach churns with anxiety. Did I take it too far? Am I going too fast?

"Baby?"

She lets out a slow breath. "Yeah. I like that."

"You do?"

"Yeah. I, um. I didn't think I would. But I really do." She pauses. "I wish I could show you just how much I like it in person."

My cock perks up at the insinuation. "Yeah?"

"Yeah." Mackenzie giggles. "Do you… do you like when I talk like that?"

"A little too much," I admit. I adjust myself and roll over. There is no way I'm going to touch myself while I'm on the phone with her. Not yet, at least.

"Maybe this week we can…" She stops.

"Yeah?"

"We can hang out in my dorm. I know it's small and cramped, and I live with the worst roommate ever but…"

"But it's not my house."

"Yeah." She sighs. "I like your house, but with all your roommates… and one in particular… maybe some privacy would be best."

"That sounds great, baby."

"And maybe…" She trails off.

My sweats are way too tight now. "Yeah?"

She takes a deep breath. "Maybe we can explore a little?"

"Whatever you want to do."

If she wanted me to stand on my head, I'd do it—because it's her.

"I want to touch you," she blurts, then giggles. "I'm sorry. I'm nervous. Which is ridiculous, because it's you, and you already know how I feel about you. But I do. I want to touch you, and I want you to touch me, and…"

I stifle my groan into my fist. "Baby, you can't talk like this."

"Like what?"

"Like you're in another state and not in your dorm on

campus right now. Because I'm about ten seconds from ordering a cab and driving up to you."

It's only two hundred and fifty miles. At this time of night, I'm sure we can make the drive in four hours, maybe less.

She's quiet. "You would do that?"

"In a heartbeat."

"Wes…"

"Yeah?"

"I know why you can't actually do it. But a part of me wishes you would. I… I miss you already."

"I miss you, too."

This is part of being a competitive athlete in the middle of their season. All of the games can't be held at home; some of them have to be on the road. And that means I have to miss her while she's gone, all the while knowing that soon, she'll make her way back to me, before she leaves again, and comes home again. It's a never ending cycle.

I spent five years living this life, traveling every weekend for college football, on top of all the years growing up. I never had anyone to miss—or anyone to miss me. As much as I wish Mackenzie was here with me, it also feels kind of nice to have a person in my life again that I want to be with all the time.

"Maybe…" She pauses again.

"Yeah?"

"I get home Sunday afternoon. Maybe you want to come over for a little bit?"

Yes. A thousand times yes.

"I'll be there to meet you at the bus." It's the least I can do. The quickest way for me to see her again, to pull her into my arms and kiss her senseless.

There's a shout on the other end, followed by some rustling.

She sighs. "I have to go. Lights out in fifteen minutes."

"Have a good sleep, baby. You're going to play great tomorrow."

"Thanks. Good night, Wes."

My traitorous cock twitches again at the sound of my name on her lips.

"Good night, Mackenzie."

I roll over and touch myself, thinking of her. And then I think of her all over again.

twenty-five

. . .

Mackenzie

ASHLEY HAS a cheer competition in Virginia, so my dad is with her and my mom has the weekend free. She comes up to Maine for my game, and we get to spend the weekend together. After the game on Friday night, she makes a point to take me and Dareesa out to dinner. It's a little weird spending time with my teammate outside of the arena or the gym. I kind of like it. It's almost like having friends again.

Technically, we have a day "off" on Saturday, but our schedule isn't our own. Team breakfast leads to mandatory study hall in the team's reserved block of banquet rooms. We have two hours of free time before we're required to gather for team yoga and then lunch. In the afternoon, we can do whatever we want—my mom and I grab coffee and wander through downtown Orono for a little bit—before we reconvene for a meeting to talk strategy, followed by team dinner. We get a few more hours of free time before bed. Pia and Amber set up a mini spa in their room and we gather to paint our nails in team colors.

It's a *lot* of together time.

Don't get me wrong—I like these girls. I like spending time with them, and the more I get to know them, the more I like them, and the more I feel like part of the team. It's not their fault we have a small freshman class. It's not their fault we aren't gelling as a group. They're trying. They're making every attempt to include me, include us. I'm just not feeling it. I don't think the other girls are, either.

"Tell me what else is new," Mom says at breakfast on Sunday before the game. It's a quiet few minutes away from the girls.

I bite my lip. I want to tell her the biggest news to happen to my personal life in—years. I want to tell her so bad. But we're keeping it on the down low, so my brother doesn't find out (and throw a fit about something that is literally **none of his business**).

"I called you last Sunday. You didn't answer and you never called me back."

That's not like me. I usually return calls right away. I don't like to keep the other person hanging. And this week has been so extraordinarily busy, I haven't had a chance to talk to either of my parents at all. Despite eating dinner with my brother nearly every day, we haven't talked, either.

"I was, um, on a date," I admit. I can tell her that much.

Mom's eyes go wide. "Tell me more."

"It went… well."

We've never had an opportunity to talk like this, mainly because I don't date. It's not that I don't want to—it's that it's never really happened for me. I guess I'm a bit of a late bloomer.

"Are you going to see them again?"

I notice how careful she is about her pronouns. Although my sister exclusively dates girls, she has never publicly, officially announced any particular sexuality. I'm not attracted to women. I'm just emotionally stunted and wasn't ready to date until now.

"I think so," I admit.

I hope so. Now that Wes and I are whatever we are, I'm

pretty sure that means we'll go out again. I like him, he likes me, and we both want to pursue this further.

"How did you meet?"

"Through the athletic department. He's an athlete, too."

Not a lie. Wes is a football player—or he was, until he "retired" at the end of last season at the end of his athletic eligibility. I'm pretty sure he would play another year or three if he could.

Mom sighs. "And what does Wes think about this? Does he know?"

My stomach flips. "What is that supposed to mean?"

"I just… well, you guys are so close. I always thought that maybe you two would…"

"Wes is probably my best friend at school," I remind her.

"I know."

"Our friendship can survive me dating. No matter who I'm dating—or not dating—I think we're mature enough that we can stay friends."

If we break up—*when* we break up—it won't be because I don't care for him. He'll be moving on to grad school and I will still have three more years here. We'll move on to the next natural stage in our lives. It will hurt like hell. But that doesn't mean the time we spend together now isn't worth it. It just means I have to enjoy him while it lasts.

Or maybe we'll be together forever and we'll live happily ever after. Who knows? I'm only nineteen and Wes is only my first boyfriend. I don't have it all figured out yet. I like him, he likes me, and we're together. That's all I know. That's all I need to know.

twenty-six

. . .

Wes

THERE'S an eerie sense of calm flooding through my veins. I feel like any other day I would probably be panicked out of my mind. With anyone else, I'd be sweating buckets.

Instead, I feel… good. Confident.

The bus pulls into the parking lot, and I shove my book into my backpack. It's been three and a half days since I've seen her. Longer still since I've held her in my arms. It doesn't matter that we've been talking on the phone every night before she goes to bed, and we text all throughout the day when she has her phone on her. I missed her.

Mackenzie is the seventh person off the bus. She darts over to me, and I wrap my arms around her. She smells like she always does, and it's comforting. Familiar. Her head fits perfectly beneath my chin. I coil a strand of hair from her ponytail around my index finger.

"Hey, baby."

It feels like my heart is about to pound its way out of my chest. My blood sings with pleasure at being near her again. It's like there's an ache in my soul that's been soothed by the simplicity of being in her presence.

She giggles and presses her face into my neck. Her warm

breath against the stubble on my jaw sends chills down my spine that coalesce into a ball in the pit of my stomach. Her open lips touch the sensitive spot beneath my ear, and my cock twitches.

"Missed you," she murmurs into my skin.

"Missed you more."

Her mouth curves into a smile. I ease back enough to meet her warm brown eyes. Slowly, deliberately, I lower my head and meet her for a kiss, soft, sweet, chaste. Her nails scratch through the hair at the back of my head, and my chest rumbles with a groan. She smiles against my lips.

There's a catcall from the general vicinity of the bus, and then what sounds like the whole team erupts into hoots and hollers.

"Your girls like this," I tell her, and she laughs.

"Yeah, they do." She locks her arms behind my neck and tries to kiss me again.

Taking a step back, I take her hand in mine. She pouts, and my chest warms with affection for her. I'm glad she's back. We have four short days before she has to travel again for her next set of games. We have to make the most of it.

Picking up the strap of her duffle bag, I sling it over my shoulder. She's perfectly capable of carrying it. She lifts heavier weights every day in the gym. I just want to do something nice for her.

The logical conclusion is that we're going to her dorm room. My house is out of the question. I'm not really in the mood to go to the library right now. There isn't exactly anywhere private at the ASC. There's no other place for us to go.

Mackenzie squeezes my hand and silently we walk in the direction of campus. After a few moments, she starts talking —and then she doesn't stop. She tells me about her games, which I watched online, and about seeing her mom, which I figured was part of her weekend plans, and about the shenanigans the senior girls of legal drinking age got into at their spa night.

I contribute minimally to the conversation. I'm more than satisfied walking with her and listening to the sound of her voice.

I still can't believe this incredible woman is interested in me. Doesn't she know there are other people out there that would be better for her? Not that I want her to go out with them—I don't want her to go out with anyone else. But I'm too old, too broken, too damaged for her. She deserves better than what I can offer her.

In three months, I'm going to graduate and move on to the next stage of my life. I can't ask her to come with me—I could never impose that on her, to give up on her own dreams and goals to support me in mine. And I don't know that I can sustain a long distance relationship. I don't even know that I can sustain an in person relationship.

All that said… Newton is still my top choice for graduate school. I already know the professors, I know the program. I know I would succeed here. What I don't know is if they will accept me.

Her dorm room is empty. Her side of the room is pristine, exactly as she left it. Her roommate's side of the room, on the other hand… yikes. I'm no neat freak, but the disorganization over there is making my palms sweat.

Mackenzie giggles nervously. Setting her bag down on her desk, I wipe my hands on my pants. She's blushing, not looking at me.

I clear my throat. "There's nothing to be nervous about."

"I'm not," she says, which is a blatant lie. She's practically vibrating with anticipation.

It's not like I'm about to launch across the room and maul her. Slipping off my coat, I toe off my shoes and then sit at the edge of her bed. Her shaking intensifies.

I pat the blanket beside me. "Sit with me."

She swallows and wrings her hands.

"Do you not want me here? I can go home."

I don't want to, of course, but if she's that uncomfortable…

She blows out a breath and shakes out her hands. Slowly, deliberately, she unbuttons her coat and slides off her boots. She sits next to me and then turns, one long leg propped on the bed between us.

"What happens now? Do we…" She purses her lips.

"Now we hang out." I have about as much experience at this as she does. "Do you want to watch a movie? Or maybe read?"

Her eyes light up. "Read."

Laughing, I squeeze her arm before digging out my book. She pulls her e-reader from her bag.

I make myself at home, stretching out on her bed. She looks lost. I pat the blanket beside me again. Gingerly, she lays out beside me.

I might not have done this for a while, but I think I still remember how to cuddle. I slide my arm beneath her neck and wrap it around her torso. I'm not trying to feel her up. I'm just holding her.

Tentatively, Mackenzie sets her head on my shoulder. A rumble of pleasure bubbles up deep within my chest. She darts up.

"Did I hurt you?"

Not in the slightest. I urge her back down and take the opportunity to place a soft kiss to her temple. Her happy sigh is answer enough.

We read our own books in quiet silence. I run my fingers through her hair, indulging in the feeling of her pressed up against me. After a few moments, she turns into me. Her cheek is resting on my chest now, her arm slung around my belly. I drop a kiss to the top of her head, and she sighs again.

"It's Sunday," she says out of nowhere.

I set down my book on my chest and crane my neck to look at her. "So?"

She sets down her e-reader, too. "Don't you have your Sunday night plans with the guys?"

"I'd rather spend the time with you."

Instead of melting like I expect, she looks even more determined. "I don't want to come between you and your friends."

"You're not."

She frowns.

"I spend every day with them. You leave again on Thursday. I would rather spend the time with you than with the guys I see all day every day."

"Wes…"

I love the way my name sounds on her lips, even when she's being stubborn.

At the end of the day, if I thought she were getting in the way of the things I wanted to do, I would tell her. She's not.

"You're the person I want to spend my time with. Whether that's Sunday evening or Saturday night or any other time of day, any day of the week, it's you. I like *you*."

Her eyes soften. "I know how important your friends are to you."

I shake my head. She's not getting it.

"You're important to me, too."

"Wes..."

I prop myself over her. The kiss is soft. Chaste. A simple brush of lips over lips, a casual reassurance of my feelings for her. I'm in this with her. I want to be with her.

Mackenzie slides her hands over my shoulders, her arms wrapped around my neck. She pulls me down on top of her, and I tuck her body beneath mine as I nonverbally assure her of how I feel about her.

Her body feels like magic pressed against me, all supple curves and beautifully firm lines. She's tall, nearly as tall as I am, so it feels like we're equals. Peers. The other girls I've been with were petite, tiny little things, a gymnast and a ballet dancer. Frail. I was always afraid I was going to break them. With Mackenzie, I know she can take it—she's strong. She can handle anything I throw at her, even my three hundred plus pounds.

My traitorous cock twitches, trying to get involved in the action. I shift my hips away from her, and she lets out a quiet sigh against my lips. She deepens the kiss. Slowly, her hips rock into mine.

She likes this. She likes *me*. I still can't quite wrap my brain around it.

I pull back to take a breath, and she moves her attention to my neck, sucking on the pulse point just below my jaw. Her hands roam over my body, caressing my arms, my back, groping my butt. My cock jerks in my jeans.

There's a sound behind us. I can't focus on that. I fold her leg over my hip and rock into her. The friction feels amazing. It's been five long years since I've gotten off with anyone other than me, myself, and my fist. This feels so good. I'm a few short minutes away from blowing a load in my pants like a horny preteen.

Let's face it. I might be twenty-two years old, but I'm still a horny preteen.

Mackenzie lets out a soft sigh. Her fingers dig into my back, her hips working against mine. She's enjoying this, too. My hands drift over her curves, feather light, a ghost of a whisper over her hips, her ass, her thighs.

There's a sound, like someone is clearing their throat. It's not Mackenzie. I try to turn and look. Her hand on my cheek forces my attention back to her. She runs her hands through my hair and rubs up against me.

"Come on," a voice says, and I nearly jump out of my skin. "Seriously?"

My heart hammers a thousand beats a minute. Miles cannot find out about this. He will absolutely kill me if he finds me rutting on top of his sister in her dorm room bed. He will straight up murder me if he finds out what kind of improper thoughts I've had about her in the security of my bed.

It's not Miles, though. There are two people standing in the doorway, a petite brunette I don't recognize and a guy I'm pretty sure was a redshirt freshman on offense last year. Jacobs? Johnson? I'm not sure. He wasn't important enough for me to remember his name.

Mackenzie leans her head around me. "Go away."

"It's my room, too," the pixie says, which makes my girl laugh.

"Yeah, like all the times you guys start fucking when I'm in the room?"

"Are you guys going to start fucking?" The guy looks interested, the piece of shit.

Joel. Eric Joel. He's a running back—and not a very good one, if I recall correctly. My eyes narrow in his direction as if we were on the field, and he flinches.

"Come on, babe," he says, slinging his arm around the girl. "We can hang out in my dorm tonight."

She frowns.

"I'll get rid of my roommate," he promises.

Her sigh is heavy, but after a moment, she nods, and he leads her out of the room.

Mackenzie's hand on my cheek forces my attention back to her. "Sorry about her."

"Not your fault. Part of having roommates."

"Still. Claire is the worst."

She's an awful person, and probably a worse person to be forced to live with, but at least she left. I don't think I could sneak her into my room—and even if I did, there's always the risk her brother would knock on my door at the most inopportune moment.

No, when we're at my house, we'll have to pretend like

nothing is happening between us. We can still hang out. We can spend Saturday nights together reading, and maybe make out if we're absolutely sure everyone is out for the night.

I'm not afraid of her brother. I'm not. But she's concerned, and I have to abide by her wish that he doesn't find out.

———

Miles pins me with a sharp stare when I walk through the door shortly before eleven. "Where have you been?"

The living room is empty, the TV paused on a video game. None of the other guys are hanging around. He's sitting alone by himself like I normally would.

"Out." Robotically, I hang up my coat on my hook.

"Yeah, I guessed that. Where were you?"

He's not my father. He's not my team captain. I don't owe him anything. I'm only dating his sister—in secret, because he can never know.

"I had plans."

Miles rolls his eyes. "Whatever, man."

Irritation creeps up my spine. Who the fuck does he think he is?

"You missed a good movie."

"Next time."

He scoffs. "We do this for you."

"Do what?"

"The Sunday night hangout. Dinner and a movie. It's for you."

I never asked for it. I never asked for anything from anyone. If they want to stay in, that's their choice. Just because I have no interest in dating, partying, drinking, or going out doesn't mean they have to abstain. I'm happy enough to hang out with my book and a mug of tea with me, myself, and I. Sure, sometimes it can get lonely. I like hanging out with them. But I never asked them to change their habits to spend time with me. Whatever they decided, that's on them.

Okay. So maybe I should have told them I wasn't going to come home for it. We have dinner together and watch a movie together every Sunday night. It's been the routine for the last two and a half years. Next year, when I'm in a new place for grad school without the easy camaraderie of my football teammates, I'm going to miss it. It's not like it's easy for me to make friends to begin with. Starting over with a new school, all while missing the place I've called home for the last five years, missing my best friend… yeah, it's not going to be pretty.

I grunt out a sound with an uplifting question at the end, and Miles sighs.

"Just tell us next time," he says.

There's no way in hell I'm telling him I'm making out with his sister. But, I guess I can tell him that I'm just going to be out.

Once I'm sequestered in the security of my room, I pull off my hoodie and t-shirt. The fabric smells like her perfume, subtle and light. My balls ache with pent-up tension.

After the interruption by her roommate, Mackenzie wasn't interested in continuing, and I don't blame her. We laid there and read and talked for the better part of two hours, until she started yawning. I wasn't going to chance staying the night. For one, her bed is far too small. On top of that, I don't want to alert my roommates that something is going on any more than we already have.

It's not that I'm ashamed. I'm not. I'd shout it from the rooftops if I could.

But she doesn't want her brother to know, and to be honest, I'm not sure if I do, either. I'm defying every rule there is in the book about roommates, teammates, and friends and their little sisters.

Mackenzie means more to me than some stupid bro

code. She's the real deal. She's amazing. And I love her. I've been in love with her for ages. So if she wants me, if she wants to be with me, I'm not going to let a pesky technicality like her brother being my friend stand in my way. She's not just Miles's younger sister; she's her own person in her own right, and she's incredible. She deserves to be cherished for who she is, not just because of who she's related to.

Even though I've spent all evening with her, even though I know she's asleep, I have to fight the urge to call her now. I satisfy myself with a simple text wishing her a good night.

I rarely use my phone for actually communicating with people. Most of the time I'm reading on my e-reader's app or checking my email for spam or keeping up with my fantasy football league. Occasionally, I'm looking for porn. But talking to people? Yeah, right. There's a group text for the house, individual texts with the guys, the messages from my sister, and now Mackenzie. That's it. Oh, and the pharmacy. They like to text me at least three times a week. Yeah, I get it, my anxiety medicine has come in, I'll pick them up eventually.

My bed feels way too empty. She's never been in my room. I would love to get her in here. I'd spread her legs and go to town on her pussy, feasting on her. I bet she tastes amazing. And if she's not ready for that, or *I'm* not ready yet, I'll hold her in my arms and let her fall asleep on my chest. I fantasize about that, too.

The raunchy stuff I dream about at night is great, and I like to believe it will happen one day when we're both ready for it, but it's the simple moments I'm looking forward to. Holding her hand. Walking to class with her. Sitting beside her and having everyone know we're together. Kissing her in public, and not having anyone freak out because I'm too old and she's too young and she's related to some random dude I happen to live with and we're not a good match. Dating, a real relationship, like any other couple on this college campus.

And, eventually, sex. The physicality of it, the emotional connection of it. I haven't had anyone I've even wanted to consider getting close to in five very long years. I wasn't ready. I'm still not sure if I'm ready now. But Mackenzie makes me want to try. She makes me want to believe I can do it again. So I'm going to try—for her.

twenty-seven

. . .

Wes

OUR SECOND SPEECH is meant to be informative. It's hard as fuck to talk about any one topic for four and a half minutes without droning on—or going so far into it that the audience isn't completely lost. Just because I'm fascinated by all the different ways a knee can functionally break doesn't mean everyone else is. As if it's not bad enough that I have to stand up in front of everyone to begin with, it's made even worse by my epic meltdown last time.

Mackenzie is researching the history of Madame Alexander doll collecting, which is obscure enough that nobody else will be researching it, yet ubiquitous enough that most people know one or two freaks who do it. Her head is bent over her computer as she types slowly. Her lips are pursed as she thinks. She taps out a few words, pauses, and then continues. Pause again. Types. Sits back. Frowns.

This is her process. From the few times we've studied together, I know this is how she works. It drives me fucking nuts. It works for her, so it's not my place to say anything. Her grades are great. She works hard for them. It's hard enough acclimating to college, not to mention being on the road every other weekend. She got four A's and one B last semester, her mother has informed me no less than three times.

My grades are… decent. Passable. Decidedly closer to average. I have a strong enough GPA that I think I can get into at least a second tier grad program. My GRE scores were phenomenal, if I do say so myself. I've always been good at tests, at being put under pressure. It's essays where I have more difficulty opening up and putting my thoughts to paper —or computer screen, as the case may be.

Today is strictly about studying. It's why we're here in the ASC, in public. There's nothing illicit about what we're doing. Everyone knows we're in the same public speaking class. Everyone knows we study together. Everyone knows we're friends.

Nobody knows we're more than friends.

Miles doesn't seem to have caught on, even after our late night together. Greg mentioned something about Mackenzie joining us for more meals lately, but her brother shut it down. He likes seeing her—it's how he knows she's okay, which is total patronizing bullshit. She doesn't need anyone to take care of her, much less an overprotective brother.

At the same time, I understand his need to protect her. She's fragile. Not mentally. Not socially. Not academically. Emotionally. She doesn't have very many friends. She hasn't found a social circle for herself yet. Even her teammates don't seem to invite her to spend time together outside of team functions.

And if she has limited friend experience, she has even less experience with guys. Dating. Sex. She's a virgin, and that doesn't seem like it's about to change anytime soon. She's not ready. And as much as I'm not ready for my own personal reasons, I respect her reasons for not being ready even more so. Sex complicates things. It's messy. It can bring up a lot of emotions, even when there's nothing traumatic or scary in the past. Some people aren't ready to handle it. There's no need to rush.

It's not like I'm ready, either. I've thought about trying therapy again. I'm not sure it will help. Tucker thinks it will. Then again, he's a psychology major, and he basically failed out of therapy himself, so I'm not sure how much weight I want to give his opinion. He's only been with one woman—okay, two. He had a one night stand with one woman shortly after Mason broke his heart, and then he spent two and a half years pining for his ex, so clearly he's not the suave Romeo he thinks he is.

Although really, Romeo was a tool. The really suave guy was Mercutio, whose life was cut all too short because of a stupid mistake, sticking up for his friend. Mercutio was the shit. He was cool as fuck. He probably had no trouble getting laid. I should want to be more like Mercutio, not like Romeo, who doesn't know how to tell his beloved-at-first-sight is in a medicated coma and not actually dead. Romeo was a fucking idiot.

Mackenzie makes a noise, and I realize I've just been staring at her with my mouth open for several minutes. I shake my head and refocus my attention on my laptop and open research. Okay, so maybe I'm killing two birds with one stone. Yes, knee injuries fascinate me, even more so than hip injuries. Knees are fragile and strong at the same time. Yes, my anatomy paper last week was on the function of the kneecap. I can reuse a lot of the same research *and* talk about something I'm already familiar with. Hopefully there will be less pressure this way. Two birds, one stone.

"I read this really great book the other day," she announces.

My ears perk up. I always like to hear about new books. Even if our tastes aren't exactly the same, if she enjoyed it, I'm going to at least give it a try.

"It was about serial killers," she starts, and I nope right

out of there. She seems to see my displeasure on my face. "It wasn't gory. It was about the psychology of—"

No. Not happening.

I've had enough death in my life. I don't need serial killers haunting my dreams now, too.

I've been cutting back on my daily book consumption. Now I'm down to four to eight books a week instead of my usual ten to fifteen. Spending time with Mackenzie, thinking about her, my free time to read has been cut down drastically. And I'm not complaining in the slightest.

I didn't think I was ready for a relationship. Dating Mackenzie has been the best decision I've ever made. We can talk, we can read, we can talk about the books we read, we can study, we can workout together… there's very little we can't do. It doesn't matter if it's just the two of us or if we're in a big group, she's still my best friend.

Now I text her in the mornings when I wake up and at night before I go to bed, which are both times when I used to think about her as it was. We talk on the phone when she has away games. We spend as much time together as we can.

Not much has changed. Everything is different.

My phone vibrates with a text. I should pull it out and check, but that would mean taking my attention off of her and the way she's scrunching her nose as she thinks.

"You should check that," she says, not looking up from her computer.

The text message is from her. *You're staring again.*

Yeah, damn right I'm staring, and I'm going to keep staring until the day she tells me not to.

———

Sarah calls on my walk home from Mackenzie's dorm. It's not our normal time for our weekly phone call. My stomach sinks.

"Hey."

"Wes, hi."

We text every morning and every night—a quick confirmation that she's alive, a message to let her know I'm doing okay—but we have one phone conversation every week. It's part of our routine.

"How are you?"

I grunt out a vowel sound. She's nervous.

"Listen, I've been thinking about spring break…"

A cautious noise. I'm supposed to fly out to Seattle and spend the week with her, exploring all of the great indie bookstores and playing video games on her couch instead of mine for a week.

"It's two weeks before midterms. It's not a great time…"

So she doesn't want me to come out there. Somehow I'm not surprised. Sarah is my sister, she's great, but we've never been particularly close. I know she sees me as an obligation as much as a sibling. I'm not her peer, not yet. Since our parents died, she's gone out of her way to be there for me. Sometimes she needs her space, too.

"That's fine."

"Don't be like that," she snaps.

"Like what?"

"Upset."

I huff out a laugh. "I'm not."

"Wes."

I haven't told her about Mackenzie. It's weird talking to my big sister about the girl I'm dating. The woman I've been in love with for way too long, someone who is definitely too young for me.

"I have other plans," I lie.

"You do?"

Mackenzie has almost a full week off. She has a game on Saturday at the start of spring break and on Sunday a week later. Her family is local—she's probably not traveling. I'll spend time with her. I'll hang out in her dorm and avoid my house. It'll be fine. It'll be great.

"With my girlfriend."

Sarah bursts out laughing. "Yeah, alright. You don't have to invent someone to make me feel better."

My throat feels tight. "I'm dating someone."

"Wes..."

"She's amazing."

Sarah's shock is audible. "She goes to your school? You've met in person? This isn't some online relationship?"

"I've known her for a while," I admit. "We started dating three weeks ago."

She's quiet for a moment. "And you didn't tell me?"

I didn't know how. Sarah is the type to overshare any and every thing, so she tells me when she goes out on dates with random guys, people she never intends to spend time with again after one night. I've flown across the country to beat up her ex who shattered her heart. She informs me every month when she gets her period. There is very little that she keeps private, at least from me.

She's been pushing me to date for—years. Ever since I locked myself away in that horrible period after our parents died, when my girlfriend at the time and all of my friends dumped me in one fell swoop. I don't generally enjoy the company of other people. Teammates, coaches, they're whatever. Roommates are a necessary evil if I want to live in free student housing.

Dating? That was something I could control, something nobody could force me into. I wasn't ready. I withdrew into myself even more so than I ever had before, hiding from the world and everyone in it.

It's not like I was sitting around, pining and waiting for Mackenzie to turn eighteen. I've always enjoyed her company, even when there was truly nothing between us.

Since she's started college, she's... blossomed. Come into herself a little bit more. She knows who she is and is true to herself.

First and foremost, we're friends. We just happen to be friends who are now dating. I like her as a person and on top of that, I'm attracted to her. There aren't many people I willingly want to spend time with. And I crave time with her. Even if all we're doing is sitting on separate couches and reading our own books, I want to do it with her. When she's not around, I miss her. I want to be with her.

My sister clears her throat. "So, who is she?"

"A friend."

She laughs. "I figured."

"Mackenzie Cavanaugh."

"Isn't there... don't you have a friend? Cavanaugh?"

"Yeah."

"Wes..."

I know. *I know.* I'm breaking like every single rule in the bro code *and* the teammate code *and* the roommate code. Don't mess around with another dude's sister.

But Mackenzie isn't just Miles's sister. She's my friend— my *best* friend. The relationship we share has absolutely nothing to do with him. We've been friends since even before she started here. We're both introverts who thrive off alone time and prefer to stay home and read than go out to a frat party on a Saturday night.

That she's gorgeous and actually likes me? That's just icing on the cake.

"She's perfect," I tell my sister.

Which... Mackenzie has faults. I'm not blind to them. She's perfectly imperfect, and I love her for that. In spite of it. Because of it.

"Well, if you're happy, I'm happy," Sarah says. "I'm proud of you, Wessy."

A growl rumbles deep in my chest at the childhood nick-name, and she laughs.

"I know, I know. You're a foot taller than me and more than double my weight, but you're still my little Wessy Poo."

I'm not above flying across the country and kicking her skin in person. I crack my knuckles.

"Okay, okay, I'm done," she says. "Don't kill me."

"No promises."

She laughs outright.

I stop in my tracks. It's almost spring break. Mackenzie is a freshman. She might actually have plans. She might be going on a trip. She might be going home to spend the week with her family. She might have basketball practice. She might have all of them at once.

What am I going to do?

Amir is going home to Wisconsin. Tucker and Mason are visiting his brother in Detroit. Barrett and Diana are going to visit her family in Amherst. Greg is going to Miami—partly because it's where his dad lives, and partly for the parties. And then there's Miles…

I'm sure if I asked, my roommate would be more than happy to invite me to his place for a week. I've visited for Thanksgiving and for summer barbecues.

Somehow, the fact that I'm dating his sister in secret means I probably shouldn't ask this time. I never want him to think I'm only using him for access to Mackenzie. My friend-ship with my teammate has absolutely nothing to do with my girlfriend. What she and I share has absolutely nothing to do with him.

Except for the fact that they're related. Except for the fact that he clearly told us the first time he introduced us that she was firmly off limits. He doesn't want his teammates dating his sisters—and I totally get that, because I had the same rules with Sarah. That she was four years older and not interested in my friends was entirely irrelevant. They still crushed on her something fierce.

My feelings for Mackenzie are more than a simple crush. I'm crazy about her. I might be in love with her. She's my friend, maybe even my best friend.

Fuck. Maybe this is more complicated than I thought.

twenty-eight

. . .

Mackenzie

WE'RE three quarters of the way through the season. We have a winning record. Playoffs are in sight. The end is near. As much as the year is flying by, I'm not ready for it to end.

The girls are great. Supportive. I feel like one of the team, like I've been fully welcomed. But they're not my best friends. I didn't immediately click with someone and create a lifelong friendship. They're teammates. I'm not opposed to hanging out with the girls.

Right now, though... I don't really want to see any of them. Dareesa and Lauren are so buddy buddy, there's no room for me. Pia and Amber are nice, but it's on a surface level. And Rebekah, Miri, and the seniors keep me at arm's length. We're too different.

So today, I'm taking some time for myself, to do the things I enjoy. I went to the library and picked out a new stack of books. I got a coffee from the (expensive) café in the quad. I read in the springtime sunshine and indulged in being outside. I went to a yoga class, just for fun, not for a purposeful workout or a recovery session.

I haven't been to the pool in—weeks. At least in the three weeks since Wes and I got together. Most of my free time has been spent wrapped up in him. Not that I'm complaining. I enjoy spending time with him. But I also need some "me" time to be on my own, to rest and recharge.

The familiar scent of the indoor swimming pool washes over me in a welcoming waft of sharp, acidic chlorine and bleach. I grew up swimming nearly as often as a fish, as much as physically possible, and if I wasn't swimming, I was playing basketball, tennis, running the track, or watching one of my siblings play their sports.

There is only one lane occupied, the far right lane. The woman is slaying in butterfly, zipping across the pool with effortless strokes. She glides through the water. There's almost no splash.

Dipping my toe in the pool, it's not nearly as warm as I expected. Oh, well. There's only one way to get acclimated: by jumping straight in. Setting my towel and bag to the side, I sit at the edge of the pool and let my feet touch the water. It's cold. Downright chilly.

I can do this.

Jumping into the water, the cold hits me like a tidal wave. Goosebumps break out over my skin. I move my arms and legs, trying to warm up and adjust. Dropping back, I let the water run over the back of my neck and my chest. The sooner I get used to the temperature, the sooner I can get back to what I really enjoy: real swimming.

It's already not so bad. I give a few careful strokes, testing. Yes, the water is moving nicely today. It could be a lot worse. My hair is tucked up into a swim cap. Lowering my goggles, I duck beneath the water until I'm fully submerged. With my ankles propped on the wall, I stretch my arms and my torso, letting my muscles get used to being in the water again. It's been a while. Muscle memory can only take me so far.

The woman at the other end of the pool switches to breaststroke. She makes this look effortless, too. I'm a little jealous.

Kicking off the edge of the pool, I launch into a simple

backstroke. The water swirls around me as I move. I feel weightless. My body is powerful and strong, buoyed by the water. My legs kick water up around me as my arms propel me backwards.

I've missed this. Once the basketball season ends in a few short weeks, I'll have to make more time for this—and for tennis, too. I don't want to sacrifice my second and third loves for the sake of my first. Just because I accepted a scholarship to play basketball doesn't mean I can't ever swim or play tennis again.

Maybe Wes and I can play a round of tennis next weekend. Or maybe racquetball. We need to do something active, something more than sitting down and reading together. We don't have to talk—we can stroll through the library or a bookstore and pick out books for all I care. We just need to do *something* that isn't sitting on the couch.

And, yeah, maybe that means making out again. I hate that we were interrupted by Claire last weekend. After this road trip coming up tomorrow, we have only a few short weeks until spring break. I'm supposed to get my period next week, which is never a particularly enjoyable five to ten days for me, and will… curtail any naked fun in the plans. Or even semi-naked. Or even fully clothed. I'm not squeamish, but I genuinely feel so crummy in the lead up to and then during my period, it's hard enough to live my regular life without adding something new and exciting to it.

I want to touch him. I want to feel his skin, the hardness of his body, the softness of his curves. Wes is a big guy, in every sense of the word. He would never hurt me, not on purpose. He's as kind and cuddly as a teddy bear and as fiercely protective as a grizzly bear. If I want to one day maybe possibly have sex with him, and I'm pretty sure I do, I need to be far more familiar with his body. I don't want to be nervous. I don't want to be scared. I want to be strong and confident and comfortable in my skin.

And that means we start out slow. Explore each other, both clothed and… less clothed.

Next time, I'm going to take off my shirt. I might even be able to persuade him to do it, too. And then we can be pressed together, skin to skin…

I shiver, and it's not just from the chill of the pool. Hitting the wall, I flip over into a butterfly stroke, stretching my arms and legs. I haven't had a good, strong swim in months. I think I've swam all of half a dozen times all school year. There was never enough time. I was always too busy with classes, with basketball, with family visits, now with Wes…

I have to make time for myself. I have to dedicate at least two hours a month to swimming. It makes me happy. Just like I want to play tennis twice a month, I want to swim with the same frequency. I won't ever be good enough to manage three sports at the collegiate level. That's not what I'm interested in. I just want to be active, to indulge in my favorite pastimes, and have some "me" time. I don't need to constantly be surrounded by other people. Sometimes it's nice to have some time by myself.

I crisscross the lane at least a dozen times before I need a break. I prop myself up on the wall and take a swig from my water bottle.

The woman from the other end of the pool is doing the same, her goggles propped up on her navy and silver Newton Wolfpack swim cap. She is all muscle and sinew, strong and capable. As if she feels my eyes on her, she turns. Her eyes scrub over me, too. She nods and then replaces her goggles, launching back into the water.

After taking another moment to breathe, I do the same.

It feels so good to be in the water again. I didn't realize how much I missed it until now. Swimming is as natural to me as breathing, as natural as dribbling a basketball, as natural as swinging a tennis racquet.

I swim for the better part of an hour, until my muscles

burn and my lungs ache. I've missed this. When I take a look around, the pool is empty. The only sound is a faint drip of water somewhere and the rush of my blood pounding in my veins.

My stomach rumbles. I need food, real food, and not just coffee. I'll grab something quick at the ASC. But first, a much-needed shower. My skin is equally pruny and tight from the chlorine.

The other woman is in the locker room when I walk in, mostly dressed in a sports bra and jeans. She's tall, taller than I realized, with abs of steel. Her dark brown hair tumbles nearly to her waist.

"You looked good out there," she says.

It's totally not weird coming from a half-dressed stranger in the locker room.

"Thanks."

"You're a swimmer?" She pulls on a t-shirt.

"Used to be." I adjust the knot in my towel. As much as I need a shower, I can take a break to make awkward small talk. It's a small school. "I'm on the basketball team, so I had to cut back."

She nods. "I get that. I had to quit soccer three years ago to focus on swimming."

"Nice to meet you."

"I'm Deisy," she says. She laughs. "I should have started with that. Deisy Cruz."

"Mackenzie Cavanaugh."

"Nice to meet you," she says. "I'm on the swim team, but outside of designated practice time, the pool is always open if you want to get a few laps in. You can keep up with us. You sure you don't want to join the team?"

It's my turn to laugh. "I have a hell of a time managing one sport as it is. Somehow I doubt I could keep up with two."

Her phone dings and she frowns, pulling it from her back

pocket. She shakes her head. "My boyfriend. He can't remember what time I'm done today. He knows I swim every Sunday from three to five."

I offer her a tight smile. I'm not sure what to say to that. Wes knows my schedule nearly as well as I do.

"Will you be back next week?"

"I've got a game on Sunday. But I'll try to get a swim in as much as possible," I promise her. I'm not sure why I feel the need to commit to her. Maybe it's a commitment to myself. "And if you ever want to try a workout on dry land, come visit us in the basketball court. It's fun."

Deisy laughs. "I would, but the squeaking of the shoes gets to me. I'll come see your game on Sunday, though. Student athletes should support other student athletes." She slings her bag over her shoulder. "Nice to meet you."

"You, too."

She starts to head out, so I move on to the showers. By the time I get out, she's gone.

———

All too soon, the team is on the road again. We have this away game, two at home, and then one away before spring break. After our week off, we have three more games before the season ends and playoffs begin. Our team has a positive record now, but something in me makes me doubt we'll make it far in the playoffs.

I want to believe in us. I'm not naturally pessimistic. I've just seen the way we've played all season, the way the team hasn't really gelled. We're okay. We're not great.

Next year will be better. It has to be.

Wes and I text through the bus ride to Connecticut. He's only slightly more verbose over text than he is in person. I know he uses his phone more for reading books or articles online than for any real communication. The only people he talks to with any regularity are his roommates and his sister, and she's the only one who calls him to actually talk.

Well, and me. I like talking to him, whether we're in person or over the phone. The deep rumble of his voice soothes me like a caress from a distance. We talk on the phone every night before I go to bed, and when in the morning, I have a few text messages to wake up to.

He cares about me. He might not be the greatest communicator, but I didn't expect him to suddenly start speaking in full, complicated conversations. He's a quiet guy. He keeps his thoughts to himself. He isn't afraid to open up with me. It just takes patience on my part, and continued effort on his.

Luckily, I have a lot of that.

I can't wait to see you tonight, he texts me shortly before lunchtime. *You're going to play great at your game today. I'll be cheering for you.*

I text him a response, but he doesn't answer before I have to get ready for the game.

And that's okay. I don't require an immediate answer. It's enough to know that he cares. That he's thinking of me. That he's going to watch the game on his computer. That he would be here if he could.

And tonight, when I'm back on campus and we're locked in my dorm, I'm going to touch him. I'm going to let him touch me. We won't go all the way—I'm not ready to even consider that possibility. But we can… explore.

This weekend, Dareesa and I are sharing a room. Lauren didn't make the trip. There's no point; with her injury, she can't play any time soon. She sits on the sidelines during home games, and cheers us on from afar by herself at away games.

I wonder if she feels like she's missing out nearly as much as I do. Dareesa gets the best of both worlds: she can play, and she made an instant best friend. I'm still waiting to feel that emotional connection to the girls. And Lauren can't play; she can barely even practice with us. She gets to travel for one of every three or four weekends away.

It's not that the girls aren't welcoming. They are. But we don't hang out outside of clearly designated team activities. Nobody has offered to go grab coffee or study together or hang out without some sort of basketball related activity going on.

And yeah, I could initiate it. I could be the bigger person and tell someone, I want to spend time with you. But that's not me. Most of the time, I'm more than happy to do my own thing by myself. I can work out, I can study, I can read, I can go for a walk.

It's just that every once in a while, I want to have someone with me. Not in a romantic sense—Wes is great, and I enjoy spending time with him, but sometimes I wish I could have a friend I could talk to about... everything. About boys. About family. About school. About basketball. About... anything, really.

I've had friends. I've had teammates. But I haven't had a best friend. Wes is the closest thing I've ever had to a best friend, and we're dating now, so clearly that worked out in that regard.

I have nobody I can talk to about him. To squeal with over the cute things he does, to gripe with about the frustrating moments, to talk out my hesitation with getting naked with him...

I'm not sure why I'm still a virgin, other than the whole "lack of opportunity" thing. I've never felt the urge to get naked with either of the guys I've fumbled around with. According to all the books I've read, sex is supposed to be something meaningful between two people who love each other—or are in lust with each other.

I'm attracted to Wes. My body reacts to him. My mind is enchanted with his brain. My heart sings when he's near. We can be sitting reading our own books or doing something active together, and I still want to be around him. I want to kiss him, like, all the time. Eventually, I want to get naked with him.

Not yet. Someday. Maybe soon.

And even if he didn't have his own hangups with sex, I'm not sure I'm ready yet. I don't know what I'm waiting for. Some giant beacon in the sky telling me it's time?

I want to explore with him. I want to experiment and discover and learn his body—without the magnitude of penetrative sex hanging over us. I've never had a social orgasm. I've never had anyone successfully get me off, or even try. I think I'm ready for more… just not everything. Where the line is, I'm not sure. I'm making the rules up as I go.

twenty-nine

. . .

Mackenzie

WES IS IN MY BED. He looks gloriously disheveled, his cheeks flushed and his hair mussed. His lips are red and swollen from where I've been kissing him.

He blinks up at me. "What?"

My heart warms with affection for him. It shoots through my veins like a fiery tornado. I shake my head. "I just really like you."

His eyes soften. "I really like you, too."

He leans forward for a kiss, and I let him pull me down on top of him. Deftly, he maneuvers me until I'm straddling his lap. His delicious hardness presses against my core, and I sigh, twisting my hips for more friction.

Wes grinds into me, his hands on my hips and his fingers in my back pockets cupping my ass. His hips thrust up into me, and I lose track of all rational thought. This feels so good. How did I not know this would feel so good?

I pull back, and he lets out a soft whine of protest. It turns into a rumbly groan when I sit upright and pull off my shirt, leaving me in just a simple bra and my jeans.

His pupils dilate as he stares at me. He raises his hand and then lowers it.

"You can touch me," I say, taking his hand and pressing it just below my fabric-covered breast.

His strong fingers close around me and I sigh, grinding into him. My nipples are hard pebbled buds in the bra cups. My pulse thuds dully between my legs.

"Wes…"

He sits up and spreads his legs for balance, his hand sliding around to my spine, as he kisses me thoroughly. I can't think, can't breathe. His cock twitches against my center as he strokes my nipple through the thin cotton.

I've never really had sensitive breasts. When I touch myself, I get no enjoyment from playing with my nipples. When he touches me, though… all bets are off. Reaching behind me, I scramble for the clasp.

"Hm?"

"Off," I murmur against his lips. I can't get the simple clasp to open.

His thick fingers caress my back as he makes his way towards the clasp of my bra. It takes him a few tries before he gets it open. Eagerly, he pulls the fabric away from me.

He pulls back enough to look down at me. I follow his gaze.

My breasts are small, more muscle than anything particularly alluring. The small, dusky nipples are pebbled tight.

Wes's eyes dilate further. "Mackenzie…"

His voice is rough, gravelly and thick with desire. It does dangerous things to my heart rate.

"Yeah?"

His palm ghosts over my breast. The thick callouses rub over my sensitive skin in the most exquisite torture I've ever felt.

His kiss is hungry. Pained. He devours me even as his fingers do dangerous things to me, learning my body. I thread my hands through his hair and rock against him.

He's moving. I'm not sure how he maneuvers us, but

somehow I'm on my back and he's leaning over me. His mouth moves down my neck and south. He kisses between my breasts before he takes one of my nipples in his mouth, his lips closing around the tight bud. A scrape of teeth.

Arching my back, I reach for him again. My legs are wrapped around his waist now. Our lower halves are pressed together in a delicious slide of friction and frustration.

Wes sucks—hard. My back lifts off of the bed, arching into him. His other hand plays with my other nipple, so it doesn't feel neglected. I don't want this to end. I never want this to end. There's only one thing that could make this better.

Releasing my firm grip on his hair, my hand starts to slide between us. I could try to help him out. I could try to bring him as much pleasure as he's giving me. But I'm not going to —not right now, at least. That's a mission for later.

Slipping my hand between my legs, I start to rub—hard. The seam of my jeans hits at the exact right place. His cock is hard against my wrist and that spurs me on.

He pulls back. He looks down.

"Are you…?"

"Yeah?"

He swallows loudly. "Fuck."

"Bad?"

His eyes are trained on my hand, still moving, tortuously slowly now.

"Good. So fucking good." His hand twitches. "Can I…?"

"Yeah?"

Wes meets my eyes. His pupils are lust-blown black, rimmed by the tiniest hint of his green irises. "Can I touch you?"

My mouth goes dry.

"It's okay if you'd rather," he starts quickly.

"Do-do it. Touch me."

The first touch of his thick fingers to the seam of my jeans is clumsy. He can't get the angle right. The second is—better.

He strokes over me carefully, his brow creased in concentration.

"I could…"

"Hm?" He looks up at me.

"I could take my pants off. If that would help."

Wes stares at me. It takes him a moment to process.

"Yes. Please. Let me take off your pants. Please."

Laughing, I undo the button and zipper, and he tugs the thick denim off my hips and down my legs. I lift up so he can work the fabric over my butt, and he groans, his hand cupping my ass.

"Are you wearing…?" He rolls me over onto my stomach, my pants around my knees. He groans again.

"Bad?"

His finger ghosts over the thin strap of my black satin thong, right where it disappears between my cheeks.

"Holy shit, Mackenzie."

I try to turn over. He pulls my pants the rest of the way off, flinging them aside.

There's a touch to my butt, and I jump. And then he's cupping my ass with both hands, squeezing and kneading firmly.

Let's be clear: I have a good butt. What I lack in the chest area has all traveled down to my ass. I do a metric fuckton of squats every day. Box jumps are fun for me. Building my glutes is my jam.

When Wes puts his hands on my ass, though… holy fuck, does that feel good.

His finger traces the strap of the thong again, whispering between my cheeks and down to my core, where my panties are drenched between my legs. He lets out a heavy breath.

"Mackenzie…"

Lifting my hips, I arch into his touch, and he gets the hint, sliding his fingers over me. He cups my core as his fingertips search for my clit.

It's RIGHT THERE. Over a bit, to the left. No, not that far. It's—

I let out a groan when he finds that magic place that sends pleasure shooting through my bloodstream. He kisses between my shoulder blades, down my spine, as he rubs me firmly. I don't know how to ask him to touch my bare skin without taking off my panties, and if I take them off, I'm worried he'll think I'm ready for penetrative sex.

I'm not. It's too soon. But I wouldn't be opposed to his thick fingers inside of me, or his mouth on me, or…

He's moving lower now. I miss his heavy presence beside me. He kisses down my spine and to the thin strap of my thong.

And then there are teeth sinking into my ass. I squeal, and he releases me at once.

"You okay?"

Propping up onto my elbows, I look back at him. "Do that again."

His grin is positively devilish. "As you wish."

This time his teeth sink into the other side of my ass as his fingers slip beneath the sodden material of my underwear. He strokes over my bare skin. He groans when he feels the wetness between my legs.

"Mackenzie." His voice is low, as rough as gravel behind me.

"Yeah?"

I can hear him swallow. "Can I taste you?"

YES. Fuck yes. After reading about this in so many books, I can't wait to experience it firsthand. I'm lost for words. My hurried nod is answer enough.

Wes moves his hands to the waistband of my underwear. Slowly, tortuously slowly, he drags it over my hips and down my legs. He flings the wet fabric to the side and cups my ass again. I might spread my legs ever so slightly. The bed dips as he moves lower.

The first touch of his tongue to my core from behind is hesitant. Cautious. Wes sighs and presses his lips against me more firmly, caressing my lower lips. His tongue comes out to taste me.

It feels… different. Not exactly what I imagined. I need a little more stimulation. The scratchy stubble lining his cheeks and around his mouth send pinpricks of sensation through me. This is great, I'm enjoying it, but I—

His thick, calloused fingers slide over my clit, and I gasp. Pleasure shoots down my spine. Tilting my hips back, I get a little more contact and I—and I—

"Wes."

"Yeah?" His voice is muffled by my pussy. The vibrations have my thighs shaking.

"I really like you."

He laughs. His tongue slips lower—*inside!*—and I nearly lose it.

"I really like you, too," he says, before he starts to lick me in earnest. His calloused fingers continue to work at me.

Butterflies erupt in my belly, sending tingles soaring through my body. My head swims and my toes curl. My fists twist in the sheets. My chest heaves as I work to get breath into my lungs. My thighs start to tremble.

The orgasm hits me like a freight train, almost before I'm ready for it. Wes grounds me through it—he doesn't let up with either his mouth or his fingers until I'm ready. When I twitch my hips away, he takes the silent hint and releases me. Boneless, I collapse onto the bed and sigh.

"You okay?" His voice is thick.

Holy fuck. My first social orgasm. The first orgasm achieved with the help of someone else. The first time I've ever been touched by someone else. I—he—we—

It takes a considerable amount of work to roll over. I'm naked in my bed, my legs splayed. Wes is hovering by my waist, his mouth swollen and glossy. He's still fully dressed.

Leaning down, I grab him by the shirt collar and drag him up to me. He's half a foot taller than me and close to double my weight, but he lets me manhandle him like a rag doll until I've got him where I want him—on top of me.

He tastes like me, a little bit salty and musky. I'm not sure if I'm supposed to like it as much as I do. I wrap my legs around his waist. He's still hard, his thick cock pressing against my core through his jeans.

"Mackenzie…" He sucks on that place just beneath my ear that makes me go crazy.

"Yeah?"

"You're fucking perfect." He sighs, pulling back to look at me again. His calloused palm cups my breast again. "I could do this all fucking day long."

I hope he does. Again, and again, and again.

"I could…"

"Hm?" Wes kisses my shoulder blade.

"I could help you out." I tighten my legs around his waist and rock into him. My hand on his cheek directs his eyes to mine. "Can I take off your pants?"

His pupils are a lust-blown black, the rich green irises nearly completely eclipsed. He swallows thickly.

"You want to?"

I nod. "I don't know what I'm doing. You'll have to… teach me."

His cock twitches against my core. He likes that. He's probably read some of the same student/teacher erotica I have.

He kisses me, a sweet, innocent peck, before he's moving back, giving himself some room. He undoes his belt and unzips his jeans. Sparks tingle along my spine at the sound.

He's wearing dark green boxer briefs, the front tented by his thick erection. It's my turn to swallow. I meet his eyes. He's nervous. He settles on the bed beside me again.

Reaching for him, I curl my hands into the waistband of

his underwear and slowly work it over his hips and down his thick thighs. His cock bobs between us, and I divert my attention.

He's thick. Bigger than I expected. Although everything about him is big, so maybe I should have guessed. He's a dusty rose color, the head red and weeping with silvery pre-come.

He's gorgeous.

My eyes dart up to his. "Can I touch you?"

His Adam's apple bobs as he swallows. He nods, a quick jerk of his head.

I ghost my fingertips over his length, and his cock twitches. When I wrap my hand around him, he lets out a gusty sigh.

"This okay?" I watch his face.

Wes closes his hand around mine, tightening my grip. His hand on mine, he moves my hand over his length, back and forth, back and forth.

His chest rises and falls, his thick belly heaving. Together we touch him as he teaches me what he likes. The tip is sensitive. The slit drips pre-come. His balls are firm and heavy in my hand, lightly covered in light blond hair. He's satiny soft and hard as steel, smooth as velvet and sticky like an ice cream cone. I wonder if he tastes like an ice cream cone.

Maneuvering around him, I start my descent. Wes groans and stops me with a hand to my shoulder.

"What are you doing?"

"Returning the favor." I give him what I hope is a sultry smile.

He chokes out a laugh, his face red and sweaty. "You don't have to do that."

"I want to." I squeeze him firmly, the way he likes.

His cock jerks in my fist and then erupts into a volcano of hot, white come. He groans and adjusts his grip, so it lands in his hand and not all over me. He's shooting everywhere, all over my hand and arm. I think it might even get in my hair a little. I'm certainly not complaining.

Wes moves his hips away. I release him, and he sighs, touching himself slowly now. His big belly heaves as he works to get air back into his lungs.

"Holy fuck, Mackenzie," he says, and it's my turn to laugh.

"Good?"

He leans over me to grab a tissue from my bedside table. It takes three tissues to wipe himself up, and another two for me. He pulls his pants back on before he collapses onto the bed beside me. His arm wiggles under mine until I'm resting on his chest.

"The best," he says. He tilts my head up until I meet him for a kiss, sated and sticky and sweet. I'm still naked, he's fully dressed, and somehow this is one of the most erotic things I've ever been part of.

I've read about all sorts of depravity. I've read about people who let themselves indulge in sex and sexual acts. Every day, every moment with Wes, I'm one step closer to being ready to take that next step with him. I don't want to do it with just anyone: I want to share it with him.

But he's not ready, and as much as I respect that, I don't think I'm ready, either.

Maybe there isn't some arbitrary sign that will go off, telling me it's time to have sex for the first time. Maybe I won't ever be comfortable with the idea. That's okay, too. I'm not going to do something I'm not ready for just to make someone else happy. I'm not going to be someone I'm not. Whether it's sex or personality or anything else, I won't sacrifice who I am and what I believe in. I refuse to compromise on my beliefs.

And he isn't asking me to. We both want to wait. We both need more time. So we'll wait. So we'll give it more time. I'm not rushing.

thirty

. . .

Wes

"WHAT'S UP WITH YOU?"

Setting down the weight in my hand, I grunt and look to Amir in silent question.

"You're, like, smiling," Barrett chimes in.

Another grunt. They're both grinning now.

"What happened to make you so happy?"

Mackenzie. She happened. She rocked my fucking world last night. I can't tell them that, though, so I lift the weight again and turn back to the mirror. We can pretend I'm trying to check my form. They both know I'm just ignoring them.

"You haven't been hanging around as much lately," Barrett says. "What, you finally find a girl?"

"Or a guy," Amir adds quickly. "We don't discriminate."

I roll my eyes. There's no way I'm dignifying *that* with a response. Just because I was purposefully celibate for five years doesn't mean I'm interested in having sex with men. I wasn't interested in having sex with anyone, period. I still don't know that I'm ready for Mackenzie and I to take that step. Then again, neither is she.

The last time I had sex, my parents died. Two weeks later, my girlfriend at the time dumped me. I didn't want to try again. I wasn't ready. I don't think I ever would have been ready, if it wasn't for Mackenzie.

In just a few short weeks, she's flipped my entire life upside down. In the few months we've been friends, she's made my whole world make sense again. She effortlessly drew me out of my shell and made me *want* to open up again.

I don't know that I'm ready to open up to other people yet. I don't know that I will ever be a super social guy. But that's not me. She knows that, and she likes me anyway. In spite of it. Because of it. She's not trying to change me; she likes me just the way I am.

We started out as friends, and I'm confident that no matter what happens between us, we'll stay friends after. I don't want to lose my best friend just because I'm inept at romantic relationships. Actually, I'm pretty inept at managing platonic friendships, too. Maybe I'm just the common denominator.

"I bet it's a girl," Barrett says with a smug grin. "She's about five foot one, short red hair, and freckles."

Or maybe she's nearly six feet tall, with long, dirty blonde hair, warm brown eyes, and a wicked sharp brain that knows how to make me laugh—and knows how to make me come like a freight train.

Amir laughs. "Who?"

"A gymnast, or maybe a cheerleader," he adds. "Why is it that football players always go for cheerleaders? I've never understood the appeal."

I'm not sure, either. Just because the two women I dated in my past—my *very* distant past—were a gymnast and a dancer doesn't mean I'm only attracted to petite women. Like they said earlier, I don't discriminate. Maybe I'm picky. Maybe I'm emotionally stunted. I'm not about to psychoanalyze myself any more than I already have. All I know is, I like Mackenzie, and she likes me, and I'm not about to change anything about what we have.

Except graduate school looms on the horizon. I have three

more interviews, one online and two in person. There are still a few more weeks until I start getting rejection notices. I don't know where I'll be headed come June.

My top choice is Newton. It always has been, even before Mackenzie. And while I'm not trying to plan the next two and a half years of my life on a three week old relationship, I can't discount the fact that she's my best friend, my girlfriend, and being around her makes me incredibly happy.

We could survive long distance. We could survive living on opposite coasts. But if we don't need to, why should we put ourselves through that? My goal is Newton. My backup is UMass Lowell, which isn't terribly far away in the grand scheme of things. BU. Michigan. Kentucky. UT Austin. UW. GW. I'm casting my net wide. I'm not limiting myself. Wherever I get in, I get in, I'll take the best aid package available, and that will be that.

Graduate school is pretty much a requirement to be a physical therapist and further my future career beyond basic entry level. Ten, fifteen, twenty years from now, I'll be grateful to myself for have put in the extra two and a half years of work. Ultimately, if I could work with a professional sports team… that would be the dream.

"We should ask Mack," Amir says. I nearly drop the weight and he snickers. "What, you haven't told her?"

She knows. She knows damn well who I'm dating—her.

Still, I refuse to admit to anything, so I continue ignoring him and finish my set.

"Mack would know," Barrett chimes in. "They're, like, best friends. It's kind of cute."

"She hasn't been hanging at the house, either," Amir says slowly. "What, is she pissed with you for dating someone?"

Seriously, has nobody put the puzzle pieces together? I didn't think we were being particularly subtle.

We've been hanging out together, mostly at her dorm, sometimes out in town, so there are fewer opportunities for us to be at the house with my five roommates. Other times, we're legitimately studying together, nothing illicit going on. It isn't all X-rated. Sometimes it's downright PG, if not outright G.

As much as I wasn't interested in dating anyone, if I had to fall head over heels for someone, I'm glad it was my best friend. We have a good time and enjoy each other's company even if all we're doing is reading on two separate sofas on a Saturday night. We have fun when we work out together, we can study together in peace, and we can be apart without the world falling to pieces. Sure, I miss her. I like being around her. She lights up my life. But I know that when we're apart—and we're apart often enough, between her road games and the general commitments in both of our lives—is good for us, too. It's going to strengthen the bond we share.

And it just means our reunions will be that much better when we do get a chance to see one another again.

thirty-one

. . .

Wes

THIRTY PEOPLE STARE AT ME. Some are bored. Some are tired. Some clearly don't want to be here. Only one is interested, eyes focused on me.

Okay, two people. One is Professor Blake. The other is Mackenzie.

Her eyes are intent on me, focused. Supportive. She mouths something I can't make out. I know it's meant to calm me down, to reassure me I can do this. Because I can do this. I can. I just have to stand here and say the words that are written on my notecards. Don't rush. Don't stutter. Just… talk.

Easier said than done.

It's not performance anxiety. It doesn't matter if there are twenty people in front of me or if we're one on one: I don't like talking. I've never been the most verbose guy, even before *everything happened.*

I wasn't in the car when my parents died. The accident wasn't my fault. I had nothing to do with it. They were out for dinner and were on their way home. My dad went instantly. My mom died in the ambulance en route to the hospital.

They never stood a chance.

They weren't perfect people. A week before, we had gotten into a stupid fight about me not doing my chores timely enough. My dad liked to crack terrible jokes at my expense. My mom treated me like a baby who didn't know how to tie my own shoes. My sister and I fought constantly growing up—her moving across the country for college was the best thing that happened to our relationship, and now, we're closer than ever despite the distance.

Sometimes I forget they're dead. Sometimes I pick up the phone to call home and realize that the number is out of service, that we sold the house and most of their belongings. We left a few things in storage. Sarah and I are both still in school. When we're settled, when we have slightly more permanent living situations, we can get the family china and heirlooms and pictures shipped to wherever we are then.

We have no real family. My mom had a sister. They weren't close. My dad's brother is fine—his wife is a total bitch, and after her actions immediately following the funeral, she will never have the title of aunt again. And that my uncle let her treat us that way… yeah, he's not on my Christmas card list anymore, either. The few cousins I have are either way older or way younger than me; we have no real relationship, either.

I'm alone in the world except for my sister and the few friends I've made along the way. I don't talk to anyone from high school. I don't talk to anyone, period. If they talk to me, I'll stumble my way through a conversation, but it's very rare that I initiate it.

I can rattle off facts about kneecaps in my sleep. I know knees. I've injured both of mine often enough to almost diagnose the lifelong problems that will follow me after fifteen or so years of playing football.

But standing in front of a group of people? Talking *to* them, and not just *at* them? That's nearly impossible.

My eyes dart from the professor back to Mackenzie. She's watching me, her smile getting more strained the longer I stand up here and stare out at the crowd like an idiot.

I swallow. I can do this. It's four and a half minutes. It's a topic that genuinely interests me. I can do this. I can do this. I can do this.

"Most people don't—don't think about the power of the kneecap," I start, and then stop. Mackenzie nods encouragingly. I clear my throat. "It's a tiny bit of muscle and cartilage that enables us to walk, and stand, and protects us from danger. The kneecap is small but mighty."

There's a snicker at the back of the room. Someone else coughs.

"You don't think about what you have until it's broken. That's where physical therapy can come into play. Whether it's in response to a surgery or a traumatic injury, supervised rehabilitation is practically required to ensure that everything functions the way that it should be throughout the healing process."

I look up from my notecards. Mackenzie is smiling now, nodding along. She's read this speech at least five times, in every variation. She might know it nearly as well as I do.

Somehow, I make it through. So what if it's a little robotic and monotone? So what if I don't make eye contact with anyone except for Mackenzie?

My stuttering is kept to a minimum through considerable effort on my part. My hands shake the entire fucking time. I'm sweating buckets beneath my extra extra large hoodie. It feels like it's a million degrees in here. My face is red and wet with perspiration.

But I finish the speech. I don't give up halfway through. Stuttering, stumbling, I deliver what is meant to be a four minute speech in a hair over five and a half, so while I'm losing points for going over on time, it could be worse. I don't care if I get a D on this speech; it has to be better than the outright zero I got on the first one. In all the chaos with Mackenzie, I haven't had the balls to check my online grade portal and see if my "extra credit" ~~speech~~ declaration of love was effective.

Mackenzie gives me a happy smile as I make my way back to my seat beside her at the back of the room. Everyone is watching me. Even though the next person is getting up to deliver her speech, I know they're still looking at me. They're wondering what a total knockout like Mackenzie is doing with a lump like me. Sometimes I wonder, too. Doesn't she know she can do better than me? Doesn't she know she could have pretty much anyone she wants? If she isn't a 10, she's a solid 9.99.

She wants *me*, I remind myself. She likes *me*.

She takes my sweaty hand and squeezes it as the next student begins her speech about canning jam, which is probably almost as boring to this crowd as the function of the kneecap.

Flipping to a new page in her notebook, Mackenzie scrawls a note in her neat cursive. She points at it.

You did great!!!, she wrote.

I shake my head.

She frowns. *You did a really good job,* she writes next, underlining "really" three times. *It went way better than last time.*

I snort. Anything would be better than last time.

Although last time did bring us together, so maybe…

You're going to rock #3. I'll be cheering you on every step of the way.

And then I fall in love with her all over again.

———

When Mackenzie said we were going to celebrate, I thought she was talking about getting ice cream. I never expected her to wrap her hand around my cock and lick me like *I'm* the ice cream cone. I'm certainly not complaining.

I'm not sure where she found the nerve to do this. After last time, I thought she was deterred. I certainly haven't intimated that it was something I wanted—even though I'm totally down with this. I would never presume that it would be something she was interested in. When we took our pants off last time, I thought it would end the same way it always had, me going home and desperately jerking off by myself. I don't want to push her into doing something she is not ready for.

And somehow when we ended up back at her dorm, making out and casually touching one another over our clothes, I never expected it would turn out like this.

Her grip is firm, tight, just the way I need it. Her mouth closes around the head and she sucks—hard. Pleasure erupts down my spine.

Mackenzie moves lower, taking more of me into her mouth. Briefly, I see stars. I can't watch. I can't look away.

As much as I'm interested in the physicality of sex, the emotional component terrifies me. I'm still convinced that if I start having sex again, my whole world will come tumbling down around me. I won't get into grad school. My sister will slip and fall and be permanently injured. I recognize that it's an irrational thought, but that doesn't make the fear any less real.

My last girlfriend and I had been having sex for less than a month when my parents were killed. We'd even done it the night they died. She dumped me two weeks later, when I didn't want to hook up immediately after the funeral.

Yeah, maybe she had problems. Yeah, maybe it wouldn't have worked out. But I can't shake this nagging feeling that if we were to have sex for the first time, my life as I know it will be over.

I'm not sure why penetrative sex is such a big deal but

oral sex isn't. I can go down on Mackenzie with no performance anxiety. While receiving wasn't part of my plan, I'm hardly about to complain. I can pleasure her with my fingers and explore what she likes. But the thought of putting my cock inside her, of the connection we would share when our souls are so intimately laid bare… it's fucking terrifying.

thirty-two

. . .

Mackenzie

MY JAW IS A LITTLE SORE. That's offset by the enormity of what I've just done. I gave Wes a blowjob. More than that, he *enjoyed* it. And I enjoyed doing it.

Who am I, and what happened to the scared, shy Mackenzie Cavanaugh I used to know?

My hands tremble with excess adrenaline. Wes gives me a tentative smile.

"I need to hit something," I blurt, and he frowns. "I'm going to play a bit of tennis today."

"Oh."

"Do you…" I bite my lip. "Would you like to play with me?"

His smile is radiant. "That would be great. Let me clean up and I can join you."

Right. *Clean up.*

He sneaks out of his room to hit the bathroom. When he comes back, fully dressed in workout clothes, he leaves the door open.

"It's safe," he says with a furtive nod, like we're on a secret mission.

I guess in a way we kind of are. Nobody can know, especially not my brother.

But as time goes on, as Wes and I get closer, I'm finding it hard to remember my reasons for not shouting it from the rooftops. Surely it's not that big a deal that he and my brother are teammates. It can't be that big a deal that they live together in student housing. They're both about to graduate; it won't be an issue in a few short months.

Wes won't be here in a few short months.

My heart thuds dully in my chest like a brass drum. Wes is leaving. We only have a limited amount of time together, and we have to spend it sneaking around and hiding. This freaking sucks.

At the same time, I wouldn't trade what I have with him for the world. If all I get with him is from now until the end of the year, I'm going to make the most of it.

The living room is empty. Coats on the hooks behind the door tell me that Barrett, Amir, and Greg are home, Miles and Tucker are not.

Amir's door opens right as I step out of Wes's room. He gives me a thorough once-over in the hallway between the two bedrooms.

"Hey, Mack. I didn't realize you were here."

"We're going to play tennis," I tell him.

He laughs. "Oh, is that what they call it?"

My eyes narrow. There's no way he heard us. We were quiet, so quiet it almost wasn't audible.

"I'm just playing with you," Amir says with a forced laugh. "You guys have fun."

"Do you want to join us?"

"Playing tennis?" He raises his eyebrows suggestively.

Wes steps into the hallway, dressed for exercise and with a tennis racquet in hand.

"Oh. You mean *tennis*," Amir says loudly. He is being

remarkably unsubtle about this. "I think I'm going to pass. You kids have fun."

I offer him a tight, sarcastic smile. "Thanks. We will."

We set out together towards the athletic compound, falling naturally into step with one another. After we clear Athlete's Village, Wes takes my hand, lacing our fingers together.

"You're kind of amazing," he tells me, squeezing my hand.

"Only kind of?" I tease.

He laughs. He tugs me to a stop and kisses me in the middle of the road. His hands thread through my hair.

"Come on," he says, taking a step back and reaching for my hand again. "We're going to be late."

Once again, we have no trouble getting a court. I grab a bucket of tennis balls and a loaner racquet, and we warm up side by side.

Okay, there might be a few kisses in there. He can't keep his hands off of me. He takes every opportunity to touch me —a hand on my back, his fingers ghosting over my wrist as he hands me the racquet, a kiss to my cheek before he heads across the net to the other side of the court.

And then we play.

I give the ball a few test bounces before I lob it over the net. Slowly, deliberately. I'm not trying to destroy him. I just want to feel the satisfying thwack of the ball on my racquet, force the small greenish yellow circle back and forth, back and forth, until I'm dizzy trying to keep up. He doesn't let me beat him—he gives it his all—and isn't a sore loser when I wipe the floor with him.

I could tire my brain out with swimming laps until my muscles ache. Basketball isn't as much fun by myself. But tennis requires a partner, and in Wes, I have a willing partner in pretty much every respect. There is very little I suggest that he's not interested in. Maybe if I asked him to braid my hair— that's more in Tucker's wheelhouse, though Wes might beat up his roommate if Tucker did actually braid my hair. He's not a violent man. The self defense lesson proved that. He knows when to stand up for other people, when to beat up on people who aren't being kind or fair. For the most part, he keeps to himself.

He opens up to me, though. I've never had to push him to give me more, never had to prompt him to say something he's not ready to verbalize. He seems to realize that being in a relationship means giving more of himself than he was previously.

All in all, he's a good boyfriend. I couldn't be happier with him. Except for the hiding and sneaking around thing, I really have no complaints. He respects me. He respects my boundaries. He's kind and giving without losing himself in the process. We have similar interests, compatible hobbies. And on top of all of that, he's my best friend. Yeah, it really could be worse.

———

After we take (separate) showers at the courts, we head to the softball field. Everyone is looking at me. They want to know what I'm doing here. All of the guys have brought their girlfriends. Wes has brought… me.

Okay, or maybe we showed up at the same place at the same time. They never have to know we walked up together.

My brother looks between us with a frown. "Hey, Mack. Glad you could make it."

I offer him a smile that's about 98% fake. "Thanks for inviting me."

He didn't. Sam did. My brother's girlfriend invites me to all of her games. This is just the first one I've been able to make work with my schedule in the last four and a half weeks since Wes and I got together. Once the season is over, I'll have more free time.

All of the guys try to support one another, and by extension everyone's girlfriends, in their respective sporting endeavors. Sam, Mason, Diana, and Jill sat with me and my family every Saturday during the guys' football games, and I've gone to Mason's track meets, Diana's soccer games, and Jill's field hockey games. They all show up to my basketball games en masse. To them, I'm not a girlfriend. I'm not part of the club. I'm just Miles's sister.

They don't know I'm dating Wes. They don't know I rightfully belong in the girlfriend club, that I want to be included in all their fun. They still include me in group activities, whether they know about that little label or not. As Tucker and Barrett have assured me time and again, I'm family, and family sticks together.

Wes likes to sit at the end of the row. He doesn't like to be boxed into the middle. Everyone knows this. So it's totally not weird when I take the spot between him and Tucker, who has his arm around Mason, who is chatting with Diana beside her. It's only natural that I shift a little bit closer to Wes. I don't want to intrude on couple time.

His hand twitches. It's like he has to remind himself that he can't touch me in public. I kind of like that. He wants to touch me. The guy who is petrified of human contact *wants* to touch me. I don't know if it's because of the blowjob earlier or if it's just because it's him and me. I like it all the same.

Miles is in the row ahead of us with Amir, Jill, and Greg. My brother turns around to face me.

"I haven't seen you lately," he says accusingly.

I meet his stare with a blank look. "I've been busy?"

He frowns.

"I'm around."

Do I sound too defensive? I'm not trying to be. I'm also not down for baseless accusations. He hasn't made any attempt to see me, either. I'm busy juggling a full course load in the middle of my competitive season, plus a secret boyfriend. I don't have a lot of time to spare for my big brother. He's a grown ass man. If he wanted to spend time with his sister, he knows how to text me and request time with me.

Miles hums. "I just haven't seen you."

I roll my eyes. "I've been here literally this entire time."

"You haven't been at the house in a few weeks."

"Yeah, it's called basketball season. I have games every weekend and I need to study."

"Claire still giving you a hard time?"

We've reached a fragile detente. My having a boyfriend who is bigger, stronger, and influential over her boyfriend seems to have made her realize that if she doesn't get naked in our shared dorm while we're both in it, neither will I. She hasn't even slept in her own bed three out of the last seven nights.

"It's getting better. She's traveling for matches so she's gone on the weekends a lot."

Wes tries to come over once or twice a week for reading and cuddling and, yes, a little making out. It's easier if he's at my place than if I go to his. Safer.

And I like the way he looks, spread out in my dorm bed. I like the way he looks in his bed, too, my hand wrapped around his cock, but I'll take what I can get.

Miles's eyes soften. "Good. I'm glad."

"We can go to dinner one night this week," I suggest. "Just the two of us. Bring Sam if you want."

He laughs. "And this new boyfriend of yours?"

I freeze. Wes goes tense beside me.

"Um, what?"

"Mom says you have a boyfriend now. I want to meet him," my brother declares imperiously.

"We're not really at the introducing to family stage yet," I say. Nerves creep up along my spine. I want to reach out to Wes, to touch his hand or his leg, reassure him I'm still all in with him. But I can't do that with Miles watching me and the rest of the guys turning in to our conversation.

"Wait, Mack has a boyfriend?" Greg demands.

"Why didn't we know about this?" Barrett chimes in from the end of the row.

"Because it's new. We're not there yet."

Tucker looks to Wes. "And you're okay with that?"

Wes looks up from the book he isn't reading. "Why would I care?"

"You two are, like, super close," Tuck says. "You don't care that your best friend is dating some random dude and you didn't even know?"

"I knew," Wes says, closing his book.

Miles looks taken aback. "And you didn't say anything?"

"None of my business," he says.

"But it's Mack," Greg says.

"She's happy, I'm happy," Wes says firmly.

My heart sings with happiness. I know he's telling the truth in this regard. He did know I started dating someone (because it's him). He's happy if I'm happy (because he knows I'm happy dating him). It's none of his business who I date (because he knows I'm dating him and not some random dude).

Amir looks at us suspiciously. "Who is this dude? How did you meet?"

"Through the athletic department." Not a lie.

Miles narrows his eyes. "What sport does he play? He doesn't play football, does he?"

I meet his stare head on. "Would it matter if he did?"

"You know how I feel about you dating my teammates."

I roll my eyes. "Well, you don't have to worry about that for much longer, do you?"

"What's that supposed to mean?"

"You're graduating."

"So?"

"So they won't be your teammates anymore."

Miles glares. "So he is a football player."

"I didn't say that."

"I don't understand why you're being so cagey about this."

"Because it's none of your business."

"Mack—"

"No. I'm not ready to bring him around to meet the Spanish Inquisition. When I'm ready for you to meet him, I will. Until then, please respect that I'm not at that stage yet."

Eventually, one day, I'll tell Miles the truth. He deserves to know that much. If I wait until the day they move out… well, that wouldn't be that bad.

Miles sighs. "I just want to protect you."

"That's not your job."

"Yeah, it is. I'm your brother. That will always be my job."

"Except I don't need protecting. Not in this. Not in a lot of things."

Wes isn't the type of guy to hurt me deliberately. He's big and strong, but he wouldn't ever lay a hand on me. Is it going to suck when we inevitably break up? Yes. Of course it will. There's no getting around that.

But that's not something my brother can shield me from. It's a fact of life. At some point, every relationship must come to an end. Couples break up. Marriages dissolve by divorce. Someone dies. Eventually, all good things must end.

That doesn't mean I won't enjoy what we have now while we have it. I won't look a gift horse in the mouth. What Wes and I have is good and strong. Eventually, whenever eventually is, we'll figure it out and go on from there.

The guys start to lose interest in me as the game starts, and they're easily distracted by the players swarming the outfield.

"Stay the night," he murmurs under the cover of the school fight song in the bottom of the third inning.

My heartbeat thuds dully in my ears. "Yeah, okay. I can sleep on the couch."

I haven't done that in a while. The guys are probably getting suspicious why I've been spending so much more time with Wes and so much less time at the house with the rest of them.

"No. Stay with me," he says. His eyes meet mine. "I want you to stay with me."

thirty-three

. . .

Wes

MACKENZIE IS IN MY BED. Holy shit. Mackenzie is in my bed. This is not a drill.

She made up a bed for herself on the couch just in case anyone comes downstairs in the middle of the night for a glass of water. Once everyone was safely ensconced in their rooms, she snuck into mine. And I'm not letting her go.

She's wearing my t-shirt and nothing else. Her smooth skin is pressed right up against mine, our legs tangled beneath the covers. Her head is pillowed on my chest as she reads on her tablet. From the few glances I've been able to peek at, it's a contemporary romance, best friends to lovers. Moderately steamy. I'll have to ask her what the title is so I can read it for myself later.

My hand threads through her hair, letting the silky soft strands fall through my fingers as I read with one hand. It's a little awkward. It's definitely cumbersome. The alternative is not cuddling with her at all, so I'll take what I can get.

I kiss the top of her head and she smiles, tilting her head up to look at me.

"What's that for?"

"Felt like it."

I'm not about to feel her up, not with a full house tonight. Sam is staying the night with Miles. Tucker and Mason are holed up in his room. Barrett and Diana are hanging out with Amir and Jill in the living room, watching a movie—I can hear them talking over it through my bedroom door. If they're wondering where Mack disappeared to, they haven't said it loud enough for us to hear. Even Greg has a date sequestered in his room, some girl from the volleyball team he's been out with a few times before.

As far as they're aware, I'm alone in here, and that's just the way I like it. The light is off, the room illuminated by my tiny bedside reading lamp.

"I'll set an alarm and go out there around five," Mackenzie says, and I startle back to her.

"You don't have to—"

"I need to be back on the couch before anyone wakes up. I know Mason has practice early tomorrow morning," she says.

I sigh. "Is it really so bad if they find out?"

"I've read this book before. The secret always gets out," she says. "It's always bad."

I've read the books, too. It's one of my favorite tropes. Maybe it was my subconscious telling me what I didn't want to face: that falling for my best friend, my roommate's sister, was an inevitability.

"It doesn't always end in disaster."

"Except it does." It's her turn to sigh. "In our case, it will."

Our relationship shouldn't have to revolve around her brother and his precious feelings. It should be about us. We are both stable, sane, consenting adults in our rational minds. We aren't hurting one another. If anything, I think we're each good for the other—she forces me to open up a bit more, and being with me makes her happy. We don't only sit around reading—we do activities together.

And, yeah, sometimes there is naked time (or semi-naked time) involved. We're exploring one another. Experimenting.

At the end of the day, isn't that what life is about? It's all one big experiment. Some things work. Some don't. But we don't know until we try. Us being together makes the two of us stronger individually and united as a team.

I don't care that for five years her brother and I played on a defensive line together. He's my friend. My teammate. My roommate. My friendship with him should have no bearing on my relationship with her.

I love her.

But even if I didn't, even if I was more hesitant about my feelings for her, that shouldn't matter. We shouldn't be denied the opportunity to explore what this could be because he's standing in our way. I know, I know, it goes against every rule in the bro book to hook up with another dude's sister.

Except I don't think of Mackenzie as Miles's sister. (Yes, technically, she is. Whatever.)

First and foremost, she's *my* friend. The friendship we had, the connection between us that eventually blossomed into a relationship, had absolutely nothing to do with who her brother is. Sure, that might be how we met. Yeah, I wouldn't have spent nearly as much time with her if we didn't have that tying us together.

Us becoming friends was serendipity. Our friendship developing into more was fate.

Neither of us were ready to date anyone, much less each other. That's why we've been able to maintain our friendship for so long. Neither of us were looking for anyone. We were actively declining to participate in the dating scene. And that's okay. That was good for us at the time.

I'm still not what I would consider "in" the dating scene. I'm dating one woman: Mackenzie. And if she decides to end it, if she decides she's had enough of me, I probably won't look for someone else. There's nobody as great as she is. She's perfect for me. We're two halves of the same soul, trapped in two different bodies.

I love this woman so fucking much, it aches in my teeth like saccharine. My heart pounds whenever she's nearby, trying to beat right out of my chest and into hers. My blood sings when I smell her perfume, subtle and light. And my cock… yeah, that thing has a mind of its own when it comes to her. It's quite fond of her.

I'm quite fond of the rest of her, too. Her smile. Her freckles. Her brain. Her voracious appetite for all things books and/or apple cinnamon flavored. Her sense of humor. Her razor sharp wit. Her long, long legs, and the way they wrap around my waist. Her, naked and trembling with desire, as I devour her.

So instead of fighting, I drop another kiss to the top of her head. "Whatever you think is best."

Her eyes are sad. "We still have a few hours before I have to leave."

Depositing my book on the bedside table, I roll over and curl up around her into the spooning position. My arm slides around her waist and she curls her legs into mine, her arm hugging mine.

"I wish it wasn't this way," she says quietly. "I want to be able to enjoy what we have."

My stomach sinks. "Do you not enjoy it?"

"No, no, no. I do. I do," she insists. She rolls over to face me. Her hand lands on my cheek. I meet her eyes. "I like you, Wes. A lot."

Hearing that settles the butterflies in my stomach. I swallow.

"I hate that my brother has any bearing on how I live my life. It shouldn't matter. I shouldn't care what he thinks. But I don't want to blow up your living situation. You're in this house with him every day. He's one of your best friends."

She's my best friend. Without a doubt, no hesitation about that. The other guys are my friends because of convenience.

Once I graduate, I doubt we'll keep in touch much beyond an occasional text message.

Mackenzie is my friend because we have the same interests. We are both quiet introverts who would rather read than go out drinking and partying, and in a college town and a raucous athletic department, that's rare. More than that, we enjoy similar enough genres that we can share book suggestions with one another. She's fun to work out with, too, whether we're doing self defense or tennis or pilates or something else. She's just fun to be around, period.

She props herself up on her elbow, staring down at me. The first touch of her lips to mine is hesitant. Cautious. I reach up and cup her cheek with my hand.

It's like fireworks going off in my brain. I have the most beautiful woman in the world in my bed, kissing me. She likes me. She wants to be with me.

Who am I, and what happened to me? When did this impossible fantasy become my real life?

Mackenzie kisses me more firmly. She adjusts the angle and with it grows in confidence. Her tongue comes out to meet me and I can't help the groan that rumbles up from deep within me.

"Shh," she mumbles against my lips. "We're going to get caught."

My cock twitches at the idea. I shouldn't like that as much as I do.

I'm not an exhibitionist. I don't have a performance kink. But the idea of someone walking in right now and catching us…

Surging forward, I wrap my arms around her and tug her onto my lap until she's straddling me. Her bare ass rests on my cock through my sweatpants.

"We can't."

"We're not going to play." I run my hand over her spine,

then slip my hand under the t-shirt she's wearing and learn each vertebrae. "We're just gonna…"

She kisses down my neck. "Yeah?"

"We're…"

My brain turns to mush.

Mackenzie giggles, burying her face in my neck. I tip her chin up and kiss her again, and again, and again, until I'm breathless and dizzy. She's squirming on my lap, trying to get more friction. Her hand slips between her legs.

"Baby, you're killing me here."

"You're killing *me*," she counters. Her hand moves beneath the baggy fabric of her borrowed t-shirt. She sighs.

That's it. I'm done. I work my hand between our bodies until it's me touching her. She's damp, a hot, wet spot on the front of my sweatpants where she's trying to ride me. When I push aside her underwear, her slickness practically drips over my fingers.

"Inside," she whispers.

My eyes dart up to hers.

She clears her throat. "Inside of me."

Adjusting my angle, I slowly circle one finger around her entrance. She's a virgin. She doesn't have a lot of experience. She's—

She's absolutely fucking perfect.

She's also really fucking tight. Her hot, wet heat clenches around my finger in a vise grip.

Mackenzie lets out a gusty sigh and spreads her legs, letting me get a little deeper. Slowly, I move my finger out and back in, and she throws her head back. Her long dark blonde hair flutters around her like a halo.

Arching her back, she leans over me and kisses me again. Her forearms brace on my shoulders as she moves her hips, working my finger deeper.

"How are you—are you—"

I want to check in, make sure she's okay, but I can't think

straight with her kissing me and riding my finger the way she is.

She moans, taking more of my hand. She's still impossibly tight. Slowly, I work the tip of my second finger in.

"You feel so good," she says, a little breathlessly. She leans back and pulls off the t-shirt, until she's naked on my lap with my fingers buried deep inside of her. My cock jerks in my sweatpants against the inside of her thigh.

She moans again.

"Wes, I—"

With my free hand, I cup her breast, plucking at her nipple. A gush of wetness coats my hand. My fingers are buried to the hilt inside her, thrusting and scissoring, looking for that special spot that will drive her crazy. I've read enough books. I know how this works. She moans— loudly.

There's a knock on the door.

"Hey, man," Miles says through the door.

Mackenzie goes white, her muscles tense. She clenches around my fingers so tightly I nearly see stars.

"Uh, hi?"

"Can you turn down the porn a bit? It's a little loud."

I clear my throat. "Sure."

"Thanks, dude," Miles says. "Have fun." He snickers and then his footsteps fade away, replaced by steps on the stairs.

Mackenzie looks at me with wide eyes. "I can't believe that just happened."

I slowly slide my fingers out and push them back in. Her eyes roll back and she sighs, so I do it again.

She bites her lip. "I can't believe he thought it was porn."

I shrug. Usually, I'm considerate enough to play it with either no volume or my headphones on. I don't want all the other guys hearing what I'm up to.

"Wes…"

I maneuver my hand so my thumb rubs against her clit,

and she lets out a low groan. She claps both hands over her mouth as she rides my fingers, taking what she needs.

Her thighs start to shake as she works her hips. Her breath catches in her chest.

And then she tumbles over the cliff of release. Breathing hard, she collapses onto the bed beside me.

"Holy fuck," she says, breathing hard. "I—you—" She rolls over until she's resting on my chest, her arm around my belly.

"Good?" Pride warms my chest that I was able to successfully help her get off.

"Fucking awesome," she says emphatically. "Give me a minute and then I can return the favor."

"That's not necessary."

She frowns, pushing up to look at me. "You want to go to sleep with a hard on?"

Well, no. Not really. But I also don't want to push her into doing anything she's not comfortable with in the name of reciprocity. I don't care that last week she gave me a hand job and then a few days later a blowjob. I'm not going to expect her to return sexual favors if she's not interested. That's not how this works.

"Trust me, I want to take care of you," she says. "I just need to catch my breath."

My cock jerks in my sweatpants at the idea of her *taking care of me*. I'm not about to turn her down. After five long years, having someone else that wants to touch my dick... yeah, it doesn't suck.

thirty-four

. . .

Mackenzie

THE DINER IS as packed as it was the last time we were here. The waitress we had last time—Tricia, says her name tag —waves us to her.

"Come on over, Wesley, baby," she says. "I've got your booth ready."

Again, there are complaints from the half dozen people already waiting for a table.

Wes ignores them all. With his head held high, he sets his hand on my back and gently leads me in her direction. It's the same table we had last time, too. He is nothing if not a creature of habit.

He guides me to the bench and takes a seat across from me before he takes my hand.

We slept together last night. We didn't have sex—neither of are ready, and especially not with a full house of roommates—but we spent seven hours in his bed, cuddling and sleeping and just—

It was perfect.

Okay, so, yeah, he snores. That's not great. And he's a sweaty sleeper. He wakes up drenched, even with a fan on and a window open in the middle of winter.

I'm an athlete. I can deal with a little sweat. I know where to buy earplugs. The way it felt to fall asleep in his arms, to wake up wrapped up in him... Yeah, I want that again. And again. And again.

I can't be the best bed partner, either. I'm a light sleeper and will be awake for hours in the middle of the night for no reason at all. Sometimes I thrash around. Claire has been known to throw stuff at me in the middle of the night to wake me up.

So neither of us are perfect. So what? He didn't complain, except for a brief whine when I pulled out of his bed shortly before five o'clock in the morning. He was snoring again a few minutes later, so it couldn't have fazed him that badly.

The waitress brings over his tea and a cup of water for me. "Can I get you anything else, honey?"

She's not looking at him. She's looking at me.

"Um, orange juice, please."

She smiles kindly. "Be right out. Y'all know what you want, or not yet?"

I look to Wes. He shakes his head, his eyes hazy.

"A few more moments, I think."

She tucks her notepad into her apron pocket. "I'll be right back."

I think I want something different this time. Not that I'm opposed to the same thing every day—I love me a routine—but today I'm ready to experiment a little.

The waitress brings me a glass of orange juice in hardly a second before she's gone again.

"So you come here often?" It's not every place that knows someone's order and brings out specialized drinks without needing to be asked.

"Every Sunday," he confirms. He clears his throat. "I couldn't sleep much at the—at the beginning. So I came here at five o'clock in the morning with my book. They let me stay until it got busy, when they needed the table."

"We could have come in at—"

"I sleep better now than I did back then," he explains. "I come because I want to, not because I'm wide awake with nothing else to do."

That makes sense. I'm not exactly a morning person—I am *so* glad to be done with six o'clock in the morning swim practice four days a week—but I'm not a night owl, either. I like to wake up, get my day going, and then go to sleep at a reasonable time. I can't stay up until the wee hours of the morning unless I'm deep in the middle of a really good book.

"We should go on a date," he says out of nowhere.

I blink. Isn't this a date? Are we not on one right now?

"A real date," he continues, "where we get dressed up and go out. Somewhere nice. You should…" He swallows. "You deserve to have a real date."

"I'm more than happy with what we're doing now. I don't need—"

"I want to." His eyes meet mine. "I can't offer you much. I can give you this."

"You give me plenty—"

"Mackenzie. Let me do this for you." He squeezes my hand. "I want to do this for you."

"Okay. So we'll go on a date."

His satisfied smile nearly takes my breath away.

The waitress chooses that moment to return. I place my order—going to try a waffle this time—and Wes grunts his acceptance of his usual. She doesn't seem perturbed by his curtness. If anything, she's charmed by it. By him.

It's not hard to be charmed by Wes. He's pretty damn great.

His fingers start to twitch, and I know he's itching for some quiet time to himself, so I pull out my tablet and open the book I started last night. He pulls out his book. He finished his in-progress novel last night, so this is a new one. I blink at the title. It's a romance novel, a contemporary story about college athletes that I've recommended to everyone I know, it's so good.

I'm not surprised he's reading romance. I know he likes the genre, even if he prefers other genres more. What's surprising is that he's reading it out in the open, without switching to his e-reader.

He doesn't care if other people see the title or cover of the book he's reading, so I shouldn't care, either. I like that he's secure enough in his masculinity to be seen reading stereotypically female-oriented books. Not that men can't read romance, and that they shouldn't read them in the open. They can. They should.

But stigmas prevail, and given how reserved Wes is in every other aspect of his life, it wouldn't surprise me if he kept this side of himself hidden. I like that he doesn't. I like that he's confident enough to proudly read the types of books he wants to read, without any regard for what other people might think of him.

We take a break from reading when the food arrives. It's hard to butter toast or cut a waffle with only one hand free. And I would never want to get maple syrup on the tablet screen.

He's quiet, even more quiet than usual, as he focuses on his breakfast. I hope last night I didn't do anything embarrassing. I woke up in his arms and— Oh, what I would give to be able to do that every day. Or even every once in a while.

Wes clears his throat. I look up from my breakfast to find Tucker and Barrett standing over us, both looking distinctly amused.

"Good morning," I chirp, way too peppy and enthusiastic. Wes raises his eyebrows.

"Morning," Tucker says carefully. "You're up early."

"Couldn't sleep. Your couch is super uncomfortable."

"Mm-hmm." He looks to Barrett, who snorts. "It looks like you guys are nearly done, otherwise I'd suggest we join you."

I force a smile. "You're always welcome to join. The more, the merrier."

"How early did you guys get up?" Barrett asks.

"Early," Wes grunts.

I laugh. "I was already up and dressed by the time he came out of his room. I was getting ready to leave and head home, but breakfast sounded too good."

Technically not a lie.

I slept wrapped up in his arms. Shortly before five, I went back out to the sofa, where I dozed for an hour and a half until I heard Mason come down the stairs and Tucker go back up. Once he was safely in his room, I got up and dressed, and Wes was ready five minutes later.

"Do you do this often?" Tucker asks, looking between us.

"Have breakfast?" I'm purposefully being obtuse. I know what he's insinuating. "Yeah, you eat breakfast with us all the time in the dining hall."

"No, I mean…" He sighs. "Forget it."

Wes grunts and opens up his book again, clearly done with the conversation.

"You guys are reading," Barrett says.

Wes laughs.

"Yeah, we like to read," I tell him, which is so freaking obvious.

"So you're not, like…"

I raise my eyebrows.

"You're reading," he says again. "You're having breakfast and reading."

"Yeah?"

Barrett shakes his head. "Nothing. Carry on."

"Thanks for your permission," I say sardonically, and he laughs.

"Never change, Mack," Tucker says, hiding his smile.

So I go back to my book, Wes goes back to his. And under the table, he nudges my foot with his. We're in this together.

thirty-five

. . .

Mackenzie

IT'S good to see my parents. It's been a few long weeks since I saw my mom in Maine, and even longer since I've been able to spend time with my dad and sister. With Miles joining us (Sam has an away game series this weekend, so his night is free), the whole family is together again for the first time in weeks.

Considering how busy we all are, it's kind of amazing that my family is able to spend so much time together. Miles did college football. I'm playing college basketball. My sister does competitive cheerleading, which is about a forty hour a week commitment. My mom plays tennis every chance she gets with the ladies at her gym. Dad swims every morning and plays basketball three times a week. In the summer and fall, he coaches youth football teams.

We're busy. Our lives revolve around sports. But our lives also revolve around each other. We make a point to meet up with as many of us as possible as often as we can. I've had at least one parent and one sibling at every home game this year. My mom travels to as many of my away games as she can, depending on Ashley's travel schedule, and Miles is always down to grab dinner together in the dining hall one or two nights a week.

Now that I'm spending so much time with Wes, I have that much less time for my brother. I don't know that he cares. I don't know that he's even noticed. He didn't realize I was dating someone until Mom told him. Sure, he might have his suspicions, but he doesn't know for sure.

I thought for sure we were busted at the diner last weekend. Then again, I'm not sure Barrett and Tucker care. They would probably think it's funny that Wes and I are hooking up beneath my brother's nose.

There should be no reason that my brother cares who I date. At the same time, I have to concede that dating his roommate probably wasn't the best idea. If—*when*—Wes and I break up, they still have to live together.

Not for much longer, though. They're both graduating. Miles is heading home for the summer to apply for jobs. I'm not sure what Wes is doing. I don't think he knows, either.

Me, I'll be at home for three weeks before I'm back on campus for summer school. I don't want to require a fifth year to finish my degree; I want to get it done on time, and for me, that means in four years (and a few summer sessions). If I take the more intensive courses over the summer, that frees up my schedule during fall conditioning and spring season.

Dareesa, Pia, and I walk out of the locker room at the same time. I wave them goodbye as I jog over to my family, waiting in the atrium. My dad opens his arms and I step into them, letting him wrap me in a hug.

"Hey, Mackie. Good game."

"Thanks, Daddy."

The guys are clustered in a half circle a few feet away. Tucker, Barrett, Amir, and Wes have come to my game, joined by Mason and Diana. I meet Wes's eye over my dad's shoulder and have to swallow at the look of longing on his face. We are so going to get busted.

I don't know how much longer I can walk around carrying this big secret when all I want to do is shout it from the rooftops. I'm dating Wes, the coolest, kindest guy I know. I'm dating a man who adores me, who would give me the world if he could. A man who treats me well and makes me feel treasured and adored.

It's a coincidence that he is my brother's roommate. It's sheer dumb luck that the guy I fell for played on my brother's right side for five seasons. His being a football player is not even in the top ten reasons why I like him. It's just a bonus.

"We're headed to the Grotto," Mom announces. "Would you boys like to join us?"

I expect them to decline. I can count on one hand the number of times the guys have agreed to join us for a meal after a game in the five years I've known them.

Instead, Amir looks to the other guys and says, "I could eat," and Barrett nods. Tucker slips his phone back into his pocket and grins.

"Wes, honey? Are you joining us?"

His eyes dart to mine before he meets my mom's. "Thank you. That would be nice."

The floor falls out from underneath me. She looks nearly as surprised as I am. He never agrees. He never wants to intrude on family time, he says.

He agreed. He's coming to dinner.

Automatically I run a cautious hand over my dirty, sweaty ponytail before I remember: This is my family. They don't care what I look like. This is my boyfriend. He likes me the way I am.

Tomorrow is hair washing day. After the game, I showered and cleaned up, spraying liberally with some dry shampoo, so at least I smell fresh. I'm not wearing any makeup, only some tinted lip balm, the same one I wear every day.

Normally we drive over to the Grotto. Since we have such a big group, my dad drives the car over and my mom walks with us through town. She talks to Miles on the walk over, letting me reflect on my thoughts a little.

Wes walks beside me, Barrett and Diana on his other side. Mason, Tucker, and Amir are directly behind us. Every so often, his hand brushes mine, like he wants to take my hand. I want him to. But I also don't want this fragile, delicate thing we share to shatter, so I'll protect it as long as I can. As long as I have to.

When we arrive at the restaurant, there is only a slight wait for a table. Somehow, through absolutely no subtle maneuvering on my part, I end up next to Wes. He has Mason and Tucker on his other side. As much as he doesn't like to be in the middle, sometimes it works out perfectly.

If my parents are surprised by this turn of events, they don't let me know it. I don't think they expected quite a large group to come to dinner. Then again, they offered, just as they do every week for my game and as they did every week for Miles's games. They want to include our friends. It just so happens that I'm friends with most of my brother's friends.

"Wes, honey, how have you been?" Mom asks. "We haven't seen you in, gosh, weeks. You haven't come out with us in—"

He clears his throat. "It's been a while."

"You're good?"

"I'm well," he nods, and then pauses. He clears his throat again. "Thank you for inviting us."

Miles looks surprised. That's more than Wes usually talks with people he doesn't know well. And as much as he might have seen my parents around a lot, he hasn't exactly spent enough time with them for them to be on his friendly conversation list.

He's getting better. He isn't nearly as reticent as he used to be. He can communicate with more than grunts and a sharp jerk of his head. His monosyllabic days are a thing of the past.

I hope.

I don't expect him to suddenly completely change who he is. He's a quiet, withdrawn guy. But sometimes, every once in a while, he opens up more. He shows a little glimpse of who he is. He lets other people see the magic and beauty he hides for me.

Under the table, I set my hand on his knee, and he jerks in his chair. He sits up straight in his seat.

"How is the hunt for graduate schools going?" Dad asks the group at large.

Mason and Tucker are both going to school for psychology. They're looking for a program that will accept both of them. Diana is looking at dietetics school. And Wes... his imminent departure for physical therapy school hangs over our relationship like a raincloud ready to turn into a late summer thunderstorm.

Wes clears his throat for a third time in as many minutes. "I have an interview next week."

"You do?" I turn to look at him.

He nods. "For Newton. My top choice."

He wants to stay here, and I'm not egotistical enough to think my being here is at least part of the reason why. Still, I like the idea that he could stay close, that he could be here next year. That there isn't an automatic end to what we have by virtue of the changing calendar and lessened proximity.

He isn't in yet. He might not get accepted. He might get a better offer. He might decide for other reasons we should break up.

My hand tightens on his knee and he looks at me out of the corner of his eye. Slowly, deliberately, he shifts in his seat so his hand falls beneath the table. He squeezes my hand and then picks it up, lacing our fingers together.

He likes me. He wants to be with me. I can't worry about what ifs and maybes and eventually. I have to focus on the here and now, and at this very moment, I'm more concerned about my brother finding out I'm dating his roommate than the fact that one day I might not be.

thirty-six

. . .

Wes

AFTER DINNER—WHICH was delicious, if excruciating, sitting next to Mackenzie and not being able to be *with* her—we say goodbye to her parents and head back to the house en masse.

"What are we watching tonight?" Miles asks.

"Oh, so it's movie night?" Amir says.

"Well, Wes is here tonight. He's not out with his mystery—"

Mackenzie flinches.

I clear my throat.

"Sure, sounds good," Barrett says, slinging his arm around Diana's shoulders. "I vote for something superhero. Maybe a Batman movie."

I could go for a Batman marathon. Maybe Michael Keaton vs Val Kilmer vs George Clooney vs Christian Bale. Then again, I don't know that I want to sit through that many movies tonight. I've got a gorgeous girl who's going to share my bed. Maybe. Possibly.

If her brother doesn't find out about us.

I know it's killing Miles that I didn't share exactly what happened a few weeks ago when he caught me coming home.

Usually I'm an open book, at least in terms of where I go and who I see. Luckily, I don't think he's cottoned on to the fact I've suddenly started having a social life right around the time his sister gets a boyfriend—someone she is refusing to introduce to him.

Her story that it's too soon is a half-truth. It is a little soon to meet the parents—or it would be, if I didn't already know and like her parents. If they like me is another story. I think mostly her mom pities me, the poor orphan who doesn't talk much. The guy who had nobody to come to his final football game for senior night because it was the same week as my sister's midterms and she couldn't fly across the country for twenty-four hours.

And now Sarah isn't even available during my spring break. I guess I'll just stay in the house for a week by myself. I'll check out double my usual stack of books from the library and make a point to go to the diner every morning for a leisurely breakfast. It'll be good. It'll be fine.

It's only a week. One week. I can survive without seeing Mackenzie for seven days. I think. Maybe.

Purposefully, I stumble over my own two feet, and her hand lands on my arm, helping me up. I set my hand on hers for a second. It's not enough. I just needed to touch her for a second.

"Steady, there," she says, hiding her smile.

Yeah, I'm not subtle in the slightest.

Miles looks between us with eyebrows raised. Mackenzie clears her throat, and I release her. My skin mourns the loss of her innocent touch on my arm.

We get back to the house in one piece. I disappear into my room for a few minutes and reset.

Mackenzie and I might be dating, but it's a secret. Nobody can know, most importantly not her brother, my roommate, teammate, and friend. She might be spending the night in my bed, which is extra reason to keep everything on the down low. I can do this. We can do this.

Fuck, she's so close, but she's so far out of reach. The guys are on the couch so she settles on the floor in front of my usual armchair. I want to haul her into my lap and kiss her. I want to hold her in my arms and breathe in the green apple and pear blossom of her shampoo. I want *her*.

Instead I take my seat and crack open a book. I'm perfectly capable of multitasking.

When the lights go out, she shifts ever so slightly over to the left, so she's leaning on the chair. Her head rests against my knee. I have to fight the urge to run my hands over her hair. She turns on her e-reader and flips to a new book, one I recommended to her last week.

Amir groans. "Ugh. You two would be perfect for each other."

Miles growls. "What's that supposed to mean?"

"Look at them," he nods. "They're both reading during the movie. They're both quiet bookworms. And they're friends. They would be, like, the perfect couple."

"Mack's not quiet," her brother protests.

Amir shrugs. "If you say so."

She's quiet around people she doesn't know or when in a big crowd. She feels like her voice isn't being heard in crowded spaces and doesn't have the wherewithal yet to assert herself. That's one of the reasons she signed up for the public speaking class, aside from the fact that it fulfilled a requirement, was that it would force her out of her shell a little.

There's no shell in sight when she's with me, except maybe when it comes to intimacy. She's not ready for sex; that's fine, I'm not pushing her. But there's a reason she's a nineteen year old virgin, and it can't be simply due to lack of opportunity. If she really wanted to, she would have had sex already.

Although I'm reading with half my brain, the other half of my attention is on her. Without a word, she gets up ten minutes into the movie and disappears down the hall. My door creaks open and some of the guys look towards me. I ignore them.

She comes back a moment later with the blanket from my bed.

Her brother looks at her. "Did you just—isn't that Wes's?"

Because Amir's door squeaks significantly less loudly than mine does. I need to WD-40 it. I keep forgetting.

"He lets me borrow it," she says. "It's not like he uses it."

It's true. I do. I have since she started staying the night last fall. I'm a sweaty sleeper; I like to sleep with only a thin sheet on me. My sister thinks this is unacceptable and insisted on buying me a full set of sheets and blankets, plus extras in case of "overnight guests," as she called it. Yeah, she spends the night, but Mackenzie isn't a guest. She might as well live here, too, with how much time she's spent here over the last few months—even before we got together.

She curls up at my feet again, the soft knitted blanket spread over her lap. She rests her head on my knee.

"And you didn't ask?" Miles won't let this go.

She doesn't have to. She knows it's hers for the taking.

"He always lets me borrow it," she says, picking up her e-reader.

"But—"

"It's not a big deal," I cut in. She is perfectly capable of defending herself. She shouldn't have to, not when it comes to this. "She knows where I keep the spares."

Of all things, this is not what they should be fighting over. I like that she's not engaging, though. She's standing up for herself, holding her ground, but she isn't caving in to him.

He grunts acceptance and folds himself back onto the armchair, his arms crossed over his chest as he diverts his attention to the movie. I go back to my book. Every so often, I feel his eyes on me.

I turn the page.

We finish the first movie and, after a break for popcorn, tea, and hot chocolate, we settle in for the second film. Mason and Tucker make out through most of it; they leave as soon as the second movie is over. Diana and Barrett are only slightly more subtle as they slip out of the room and up the stairs.

Miles looks at Mackenzie. "Are you staying the night?"

Don't look at me. Don't look at me. Don't look at me.

She clears her throat. "I had planned on it, yeah. It's late. I don't want to walk back to my dorm."

Perfectly plausible excuses. It's after midnight. I want her to stay the night—in my bed. We were able to pull it off last weekend. There's no reason we can't manage it again.

Miles nods. "I'll get the blankets and a pillow for you."

"Thanks."

Not that she's going to use them. She says she prefers my extra pillow to the one he keeps here for her. She's wrapped up in my blanket like a cocoon. She yawns and laughs.

"I'm pretty wiped. If you guys want to watch another movie, you can, but I'm going to crash on the couch while you're doing it."

"I'm done," I announce, closing my book. I force myself to my feet and lift my empty mug of tea. Reaching out my hand, she passes over her cup of what used to be hot chocolate. After a second, I clear my throat and take Amir's cup, too. I can be polite. I can not obviously favor the girl I'm dating in secret. Whatever. Dishes washed and put away, I run through my regular nightly routine and get ready for bed.

My door creaks open about fifteen minutes after everyone else goes upstairs. I'm tucked up in bed, a book in my hands. I was not so casually waiting for her to decide it was safe.

"Hey," Mackenzie says quietly, hanging out in the doorway. She's wearing pajamas—a large t-shirt she stole from my closet, and a pair of Newton sweatpants

"Are you coming in?"

"You want me to?" She blinks.

Um, yes. A thousand times yes.

"Get in here, baby."

She beams and closes the door, practically leaping into my bed in two quick strides. In the blink of an eye, she's slipped under the covers and curled up to me.

"Hi," she whispers, sliding her arms around my neck, before she kisses me.

Tossing aside my book, I roll towards her, pulling her body into mine. She's all long, lean lines, tightly packed muscle evenly dispersed through her six foot tall frame. My hand glides down her spine and cups her ass. She sighs.

"Not tonight." I steal another kiss. "It's late."

She pouts.

"In the morning, we can play all you want. We can even go to breakfast again," I suggest. "You, me, the diner. Nobody will know where we are. It'll be great."

Mackenzie smiles. "It's a date."

"Hell yeah, it is."

She kisses me again, a sweet, chaste peck, before she rolls over and sets her glasses on the bedside table and snuggles up to me again. She piles three blankets onto her torso, leaving me with only a top sheet—just the way I like it. Her head on my chest, her arm around my belly… yeah, it doesn't get much better than this.

She falls asleep first. I'm content to lie here, holding her in my arms.

thirty-seven

. . .

Mackenzie

I SNEAK out of Wes's bed around six-thirty. Nobody else should be up at this time. Nobody has early morning practice or anywhere to be. The guys usually don't get up before eight at the very earliest on the weekend. Still, I don't want to push my luck.

He whines deep in his throat as I slide out of the bed. I give him a quick kiss, and he tries to pull me back onto the mattress. I laugh and tuck the sheet up around him. He pouts, still half asleep.

Gingerly, I shut the creaky door and creep to the bathroom for a quick rest and reset. Splashing some water on my face helps. It's early, but I'm awake. I might be able to snooze for an hour or two, until everyone gets up.

My brother is sitting on the couch, right in the middle of my supposed bed. The one I didn't sleep in last night. His eyes narrow.

"Where have you been?"

"Um, the bathroom?" Not a lie.

"I've been down here for an hour."

"I really had to go."

"Mack."

"What?"

"Where did you sleep last night?"

"Here." Not a lie, if here is this house, and not referring to the sofa.

Miles glares at me. "Why are you being so difficult?"

"Why do you care?"

"You're hiding something."

Well, finally, he gets it.

"Can I please have my bed back? I want to go back to sleep."

He rolls his eyes. "Yeah, the bed you don't sleep in."

Wes's door creaks open, and he pads down the hall. I can't see him, but I can hear his footsteps as he makes his way to the bathroom and shuts the door.

"I'm going to kill him," Miles says slowly. "I'm going to fucking kill him."

"Kill who?"

His eyes meet mine. "Tell me you didn't sleep with Wes last night."

I look away.

Faced with the truth, I can't lie. Last night I slept in Wes's bed. Nothing happened, at least nothing that hasn't already happened. We didn't have sex. We only kissed a bit, which I would think is fairly natural for couples who are tucked into bed together.

The toilet flushes and water runs. The bathroom door opens.

Wes looks over to us and stops, a deer in the headlights look on his face. There's a love bite on his neck. Shit.

"Morning?"

Miles lets out a growl and charges at him. Wes can't move away in time. In seconds, he's pinned against the door frame, his broad shoulders pressed to the wall and an arm across his throat.

"Did you sleep with my sister?"

Wes looks to me.

Miles screeches in frustration. Before I know what's happening, he rears back and punches Wes in the face.

I shriek.

That seems to wake Wes up. He ducks the second punch. The third lands on his shoulder. In a few short maneuvers, he escapes Miles's hold and has my brother in a headlock.

"What the fuck," Miles yells.

"I let you have one punch," Wes says calmly. "That's it."

"She's my sister!"

I snort out a breath of disbelief.

"She's a kid!"

"I'm nineteen," I remind my brother, crossing my arms over my chest.

Miles looks to me with pain in his eyes. "Mack."

"This is none of your business."

He frowns.

"Who I date is none of your business."

"You're—you're dating? *Him*?"

I roll my eyes. I know it's early, but I thought he would have cottoned on by now.

"No, I just hop into bed with any random guy I know," I tell my brother, and he growls. I roll my eyes again. "Nothing happened."

"You slept with him."

"Yeah, slept," I point out. "We fell asleep. That's all."

"But—"

"We're not—I'm not—" Miles looks to Wes.

"I love her," he says, and my stomach drops. He wouldn't lie about this. He wouldn't use those three important words as a cop out. Wes looks at me. "I love you, Mackenzie."

It's only been five weeks. We haven't even gone on a real date yet. We—

He's my best friend. My favorite person.

This is Wes. When he commits to something, he goes all

in. He doesn't do anything in half measures. He finishes every book he starts. He does his homework without complaining. He dedicated years and years to perfecting his body and his mind for football.

"I know it's soon," he says. "I've been holding back for a while now. You deserve to know. I love you, Mackenzie."

Miles lets out a grunt of frustration.

"Nothing happened last night," Wes tells him. "We fell asleep together."

"You—him—I can't—Mack—"

"I'm sorry for hiding it," I admit, because I am. I'm ashamed we snuck around for so long. "I'm crazy about him. Who I date shouldn't impact your life whatsoever. He might be your teammate, but he's *my* boyfriend."

My brother flinches.

"This isn't some fling," Wes says seriously. "I care about her. She's important to me."

"You're seriously together?" Still in the headlock, Miles looks from me to Wes, his face drawn.

"We're dating," I confirm.

"So this new boyfriend of yours…"

"Wes."

"And the reason you've been coming home late?" He looks to Wes again.

"We've been hanging out." Wes clears his throat and releases Miles from the headlock. When my brother doesn't immediately charge at him, he lets out a sigh of relief. "I know it breaks every rule of bro code, but—"

"Hang on a second. Bro code?"

He looks to me. "Yeah. You're not supposed to date your buddy, teammate, or roommate's sister," Miles explains, like I'm a child. "It's against the rules. Sisters are off limits."

"So the whole reason you were opposed to this was some antiquated patriarchal bullshit bro code?"

I am going to murder him.

"We were friends for a long time," Wes tells him. "Our friendship had nothing to do with you. Our relationship didn't involve you. I would still want to be with her regardless of whose sister or daughter she is. She's great, man. She's perfect."

I laugh. I'm not perfect.

Wes meets my eye and grins. "Okay, so maybe you're not perfect. But you're perfect for me, and I like to think I'm a good fit for you, too."

It's a risk, but I cross the room to his side. Wes reaches for me, and I take his hand. He pulls me close, his arms wrapped around me.

"I'm in love with you," he says quietly.

"I—"

"It's okay if you're not there yet. I'm not pressuring you to say something you're not ready for," he says. "It was time you knew. I'm fucking crazy about you, Mackenzie."

Miles growls.

"I'm pretty crazy about you, too," I admit.

He grins, his forehead pressed to mine.

Slowly, gingerly, I press my lips to his in a sweet, innocent kiss. My brother makes a noise of disgust behind us. I ignore him.

Wes kisses me back, a simple brush of lips on lips. Teasing. Innocent.

"I can't believe you two are actually—"

I flip him off.

"Nice. Real nice, Mack."

Wes breaks the kiss and takes a step back, though his hands remain on my hips. "Now, as fun as this has been—"

Miles snorts.

"—I'm going back to bed. It's too early to be up for the day. You're welcome to join me," he says, directing this to me. "We can still go on our breakfast date in a few hours."

"A nap wouldn't be the worst," I agree. I take his hand

and ignore my brother's huff of annoyance. "Let's go back to bed."

I let Wes lead me down the hall to his bedroom. The door creaks open and shut. Once the door is safely closed, he lets out a slow breath.

"You okay?"

He frowns. "I should be asking you that. He's your brother."

"Yeah, and he punched you in the face."

He waves it away. "Didn't hurt."

"Uh huh. Sure." A punch to the face doesn't not hurt just because he wants to look strong and tough in front of me, but I let it slide. There are bigger battles to fight.

"Come to bed." Wes's voice softens. "Let me hold you for a bit."

thirty-eight

. . .

Interlude

"I KNEW IT."

"You didn't know shit."

"I knew he was hooking up with someone."

"Yeah, but you didn't know—"

"Mackenzie?!"

"Dude, where have you been? Didn't you hear the fight this morning?"

"No?"

"They're totally hooking up."

"And Miles is okay with this?"

"I guess so. I mean, look at them."

"It's none of his business, anyway."

"Shut up. So you're saying you wouldn't care if one of us dated your sisters?"

A laugh. "You can have them. Doesn't mean they'd be interested in a scrub like you."

"What's that supposed to mean?"

"Besides, don't you have a girlfriend?"

"This is all hypothetical."

A pause.

"They do look happy, though. Don't they?"

"They look good together. She'll be good for him."

"I wonder how long this has been going on."

"Long enough if they're sleeping together. He hates to be touched, but look, his arm is around her. They're curled up together."

"And that thing with the blanket last night…"

"Yeah, that was weird."

"They were sitting next to each other at dinner, too. And have you noticed she's been joining us more often lately? Not that I'm complaining. I like having her around."

"I think he does, too."

thirty-nine

. . .

Mackenzie

AS MUCH AS I want to give my brother space to process, now that my secret is out in the open—and *all* the guys know —I see no reason to hide anymore. Wes is gone when I wake up a little after nine o'clock. The shower is running in the bathroom next door, so either he or Amir are up and getting ready.

Stretching my arms over my head, I look around the room and assess. It's like a weight has been lifted off my shoulders. My stomach doesn't churn with anxiety. I feel… good.

The water turns off next door. I can hear the curtain being pulled aside—fuck, these walls are *really* thin. And that day Miles heard us, heard *me*… just how loud was I? Do all the guys know now what it sounds like when I come?

I can't be ashamed of the way Wes makes me feel. He makes me feel beautiful and sexy and, yes, loved. He sees me for who I am. He listens when I talk. He's never made me doubt his feelings for me. Right from the beginning, he's made clear that he's in this for the long haul. This isn't some spur of the moment, flight of fancy fling for him.

He loves me.

And I… don't know. I've never been in love before. I don't

know what to expect. How will I know if I love him? I have virtually no experience when it comes to this. Aside from a few fumbled kisses, I've never so much as pursued a crush. I've never had the nerve.

And now I have a boyfriend, we are in a committed relationship, and he loves me.

Where do I go from here?

The door creaks open. Wes pokes his head in before he catches sight of me and grins. His sandy blond hair is wet and sticking up in every direction. A towel is wrapped low around his waist, his broad chest and big, hairy belly on display. He is confident in his skin—it's only one of the many, many things I admire about him.

"Good morning," he says, closing the door behind him. "Have a good sleep?" He crosses the room and kisses me, sweet and innocent.

"Very. It must have been the person in the bed beside me."

He laughs and his whole belly shakes with it.

"So I guess everyone knows now."

"Is that a problem?"

I let out a slow breath. "No. It saves us from having to announce it. I just wish it was on our own terms, not his."

"I'm not ashamed about how I feel about you," he says seriously. "I would tell the whole world."

My stomach twists.

"My sister knows," he says, and my stomach drops. His last remaining family member... I know how close they are. He values her opinions. "She's happy for us. I don't know when she can get out, maybe not until graduation, but I want you to meet her."

Graduation. It looms over us.

I clear my throat. "Any luck on your grad school applications?"

His tight smile is pained. "I have the Newton interview coming up."

I don't want him to leave. Never, ever, ever.

But of course the world doesn't work that way.

"Let's grab breakfast," he says. "The diner, just the two of us, or the dining hall with everyone?"

"I don't care. Whatever you're in the mood for."

I really don't. As much as I want to flaunt our "new" relationship in front of all of our friends, I also relish our time alone together. Maybe now that we're out of the so-called closet, we can arrange for more dates and time together. And maybe that means we can organize a few more sleepovers, too...

Wes crosses to his dresser and pulls out clothes. His shirt goes on first, then he shimmies a pair of boxers beneath his towel—like I haven't seen it before.

"I'll get dressed," I announce. Careful so as to not expose him, I crack open the door and slip out in pursuit of my overnight bag.

Tucker lets out a catcall when he catches sight of me. "Well, well, well. It seems someone has been holding out on us."

I laugh. "Oh yeah?"

He's lounging on the couch, his phone in his hand. He shoves it into his pocket and stands to give me a side hug. "Congrats, I think? I'm happy for you two."

"I'm happy for us, too."

"We'll have to arrange a double date, you guys and me and Mase," he suggests.

There's a fluttery feeling deep in my chest.

"That would be nice. I... I would like that."

Does it really matter if all of my friends are poached from my brother? Does it matter if they're only my friend by circumstance? Still, Tucker is extending an olive branch of comradeship—we're both in relationships now. We can hang out as two couples. Equals.

Ducking into the bathroom, I race through a shower and

get dressed. When I emerge, Wes is sitting in his armchair with a book. My chest warms with affection for him.

He looks up, smiles, and marks his page. "Hey."

"Hi."

There's a cough, and I only now realize that the rest of the room is packed full. Amir and Tucker are on the couch. Barrett is in another armchair, Diana perched on his legs. Greg is in the doorway, peeling a banana.

And Miles is looking like he's sucking on a lemon.

Mason barrels down the stairs and stops short. "Were you waiting for me? I told you to go ahead."

Tucker stands and reaches for her, tucking her under his arm. "I'll always wait for you, sunshine."

Barrett laughs. Diana swats him gently in the chest.

Everyone starts to get up and pull on coats. Wes grabs mine and shoulders through the crush of his roommates. He helps me into my coat and ducks down, kissing my cheek.

The room goes silent.

"Ready?" he asks.

Fisting my hands in his hoodie, I pull him down to my level and kiss him properly. The guys erupt into catcalls.

"Now I am."

He's grinning at me, with a bewildered look in his eyes like he can't believe I just did that. I can hardly believe it, either. He takes my hand and laces our fingers together.

Miles scoffs. "Seriously?"

Greg rolls his eyes. "Leave them alone. They're cute together." He winks at me. "Now I know why you never want to party with me."

I laugh. "Maybe because frat parties suck and football parties are lame?" Wes's hand tightens on mine. "Besides, I've got someone else I'd rather spend my time with."

"I can see that." Greg grins and pulls on my ponytail. "He doesn't treat you right, you let us know. We'll set him straight."

Wes clears his throat. "I'm right here."

Amir claps him on the shoulder. "And you're dating our collective sister. So if you break her heart, we break your face."

"Gladly," Wes says. I blink up at him. "I don't want to hurt her. Not now, not ever."

Some of the guys are mollified by this. Miles, however, is not. "You—"

"You don't get to dictate anything about our relationship," I interrupt loudly. "It has nothing to do with you. I'm not dating you."

Miles makes a face. "Gross, Mack."

"Well, why the hell do you think you get any say in what happens? It doesn't involve you."

He frowns.

"I didn't get upset when you started dating Sam. I was happy for you that you found someone that you liked, and liked you back," I remind him. "So why can't you just be happy for me?"

Miles opens his mouth and closes it abruptly.

"We aren't dating *at* you. We aren't purposefully trying to piss you off. We were friends, we decided we should be more, the end."

My brother crosses his arms over his chest and looks away, an uncomfortable expression on his face. He doesn't like being called out. He especially doesn't like being called out in front of all his friends. He's in the wrong and he knows it.

"Sorry," he mutters, still not looking at us.

I cup my hand around my ear. "What was that? I didn't catch it."

Miles groans. "Mack."

"What?"

"Don't make me say it."

"Say what?"

"I'm sorry!" he yells. "Are you happy now? I'm fucking sorry."

"For what?"

"For…"

"For making our relationship about you? For trying to convince me somebody who loves me is going to hurt me? For being a patronizing asshole who thinks he gets to control my every decision? Hm?"

Wes barks out a laugh. He ducks down and drops a kiss to my cheek. "I love you," he says casually, like he didn't announce it for the first time only a few scant hours ago. "You're perfect."

"Thank you." I smile prettily up at him, and he laughs, tugging me into his side and wrapping his arm around me.

We finally get to do this now. We get to act like a regular couple, like any other two consenting adults who have mutual affection for each other. We don't have to hide.

In short order, we make it to the dining hall. Greg holds open the door for everyone, and Wes places his hand on my back, guiding me inside. I live for these little touches, the innocent displays of his feelings for me. He's proclaiming to the world that we're together with this subtle little display. We're intimate in ways that have nothing to do with sex.

We fill our plates and wind through the cafeteria lines. The table at the back of the dining hall is unofficially reserved for the defensive squad. Everyone settles into their regular seats. Wes is on the end. I sit across from him, next to Amir today. Wes unloads his plate, mug of tea, and a separate mug of coffee before he reaches out for my empty tray.

"Holy shit," Barrett says.

"What?" Wes looks up, confused.

"You make her coffee."

"Yeah?"

"Every morning, you make her coffee," he repeats. "How did we not see it?"

I laugh. "We really weren't trying to be all that subtle. I was practically stalking this table."

"So you've been dating all this time?" Diana asks, looking between us. She nods to the books we're both holding. "Is that a thing?"

"It's been a few weeks," I explain. "We really were just friends for a long time."

Wes snorts.

"Okay, so maybe we both wanted it to be more," I relent. "He was waiting until I turned legal—"

"I was not," he protests.

"Oh, so last year, you would have—?"

He makes a face.

Last year I was in high school. Sure, I was eighteen, but that's only by virtue of having a birthday early in the year. I was still a kid.

"I waited until we were both ready," he finally says. "You weren't ready, and neither was I."

This is true. Even that night we officially got together, he tried to convince himself it wasn't time yet. There was no dissuading me, though. Once he made it clear he had feelings for me, feelings he was trying to repress, I knew I had to make my move. Not that I had any idea what I was doing. I can count on one hand the number of guys I've kissed, and still have three fingers left over if I only include the ones that knew what they were doing.

And boy does Wes know what he's doing. My pulse sings when he's near. My heart pounds and my palms get sweaty, and I have to remind myself that he likes me, he really likes me, he wants to be with me. When we're lying together mostly naked in bed and his fingers are buried in me… yeah, I like that, too. My face heats and Diana laughs, not unkindly.

"Seems like it's worked out for the both of you, then," she says casually.

Wes winks at me from across the table. "Yeah, I think so."

forty

. . .

Mackenzie

SAM SEEMS GENUINELY happy for me and Wes. The first time I see my brother's girlfriend after the secret is out, she shrieks and throws her arms around me—right in the middle of the dining hall.

"Oh, I'm so happy for you," she says, rocking me back and forth, despite the fact that I'm a solid six inches taller than her.

"Thank you?"

"You and Wes! I knew it! It was only a matter of time!"

I laugh. That's what everyone has been saying. They all saw it coming. So why didn't anyone tell either of us?

"Thanks, Sam," I say sincerely.

"We should go on a double date," she chirps.

Out of the corner of my eye, I can see my brother make a face. He's not wild about the idea.

"Sounds perfect," I say, just to make him squirm.

"Everyone is coupling up."

Together we look around the table. Miles has Sam. Tucker is with Mason. Barrett and Diana are attached at the hip. Amir and Jill seem happy. And now me and Wes are together…

The only odd man out is Greg, who doesn't spend the night with the same girl twice. Of all of them, he's the one most likely to be at a party, always ready for a good time. He has the greatest chance of all five guys combined to go pro. His dad was a professional football player, so it stands to reason that after his senior season, Greg will enter the draft and someone will select him based on name, size, and legacy alone.

"Don't look at me," he says quickly. "I'm happy on my own."

"If you say so," Sam says, refusing to let him bring down her mood.

"I'll let you know if that changes," he promises, and she grins.

Wes arrives at the table with a tray laden with snacks for us to share. He's made us a veggie platter with hummus, fruit and cottage cheese (no strawberries in sight), apples and peanut butter, and a stack of toast. He's even made me a hot chocolate, though he had to forgo the marshmallows this time due to lack of availability.

He watches us warily as he unloads the tray, organizing it between our two usual seats. He picks up his tea and his book. My e-reader is already at my spot at the table.

"Tomorrow night, before your game on Wednesday," Sam says to me now. "The four of us can go to the pub for dinner and hang out. Somewhere that isn't here." She waves at the dining hall.

I glance to Wes. "You okay with that?"

He shrugs and opens his book. "I get to spend time with you? Count me in."

Sam swoons, her hands clasped to her chest. "Wes, you know all the right things to say."

He cracks a grin, not looking up from the page. "It's all the books I read."

"I'll say," Sam says with an appreciative leer, only half joking.

Miles scowls.

She's not the only one who's noticed he's different lately. He looks happier, too. He smiles more easily now. He's more talkative, too, especially in mixed company. Whatever is going on with him—whether it's the graduate school interviews all having been completed, his football career finally being finished, or even getting together with me—it seems to suit him.

"I'm going to wash my hands," I announce to the table at large. I need a minute to regroup. It's all a little much right now.

He looks up, a furrow between his brows, and I kiss his stubbly cheek.

"I'll be right back."

Wes nods, returning his attention to his book.

Taking care of business, I rinse my hands and fix my hair. Sam's unconditional support only serves to highlight how lukewarm my brother has been about this. He's taken to ignoring me most of the time, and pretending nothing is going on the rest of the time.

In the bathroom mirror, I can see someone else come up behind me, tall and broad and tanned. Moving aside, she takes the sink beside mine and recognition dawns. The girl from the pool.

"Basketball girl," she says.

"Hey. Dalia, right?"

"Close. Deisy," the swimmer says.

"Mackenzie. Nice to see you again."

"You, too." She grins. "Haven't seen you at the pool lately."

I laugh. "I've been trying to make it back. I miss swimming. My schedule has been insane lately."

"Tell me about it." She dries her hands. "Our season is over next week. I already miss it."

"I've got another month and a half of basketball. And then I'm done!" We both laugh.

The end is in sight. The intense demand on my time, the physical wear and tear on my body… I'm looking forward to a week of doing nothing except go to class, study, and wrap myself in Wes's arms. Maybe a light workout here and there, some tennis or a swim or a yoga class. Not the insane ten hours a week of gym time and another ten to fifteen on the court.

"My boyfriend and I are planning on going to your game on Wednesday," Deisy says. "We haven't had a date night in ages. It'll be nice to take in a sporting event."

"We might not be as popular as men's basketball, but I promise we're just as fun to watch."

"I'll hold you to that," she grins.

Together we make our way out of the bathroom and into the dining hall proper. She waves at a table full of women, most of them tall and broad shouldered. Probably her fellow swimmers.

"It was great running into you," she says. "We should do it again sometime. Not in a locker room or a bathroom. Somewhere we're both fully dressed."

"I'm going to a hot yoga class this afternoon, if you want to join."

I'm not sure why I offer. I've met this woman twice. She plays a different sport. We have almost nothing in common—we haven't even had a deep enough conversation to know what we do and don't have in common yet.

At the same time, I feel some sort of kinship with her. Maybe it's that we're both tall—she's got to be close to 5'10", and I'm a hair under 6'—and student athletes, both swimmers (or former swimmer, in my case) trying to balance the insane demands of school and sports and everything else.

Deisy grins. "Sure. Sounds like fun. Here at the ASC?"

"Studio three. Four o'clock."

"I'll be there."

Wes looks up as I approach the table. He sighs in what looks like relief and visibly grows more confident.

"Everything okay?"

I nod. "I think I might have just made a friend?"

He beams with pride. "Congrats, babe. That's amazing!"

Down the table, Miles gags. I flip off my brother and settle into my seat across from Wes, who laughs.

I take an apple from the slices he's prepared for us and drag it through the pile of peanut butter. "Thank you for making this."

"Any time." His eyes linger on mine before flicking down to his book and back to me. "You sure you don't want to come to pilates with everyone today?"

"I'm going to try to get some work done before hot yoga," I explain. "I don't think I'm up for both today."

He nods, accepting this.

As much as I want to spend time with him, it's important that we have some time apart to focus on our own interests. Every Sunday, he and the guys do a pilates class. It's a nice, low impact workout that gets their heart rate going and gives them a chance to spend time together without TV and phones and away from the football field. I need a hot yoga class to stretch and relax my muscles after yesterday's game. I can't be everywhere at once, and I can't ask him to give up something that's important to him. I already cut into his weeknight Jeopardy! and Wheel of Fortune watching with his roommates, and he's skipped three of their Sunday night movie marathons. Of his own volition, of course. I would never ask him to. He needs time with his friends.

We still have a little bit of time before the guys leave for pilates, so we have a leisurely lunch and read our books while the rest of the table chats. Occasionally I jump into the conversation. More often than not, I let it go on around me, surrounding me in the camaraderie without forcing me to participate more than I want. Most of the time, the guys are good about respecting my boundaries, my brother excluded.

Sam catches my eye and grins. She's happy for me, even if he isn't. She'll work on him. I can't press a button and magically undo the last week. I can't pretend we weren't sneaking around behind his back. The fact that we had to in the first place irritates me. The fact that he still is acting like a baby about something that has nothing to do with him makes me want to shake him.

———

I recognize about a dozen of the student athletes taking this hot yoga class, mainly from seeing them around campus. There are two gymnasts—I think Greg might have gone out with the one on the left last semester. There are a cluster of three volleyball players, long and lean, and two more women I recognize as Sam's freshman softball teammates. There are four baseball players in the corner, so identified by the Newton Baseball shirt they're wearing, and an *extremely* well-built guy wearing nothing but a tight pair of shorts and socks.

I can look, but I have no interest in touching. Most of my life is spent with athletes. I know six (or eight) pack abs have nothing to do with how strong someone is, how good of a runner they are, or how effective they are at their game. Different sports require different builds. Having visible abs just means the person has a low body fat percentage; it has nothing to do with who they are as a person.

Pia, Jacki, and Miri, three of the juniors on the basketball team, walk in together, wearing skintight leggings and sports bras showing off their perfect abs and toned torsos. They wave at me, and I smile back. On their heels is Deisy, who grins when she sees me, and I breathe a sigh of relief.

"Hey, girl," she says, dropping her yoga mat beside me. "Thanks for suggesting this."

"Yeah, of course."

"I had a meet yesterday and my shoulders are, like, so sore," she says, sinking down and stretching out.

Managing fatigue and injuries is one of the hardest parts of all of this. I want to play my best, and that means resting tired muscles, getting regular physical therapy, and taking care of myself. At the same time, I'm fighting for playing time, so I have to fight that instinctive competitive itch inside of me to push through a twinge in my hamstring or an ache in my labrum. If I injure myself, if I burn myself out, I'm only putting myself at more risk.

It doesn't feel good to sit on the sidelines while the other girls play without me. It doesn't feel good to not play my best. It sits heavy on my chest like an unbearable weight, knowing I am capable of performing better than I have been. It's a new team, a new system, a new coach.

They're excuses. I can do better, and I haven't been playing to the standard I know I am capable of. I can do better. And so I will.

The instructor begins class, and I lose myself in the stretches he sets for us. The heated room adds an element of intensity I need right now.

It's kind of nice having someone at my side while we torture ourselves together. Sure, my teammates are on the other side of the room, but it's not the same. Deisy and I can't talk—not in the middle of class—but we're both struggling through the different poses. Some are decent. Others make my limbs shake and my muscles ache as they stretch. I need to work more on my hamstrings, they're so tight I'm afraid they're going to snap.

I don't know how to make friends. I don't want to push her too much.

I'm a little less lonely now that Wes and I are together. I'm dating my best friend. At the same time, I'm all too aware of the fact that he's most likely leaving in a few short months. I don't want to be alone again. I have to put the work in now, build the friendships I want to have, if I want to have a support network next year.

That makes it sound like I'm using any potential new friends. I'm not trying to. I want people that I can relate to, people that have the same interests as me and like the same hobbies. I don't expect to find too many other student athletes who are also bookworms. Maybe I should hang out more in the library. Although… I don't think I'd take too kindly to someone interrupting my reading time, and I doubt any potential new friends would, either.

Why is this so hard???

I miss kindergarten. All you had to do was play with a kid for five or ten minutes and then you were friends. Everyone in your class was your friend. Everyone on sports teams were friends. It was easy.

Somewhere along the way, all of that changed. I don't know how to maintain friendships. I've never had the time—I was always too busy. Sure, I got along with my teammates, but I wasn't invited to the sleepovers. I was only begrudgingly invited to the birthday parties that the whole team was invited to. Nobody ever suggested getting coffee or going to a movie or hanging out. And I was too scared to initiate.

The girls on my team are fine. I like them fine. Nobody has made me feel unwelcome or unwanted, the way my roommate has. Dareesa and Lauren met and instantly clicked. It helped that they live together and were corresponding all last summer before getting to campus. I didn't have that. Pia, Jacki, Miri, and Rebekah have been nice enough, inviting the three of us freshmen to parties at their house in Athlete's Village and to team sleepovers.

Still, it has the underlying sense of mandatory fun; it's not like I can say no. I don't want to say no. I want to be one of the group. I want friends, people who want to be friends with me because we actually like each other and not just because we play the same sport or live in the same dorm or take the same classes.

Although... isn't that how friends are made? Degrees of commonality, shared interests and circumstances.

Wes and I fell into a friendship naturally. We both like to read, and we don't mind reading in one another's presence. Neither of us wanted to go out to a party on a Saturday night; we were happy enough to sit in the same room and not talk for a few hours as we read our own books. It was easy and painless. Neither of us put any particular effort into it. It just... happened.

Sam, Mason, Diana, and Jill invite me to things, group activities. But that's because I'm Miles's little sister, and now Wes's girlfriend, and we're bonded together by the five guys who live in the same house and not by any particular affinity they have for me personally.

Sam is fine; as my brother's girlfriend, I've gotten to know her over the last two years, and I like her. I like them together even more. Mason and I got off to a rocky start—she thought I was dating Tucker for a millisecond before they got back together, so it started out a little chilly. Diana has always been welcoming. She was new last semester, too, a fifth year transfer, so we navigated the new environment together. She had Barrett to lean on, though. Jill and Amir haven't been dating very long, so I don't know her very well yet, but the little I've seen from her so far I like. She certainly seems devoted to him.

The girls don't like me as a person. They're nice to me because I'm dating someone in the house and because I'm Miles's sister. I'm invited to group activities because they don't want to slight me; nobody ever invites me to hang out one on one or grab coffee, to study at the library or go for a walk. I know Mason and Diana are friends outside of their boyfriends; they get lunch at least once a week and take pilates class together. Sam and Jill are both in sororities, albeit different ones. It's not the same as having friends of my own.

But maybe with Deisy, I can start something new, something that is entirely independent of the guy I'm dating. Maybe I can finally learn how to make friends of my own.

forty-one

. . .

Wes

IT'S like there are four chapters in my life: before my world ended, before Mackenzie waltzed into my life, hiding our relationship, and now being out in the open about it. Now that we've turned the page, I find myself enjoying this new chapter quite a bit.

Every morning for the last week, I wake up with her in my bed. We walk to the dining hall hand in hand and eat breakfast and read our books. Most days, I walk her to her first class of the day—except for Wednesday, when my schedule has me on the opposite side of campus at the same time as her class starts, so I meet her after class instead. We eat lunch together as often as we can. She goes to practice, I go to the gym, we meet in the library or a study room and put our heads down for a while. Dinner.

And then we go back to my house, and instead of sitting in my chair and reading, we make out in my bed. Okay, and sometimes we read in my bed, too. Naked reading, where we reenact some of our favorite foreplay scenes from some of the romance and erotica books we've read over the last few months. We fall asleep wrapped up in each other, and then we do it all again.

Miles isn't happy, that's to be sure. He's also not saying anything out loud where either of us can hear it. I give him as wide a berth as I can, and he spends a lot of time this week at Sam's place. We need a little distance. He's my friend, I like hanging out with him, but if I had to pick between him and Mackenzie, the choice is her every single time. There's no question about it.

I'm in love with her.

The more we play—naked—the more comfortable I get with her. I still can't shake this nagging feeling that as soon as we cross the finish line, she's going to up and leave. Logically, I know she has no intention of dumping me. Realistically, I know she's not ready yet, either.

But logic and reason don't listen to feelings, and I can't escape this feeling of dread in the pit of my stomach.

I can't talk to any of the guys about this. Miles is out of the question. Amir would give me too much shit. Barrett and Tucker have gone through difficulties in their relationships, yeah, but nothing like this. And Greg is more content to be single than to see the same girl two nights in a row, so I can't really rely on his viewpoint on this.

There's no way I can talk to Sarah about this. Just... no. My sister and I discuss a lot of things. She reveals a whole lot more about her sex life than I'm comfortable with. That doesn't mean I'm about to do the same to her.

I've always been a private person. I keep my cards close to my chest. Even in the "before" times, it was hard for me to open up to people, especially those I didn't know well. It was nearly impossible to make new friends. Sure, I hung out with the guys I grew up with, guys on the teams I played on, but I've never had a real best friend, like the kinds of friendships modeled in the books I read.

Until Mackenzie. She gets me in a way nobody else ever has, not even Sarah or my parents. She understands the way my brain works. She understands the way I need books in my life like other people need oxygen, and that just because I have my head in a book doesn't mean I'm ignoring the world around me—but, yes, sometimes I am.

She knows when to push me and when to leave me be. She knows that sometimes I need space, even from her, and it doesn't mean my feelings for her have waned. Because they haven't—not in the slightest.

Sometimes the commotion and trivialities of everyday life get too overwhelming. I can't think, can't breathe, can't process. So I retreat into a book, and all is right in the world.

forty-two

. . .

Mackenzie

SAM AND I ARRANGE EVERYTHING. My brother puts absolutely no effort into this double date. When it's time for us to meet, he comes down the stairs in a hoodie with a sullen expression on his unshaven face. It's clear he doesn't want to do this.

Wes, in contrast, is wearing a nice collared shirt and dark jeans. His sandy blond hair is styled with slightly more effort than usual. He's freshly shaved and smells amazing.

My brother's girlfriend looks peeved. Frankly, I am, too. I get that he isn't a fan of my dating Wes. Fine. Whatever. But nothing he says or does is going to make me suddenly decide to end this relationship. The time has passed for him to get on board with this. They don't need to be best friends again. They just need to coexist relatively peacefully.

It's been almost two weeks since our secret was revealed to the world. I'm not sure why my brother can't get with the program. Him being a dick isn't going to make me suddenly change my mind and stop dating his roommate.

Wes grins when I walk in the door and closes his book. He heaves himself to his feet and crosses the room to greet me, kissing my cheek.

"Hey, baby. You look great."

My brother scowls.

"Thanks. You clean up pretty nice yourself." I let my fingers trail down the column of buttons in the center of his shirt. He stops my hand when I get to the middle of his sternum, taking it in his and kissing my knuckles.

Miles clears his throat. "You ready?"

I chance a glance at Sam, who looks more resigned than excited. She was decidedly more enthusiastic when we met for coffee this morning to go over the plan.

He reaches for her, and she stands just outside of his grasp. She tugs on the zipper of her coat.

"Yeah, let's go," Sam says.

Miles frowns, but he doesn't call her out on her uncharacteristic evasiveness.

The walk to the pub is silent. Nobody is in the mood to talk. Wes takes my hand in his, and we walk slightly behind my brother and Sam, who has her hands in her pockets, her head down.

The awkwardness continues as we make our way to the restaurant and find a table for four in the slightly less loud back room. Wes pulls out a chair for me and then hands me a menu. We've been coming here after every home football game for five years, so I've pretty much memorized the menu.

Sam looks around the table. "I can't believe I missed all of the commotion of the weekend."

Wes smiles at me. He takes my hand and brushes a kiss across my knuckles. "Yeah, I guess it was kind of exciting."

"So you're officially together?"

"Official and everything," I confirm. "We didn't want to hide it, but circumstances being what they are, it felt necessary." Avoiding my brother's frustrated gaze, I take a sip from my water glass. "It feels so much more freeing to have everything out in the open."

"Good," Sam says loudly. "There was no reason to hide in the first place."

Miles coughs.

We're interrupted by the waiter, who comes over to take our order, and leaves us in an awkward silence.

My brother used to be one of my best friends. From day one, I've known he's kept an eye out to protect me. Part of it is that he's my older brother. I'm sure he still sees me as the weak little baby missing half my front teeth. But I'm grown now. I'm not that same little six year old kid with knobby knees who got called giraffe by the mean girls on the playground. I'm nineteen. I don't need my big brother to protect me from a guy who loves me and treats me right. I need him to respect my decision to be in a committed, loving relationship with someone who cares about me.

Sam and I carry the conversation, talking about her job applications—not a good response so far—and her plans for the mythical creature of "free time" once her softball season is over. Wes contributes minimally, which isn't abnormal. To be honest, I'm a little surprised he hasn't pulled out a book. He's making an effort to be sociable.

My asshole brother scoffs or rolls his eyes every time Wes opens his mouth. It was easy enough to ignore at the beginning of the evening. As we receive our dinners and start to eat, it only gets more pronounced.

"Do we want to get dessert?" Wes asks as the plates are cleared away.

Miles snorts in derision.

"You need to get over this," I tell my brother hotly. "We're together. We're happy. Why can't you just be happy for us?"

"You're my little sister. You're not supposed to—"

I roll my eyes. "You don't care when Ashley dates."

"Ashley dates girls."

"What's that supposed to mean?"

"She's been dating for a while. She knows what to do."

I blink. "Um, what?"

"You've never dated before," Miles says calmly. "He's leaving. I don't want you to get attached."

Slowly, I let out a breath. "So your whole opposition to this, to me having a boyfriend who loves me and wants to make me happy, is that you're worried he's going to hypothetically break my heart when he graduates in a few months?"

"It's not that hypothetical," he mutters.

"You don't think maybe we could make it work?" I ask. Wes reaches for my hand, and I squeeze it, grateful for his silent display of support.

"No," Miles says bluntly. "He's going to move on and leave you here, alone, to deal with the consequences."

I want to shake him. "You don't get to have an opinion on this."

My brother raises his eyebrows. "Excuse me?"

"I'm happy. I'm so freaking happy, and you're being an asshole about this," I snap. "Why can't you just be happy for me? If I cared about your opinion, I would have asked for your input."

Miles frowns. "I worry about you. You haven't dated a lot and—"

"And neither did you. And then you found Sam, and you don't see any of us complaining. We like her," I remind him. "She's really cool and way out of your league. We didn't say shit to you when you first got together."

He scoffs. "That's different."

"How? Because I fell for my best friend?" I demand. "Because I found someone that's perfect for me without having to date a million people first? We're happy. Why can't you just be happy for me?"

"Mack—"

"You're being a dick," Sam snaps.

Miles blinks back the hurt on his face.

"This is your sister. This is your friend," she reminds him. "You live together. You played together for five years. He's in love with your sister. And this is how you react? This is how you treat them? You're making me reconsider the last two years. I don't know if I want to be with someone who acts like this with the people they love, the people that are supposed to be important to them."

His face falls, crestfallen. "Baby…" He reaches for her.

She flinches and pulls away. "No. I can't do this right now."

"Sam."

She scoots her chair back from the table. "I think I need a little space."

She reaches for her wallet. A discreet shake of Wes's head. He'll take care of the bill.

"Have a good night," she says firmly. Miles moves to stand up, and she shakes her head. "I'm going home. Alone. Don't follow me." She stomps away.

My brother throws his napkin on his plate and shoves back his chair. "Now look at what you've done."

"Oh, no. This wasn't me. This was all you," I tell him. "Go ahead, chase after her. Directly ignore what she just told you not to do."

He lets out a sigh. Sinking back in his chair, he scrubs a hand over her face and groans. "Fuck."

Yeah, I'll say.

Miles looks to me, pain in his eyes. "What do I do?"

"You get on board," Wes says firmly.

Miles's nostrils flare.

"I love her. I'm in love with her. I treat her well. I don't care that she's your sister. She's my best friend."

"And when you leave in three months?" he demands. "What happens then?"

"We'll figure that out, the two of us," Wes says. "We're a long way away from that."

"You're going to go off to some other school and she—"

"I might not."

"What?" I turn to him in surprise. "But… grad school…"

"Is not the be all, end all," he says. He squeezes my hand. "I'm applying to externships in the city. My future is still open. I'm not deciding anything now."

"But—"

"It's always been my backup plan," he explains. "Originally, I was going to move to Seattle, but I'd rather stay here with you and my support network than go to where my sister is."

I frown.

"She graduates next year, anyway, so I would have to pick up and move in a year and a half regardless."

Miles forces out a hollow laugh. "I literally don't think I have ever heard you say this many words. Like, ever."

"Because you don't listen," I snap.

He frowns.

"I've never had any difficulty understanding him. He communicates perfectly well."

Wes punctuates this with a grunt, which makes me laugh. He's a far cry from the shy, insecure guy grunting and hiding from behind a caveman mask for so long. He is perfectly capable of making his point known.

"No matter how much you fight this, we're still going to be together," I tell my brother. "He's exactly the type of guy you should want me to be dating. Wes is honest and trustworthy. He's not going to take advantage of me. Would you rather I go out with someone like Sully?"

The safety is known around campus as the team's bicycle. Everyone has hooked up with him, or wanted to. I never have. There's no appeal there.

Wes growls and squeezes my hand. Miles turns white.

"N-no. Not Sullivan," he says quickly.

"Wes and I work because we started as friends. We have a solid foundation. We care about each other."

My brother sighs. "I know. I *know*. But—"

"I'm not a child. It's not your responsibility to protect me, not when it comes to this. I'm perfectly capable of handling my love life on my own."

He makes a face. "Gross, Mack."

"What? We're not having sex. It's not like we don't know you and Sam sleep together all the time," I remind him. "You're in a relationship. It's not out of the ordinary for you two to, you know…"

Miles looks to Wes. "And you're really not…?"

"I'm not ready," Wes says honestly. "Neither is she. Even if she wanted to, I don't know that I'm ready for that, either."

"But you've done it before," Miles checks.

Wes takes a deep breath and straightens his shoulders. "The last time I had sex was before my parents died. I lost all interest after that."

He never talks about his parents, not ever. I squeeze his hand. He lifts mine to his lips and brushes a kiss across my knuckles.

Miles sighs heavily. "Yeah. I can see how that would complicate things."

"So yeah, I want to wait, and she wants to wait, so it's an easy decision for us," he finishes. "When we sleep together, we really are only sleeping."

And maybe kissing and touching a little. I don't know why I'm okay with his fingers inside me and not his cock, but that's crossing an arbitrary line in my head that I'm not ready to broach.

"I'm not asking for your permission. I don't need it," I tell him. "What I'm asking for is your respect. I'm nineteen. I'm old enough to decide for myself when I'm ready to date and when I'm ready for things to turn physical. None of that is your business. I'm sorry we went behind your back, I am, but we shouldn't have had to in the first place."

"Yeah. Yeah, I know. I—" He blows out a breath. "I am sorry, Mack. I didn't intend to force you to hide what you were doing. I just wanted what's best for you."

"And I'm entitled to decide that. Not you, not Dad, not anyone. Me."

"I get that," he says, meeting my eyes. "I really do." He sighs. "I'll work on it. I will."

I want to believe him, but I'm not sure I do. Talk is easy. Actions require effort.

forty-three

. . .

Wes

MR. CAVANAUGH DOES NOT LOOK happy to see me. At all.

"So you're the asshole dating my baby girl," he says.

Ashley, the youngest of the three siblings, rolls her eyes. She's seventeen and precocious as fuck—she's been dating for at least the last four years I've known her, if not longer. She rarely goes more than a few weeks without a new girlfriend. Somehow, I doubt Mr. Cavanaugh has displayed this much emotion over any of the girls she's dated in the past.

"Steve, be nice," Nancy says, laying her hand on her husband's arm. As much as Steve likes to pretend he's a big tough macho guy, we all know she's the one that runs the show. "We like him, remember?"

Steve grunts. I lift my chin under his inspection, my spine straight and tall. I've stared down three hundred plus pound men intent on getting past me. He doesn't scare me. He's a former running back, shorter than me and at least a hundred pounds lighter. He's only my girlfriend's father.

He scoffs and looks away.

"Well, Wes, we're pleased as punch you and Mack have decided to be together," Nancy says.

Miles clears his throat. We all turn to him. His cheeks are tinted pink, his attention firmly on the court below us.

In the twenty-four hours since that disastrous double date last night, he hasn't done anything to show he supports us. On the other hand, he hasn't done anything to stand in our way, either. Maybe it will take more time. His displeasure at our being together is really starting to frustrate me. Still, I abided by Mackenzie's wish not to say anything to him. I stayed out of it.

And then she exploded. Fuck, was that fun to watch.

Miles doesn't complain when I settle into the seat beside him. I don't even pull out my book, no matter how much I want to. I will be... sociable. It won't kill me to make small talk for three and a half hours.

I hope.

The Cavanaughs talk amongst themselves. I'm sitting on the end, so it's a little hard to hear and partake in the conversation, even if they were addressing me. Which they're not. They aren't excluding me. But they aren't particularly going out of their way to include me, either. Nancy and Ashley talk about their plans for the week and the big cheer competition day after tomorrow. Miles and Steven chat about the math midterm he took this morning.

I really want my book.

My hands are jittery, and not just from being in a crowded arena with people who aren't particularly welcoming.

These are Mackenzie's parents. Her family is important to her. She cares deeply for them. She would want us to get along.

She's sitting on the sidelines, still wearing her warmups. She doesn't look happy. The team is up by about eight points. That's not enough of a margin for the coaches to play her. She's a freshman; she has to earn her playing time in practice, and by her own admission, she's not good enough. Not yet.

I think she's a little hard on herself. She's a great basketball player, and she works her ass off. She is a phenomenal asset that the team is neglecting in favor of the other more veteran players. I wish it were different for her.

Coming into college, I knew my first year I would have to red shirt and my second year was when the fun would begin. I started out getting sheltered minutes, until I broke two vertebrae in my back and needed to take a season to recover. By the middle of the season after that, I was a bonafide starter. A combination of size, dedication, and injuries to other players elevated me higher in the roster. It was luck—for me, not for the other guys.

She has to keep busting ass in practice and show the team how much she wants this. It will happen eventually. Whether eventually is as soon as she wants it to be is a different story. Mackenzie is used to being the best player on her team, the one who gets the most minutes and scores the most baskets. To go from being top dog to a small tadpole in the pond is a difficult transition. It's a mental battle almost as much as it is physical.

I'm distracted by the bombshell on my phone. It's about to detonate my entire life. Now is not the time to bring it up. Now is not the time to destroy everything I've worked so hard for in the last few years.

This is not how I want to spend the rest of my life. I want to stay here in the city that's come to mean so much to me the last few years. This is my home now, as much as Michigan is.

The final quarter of the game, Mackenzie gets a solid nineteen minutes of playing time. She scores three baskets within five minutes, and two more assists. When the final buzzer sounds, she's grinning from ear to ear.

After the game is over, we loiter in the lobby while the ladies get cleaned up. Ash and Miles are ribbing each other, their barbs on the prickly side of taunting, and their parents watch fondly and referee when needed.

At long last, she emerges from the locker room with a

cluster of her teammates. She's fresh-faced, her cheeks pink and her lips a shimmery petal pink, her long dark blonde hair pulled back in a sweaty ponytail.

"Mack! Honey!" Nancy waves at her daughter.

She breaks off in the middle of her conversation with Pia and grins. She waves, says something to her teammate, and jogs over to us. After every game, she gives her dad a hug. That's part of the routine.

Today she doesn't, though. She throws her arms around my neck, and I only just manage to get my arms around her in time.

"Hey, baby," I say quietly in her ear, and she smiles into my neck.

"You made it!"

"I promised I would." It was uncomfortable as fuck, but I made it through. I clear my throat and raise my voice so they can hear us. "You played great."

"Thanks." She smiles up at me, unexpectedly shy.

I kiss her forehead and release her. It's time to face the music.

Steve looks... sad.

"Come here, baby girl," he says, opening his arms to her. He wraps her in a hug. "Great game."

"Thanks, Daddy."

It's Nancy's turn next. Ashley gives her a high five. Miles claps a hand on her shoulder.

Mackenzie drops back and searches blindly for my hand. I take her hand and squeeze.

"Dinner?" she suggests.

Nancy looks at our entwined hands with a strange expression on her face. "Sure, honey."

There's barely enough room in their SUV for all of us. Even with the third row bench, when one of us is six feet tall and two more are close to six inches taller than that, it gets cramped.

We go to the Grotto, a decently nice family owned Italian restaurant just off of the main drag in town. It's the kind of place people bring their parents to because it's outside of a regular student's everyday budget. From Mackenzie, I know it's where they go after each one of her games. With Miles, they used to go to the pub after football games, but she wanted to start her own variation of the tradition.

They already have a table waiting for us. The server seems surprised they have a plus one with them this time, nearly as surprised as they were when the whole gang joined in for dinner a few weeks ago.

Mackenzie sets her coat on the back of a chair, and I step closer, pulling the chair out for her. She smiles up at me, and I quirk a smile of my own back at her, getting momentarily lost in her eyes. She's so pretty. She's fresh-faced and red-cheeked, her sweaty hair pulled back into a ponytail, and wearing a team hoodie and jeans. Not a special outfit. She looks absolutely gorgeous.

My heart skips a beat, and my stomach twists. I care for this woman so fucking much. We have one more week of classes before spring break. What am I going to do without her for a week? I don't want to think about it. It will be the longest stretch of time that we've been apart so far. I'm not looking forward to it.

Our time together is limited. The clock is ticking. One day soon, I'm going to have to go away for grad school. I can't expect her to wait for me forever. I would never ask that of her.

Michigan accepted me into their physical therapy program. I should be elated. I should be over the moon. Instead, I feel… numb. I don't want to go back to the state of Michigan, not really, even though I know the program at the University of Michigan is one of the best in the country. I even qualify for financial aid, so I would have to take out that much less in student loans. I can get an internship to help pay for living expenses.

The acceptance email came in only a few minutes before the game started. It didn't feel appropriate to tell her before. It doesn't feel right to tell her now. Carrying this secret is like a weight on my back, impossibly heavy. It's a burden I don't want to share. I don't want to impose.

I've applied to other programs. Michigan isn't my top choice. But I'm in. That's at least half the battle. I have a guaranteed acceptance. Someone wants me. I have worth outside of football.

The Cavanaughs make small talk. Ashley and Miles carry the conversation, which isn't atypical. Mackenzie is quiet. I set my hand on her knee, and she smiles at me, but it doesn't reach her eyes. Exhaustion lines her face. There will be no playing tonight. I'm going to take her home and tuck her into bed. She looks like she needs a good night's sleep. Maybe a week's sleep.

The conversation moves to spring break. Sam has an away game on the first weekend and a tournament on the second weekend, so she's out of town. From the little I've been able to glean, she and Miles have made up, but things are still a little tense between them.

"What are you doing for spring break?" Nancy asks, her question directed at me.

I swallow. My stomach lurches with a deep sense of foreboding. "Not much. Hanging around here."

Steve grunts, a warning sound. Nancy waves his concern away.

"You should come stay with us," Miles says. "We can hang out."

The accusation that we haven't been lately hangs in the air between us. I've been neglecting my friends in favor of my girlfriend. Not cool. Totally a violation of the bro code—an even bigger offense than dating my roommate's sister.

Nancy nods, a bright smile on her face. "It will be great to have you. You're part of the family now, after all."

My chest gets tight. My throat closes. "I—that would—"

Mackenzie squeezes my hand. "Only if you want to. If you need alone time, we understand."

"Do you not want me to…?"

"I do. No, I do," she assures me quickly. "I want you to come home with us. With me."

My heart hammers a thousand beats a minute. "I got into Michigan."

Her face falls. "You did?"

"Wes, that's amazing!" Nancy says in the background.

My eyes are focused on Mackenzie's. "I haven't accepted yet. I'm still waiting to hear back from some other schools."

Including Newton. I haven't hidden the fact that staying here would be my top choice. It's only slightly because of her. I truly want to stay in this program. I'm comfortable here. I know the school, the community, the town. I like it here.

Michigan is where I came from. I didn't want to have to go back there. I don't want to go backwards: I want to move forward.

Mackenzie swallows, her eyes sad. "So you're coming home with us for spring break. You're not staying on campus for a week by yourself."

I squeeze her hand and she quirks a small smile. I turn to Nancy. "Yes, thank you, I would love to stay for spring break."

forty-four

. . .

Wes

MR. CAVANAUGH PICKS us up from campus in his enormous SUV. He claps Miles on the shoulder and tugs Mackenzie into a hug before he stops when he gets to me. I offer my hand for a shake, which seems to impress him, because he gives me a little head nod.

Spring break has started with a freak snowstorm, because especially in East Boston, the weather hasn't gotten the spring and sunshine memo yet. I've been to the Cavanaughs' house a few times—Miles invited me home for Thanksgiving one year, and I've been invited for summer BBQs and Super Bowl parties and various festivities over the past five years. Usually, I sleep on the couch or in a sleeping bag on the floor for the night with a bunch of the guys.

I've never stayed for a full week. I've never stayed while dating their daughter. Just because Miles is begrudgingly okay with us sharing a bed doesn't mean her parents will be.

Miles sits in the front of the SUV, leaving Mackenzie and I in the backseat. She sets her hand on my knee and lays her head on my shoulder for the half hour drive in traffic. Her parents' house is only a handful of miles from campus, too far to walk unless we were really, really ambitious on a snowy day like this. They live so close, if she wasn't a student athlete, she wouldn't even qualify for housing in the dorms. They try to prioritize the needs of the out-of-town students, of which there is a considerable percentage in the student body population, over the people that technically could commute from home if they so choose. For a student athlete, though, the demand on our schedules is too intense to balance commuting, especially from a long distance in traffic; the housing in the dorms or Athlete's Village is part of our scholarship, and one that is very much appreciated.

Nancy and Ashley are just getting out of their minivan as we pull up to the curb. They pop the trunk and display a full load of grocery bags.

"Drop off your stuff, then bring all this in if you want to eat this week," Nancy announces.

My chest gets tight. My mom used to say that all the time.

Mackenzie sets her gloved hand on my arm. "You okay?"

Swallowing the lump in my throat, I nod and manage a weak smile. "I'm great." To her parents, I raise my voice. "Thank you for inviting me. It was very kind of you to include me in—"

Nancy rolls her eyes. "Come on, Wes. You're dating Mack. Of course you're welcome. You're practically family now."

Still, they don't have to include me; they are *choosing* to do so. My parents weren't nearly as nice to Sarah's boyfriends. Then again, she typically goes for douchebag frat guys who treat her like shit, so maybe they weren't being rude and were only trying to protect her.

The Cavanaughs know me well enough. I'm a decent person. I want to treat Mackenzie well. I want to make her happy. I'm not going to cheat on her or make her feel bad about herself. I'm committed to her.

Slinging my duffle bag over my shoulder, I grab three of the grocery bags in one hand and a gallon of milk in the other. I work out hard in the gym; I can lift a measly few bags of potatoes. Miles snorts and shakes his head before he grabs two of the bags in each hand. There's only one bag left, which Ashley hefts easily.

"I can help, too," Mackenzie protests.

I duck down and kiss her cheek. "There. Now you're helping."

Laughing, she rolls her eyes and closes the trunk before wheeling her bag into the house. Following her into the house, I take Miles's lead and deposit the bags on the kitchen table.

Nancy smiles kindly at me. "Thanks, Wes. You'll be staying in Mack's room."

"Seriously?" Mackenzie stares at her parents. I know they're welcoming me into their house, but I didn't think they were nearly that progressive.

"Yep. And you'll be sleeping on Ashley's trundle," Nancy continues.

She frowns. "Why do Sam and Miles always get to stay together in his room?"

"You're bunking with Ash," Steve says firmly.

Mackenzie shuts her mouth, clearly peeved. "Come on, I'll show you where my room is."

"Thank you for allowing me to stay," I say again.

The narrow house is three levels. The three kids' bedrooms are all on the second level, and from my previous visits, I know the master bedroom takes up the entirety of the top floor. The bottom floor contains the cramped galley kitchen and open living and dining rooms. That's where the family spends most of their time, or at least they have on the few occasions I've visited. It's a far cry from the three thousand square foot Michigan mansion my parents had in a little town in Nowhere, Suburbia.

This is so much better. This house has character. Personality. Warmth. All the things my parents house was lacking, this place has in spades.

Mackenzie's room is painted an army green color with white trim. Her bedspread is a flouncy, lacy white thing that is so unlike her, I have to do a double take. The walls aren't covered in pictures or posters; they're plastered with book-shelves, each one packed so full they're practically groaning.

"So, this is my room," she says.

"I like it."

I set my duffle bag down beside the bed—I don't want to put my dirty bag on her pretty white bedspread—and survey her shelves. I recognize many of the titles. There are some I've been meaning to read for a while. I stop in front of a title I remember and pull it from the shelf. *Of Mice and Men.* It's dog-eared and littered with post-its. Flipping through, I see passages are highlighted.

"You liked this one?" I'm surprised.

"Not really," she admits.

"You kept it anyway."

Mackenzie blushes. "It was the first book you ever recommended to me. Of course I had to keep it."

She absolutely *detested* this book. The next time I saw her, meek, quiet little Mackenzie tore me a new one over this book. She didn't hold back.

And it made me sit back and take notice. She was young then, way too young. I never would have done anything to make her uncomfortable. I just… paid attention. To her, to the way she hid away in her books, to the way she came alive when she talked about them or her sports. And then I gave her opportunities to open up. Listened patiently as she talked about anything and everything. Befriended her, really and truly.

I never thought anything would happen between us. It wasn't something I was planning. It wasn't even on my radar. From a distance I respected her and adored her. Being her friend wasn't a hardship, it wasn't second place, I wasn't settling; it was all I was capable of.

forty-five

. . .

Wes

AFTER WE HAVE a bit of time to rest and recharge, Steve and Ashley disappear into the kitchen to make dinner, Miles takes a quick power nap, and Nancy catches up with her middle daughter. I'm not sure what to do; I don't want to hide in her room, especially without her there. I stand awkwardly in the doorway to the living room until Mackenzie grabs my hand and physically leads me to the couch. Once I'm seated, she curls into my side, her head on my shoulder as she talks to her mom about the past week's drama and fun.

I content myself with listening to the pleasant sound of her voice and concentrate on the scent of her shampoo and the softness of her body pressed to mine. It's all completely appropriate. I wrap my arm around her and play with the end of her braid. She gives a happy sigh and sets her hand on my knee.

Yeah, I could get used to this.

I must doze off, because the next thing I know, Mackenzie is shaking me awake, the table is set, and dinner is ready. I should have offered to help; I'll do the dishes after to make up for it. It's the least I can do.

Steve and Ashley prepared a veritable feast. In addition to the two roasted chickens, there are three kinds of vegetables, rice and quinoa, and what smells like fresh French bread. Mackenzie points to a chair and, after helping her into hers, I slide into mine. Nancy and Steve are at either end and Miles and Ashley are across the table, groaning from the plethora of dishes spread everywhere.

I'm quiet, concentrating on my meal, as the five family members make conversation around me. Tomorrow, they have some chores to get through before they can do whatever they want. Miles wants to hit the gym before lunch; Mackenzie would prefer a workout after eating. They compromise with a middle of the afternoon workout session at the gym three blocks away. Ashley has a term paper to work on most of the day; she could use her brother's help with her math homework, too, if he has time. Nancy works from home, so her schedule is flexible, and Steve is on half days at work this week, so there will be plenty of time for family togetherness.

"So, Wes, you're awfully quiet," Steve starts, and I look to him. "Are you in love with my daughter?"

Mackenzie chokes. Deliberately I set down my knife and fork and meet his eye.

"Yes, I am."

Steve jerks his head in a semblance of a nod. "And what are your intentions with my daughter?"

"Daddy…"

I set my hand on hers. I've got this.

"I'm going to treat her well. I respect her boundaries and autonomy. I'm not trying to change her into someone she's not. I like Mackenzie for who she is. As long as she wants me, I'll be here for her."

———

After dinner, I do the dishes—I insist—and Mackenzie helps dry. It's easy standing here with her, peaceful. It's the little things that make me envision a life with her. I can see us five years from now, doing the dishes just like this in a house of our own. Maybe we have a dog. Maybe we have a little baby screaming its head off. Maybe it's just the two of us.

I never thought I was the type of guy to get married. I never wanted that. I don't know if I want to have kids. I've been more focused on getting through every day, one day at a time.

Mackenzie makes me think about the future. Mackenzie makes me want more. She makes me want to live my life, not just endure it.

I don't know what's going to happen next year. I've been accepted to two more programs and rejected from three. I'm still waiting to hear back from two: Boston University... and Newton. I would be happy with either at this point. Both of them would keep me in the greater Boston area for the next two years. BU is only seven and a half miles from Newton's main campus—not a bad commute at all. I could be at Mackenzie's side in half an hour or less, depending on congestion on the T. It's entirely doable. I just need to get accepted to either school first.

Once the dishes are dry and put away, Mackenzie wraps her arms around me from behind and buries her face in my back.

"I'm sorry my dad was such a jerk," she says to my shirt.

"He wasn't."

"He was. He had no right to question you."

Taking a step forward, I turn around so we can face each other. My finger on her chin forces her head up to meet my eyes.

"I love you, Mackenzie. Your dad is concerned. I'm three and a half years older than you. I don't mind his questions. It's his way of showing he cares," I explain. "Is it infantilizing and misogynistic? Yeah. You're old enough to make your own decisions about your love life. He doesn't get to dictate how you live your life. But he's allowed to worry about you."

She frowns. "It's insulting."

"Oh, yeah. Definitely," I agree readily. "He doesn't see us every day. He doesn't know me, not really. Hell, I live with your brother, I've known him for four and a half years, and he still had an issue with us being together. So, your dad asking a few questions that are none of his business? That's fine. It comes from a good place. He cares."

I wish I had parents that cared. Even when they were still around, my parents never gave two shits about who I was dating. It was expected that I would date. I was a highly ranked football player with the world at my fingertips. They thought something was wrong with me when I didn't go out with anyone in the six months between my first girlfriend and I breaking up and when I initially began dating my second girlfriend. They were highly critical of every guy my sister went out with, until Sarah simply stopped bringing anyone home to meet them.

Mackenzie sighs and bows her head forward, burying her face in my chest. I wrap my arms around her and indulge in the simple pleasure of holding her. I lose track of how long we stand there, wrapped up in each other. I don't want to let her go.

Someone clears their throat and I look up to see Steve in the doorway to the tiny kitchen, a sad expression on his face. Releasing her, I take a step back and meet his gaze head on.

"We're going to watch a movie," Steve announces. "Do you want to make the popcorn?"

"Sure," she says, not moving.

"Great."

The air is uncomfortable with tension so thick it can be cut with a knife. We weren't doing anything wrong or inappropriate. I wasn't taking advantage of her. We weren't fucking over the kitchen counter. We weren't even making out. All we were doing was hugging.

Still, it's a very stark reminder for her father that I'm now the most important man in her life. I'm the one she turns to when she's sad, when's hurt, when she doesn't feel good, and the first person she shares her good news and happiness with. She doesn't need her dad to hold her hand anymore.

Because I've just put away the dishes, I know where the big bowls are stored. I grab two and she takes the popcorn out of the pantry, sticking the first bag into the microwave. Ducking around me, she grabs another smaller bowl from the cabinet. She drops a kiss to my shoulder and begins emptying a sleeve of cookies into the bowl.

Her parents are cuddled together on one side of the sofa, Ashley sprawled on the chaise at the other end. Miles is in the armchair. There's a loveseat sofa just big enough for two. Mackenzie sits closer to me than I would expect, given that we're in a room with her parents. She folds her legs underneath her and tucks my arm around her shoulders, so she's curled into a ball beside me, her head pillowed on my chest. She cuddles into me and into the soft chenille blanket spread across our laps.

"Comfy?" I ask quietly, and she grins up at me.

"Always."

Fighting a smile, I kiss her forehead and turn my attention to the TV. Out of the corner of my eye, I can see Nancy watching us, a soft smile on her face. Steve is stoically focused on the previews we can't skip through.

It's a superhero movie, one I've seen at least twice in the last six months. I'm not complaining. It's not a bad movie, made even better by the gorgeous woman curled into my side. Yeah, life could be a lot worse.

forty-six

. . .

Wes

THERE'S a soft knock on the bedroom door shortly after midnight. Normally I wouldn't be up this late, but adrenaline and the unfamiliar environment have me wide awake. I've been go-go-go all day. I need a little reading time to rest and recharge.

"Come in," I call, expecting it to be either Steve or Nancy telling me to go to sleep already.

The door creaks open and Mackenzie pokes her head through. "You're still up."

"Can't sleep."

She frowns and pushes the door open. "Me, either."

We've spent the vast majority of the last few weeks sleeping with one another at almost every opportunity. It almost feels weird not to fall asleep beside her. I can see now why Tucker always complains about not sleeping well when Mason has away meets.

Mackenzie pads into the room. She's wearing a shirt she stole from my dresser, a pair of short black shorts playing peekaboo beneath the hem of my t-shirt. Her hair is pulled back in a no nonsense braid, the way it usually is when she goes to sleep. In her hands is her e-reader.

"Can I..." She swallows and looks up at me. "Can I hang out with you for a bit? Ash is asleep already and I... I just..."

Pulling back the covers, I scoot over and pat the spot beside me. She leaps onto the bed and beneath the covers, her cold toes pressed against my bare leg.

"We're not going to get in trouble?"

"My parents are being hypocritical. They let Miles and Sam stay together all the time."

"They're your parents. It's their house. They're allowed to—"

She sighs heavily and pillows her head on my chest. "I know, I know. I won't stay long. I'll go back soon."

Somehow, I doubt that will happen.

"If I fall asleep, I'll wake up early and sneak back to Ash's room."

I laugh. I've heard that from her before.

"This is my room. My bed. They can't kick me out of it."

I kiss the top of her head. "Okay." This is her fight.

Rolling over, she tosses her arm across my belly and tilts her face up, silently requesting a kiss. I oblige her, soft and chaste. She curls into my side and turns her e-reader on.

We read in silence for the better part of an hour, both of us occupied with our respective books. I toy with the end of her braid. She draws circles on my sternum with her fingertips. I know when she gets to a suspenseful part because she holds her breath, bites her lip, and flips through pages at a rapid pace. She doesn't like suspense, especially not before bed. I run my hand over her shoulder, trying to relax her tense muscles.

Without warning, Mackenzie buries her face in my neck, unable to look at her e-reader. She takes a few deep breaths before she's ready to pick it up.

"You okay, baby?" My voice is low and gravelly. I clear my throat.

"If I have nightmares, I'm blaming you."

"What did I do?" I don't know how this is my fault. Or is she just teasing?

She pouts up at me. "You're the one that recommended this book."

"I did?"

"Yeah. Your book club recommended it, and you refused to read it."

"Oh, is this the Scottish murder book? Or the Florida Keys assassin book?"

She shudders. "The Australian outback serial killer book. Why do I let you convince me to read these? I know I don't like them. I like romance. Happy, fun, sexy stories. Not... death and dismemberment."

Chuckling, I drop a kiss to the top of her head. "I'm sorry it's scaring you."

"No, you're not." She shoves me lightly. I don't move an inch.

"Yeah, I am. I don't want you to be scared. I thought you would like them."

She grumbles quietly to herself. "You're the worst."

I laugh outright. "Yeah, okay."

Mackenzie heaves a sigh. "That's it. I'm staying here. No way am I sleeping alone tonight, not after this murder spree."

She closes her e-reader and twists to place it on the bedside table. She snuggles into my side, her head on the pillow now, her arm across my belly.

"You can stay here as long as you'd like," I tell her. I can always sneak out to the couch in a few hours. Eventually. Maybe.

"You're not the worst, Wes," she says quietly, around a yawn. "You're the best."

My chest nearly bursts with pride. "I love you, too, baby."

forty-seven

. . .

Wes

WE WAKE up wrapped up in each other, like we normally do. I'm the big spoon, like usual, because even when we start out with my back to her front, we always roll over the other way. My arm is draped over her torso—above the blanket—and we're both fully clothed. I'm fully drenched with sweat, as usual.

There's a knock on the door and ice shoots through my veins. It's still not enough to kill the raging morning erection tenting my sweatpants.

"Wes?"

It's Nancy.

I clear my throat. "Yeah?"

"Have you seen Mack? I can't find her anywhere."

"She's here."

She shoots me a betrayed, baleful look. I'm not about to lie to her mother, not while I'm literally in my girlfriend's bed against her parents' wishes.

"You can come in. We're both decent," I tell Nancy, and the door creaks open.

"Mackenzie Anne Cavanaugh. Did we not tell you—"

"I'm sorry," she blurts. "We were just reading, and we fell asleep and—"

Nancy sighs, shakes her head. "You wait until I tell your father."

I struggle to a sitting position and pull the blankets around my waist. "With all due respect, nothing untoward happened. We were reading. We fell asleep. I'm not about to take advantage of your daughter, especially in your home."

She frowns. "I understand you're young, you want—"

"This has nothing to do with age. I'm in love with your daughter. She doesn't have nearly as many night terrors when I'm there. We both sleep better when we're together," I tell her. "We aren't fooling around. We read our books and fell asleep. That's all that happened."

"You let Sam bunk in with Miles on her last three visits," Mackenzie adds, sitting up as well. "Why do they get to and we can't?"

Nancy opens her mouth and then closes it again.

"I'm not asking for special treatment," she says. "All I'm asking for is equal treatment. Am I not entitled to parity?"

Nancy frowns. "You are. We're not treating you differently. It's—"

"Then why does Miles get to sleep with Sam, and suddenly it's a big deal if Wes and I sleep in the same bed?"

She has no answer for that. "Breakfast is ready," Nancy says instead.

It's a total cop out, sidestepping the issue. I'm not about to fight her on that. This is Mackenzie's battle. I'll stand by her side, I'll have her back, but I won't initiate an argument over this.

She slips from the bed and stuffs her feet into her slippers. With a sigh, Mackenzie grabs her e-reader and her glasses. As an afterthought, she leans across the bed and kisses my cheek.

"Good morning," she says, a defeated expression on her face.

"Morning. How did you sleep?" She only thrashed in the middle of the night a few times that I noticed, way less than usual.

"Better than I would have if I was by myself," she admits. She raises her eyes to meet mine. "I'm sorry I—"

"There's nothing to apologize for."

"No, I told you I would leave before we were found out. I promised. And now..." She sighs heavily. "It's too early for this."

Reaching for her hand, I squeeze it and give her a tentative smile. "It will all work out. And we'll get some coffee in your system, like, ASAP."

This coaxes an actual smile from her. "How did I get lucky enough to find you?"

I shake my head. "If anything, I'm the lucky one."

Mackenzie blushes. "You're pretty fantastic yourself."

Slipping out of bed, I peel back the blankets. Yep, they're drenched. How she likes to sleep next to a perpetually sweaty mess like me, I have no idea. My shirt and shorts are soaked through. The sheets are a sodden mess. All of the blankets are gross. I'm sure I smell delightful right now.

From my open suitcase, I grab a set of clean clothes and my towel, heading to the bathroom shared with Ashley. There's nobody inside—good. Hopping in the shower, I do my best to scrub away the funk and grit of the night. By the time I emerge, towel around my waist, Mackenzie is brushing her teeth at the sink, her glasses traded for daytime contacts.

"I don't want to go out there," she confesses.

"It'll be fine."

Her parents will probably yell some more. Her father will be disappointed in me. I don't think he'll kick me out, not after the conversation last night. If anything, it's only endeared me more to him. I care deeply about her, and she cares about me.

As I'm getting dressed, she starts taking off her pajamas.

My cock twitches in my jeans at the sight of her supple naked body, her pert breasts and puckered nipples and the curve of her ass. She's doing nothing salacious—she's getting ready to take a shower—but my body reacts to her all the same.

"Fuck."

Pulling back the shower curtain, Mackenzie grins at me, before she disappears behind the frilly pink curtain. Adjusting myself, I head back to the room and strip the bed. Maybe it's a good thing I'm not sleeping on the couch—even the mattress pad is a little sweaty.

I can't delay for much longer, no matter how much I want to. Eventually I have to emerge from the safety of her bedroom. My stomach rumbles. And food. I need food.

Miles and Ashley are sitting at the table. He grunts as I approach, his attention focused on his cereal. She smiles briefly at me and returns her focus to her phone. Steve emerges from the downstairs bathroom and startles at seeing me.

"Good morning," I venture.

"Morning," Ashley chirps.

"There's tea in the kitchen," Miles says.

Nancy is at the stove, cracking eggs into a bowl. Bacon crackles in the hot skillet.

"Help yourself," she says, more shortly than she might have if she *hadn't* caught her daughter in bed with me this morning.

"Thank you." Fixing a cup of coffee, I add a little bit of hot chocolate powder and milk to the mug. I also make a cup of English Breakfast. The tea selection is a little lacking. I'm not about to say anything.

Miles frowns when I return with two mugs. "You don't drink coffee."

"No, I don't." I set a mug down at each of the two seats before going back into the deep end. Nabbing a bowl, I indulge in some Special K—they don't have it at school—and top it with some yogurt and fruit.

By the time I'm back at the table for the second time, Mackenzie has emerged, dressed for the day and her hair loose from the overnight braid. She spies the cup of coffee I've prepared and sighs.

"Thanks," she says, squeezing my arm.

I drop a kiss to the top of her head and slide into the seat beside her. Steve gives a full body twitch.

Ashley melts. "You made her coffee?"

"Every day," Mackenzie confirms, and her sister sighs.

"That's so sweet."

My eyes are on my cereal, trying to be as inconspicuous as possible. It's not a big deal to make Mackenzie's coffee every morning. She likes it prepared a specific way, and once I learned how, it's an easy thing to do each day. And it puts a smile on her face.

I like when she smiles. I want to spend my whole life making her smile more often.

Rain falls steadily against the window. It's soothing. I'm stretched out on the armchair with a decent book. Mackenzie is curled into my side, her head pillowed on my shoulder. I'm not exactly sure when she fell asleep. I'm not complaining. I close my eyes and inhale the bright green apple and pear blossom scent of her shampoo, letting it wash over me. I feel at peace. At home.

The front door opens. Miles and Ashley step through the threshold, shaking off their rain coats. He stops short at the sight of us curled up on the armchair and lets out an aggravated sigh.

"So this is a thing."

Ashley rolls her eyes. "Shut up. They're so cute."

"You don't have to live with this."

She scoffs. "They're adorable. Leave them alone."

I stroke a hand over Mackenzie's hair. She stirs and burrows deeper into my chest, her face buried into my neck. She makes a soft sound that goes straight to my cock.

It's been a while since we've been able to fool around. It's been a busy few weeks since we were found out. Aside from a few quick make out sessions, we haven't been alone long enough for anything more… productive, and once we finally had some time to ourselves, she was on her period and wasn't in the mood. After years of only having my hand for pleasure, I've rather grown accustomed to her touch. I don't mind occasionally taking care of my physical needs. I would much rather the two of us indulge in each other than on my own. It's much more enjoyable to make sure she's having a good time.

We've had the house to ourselves the last few hours… and we spent it reading. No, really. Until she fell asleep a little bit ago, we were curled up together reading our respective books, fully clothed, not one ounce of inappropriate touching going on.

It doesn't feel right to feel her up in her parents' house. I know this is a me thing, a carryover from the patriarchy, but I'm also going to respect her parents' boundaries by not mauling their daughter in their home. Even if it is with her explicit consent. It's bad enough we're defying their wishes by sleeping together.

Nancy is running errands, and Steve is at work. Miles and Ashley went to a cousin's house a few blocks away. Mackenzie wasn't interested, so she stayed home, and I'm not going anywhere without her if I don't have to.

Mackenzie shifts on my lap, her cheek pressed to my chest. She sighs heavily. "What time is it?"

"Hey, baby." My voice is rough and gravelly. I clear my throat a few times. "How'd you sleep?"

She blinks up at me. "I fell asleep on you."

"You did." I can't hide my smile quick enough.

"Sorry."

"Nothing to apologize for."

She frowns up at me, her brain still processing after her nap. I lean down and kiss the top of her head.

"You can sleep on me anytime," I tell her seriously, and her soft smile sends my stomach on a roller coaster ride.

"I should get up," she says, sinking back into me and resting her cheek on my shoulder. "I don't want to, though."

"You don't have to."

There's a click and we both look up to find Ashley grinning at us, her phone out and aimed at us.

"Ignore me," the cheerleader says. "You were just so cute. I had to."

We don't have any pictures together. Memories are great, but there is nothing like tangible photographic proof to reminisce over. Time is all too fleeting. These could be the best days of my life, and I wouldn't even know until they were over.

"Take another one," I tell her.

Mackenzie turns to me with a frown.

"We don't have any photos together."

If I have to go away to Michigan next year, I'm going to want mementos to remind me of her. I'm going to want a touchstone to help get me through the lonely winter nights. As much as I don't want to do long distance for three years, I know that in the course of our relationship, three years could be a blip when we have forever stretching ahead of us.

We just have to get through the painful distance before we get to the good parts again.

She leans back against my chest and smiles up at the camera. Ashley takes half a dozen photos.

"Send them to me, please," I request, and she nods.

I'm going to want to remember this.

forty-eight

. . .

Mackenzie

ALL TOO SOON, spring break is over and it's back to real life. School. Homework. Practice. Games. It never ends.

But first, we have a formal dinner: the Athletic Department gathers for a formal, sit-down dinner in one of the ASC's ballrooms, a chance for the entire department to get together. All sports, all staff, everyone is required to attend. And we have to dress up in nice dresses and full suits for the guys. I heard one girl got in trouble for wearing a denim jacket with her dress a few years ago. They take the dress code very strictly around here.

Wes is wearing a sharp blue suit and looks good enough to eat. His sandy blond hair is brushed back away from his face, and I have the most irrational urge to run my hands through it and muss it up. I want to cover his winter pale skin with kisses. I want to slip my hands into his pants and stroke him to completion. I want—

I want what I can't have. Even if he was in the mood to fool around, we don't have time. The dinner starts in ten minutes, and it's at least a fifteen minute walk to the ASC, and I'm not about to run in heels. Everyone is waiting on Greg to finish primping and make his way down the stairs, the rest of the gang gathered and ready. When he finally does, wearing a full suit and his long hair slicked back into a bun, we're beyond late.

By the time we make it to the Athletic Student Center and into the ballroom, it feels like everyone else is already there. The room is thick with humidity and the stale odor of sweat —this room doubles as a basketball court most of the time.

Most of the tables are full. There's no assigned seating— good, we can sit wherever we want. Even though we've just spent a week together, I want to sit with Wes. It's going to be a busy couple of weeks until playoffs, and then when I finally have some freedom in my schedule, it's almost time for him to leave.

Michigan.

No. I can't think about that, not right now.

Pia waves me over to her table and gives me a hug. "Damn, girl, you clean up good."

"Thanks." My cheeks heat. I'm wearing a simple green and blue dress with tights and booties, enough to give me a lift but not enough to put me taller than Wes, who stands six inches taller than me. It's an outfit my sister picked out for me. I'm not a fashionista; I would much rather wear jeans or leggings and a sports bra than get dressed up any day.

"And this is the boyfriend?" Her eyes scrub over his form and our entwined hands.

"This is Wes. He's on the football team."

"Nice to meet you. I think I've seen you around before."

"This is Pia, she's a junior," I introduce.

He nods, clearing his throat. "Nice to meet you, too."

"Do you want to sit with us?" Pia asks.

"Oh, we were..." I glance over my shoulder, at the place where the group was clustered a few moments ago. Sam and Miles are sitting with her teammates, Tucker and Mason with the track people. Greg, Amir, Jill, Barrett, and Diana have found a table. There's only one open seat, not room for two. "Sure, that would be great."

The table is mostly women's basketball players—Pia, Miri, Jackie, and Ericka—plus Miri's boyfriend and Ericka's girlfriend, and two guys from the basketball team, Mark and Lucas. I've met them before, I'm pretty sure, at a joint men and women's basketball team function. Thankfully, we don't have events too often. They're pretty uncomfortable. I'm not close enough to my teammates to hang out with them without feeling like a wallflower, and I have met enough macho tough guy basketball players to last a lifetime.

Even now, Mark and Lucas are sizing Wes up like he's the competition. They're about the same height, or as far as I can tell when we're all sitting down, but he outweighs them by a good eighty pounds or more. He treats them like the insignificant gnats they are, unimportant to him. His only attention is on me. He doesn't like crowds. He copes by reading his book. He's not allowed to escape into his books, not right now.

So he gloms onto me, and it's my job to help make sure he doesn't get overwhelmed by the crush of people around us. I hold his hand and check in on him, even as I participate minimally in the conversation with my teammates, and he's silent and closed off.

Wes squeezes my hand. I turn to look at him, and he leans over, kissing my temple.

"I love you," he whispers, and my whole body lights up. "Thank you."

Pia and Jackie sigh. "Aw, you guys are so cute," Miri says.

Wes's shoulders get tense, the only outward indication of how uncomfortable he is. He clears his throat. "Thank you."

"How long have you been together?"

He smiles at me. "Not long enough."

Okay, as much as I'm not a fan of public displays of affection, that deserves a kiss right here and now. I lay one on him, and he smiles against my lips, keeping it short and chaste.

The room goes quiet as the Athletic Director stands at the front of the room and gives the world's most boring speech about teamwork and unity and physical effort. It's a remix of the speech every coach gives before every tough match, the speech parents give when the score isn't ideal. I've heard all of this before, as has every single athlete in the room.

Finally, at long last, we're released to get food a handful of tables at a time. It's the same selection as we'd get in the dining hall, just in chafing dishes instead of the cafeteria line: a chicken dish, a vegan entree, pasta, salad bar, and two vegetable dishes. Following Pia through the lines, Wes and I fill our respective plates and head back to the table.

Pia, Miri, Jackie, and Ericka keep the conversation flowing. I try to keep up. Small talk isn't really my thing, and rehashing what I did over spring break isn't all that interesting. Mostly, Wes and I hung out. We worked out, we went for a few runs, we went to a hockey game with my family. We spent a lot of time at the house reading and playing board games with my siblings. It might be boring to some, but it was exactly what we needed.

forty-nine

. . .

Mackenzie

TUESDAY THE WEATHER dawns bright and clear. It's a rare warm day in early spring, so Sam arranges for all of the girls to go to Jill's field hockey game while the guys have a mandatory workout, so she has some support in the stands. I've been included in the group chat since school started in the fall, but this is the first time I'm being treated as one of the girlfriends and not just a little sister tagging along. Sam, Mason, Diana and I are huddled together against a strong breeze, a flannel blanket strewn across our laps.

"I haven't gotten laid in two and a half weeks," Sam announces out of nowhere, and I cringe. That's my brother she's talking about. "I can't wait for this stupid sinus infection to go away. I need an orgasm that isn't self-induced."

Mason laughs. "Tell me about it. King went to visit his brother over break, and I was with Micah. We tore each other's clothes off the second we got back to town."

"Yeah, we all heard you," Diana teases. "I think the people in the next town over heard you, too."

"Oh, shut up," Mason says, shoving her gently. Diana and Sam laugh. Mason isn't known for being quiet in the bedroom. We've all heard what it sounds like when she comes. We know it's her because she chants Tucker's name like she's saying a prayer, and we doubt someone as devoted as he is to her is messing around with someone else.

I swallow. "How did you know it was time?"

"Time for what?"

"Time to… take it to the next step."

"You mean sex?" Mason raises her eyebrows.

My cheeks flame red. I nod.

"You're still a virgin, right?" Sam asks, and slowly I nod again. She winces. "Yeah. The first time in a new relationship is tough. The first time ever? That's a lot of pressure."

"And for someone like Wes…" Diana adds.

I sigh. "I don't know if I'm waiting because I want to wait, or if I'm building it all up in my head and I should just get it over with."

"That's the wrong attitude," Mason says. "You don't get it over with. It's not something painful to endure, especially if it's with someone who loves you."

"Isn't the first time supposed to hurt?"

"It can feel uncomfortable, but if you're secure in how you feel about him, the physical discomfort will fade. The mental discomfort doesn't."

"Oh. I didn't even think about mental discomfort."

"Besides, if you've used tampons, it probably won't be that bad," Sam adds. "It feels like—"

I cringe. "I don't know that I want to hear from you what it feels like. That's my brother."

She laughs, not offended. "I've had sex with other people before I met your brother. But I get it. I'll stay out of it."

"It feels like fullness, and pressure, and if he knows what he's doing it feels good," Diana says. "And if he doesn't know what he's doing, if he's fumbling around, it might not be so great. But Wes isn't a virgin. He's done this before. He knows at least the basics."

I don't know that I want to think about him having sex

with other women, either. I want us both to start with a blank slate.

"The first time, you don't really know what you're doing and you're kind of going with the flow," Mason adds. "But that second time? Shit, that feels good. Better if he makes you come before you get down to business. Tucker is good about making sure I enjoy myself, even if he doesn't."

My face is so hot, it could probably melt the sun. "Wes doesn't have to worry about that. He likes making me... you know..."

Sam sets her hand lightly on my arm. "If you can't talk about sex, you might not be ready to have it," she says gently.

"It feels like I'm betraying his confidence, talking about what we do behind closed doors," I admit. "I would never impose and ask you guys to share about what you do."

Mason shrugs. "You only have to ask. King and I fool around a lot, but we don't always have sex. I'm going to therapy to try to work out some stuff. I love him with my whole heart, but sometimes sex with him gets a little too emotionally intense for me to handle. So we rely a lot on foreplay. Everything but penetration is fair game."

Diana laughs. "Barrett and I are an open book. He doesn't want his sex life blasted out to the whole world, but he doesn't care if I talk with my friends. And you're my friend. So anything you want to know, ask."

"And I won't tell you anything about what Miles and I get up to," Sam says with a grin. "Repeatedly, sometimes twice in one night."

We all hear Amir and Jill—neither of them are exactly quiet. They seem to prefer morning sex over doing it at night. Greg is the only guy in the house who doesn't have a steady girlfriend. He never goes out with the same girl twice. He definitely has a lot of one night stands, if the girls I see sneaking out of the house at six o'clock in the morning are any indication.

I blow out a breath. "I've built it up so much in my head, you know? I've read about it in books. It's supposed to be this magical, earth-shattering thing, this impossible closeness you feel with your partner, and I don't know if I'm ready for that."

"You guys fool around, right?" Mason asks. "He's made you come?"

I swallow. "With his… with his fingers, and his mouth, and once with a toy."

Diana pats me on the shoulder. "It took me ages before I was ready to add toys to the mix. Once I did, there was no going back. Barrett especially likes to watch me use toys on myself."

I consider this for a moment, putting on a show for Wes, him stroking his cock while I slide the vibrator inside of me… My face heats.

"Yeah, you'll be fine," she says.

"And if you're not ready, there's no need to rush," Sam says rationally. "Wes isn't pressuring you."

I shake my head. "He hasn't even brought it up. I'm sure he's not ready. But I can't stop thinking about it."

"That's normal, especially when you're in a new relationship," Mason says. "King and I were together for two years before we had sex."

"You were also, like, children," Diana points out.

"We started dating when we were fourteen, almost fifteen, and we had sex for the first time a month before his seventeenth birthday," she explains. "Neither of us were ready. His moms are super sex positive, they had condoms and lube available—don't forget the lube, it's so important, especially the first few times," she adds. "They didn't care if we fooled around or had sex. They only wanted us to be safe."

"And your parents?"

"They didn't give two shits. They probably thought we'd been doing it for at least a year before we actually started," she admits. "My brother was the problem child, so he took most of their focus off of me." She laughs. "That's the good thing about having a playboy for a twin brother. They were so worried about him knocking up some random girl, they didn't think twice when I asked to go onto birth control."

"I've been on birth control for five years. I need it to regulate my cycle," I explain.

"Then if you skip the condoms, it's probably not the worst thing in the world," Mason says. "King and I still use them. There's less mess. And even with the meds, my cycle has always been irregular, so it helps us make sure there aren't any accidents."

Diana shrugs. "Barrett and I don't use them. But I have an IUD and honestly, as much as I don't want a kid at this stage in my life, I would love to have Barrett's kid. And I want my dad to see his future grandchildren. I think we might start sooner than either of our parents would like, but he'll have a guaranteed job after graduation, and I haven't decided on grad school yet. So… maybe."

Sam shakes her head. "I can't even imagine being a mother right out of school."

"A lot of women do it. They have kids even younger than we are now."

"Yeah, I guess. I'm just nowhere near ready. I can't even think about what happens after graduation," she says.

"What do you mean by that?"

"Well, do I stay here, or do I go back to Mississippi? Miles is from here, he wants to stay here. We both need to find jobs. We need to find a place to stay. Do we move in together? Do we live separately? He can always move back home. If I go back to Mississippi, I don't know that I'll be able to leave."

"Like, they'll keep you there?" I raise my eyebrows.

"I've been away from home almost four years. I miss my family, my friends. I don't know that I'll have the strength to leave again," Sam admits. "Plus, I don't have a place to stay. I don't have a job. I don't have—I don't know. It's all up in the air."

"You can totally stay with my parents."

She grimaces. "I love your parents, don't get me wrong. It's one thing to stay with them for a week or two over summer break. It's something else to move in with my boyfriend and his parents indefinitely."

I wince. "Yeah, that might not be so great."

Not that my parents wouldn't open their home to her. They would, in a heartbeat. Their quick acceptance of Wes proves that they would do it without hesitation. My parents have always adopted strays.

But it's different when that stray is a fully grown adult who should be setting out on her new post-grad life.

I don't want to think about what this spells for Sam's relationship with my brother. I like them together as a couple. He's clearly in love with her, and she obviously feels the same. Minor disagreements like his treatment over Wes aside, they're entirely devoted to one another, and have been since the very first moment when he punched out a guy harassing her—and nearly lost his football scholarship, to boot.

Since they started dating a year and a half ago, he's opened up a lot more, even to me. He is actually capable of human interaction now. He doesn't hide away in his room. He doesn't lock everything up inside. He isn't shy about sharing the things that interest him. Even with the family, he was reserved. He isn't anymore.

Sam sighs and cracks her knuckles. "I don't want to think about graduation. You and Wes. Sex. Are you ready?"

I swallow. "I don't… I'm not sure."

"What is making you hesitant?"

"I don't know why I'm waiting anymore," I admit. "At first, it was just because I was new to this whole relationship thing. I've never had a boyfriend before, and he's older. He's been with other people. He probably has expectations."

Mason opens her mouth.

"But Wes is… damn it, he's perfect." I sigh. "He's kind and considerate and loving and exactly what I always thought a partner should be. He makes me want to be better, to be the best possible version of myself. He loves me. And even ignoring his own baggage with sex, he's been perfectly agreeable about waiting."

"Except…"

"Except now I can't remember why I'm waiting. Have I read too many books? Am I pining for some happy ever after?" I look to the girls, my friends, my peers. "I don't want to have sex with any other guy. I only want to have sex with him. I don't even want to look at other guys."

"That's part of being in a relationship," Diana says gently. "If you were still interested in other people, you wouldn't be together, or you wouldn't want to be with him anymore."

"Maybe. I don't know. Maybe I'm overthinking it all."

Sam nods. "I know you don't want to hear about it, but I've had sex with plenty of other guys before I met Miles. It was—okay, some of the guys were pretty great. I had fun. But having sex with someone who loves you? And you love them? That's, like, amazing. It changes you."

I frown. I don't want to be changed. I don't want Wes to change me. I don't want to change for him. I want us to be ourselves.

"It's not always perfect," Mason adds. "Sometimes it doesn't feel good or parts don't line up right or emotions get in the way. The connection that you share, that's the important part. You have to be able to laugh when things don't go right, and if that's not what he is for you, then you need to find—"

"He is," I tell her, because of that, I'm sure. "Wes is the guy for me."

"Then it's only a matter of time before you two have sex," she finishes. "Whenever you decide you're ready, whenever he decides he's ready… there's no magic time. There's no flashing sign that tells you. It's when you feel comfortable with it, and he does too, and you're both in the mood and want to explore. Because Sam is right. Sex is fun in general. It feels good. Sex with someone who loves you? That's what all those romance novels are about. That's why we keep dating, keep searching for the right person. Because all we want is to love someone, and be loved in return."

fifty

. . .

Wes

SOMETHING IS DIFFERENT WITH MACKENZIE. Ever since we've been back from spring break, she's been more quiet and withdrawn than usual. She's trying to work something out, I'm sure of it. What I don't know is why she won't tell me about it.

Oh, that's right. I haven't asked. A part of me is terrified she's about to break up with me. I have no rational explanation for why I think it's about to happen. We haven't been fighting—we've never so much as had a minor disagreement, except over books. She's just… distant. And I'm not sure why.

Is it because I went home with her over break? Does she need some alone time? On Tuesday, she went to Jill's field hockey game and then didn't stay the night, and Wednesday she had to leave for an away game, so I didn't get to see her again until she got back to campus Saturday afternoon. She's been abnormally quiet over text, too. I miss the long, rambling messages she used to send me as recently as a week ago.

If she needs space, I'll give her space. I would much rather she just open up and *talk* to me.

And yes, I realize how the tables have turned. The guy

who was incapable of communicating in any meaningful way has now realized how integral effective communication is to a relationship.

When I meet Mackenzie at the lobby of her dorm, she gives me a soft kiss that leaves absolutely no room for a follow through.

"Can we go on a walk?" She looks down at her shoes.

My stomach drops. We were planning on heading to the library for a little date to pick out books we can read together, an activity I thought we both enjoyed. Maybe I'm wrong about that, too. Maybe I've been reading this whole situation wrong.

"Sure."

"We should talk," she says, buttoning her coat, and my blood runs cold in a way that has nothing to do with the freezing weather outside.

"O-okay. Yeah. If you think that's… yeah."

She gives me a weird look as I take her hand and lead her out of the lobby. There's a brisk wind rattling through the trees that settles deep in my bones, chilling me from the inside out.

We head to the main campus and the general direction of the library. It's fairly empty on a Saturday afternoon. I don't know how to start this conversation. She wants to talk, but she's not talking.

I thought she was happy. I thought we were happy. Before spring break—before the interrogation by her parents, before we spent a whole week together—we were in a good place. We could talk about anything. We spent time together, quality time, and we did more than make out or touch each other. We did activities. I thought we had a good thing going.

After a solid twelve minutes of silence—I've been counting—she opens her mouth. "Listen, Wes, I've been doing a lot of thinking," she says, and then stops. She sighs. "I think we should—"

"I don't want to break up," I blurt.

Mackenzie blinks. Hurt crosses her face. "I don't want to break up, either."

"So then why are you trying to break up with me?"

"I'm not. I'm trying to say I think we should have sex."

Oh.

Oh.

"I know you're not ready," she says quickly. "I'm not trying to rush you. But I've been thinking it over, and I think I'm, well, if I'm not ready right this minute, I will be very soon. So I think we should work our way towards a future in which we're able to have sex. Whatever you need to do on your end to be okay with it..."

"I've been thinking about it a lot, too," I admit. "Especially after that conversation with your father."

A brief look of annoyance. "He was out of line. I'm sorry. He was—"

I wave it away. "It got me thinking." I reach for her hand. "I can see a future with you. I know we're young, you're young, but I'm not worried about what happens after graduation. If I have to go away, we can make long distance work. Because I want to be with you long term. I see a future with you."

She swallows. "Wes..."

I take a deep breath. "So if you feel the same or even slightly similar, I'm okay with taking the next step. Sex is a big deal. I'm not going into this lightly. If you don't see a future for us, if you don't want to do this long term, maybe we should—"

"Stop. Stop!" She closes her eyes and breathes deeply. "Wes, I'm nineteen. You're my first boyfriend."

A pang of hurt ricochets through me. She doesn't feel the same.

"I know." My voice cracks. I clear my throat.

She meets my eyes. "I can't think about long term. I can't

think about marriage and babies and everything that comes with it. It's great that you're graduating and looking at grad school and internships and everything. But I'm a freshman. This time last year I was still in high school. I'm so far removed from that stage of my life, I can't even wrap my brain around it. If you have to move away for grad school, I'm okay with trying long distance, but anything more long term than that? That's too much for me to wrap my brain around, at least for now."

My heart is in my throat. "I understand."

It sucks to love someone who isn't on the same level. Even if she adores me, even if she is completely happy being with me, her being unable to verbalize how she feels about me hurts.

Mackenzie exhales slowly. "I'm not trying to worry about what happens later. I'm thinking about the immediate future, and sometime soon, I want to have sex. With you. I want you to be the first person I have sex with. It—I want to be with you. But if you're not ready, if you don't want to, I can wait until you're ready."

Am I ready? We have different ideas of how our future will turn out. She's not thinking about the same things I am. We're at completely different stages in our lives.

But I love her, and if nothing else, I can love her until I have to go away. I can love her for as long as she'll let me. She isn't going to willingly leave me until the situation requires it.

I take a deep breath and square my shoulders. "If you're ready, I'm ready."

"Really?" Her voice cracks. "You would… you want to… how long have you felt this way?"

Not long.

"I've been coming to terms with it for a while," I admit. I've been wrestling with it since our first kiss. Realistically, I know she isn't going to dump me the next day and the rest of my family isn't going to die and my life isn't going to end.

Rationally, I know my anxieties are rooted in a fear-based reaction to a terrible, once in a lifetime freak accident and aren't likely to be repeated.

But reality and reason have nothing to do with trauma.

She has to check again. "You're ready to have sex?"

"I mean, not right this minute." We're in the middle of campus. "We can… I'll make it special. Your first time should be special."

She winces. "You're not going to do, like, rose petals and candles and—"

The wariness on her face makes me laugh. "If I thought you would appreciate it, I would, but I like to think I know you better than that. If you want me to recreate a specific book scene, we can always try something, but—"

"It should be organic," she decides. "I'm going to be nervous, there's no way around that. But I want to do this with you. I want us to do this together. A little romance isn't the worst thing in the world."

Got it. Walk the line between cheesy and romantic. Seduce her and simultaneously make her forget about every romance novel she's ever read, so she doesn't compare fiction to the real thing. Treat her like a queen, because she's fucking amazing, and make her come at least twice before we get down to business, because she might not during the act itself. Somehow, make this the perfect first time.

It's a tall order, but I'm up for the challenge.

fifty-one

. . .

Mackenzie

I'M PRETTY sure I understand the mechanics of sex. The physicality of it, the back and forth. What I can't wrap my brain around is what it will feel like emotionally. I don't know how to prepare. From what I've read, I know it will be intense and maybe overwhelming. I don't know what that will mean for me.

Wes and I have fooled around at least a half dozen times. He's made me come using his fingers and his mouth and, once, with a toy. I feel a special closeness to him, in part, because of the orgasms he's given me. What will it be like when he's inside me? Will it feel different?

Will I know what I'm doing? How will I know if I'm doing it right? I don't want to be a passive starfish. As much as I want this to be a good experience for me, I want this to be good for him, too. It's been a long time since he's had sex, but more than that, it's been a long time since he's been able to open up to anyone. He's told me things he's admitted he's never told anyone before.

Since we've started dating, he's a different person. He doesn't speak solely in grunts and monosyllables now. He lets me hold his hand or wrap my arms around him. He occasionally puts his book down at meals. He's starting to engage with the world around him. I don't pretend to think it's because of me: this is all because of him. He's putting in the work to heal his shattered heart.

When his parents died, he shut down. I won't ever know the guy he used to be before his world ended. What I know is the man he is now, and I like the man I see. He's kind and considerate. He cares about his friends, and when he loves, he loves deeply. He devotes himself to the passions that interest him—books, yes, but also football, and a career in physical therapy, and his friends.

Because my life doesn't solely revolve around my boyfriend, I make time to go to the pool and indulge in some much needed alone time. It feels good to be in the water, to stretch my tired muscles.

The last few days have been brutal, and I'm not exactly sure why. Everything is hard right now. It's like since I made up my mind that I'm finally ready to have sex, the rest of my life has gone to shit. I completely bombed my geology midterm. I got the due date wrong and turned in my English paper a day late—luckily, the professor was kind enough to allow me a 24 hour extension. I missed nearly every free throw in practice yesterday. The toilets in my dorm keep overflowing, rendering only one stall out of six usable, and it is always occupied.

I swim back and forth for a while and then I float in the middle of the lane, letting the water rush by me. I come out of my trance to find someone standing at the edge of the pool, watching me. It's not creepy. When my eyes are ready to focus, I find that it's Deisy, my new swimming buddy. She sits at the edge of the next lane over and lets her feet dangle in the water.

"Hey, girl," she says. "I should have known I'd see you here."

I laugh. "Am I that predictable?"

She shrugs. "Not many people realize the pool is open to the public. You have to really like swimming to come here."

"You getting a workout in? I can race you."

It's her turn to laugh. "You can try."

"Bring it on. There and back."

She tugs on her goggles and drops fully into the pool. A quick dunk under to get her swim cap wet and then she's clutching at the wall, steadying herself. We make eye contact. She nods.

We launch into motion. I swim as hard as I can, as fast as I can. She's at least a full body length ahead of me. She flips around and is reversing course before I've even touched the wall. I'm swimming my hardest. My strokes might not be pretty, but they're quick.

Deisy beats me. Handily. Then again, she's on the swim team and does this every day, and I've been out of practice for nearly a year. I don't feel upset at having lost. If anything, I'm feeling pretty pleased I was able to keep up as well as I have.

"Good job," she says heartily.

It doesn't feel condescending. If anything, she sounds happy for me. We aren't at the same place. She's miles ahead of me, and that's okay. We're all at different places at different times.

She kicks out her legs and floats in the water for a bit.

"I don't want to work out today," she announces. "I know once I do it, I'll feel better, but I don't want to start."

"Do you not feel well now?"

She lifts a shoulder, accidentally splashing me in the process. "I feel fine. I just don't want to do it."

"You're already in the water. That's half the battle."

She nods, conceding the point. "Want to race a bit more? That always gets the competitive juices flowing."

I laugh, because I'm the same way. My ego can handle coming in second best a few times, especially to what amounts to a professional. Besides, I can use the extra reps.

She definitely isn't trying her hardest—I'm only a few strokes behind her, and I'm sweating in the water, my limbs shaking like jello. My shoulders ache from the effort exerted in nearly an hour of swimming.

Deisy pulls up on the wall and takes off her goggles. She's breathing hard, her face and chest bright red as she works to get air into her lungs.

"That's it," she says. "I quit. I'm done."

"You did a great job," I tell her. Better than I did.

"So did you," she says. I wave it away. "No, really. I think you should reconsider trying out for the swim team next year. Or at least try for the Masters."

"I'm not ready to make that kind of commitment yet." The swim league for adults sounds like a fun idea… for the future. I'll definitely join in a few years. I'm not ready yet. I have enough on my plate trying to balance basketball and school.

Chugging from my water bottle, I bury my fears and insecurities for the moment.

"I need coffee," Deisy announces. She glances at me. "You game?"

I could always use some extra caffeine in my system.

"Sure."

Together we lift ourselves up from the pool and, gathering our towels, head towards the locker room. It's totally not weird to strip off my suit and head to the showers—she's doing the same thing. We take our places in separate stalls. When I'm done, I towel off and return to my locker. I'm eighty percent dressed by the time she emerges from the showers, her towel wrapped around her body.

"My shoulders are so sore," she complains, taking a seat on the bench as she digs through her bag. "Fuck. Maybe I shouldn't have skipped physical therapy this morning."

"They give you a choice?"

Our coaching staff is militant with our physical therapy. If the athletic trainer says we need it, we go. The only concession is fitting the sessions around classes. Other than that, they own us.

When she's dressed, I realize I have no idea what happens next.

"I realize I barely know you, but something tells me we should be friends," Deisy says.

"Oh."

"If that's not something you're interested in."

"It is. I want to be friends," I assure her quickly. "I just don't know how to make friends anymore. I'm out of practice."

She laughs. "I think this is it. We hang out. We work out. We're going for coffee."

"All things I like," I add in.

"So that decides it," she says with a grin. "We're friends."

fifty-two

. . .

Wes

WE AREN'T DOING anything illicit or inappropriate. I'm sitting on Mackenzie's bed reading my book while she folds her laundry. I offered to help. She doesn't like the way I fold things, and try as I might, I can't get the intricate folds she prefers to work. So she's sorting and organizing her clothes, I'm reading, and we're both happy.

There's a click as the lock disengages and the door swings open. Claire stops short in the doorway and lets out an aggrieved sigh. "Seriously?"

We aren't doing anything wrong. We aren't even going to stay here. But now that we're here, now that I know how much our being here bothers her, I'm tempted to stay the night. As it is, Mackenzie spends four or five nights a week at my place, and if she's not in my bed, she's probably traveling for an away game. She's barely ever at her dorm for longer than it takes to change her clothes and switch out her library books. She has a drawer in my dresser and a dedicated charger for her phone and laptop on what's become her side of the bed. She hasn't moved in—neither of us are ready for that, and it would violate the terms of my housing allowance —but she's made herself at home.

And I like coming home to her. Twice now I've come back after classes to find her in my bed, wearing my t-shirt, either studying or reading. I like that she feels comfortable enough with me to relax and let her guard down. I certainly have let mine down. It makes me think about a future, a time after we're done with school and have moved on to the next stage of our lives. It makes me think about what could be.

Until she waltzed into my life, I never really thought about the future. It never occurred to me. The time after grad school was a hazy gray area. I never thought about dating or marriage or settling down. I thought I would be alone forever. I thought I was okay with that.

All those years being afraid of human contact had me craving it. All those years of being on my own made me realize I don't want to live this life by myself. I want a partner, an equal, someone who I can rely on and who lets me into their life. Someone who I can lean on when the going gets tough, and someone who lets me in when they're needing some support.

I'm twenty-two. I'm at a very different place in my life than Mackenzie is at nineteen. She's just starting out. She has her whole life ahead of her. I don't know that I can realistically expect her to wait for me. She's never had a boyfriend before. She's never had sex before. How does she know she wants to be with me? How does she know there isn't someone less damaged waiting for her?

I've dated before. Sure, it was in high school, but I've been with two other partners, enough to know that Mackenzie is it for me. She's perfect. She's funny, and smart, and sarcastic. We like the same things. We have compatible interests. Simply being around her makes my palms start sweating. The scent of her perfume has my cock as hard as a rock. And when she kisses me? My whole world goes haywire.

I don't want her to look back and regret being with me. I don't want her to resent me for holding her back from experiencing life. I want us to succeed. I want us to thrive—together. As much as I enjoy having her in my bed, I have to worry that we're moving too fast too soon. We spend most of our nights together. We barely ever spend time on our own that isn't because of her traveling for basketball.

I want her to grow and learn in college as I've had the opportunity to do the last four and a half years. I don't want to take that away from her. It's important. These next few years are crucial for her development as a person. It's terrifying to think that something I say to her or do with her now can have a lasting impact on the rest of her life as an adult. Her experience with me could color all of her adult relationships. That's a lot of pressure to put on someone who hasn't dated for five years and has avoided all human contact for nearly as long.

At the same time, when I think about my future, about five or ten years down the road... I see her. Maybe we're married. Maybe we have kids. Maybe we're thirty something and child free by choice.

I have no qualms about living in Boston long term. Maybe not in the city proper. That might be fun for a few years, but I'm from suburbia, and I want to live in suburbia long term. We would have to be close enough to Charlestown that we could visit often with her parents. I know how important her family is to her. We couldn't move too far away that we couldn't drive in for Sunday dinners or to watch a ball game.

Her family is important to me, too. Losing two thirds of mine in one night has made me all too aware how fleeting life is. Her parents have opened their home to me time and time again. They have made it clear I'm welcome there. The last thing I want to do is take her away from their unconditional love and support.

I don't know what Mackenzie wants to do for a career. I'm not sure she knows, either. Maybe something with sports. Maybe something with books. Maybe something completely different. She has the luxury of time to decide. I'm not about to push her into something just because I'm at the stage of my life where I need to find a job, like, ASAP.

Boston University is only a few miles away. It wouldn't even be considered long distance. We might not be able to spend every night together—grad school is tough enough as it is, I can't afford a distraction like having her in my apartment every night, and with the terms of her athletic scholarship's housing allowance, she's not allowed to have off-campus visitors in Athlete's Village.

We'll make it work. It's only three more years. We can get through this. In my bones, I know we can get through anything as long as we're doing this together.

———

Once upon a time, it used to be the six of us guys who did everything together. Over the last few years, that's changed, and I'm not sure how I feel about it. What used to be a group of six relatively quiet, relatively antisocial loners has turned into a raucous group of eleven friends who enjoy spending time together and are perfectly happy going their own ways. Since I started seeing Mackenzie, even our sacrosanct Sunday evenings with my roommates have become less of a priority.

I still make time for pilates class on Sunday afternoons, though. It would take a lot for me to give that up. Now I simply convince Mackenzie to come along with us, instead of ditching the guys to spend time with her.

Barrett's the one who got us into this, and he blames Diana, but it was really when Tucker and Mason first got back together that we started doing this as a group. Pilates is a good in-season workout because it challenges the core without putting high impact on the joints. It's more strenuous than a yoga class, which moves too slowly for me. It's even better in the off-season, when I'm not working out as often and challenging myself nearly as much.

And the eye candy? Not bad.

Mackenzie is stretched out on the mat beside mine, wearing a tight blue sports bra, tight black shorts, and nothing else. Her legs are spread about forty-five degrees, a pilates ring squeezed between her thighs. Her toned stomach ripples as she raises and lowers her legs and, with it, the ring. Me, I'm huffing and puffing and sweating like a pig, but the only sign she's working hard is the redness in her cheeks. She's intensely focused on what she's doing.

Most days, my workout consists of heavy lifting, with a few days on the bike tossed in for cardio. I'm used to big, heavy weights, not these dinky little baby weights. They're surprisingly heavy when doing over a hundred tricep kick-backs in a row without pause.

The class skews about thirty percent male, mostly our group of six guys and a few straggling baseball players and gymnasts. It's a difficult workout. Everyone here is a student athlete in the best shape of their life or close to it, and I can still barely get through it. I can do bicep curls with sixty-pound weights, but change them for five pounds and increase the reps from ten to a hundred and fifty and I'm seriously struggling.

Mackenzie rolls her head to the side, and we make eye contact. I give her a tired smile as I lift my legs into tabletop. She breathes out a breath of laughter and puckers her mouth into a facsimile of a kiss before she refocuses her attention on what she's doing.

She is the best thing to happen to me. It might just be timing, it might be a coincidence, but since we've been together, I walk taller. I'm more comfortable in my skin. I feel more confident in my everyday interactions with people. Communication comes easier—I don't have to rely on grunts and body language to get my point across, I feel comfortable using my voice.

After class is over, I'm drenched. All I want to do is shower off the grit and funk of an hour of intense sweating. Mackenzie has other plans. The pilates class has energized her. She's practically bouncing off the walls.

I'm energized in other ways. My blood flows a little too freely, centering in my cock as she bounces in her tight sports bra and barely there shorts, her long, lean body on display. She startles when I grab her hand and pull her into me.

"Wha—"

The kiss is rough. Inelegant. I need my lips on hers like I need air in my lungs. She sighs and melts into me, winding her arms around my neck. My hands land on her hips until we're flush together. I deepen the kiss, my tongue licking into her mouth and meeting hers.

"Ugh," a voice says behind us. "Get a room."

Without breaking the kiss, I reach up and flip off the speaker. I think it was her brother.

Her hands fist in my sweat-soaked shirt, pulling me impossibly closer, until there's a hair's breadth between us. She can most definitely feel my cock pressed into her hip.

Mackenzie pulls back ever so slightly. "You wanna?"

"Hmm?"

She meets my eyes. "Do you want to get a room?"

Sweat slicks my skin, making me all too aware of how gross I feel. "How about a shower?"

fifty-three

. . .

Mackenzie

THE MOOD IS DAMPENED ONLY SLIGHTLY by the walk back to the house. Nothing puts a damper on the mood like a mile and a half walk with a large group of people, one of them being my brother, and all with an idea of what's about to happen. Or might possibly happen.

When I imagined my first time, I never once thought it might happen in the shower. Usually I pictured a bed, maybe some soft music playing, and being with someone that I love.

I stop in my tracks. Wes, his hand in mine, is forced to stop as well.

"What's up?"

Do I love him?

I like him. I like him a lot. My heart goes pitter patter when he's around, great big giant thumping thumps. When he kisses me, my stomach swooshes like I'm on a roller coaster and my brain goes fuzzy. If we're not together, it's usually because we're in class or I have basketball, and when he's not around, he's constantly on my mind. My day gets instantly better when I get to lay eyes on him.

But am I in love with him?

I don't know. I've never been in love before—never even

came close. And he professes to love me, and I believe him. So is it really that crazy to think that I'm in love with him too?

He's my best friend, my favorite person to be around, and not only because he gives me orgasms. As much as I like when we fool around, I'm perfectly happy to sit with him and read or go play tennis or do pretty much anything under the sun. He's the person I want to spend my time with, whether I'm happy or sad, and when I'm in a bad mood, he's the one that can make my world make sense again.

So maybe I'm not in love with him, not yet. I wouldn't know one way or another. What I know is that I love being with him. He makes me happy. And maybe that's enough for now.

"Mackenzie?" Wes is staring at me, his brow furrowed.

"I'm fine. I'm good," I tell him, squeezing his hand.

He frowns.

"I had a thought. I'm better now."

He casts a glance over his shoulder. The rest of the group has gone on without us.

"If you don't want to, we don't—"

"I do. I want to." My stomach flips at the tension on his face. "Unless you're not ready…"

He flushes pink. "I think you felt how ready I am."

I pull him to me, right in the middle of the road. My hands fist in his t-shirt as I pull him bodily towards me.

"I'm crazy about you, Wesley Bradford," I tell him seriously. "I want to do this with you."

He kisses me roughly. His mouth seals over mine, and his hands grip my hips tightly. "I love you, Mackenzie Cavanaugh. So, so much."

I kiss him, again and again and again, until we're interrupted by an errant catcall. We break apart. There are about a dozen people milling about the street around us. None that I recognize. I can't identify the culprit.

"Let's head home, baby," he says, offering his hand. I take it and he squeezes mine.

I'm in my head as we finish the walk back to his house. There's nobody in the living room. The pipes hum overhead as the guys take their individual showers. Amir exits the shared downstairs bathroom in a towel. He catches sight of us and snickers.

"Don't forget to clean up after yourselves," he says, and Wes punches him in the arm as we walk by.

He stops in his room for two towels. Normally, he undresses in his room. This time, he heads to the bathroom fully clothed. Intrigued, I follow him.

As soon as the bathroom door is closed, Wes pins me against the door and kisses me again. His hands slide into my sweaty hair as he brings our bodies into direct intimate contact. I fist my hands in his shirt and slowly drag the fabric up. We have to break the kiss to get his shirt off. This is my favorite sports bra, not only because it comes apart with a convenient zipper down the front. I shove my shorts off my hips as Wes removes his own. His hard cock bobs between us.

It's a tight fit in the small shower. Wes is big, and we're both tall, so as we both try to stay under the spray, it takes some efficient maneuvering. He angles me so I'm under the water and my hair remains mostly dry before he kisses me again. His bulk presses against me in all the right places. His cock is hard against my belly.

Planting my hands on his shoulder, I lift one leg and wrap it around his waist. I have to clench my abs to keep from falling over. Wes groans against my mouth and shifts his pelvis, until his cock slides between my legs, hot and slick from the water and pre-cum. It's my turn to moan.

I'm not sure how he manages it. A second later, there's soap in his hand, and then he's lathering my breasts, paying special attention to my nipples. His mouth moves down my neck, licking and sucking at the pulse point. A tremor shoots through me, and I start to shake.

His hand moves down my torso, angling between us so he can ghost over my clit. With my hand, I direct his mouth back to meet mine. His finger presses against my opening before slowly sinking in. I clutch at him as my eyes roll back into my head. He's solid and hard against me in all the right ways, soft in all the ways that matter. His big bulk presses into me on all sides as his finger works at me.

"Wes?"

"Yeah?"

"You're fucking perfect."

He laughs against my lips as he adds a second finger. "You're pretty damn perfect, too, baby."

That elastic band inside of me stretches taut. When he plunges his fingers deep inside me, my whole world starts to tilt thirteen degrees sharply to the left.

"Wes—"

"You're okay, baby, I've got you." He gives me a soft, sweet kiss, in direct contrast to the terribly dirty things he's doing to me. "Let it go."

When the orgasm hits, I don't try to hold it back: I clutch at his shoulders for balance and let it take me. He grounds me through it, his fingers working at me until it's too much.

I want to touch him. I want to bring him as much pleasure as he's brought me. Reaching for him, he shifts his hips—and his hard-on—out of my grasp.

"I need to wash," he mumbles.

"You're fine."

"I stink."

"I don't care."

"Mackenzie…"

Is it weird that I like the scent of his body odor? It smells like hard work. It smells like safety, like being held in his arms overnight. It smells like comfort and home.

He wants to wash? I'll help him wash. I squirt some soap into my hand and work it into a lather between my palms. He watches me with apprehension.

Slowly, deliberately, I place my hands on his chest, above his pecs. My nails scratch through his chest hair and his eyes fall closed. He sinks back against the shower wall. My hands cover his chest, covering him in soap, before I let them coast down his belly to his cock.

When I wrap my fingers around him, he lets out a groan. When I squeeze him firmly, his eyes fly open, hazy and lust-blown.

"Baby…"

"Tell me if you want me to stop."

He swallows hard. "Don't… don't stop."

"We didn't bring any condoms with us."

That seems to bring him back to the reality of our situation. He stands up straight and widens his stance. His hand covers mine and tightens my grip. He uses my fist to stroke himself.

"We're not having sex in the shower," he says.

"We're—we're not?"

Wes shakes his head. "No. We're going to do this properly, in a bed, where I can devour you like you deserve. This is only the appetizer."

fifty-four

. . .

Wes

IT TAKES ABOUT seven strokes for me to come. Almost before I'm ready for it, I erupt all over our combined fists and spurt all over her belly. Because we're still in the shower, I'm less hesitant about spilling all over her than I would be otherwise. She looks good covered by the pearlescent evidence of my desire for her.

Oversensitive, I pull her hand off of me and cover her mouth with mine. Slowly, her hands come up over my chest and pull me to her. Our bodies slide into direct intimate contact. I map the curve of her ass with my hands, memorizing her perfect body as I come down from the high.

Eventually, the water runs cold. Shutting it off, I reach for a towel and wrap it around her before I grab the second one and throw it over my body.

"I don't want to leave," Mackenzie says.

"Why not?"

She meets my eyes. "Because this was perfect, and I don't know how we're going to top this."

"Trust me, baby, it will get better."

She doesn't smile at the pet name like she normally does.

She worries her bottom lip with her teeth, her fingers clenched around the knot of her towel.

"We don't have to do anything you don't want to do," I remind her. I'd be perfectly happy crawling into bed and reading with her in my arms.

"I want to do this. I'm ready. I want to. I'm just… nervous." She lets out an awkward laugh. "Which is ridiculous, because this is you and me, and we've done…" She gestures between us. "We've done plenty. I'm not sure what my mental hangup is over your cock inside of me instead of your fingers or your mouth."

I'm not sure what to tell her. My concern has always been with the emotional aspect, not the physical. The act itself of sex isn't a big deal. Letting my guard down, letting her in… that's what terrified me. It still kind of does, if I'm honest with myself. I trust her not to break my heart and shatter my spirit.

I poke my head into the hall. Nobody's around. Opening the door all the way, I usher her through and follow after her the few feet down the hallway to my room. Once the door is closed, I lock it. The sound is ominous in the quiet room, like a gunshot going off on a quiet night.

Mackenzie discards her towel and climbs onto my bed. She kicks the sheets and blankets down to the foot of the bed.

"Do you need more time?" She clears her throat, her face red.

Do I need more recovery time? Yeah. I'm game for round two, but I need a pause in between. Luckily, we can play before we get down to business.

Dropping my towel, I crawl onto the bed after her. I cover her naked body with mine and slide my hands into her hair. Lowering my lips to hers, I offer a soft, slow kiss. We have plenty of time. I don't want to rush this. She tries to up the ante, and I slow it back down. Either this happens tonight or it doesn't; either way, I need more time.

There's only one chance at a first time. I have to make this right for her.

We make out for a while. We deserve to enjoy the afterglow a little. There's a little urgency in her kisses, in the way her hand gropes my back and slides down to my ass, grabbing a handful. I cup her breast and stroke my thumb over her pebbled nipple until she gasps and bites down on my lower lip.

She wraps her legs around my waist and brings us into direct intimate contact. My cock twitches against her, making me dizzy. It's been a long time since I've gone for two rounds in such quick succession.

I break the kiss, and she gives a little whine of protest. She doesn't complain for long when I kiss my way down her neck and down to her other breast. My questing fingers slide between her legs again and she spreads them wide, eager.

Taking her nipple between my lips, I tug ever so slightly. She gasps and then sighs, her hands sliding into my hair and directing me ever so lightly to the left.

Continuing my descent, I kiss my way down her belly to her mound. Her clit is just begging to be sucked. I pay some attention to each of her lower lips before I return to her clit, devouring her. We've done this enough times that I know what she likes, what she needs.

The build up this time is slower. I'm not rushing, and neither is she: we have all day. If she doesn't get there, we can try something new... but I'm confident I can get her there.

I'm not sure why there's a difference between oral sex and penetrative sex in my mind. Maybe because this focuses on only one of us at a time versus both of us sharing an intimate connection by our bodies being fused together. My fingers inside of her is different than my cock being inside of her, both of us seeking pleasure at the same time. I can't quite explain it.

Her body clutches at my fingers in a punishing grip. Her

legs start to tremble and then she throws back her head, riding the wave. She moans out loud, I think louder than she intends. Her face and chest flush a brilliant rosy color.

Her release coats my fingers. Moving lower, I lap up of the evidence of her desire as her limbs flail and shake. Her legs are clamped tightly around my ears. With a breathy sigh, she relaxes onto the bed, her body going limp.

"You okay?" I lick her clit, and she twitches her hips half-heartedly.

"Fuck."

I pull my fingers out of her, and she sighs again.

"Wes?"

"Yeah?" My voice cracks.

"Can you hold me?" Her eyes are big and round. "I need… I want you to hold me."

"Anything you want, baby." I collapse beside her and pull her into my arms. Her skin is flushed and slick with sweat. She rests her head on my chest and wraps her arms around me. Our legs tangle beneath the sheet.

"That felt really good," she says. "You're good at that."

"You like it. I like doing the things you enjoy."

She swallows. "Does it bother you?"

"Hm?"

"That you've gone down on me a bunch and I've only given you one blowjob?"

I brush her hair out of her face. "I'm not keeping score. Do I like blowjobs? Sure. Do I need one every day? No."

She goes pink. "I don't need you to go down on me every day."

"Even if I want to?"

Mackenzie reconsiders. "Well, I'm hardly about to stop you…"

With a laugh, I tug her closer and press a kiss to her forehead. "I like bringing you pleasure. Whether that's with my fingers or my mouth or a toy, what's important to me is that you enjoy yourself. We can experiment as much as you'd like. We don't have to have sex every time for both of us to have a good time."

She wraps her hand around my length and squeezes. She strokes a few times, and my eyes fall closed for a second before I snap back to it and kiss her properly. With a push to my shoulder, she convinces me to lay on my back. She splays over my thighs, my cock rising between her legs.

This is it. It's time.

Reaching over to the bedside table, I grab the condom from the box I bought this weekend and come back to her.

"You're sure?" I meet her eyes again.

Mackenzie takes the foil square from my hand and rips it open. Gingerly, she pulls out the latex circle like she's never seen one before—which she might not have.

Gently, I take the condom from between her fingertips and guide her hand to my cock. I roll it over my length and then use her hand for a few quick strokes.

"It feels… different," she says.

"Bad?"

"No." She shakes her head. "I'm not sure what I expected. Reading about it in books… it's way better in person." Her hand squeezes my cock again before she reaches down and cups my aching balls. I might groan out loud. Her eyes dart up to mine, worried, before she relaxes and smiles with pride. Even when I'm flat on my back, she can bring me to my knees.

My fingers slide into her again, three now, and my thumb over her clit. She inhales sharply and spreads her legs impossibly wide. Balancing her hands on my chest, she lifts her hips higher.

I urge her up a little more, enough for me to notch my cock against her opening.

"Take it as slow as you need," I warn her. "We don't have to rush."

She swallows hard. Her nails curl into my pecs as she slowly sinks down an inch. She gasps. The head of my cock is engulfed by her hot, wet heat, and it's my turn to swallow. Her head hangs low as she breathes slowly. She's impossibly tight, even with all the prepping we've done.

It's been five long years for me, and an eternity for her. She's never done this before.

I have to concentrate on the physical aspect of this, because if I start worrying about the emotional component, I'm going to spiral into a breakdown. She's trusting me with something so intimately familiar, so precious. She's never going to have another first time. She might have sex with other people—and I don't want to think about that, especially while I'm half inside of her—but this first time will always be the first.

Mackenzie walked into my life and turned my world upside down. She made me open up, both to her and to my other friends. She convinced me that I don't have to lock away the parts of me that make me interesting. She taught me I don't have to hide behind my books. She showed me how to love again.

And I love her. She makes my whole day better. The few hours I get to steal with her are the best parts of my day.

My hands are on her hips, holding her steady, as she slowly lowers herself bit by bit. She bites her lip. My eyes fall closed, and I have to fight to keep them open, to watch this perfection personified. She sinks down further, each inch torturously slow, until her legs are spread wide, and I'm buried to the hilt inside of her.

She swallows hard, her eyes slowly rising to meet mine.

"You're okay?" My voice cracks.

She nods. "I'm… this… you feel amazing."

I let out a breath I didn't realize I was holding. "It doesn't hurt?"

"It feels like… pressure," she says. She lifts her hips a little and slides back down. "Like fullness. In a good way."

"What about when I do this?" I run my thumb over her clit, firmly, the way she likes.

She shudders. "I like that, too."

My hands on her hips help her up a little before I lower her down again. If I stretch my fingers, I can rub at her clit at the same time as I arch up into her.

She feels amazing, this is fantastic, but the angle isn't working for me. Spreading my legs a little, I rotate my hips to get more leverage. Mackenzie gasps.

"That feels… Ohhhh."

Coaxing her forward, she puts more weight on her hands, her knees on the mattress. I encourage her closer, so that I can kiss her while I thrust into her. Her hands slide from my chest to my shoulders.

It's like a piece of me I didn't know was lost has finally been found. I didn't know what I was missing until I found it again. My hands on her ass, my cock buried deep inside of her, her tongue in my mouth… I'm overwhelmed by the sensory at the same time as the emotional starts to hit me.

She likes me. She cares for me. She isn't selfish. She isn't going to shatter my heart at my lowest point just because she can. I trust her. I *love* her.

So why can't I shake this nagging feeling that something is wrong? Why does it feel like my whole world is about to implode?

fifty-five

. . .

Mackenzie

WHEN I WAKE UP, it takes me a second to remember what happened last night. Wes and I had sex. We had a *lot* of sex. I'm not a virgin anymore. I can't decide how I feel about that. Happy, maybe, and a little anticlimactic, despite the intense climax(es) he gave me. The muscles between my legs are sore, like I've gone horseback riding or rode a bike for fifteen miles with inadequate stretching. Overall, I feel… good.

Wes is fast asleep next to me. The sheets are soaked with his sweat, like they are every morning, a pile of blankets layered on top of me. I slide out from under his arm and he lets out a soft whine of protest.

When I get back, he's awake and not looking happy about it. "Come back to bed," he says impetuously.

"I have class in two hours."

"Just a nap."

"I have to go back to my dorm, I need—"

I stop at the look on his face, worry and apprehension and a little bit of disappointment.

"How are you feeling?"

He swallows loudly. "I'm okay."

I sit on the edge of the bed, resisting letting him pull me

back onto the bed. "I'm feeling good. I'm glad we—it was—I—"

Wes rises up onto his knees. He reaches for me, and I let him tug me into his body. His kiss is soft and sleep sour.

"I love you," he whispers softly.

It's my turn to swallow. "Wes, I…"

"I don't want you to say it back, not if you're not ready," he says. "When you say it, if you say it, I want you to mean it."

Do I love him?

"I'm getting there," I concede. "I'm not there yet. But I can see… soon…"

He squeezes my hand. "It's okay."

"I want to. I just—"

Wes cracks a smile. "It took us all this time to be ready to have sex. It's okay if this takes more time. I'm not going anywhere."

Except grad school. He only has one more week before he has to give Michigan his final answer.

"I need to take a shower."

He pouts.

"By myself. I'll be right back," I tell him. I give him another quick kiss. "You'll hardly notice I'm gone."

"I'll be here," he says, flopping back onto the bed.

The bathroom mirror doesn't lie: I don't look any different. It's not immediately obvious that I had my whole world rocked last night. Looking at me, nobody will know I'm not a virgin anymore.

Except for the fact that I want to scream it from the rooftops. Yeah, I probably shouldn't do that.

I keep waiting for the other shoe to drop. In romance novels, this is where everything unravels. The morning after is always the start of drama and leads to the breakup. I don't want to break up with Wes, not now and maybe not ever. I'm crazy about this guy. He's the perfect first boyfriend. He's the perfect boyfriend, period. So maybe sometimes he's a bit moody. He broods. He clams up. All in all, he's a good partner. He treats me like we're equals. The age difference doesn't matter. We make a good team. I couldn't ask for a better introduction to the world of dating.

There's a love bite on my clavicle that I'll have to strategically hide with my clothes. More marks on my breasts that won't show except when I have to get changed for practice. The girls on the team won't care, not like my brother will if he spots them.

When I get back to Wes's room, he's stripped the bed and is putting on a new set of sheets. It's part of his morning routine every single day. With how much he sweats in the night, he needs to do it every day... even if we hadn't made a mess of the sheets last night.

He kisses me on the cheek before he lumbers past me towards the bathroom. He's not particularly chatty in the morning on a good day, and today of all days, he's probably in his head a little. I should give him space to come to terms with what we did. He's been considerate enough to give me time to process; it's the least I can do for him.

Dropping my towel, I slip into my clothes. Wes has been kind enough to let me keep a few essentials in his dresser, so I don't have to wear wrinkled, smelly clothes that have been stuffed in the bottom of my backpack for three days in a row.

There's a knock on the bedroom door.

"Yeah?"

No response. All of the guys respect Wes and my privacy, but for them to drop in on us this early in the morning... I open the door.

There's a pretty blonde woman standing on the other side. She's short, nearly a foot shorter than me, with light green eyes and freckles across the bridge of her nose. Her mouth drops open at the sight of me.

"You're not Wes."

There's a rock in the pit of my stomach.

"Can I help you?"

"I'm looking for Wes."

He's standing at the end of the hall in a towel, surprise written all over his face. "Sarah?" His voice cracks on the second syllable.

Relief floods through me. This is his sister.

"What are you doing here? What's wrong?"

"Nothing is wrong," she says immediately. "Why don't you get dressed and then we can talk?"

He turns sideways to scoot past her and into his room. I step aside, and he edges past.

Wes lets out a heavy breath. "I didn't know she was coming."

"So I gathered."

His eyes lift to mine. "You're okay?"

"I'm great."

"Great. That's… great." He exhales heavily and turns to his dresser, rummaging through the drawers for clothes.

"Do you want to talk about it?"

"I don't know why she's here." His hands are shaking, and he balls up the clean t-shirt in his fists.

"It might not be bad. It might be a good thing."

"Yeah, maybe," he hums.

"Wes."

He looks up at me, his face pale.

"It could be okay," I remind him.

He exhales slowly, shaking out his arms. "Yeah. It could… yeah."

Crossing the room, I step in front of him and set my hands on his shoulders. He swallows and raises his eyes to meet mine.

"Everything will be okay," I tell him. "You'll spend time with your sister, who you love. You'll catch up and have breakfast and talk about however long she'll be in town.

After, you'll go to class, go to the gym, and have a fucking awesome workout to get out of your head a bit. And then tonight, when we come back here, I'm going to give you a blowjob, so you have that to look forward to."

He opens his mouth and closes it again. "Mackenzie..."

"If you're not in the mood, we don't have to, but I want to do something nice for you. Something you enjoy. And if you need a few days before you want to try again, we can—"

His lips descend onto mine. He wraps his arms around me and pulls me close.

"I love you," he murmurs, before he kisses me again. His cock pulses against my hip, trying to get in on the action. He twitches his pelvis away. He's still naked, and I'm fully dressed.

"Wes..."

Breaking the kiss, he pulls back and takes a step in retreat. He ducks down and picks up the boxers he dropped to the floor, stepping into them. He drops a kiss to my temple before he pulls on a pair of jeans and drags a shirt over his head. He cracks his knuckles.

"Okay, let's do this." He takes my hand.

I've been so focused on Wes's feelings that I haven't had time to process that I'm about to meet my boyfriend's sister, his only remaining family and the person whose opinion he cares about most. Hell, until a few weeks ago, his backup plan if grad school didn't work out was to move to her city and establish himself there.

As far as I know, that's changed. It sounds like his plan now is either BU or Newton or an internship in the greater Boston area if he doesn't get accepted. He doesn't want to go back to Michigan, and I don't blame him. Selfishly, I want to keep him here.

Sarah is sitting on the couch that used to be my bed, making small talk with Greg and Miles. The guys look interested in the story she's telling.

"Hey."

At the sound of her brother's voice, Sarah stops and turns to him. She grins and stands, wrapping her arms around him.

"Hey, Wessy."

He growls, tugging on a lock of her hair. "Don't."

"I can't call you my little Wessy-poo?"

I snicker, and he goes beet red. Greg and Miles are certainly enjoying this development.

"No. What are you doing here?"

She laughs and steps back. "No hi, how are you? We launch right into—"

"It's a Monday in the middle of term," he says flatly. "Your spring break was two weeks ago. You have classes. What are you doing here?"

"My friend is getting married."

"Now?"

"This weekend, in New Hampshire," she says, retaking her seat on the couch.

Wes slips into his regular armchair, and I take the one beside it. I don't know what to do with my hands.

"It was easier to fly out now and spend the week here than to come out on Friday."

He frowns.

"And I get to see you a little bit," she adds. "Let me tell you, getting into Athlete's Village was insane. The guard didn't want to let me in. Someone took pity on me and signed me in as their guest."

"How long are you here?"

"Just today. We go to New Hampshire tomorrow morning."

"Why didn't you call?" His mouth is a hard line.

Sarah rolls her eyes. "Because I knew you would freak out."

"I wouldn't—"

"I didn't want to be interrogated," she says firmly. "I have stuff to do today in the city, but I wanted to come out and visit with you for a bit."

For the first time, I notice the suitcase by the door. "Did you just get in?" I ask politely.

Sarah inclines her head. "I took a red-eye." Her eyes flick back to her brother. "Is this...?"

"Oh. Right." He clears his throat. "Mackenzie, this is Sarah. My sister. Sar, this is... this is Mackenzie."

Standing, I reach over and shake her hand. Her shake is strong, firm.

"It's nice to meet you," I say, because it is.

"I've been looking forward to this for a long time," she says, and I have to laugh.

My alarm goes off, reminding me that I have class in an hour. If I want to grab breakfast, I need to jet.

"I would love to stay and chat, but I've got to get going. Classes don't—"

"Oh, no, of course, I totally get it," she assures me. "Maybe we can have dinner? The three of us?"

I look to Wes, who swallows. He nods.

"Sure. That sounds great."

She beams at me, and I'm taken aback by the resemblance between them.

Wes stands and pulls me into a brief hug. His lips land on my forehead in a brief kiss.

"Love you," he murmurs quietly, like he's trying to remind himself. "I'll see you after practice?"

I nod. Those three little words are on the tip of my tongue, but I'm not ready to say them. Not yet.

"See you."

Grabbing my bag, I kiss his cheek, punch my brother in the shoulder, and all but run out the door.

fifty-six

. . .

Wes

SARAH LOOKS GOOD. Tired, maybe.

"Why are you here?"

"I told you, I'm here for a wedding."

I roll my eyes. "On a Monday?"

"The wedding is this Saturday," she explains. "I flew out last night. I'm taking my classes remotely all week. That way, I don't have to miss a day of school for the flight."

"Yeah, okay."

Tricia, our regular waitress, frowns at me. She drops off the menu for my sister and speeds off in the opposite direction without so much as a pleasant pleasantry.

"So you come here often?" Sarah laughs.

"Every Sunday morning," I tell her. Whether I come with Mackenzie or by myself due to her schedule, it's part of my every weekend routine, just like going to pilates class and movie night with the guys. I don't usually make it over here on the weekdays. The food is great, but certainly not what I'd consider healthy, and I get free meals at the dining hall with my athletic scholarship. I'm not about to make my sister eat dining hall food when we can just as easily go out.

"What does your day look like?"

"Class at ten, half hour break, and again at twelve-thirty." My stomach churns. "I have a big speech today, or I would offer to hang out a bit. I'll hit the gym and be done for the day by three or four." I can do my homework later. She's only here for a short amount of time; I want to make the most of it.

Sarah plays with the edge of her menu. "I wasn't entirely truthful, when I said I was here for a wedding."

I give her a flat look. "No shit."

"I have a job interview for an externship this summer."

"Sarah!"

"It's a good one, but I don't know if I'm going to get it," she says. "I'm not sure if it's a speciality I want to go into."

"It's local?"

She nods. "Corporate law. I have three interviews this week in the area, but this one… it's my top choice out of the three. I like the firm, if nothing else. They have a lot of opportunities down the line."

"You want to move here?!"

"Well, you're staying, aren't you?" She blinks at me.

"I…"

"You haven't committed to Michigan. You've mentioned taking a gap year or an internship if you don't get into Newton," she says.

I sigh.

"And she's here."

"I'm not—"

"I know, you haven't been dating long. But you're in love with her, and she's from the area, so even if she didn't have a few more years of school, I kind of expected you to stick around here," she says.

I clear my throat.

Tricia descends upon us. "What can I get you?"

"Oh. Um." Sarah looks at the menu for the first time. "A veggie omelette, please."

She turns to me with a dour look. "And you?"

There's a frog caught in my throat. "The usual."

Tricia gives me a clearly forced smile. "How's Mackenzie? I haven't seen you two in a while. Did you have a good spring break?"

"She's good."

She gives me the side eye.

"This is my sister. Sarah."

A look of relief crosses her face. "It's nice to meet you, sweetie. Can I get you some coffee? A side of pancakes?"

"Coffee would be great," Sarah says politely. "Thank you."

Tricia walks away to the back of the diner, where two other waitresses are gathered. She whispers with them and all three of them glance over in our direction.

"So I take it you're popular here," my sister says.

"What?"

She rolls her eyes. "She thought you were cheating on Mackenzie."

My stomach drops. "Um, what?"

"They didn't realize we're siblings. She thought you were on an early morning date with someone who isn't your girl-friend, someone they are clearly fond of."

"I like Mackenzie."

Her smile is pitying. "I heard you love her."

"I... I do."

"And how does that make you feel?"

Terrified. Breathless. Content. I scratch idly at my clavicle. It doesn't help the itch beneath my skin.

"It gets better, Wessy," she says.

I kick her foot under the table, accidentally on purpose.

"So let's get back to the whole you're moving here thing."

"Maybe. Maybe moving here," she warns. "I'm also applying in D.C. and Connecticut."

"Not New York?"

She makes a face. "I don't want to live in the city."

"But you'd live in the city here."

"It's different. New York is… no, thank you. I can deal with Boston."

I frown. "I don't want you to deal with it. I want you to love it here."

She blows out a breath. "Anyway, so I figure we should at least try to live on the same coast, and since you're stuck on staying here, I have to get used to it. I'm keeping my options open."

"If I don't get in here…"

"Then you'll zig instead of zag," Sarah says. "We don't get to plan how our lives will turn out, not with any degree of certainty. Shit happens. Parents get into car crashes and—"

A sharp inhale.

"I'm sorry, Wes. I should have—I—"

"I don't want to talk about it," I tell her firmly.

"Eventually…"

"Mackenzie and I had sex last night," I blurt.

Her eyes go wide. "Wow. Okay."

"It was the first time since… since Mom and Dad…"

"The world isn't going to implode," she says kindly. "You're a grown man. You're in a mature, consenting relationship. You're allowed to have sex again." She pauses. "You were safe, right?"

Nodding, I wrap my hands around my tea. "We're using condoms, plus she's religious about taking her birth control, so we're doubly safe."

"And you've been tested recently?"

"Since my last partner, yeah. And she's…" It's none of Sarah's business how many partners Mackenzie may or may not have had. Besides, the school requires STD checks with our annual physical before we can play each season. "We're all good there."

"Good. That's… good." My sister gives me a weak smile. "Little Wessy, all grown up."

I scowl at her, and she laughs.

"Seriously, this is not the end of the world. If anything, I'd say this is the start of a new chapter in your life," she says. "You're heading into something new and exciting and challenging. For the first time in your life, you don't have football to distract you."

I frown. Football isn't a distraction.

"Graduate school is hard. It's not for everyone. But I believe you can do it, and I believe you'll succeed there," Sarah says.

"If I get in," I add sourly, and she sighs.

"If you get in."

I sit with that uncomfortable thought for a minute. There's a very real possibility I won't get in to either BU or Newton. There's a very real chance my only options will be moving back to Michigan or staying here without a guaranteed job. Both prospects are equally scary. My parents left me a little bit of money, but it's not enough to support me for the rest of my life. I'm also not the kind of guy who would enjoy a life of leisure. Sure, having unlimited time to read might be nice at first, but I know that after a few days I'll get bored. I like to do something.

Graduate school is practically required if I want to have a career in my chosen field. It'll be easier if I go straight from undergrad to grad school, but not impossible if I work for a year or three in the field. We have the Student Work Office to help connect us with internships and job opportunities. There are mixers and job fairs with recruiters and companies hiring. There are options.

"Have you checked recently?" Sarah asks.

I shoot her a disgruntled look, and she laughs, adjusting her grip on her coffee cup. "You won't know until you know."

Pulling out my phone, I scroll through my email until I

find the automated notice from Newton. I log into their portal. Decision: To Be Determined.

I show her the screen. "Too soon."

"Try the other one."

I don't have to. When I search for my most recent emails from Boston University, the one I didn't want is at the top of the list, timestamped for fifteen minutes ago.

Dear Mr. Bradford, we regret to inform you that...

Handing my phone to my sister, I cram a too big piece of toast into my mouth.

Rejected. Declined. Not accepted.

It hurts to swallow. I nearly choke and moisture rises to my eyes.

Five seconds ago, I was on top of the world. My whole life was an open book, a story yet to be written. The world was my oyster: I could do anything. I could stay here. I could stay with Mackenzie. I didn't have to go back to the frozen hellhole I came from.

Sarah's eyes are sad. "What are you going to do?"

I clear my throat. "I have until Sunday to tell Michigan. If I can't find a job or internship by then, I guess I'll have to move back home."

"It might not be that bad," she says.

"Or it could be worse."

She yeahs. "Yeah. It might be worse."

Because now I don't have a support network. Now I don't have a family to rely on. Now I have nobody except my sister, who is stuck on the other side of the country, and a girlfriend who will live twelve hours away for the foreseeable future. I don't want to go back to Michigan. I want to stay here, find a job, and work my ass off. I want to stay with my friends, the guys who have become like my brothers.

But we're all standing at the precipice of now and what is to come. Half of them are graduating and moving on to parts unknown. They won't be staying here, even if I'm lucky enough to get accepted to Newton. Tucker and Mason are off to grad school. Barrett and Diana are moving to the city. Miles and Sam? Their status is still unknown. Amir and Greg still have at least another year left; Mackenzie has three, minimum.

Do I want to put my life on hold for her? We've only been dating for a few weeks. It seems crazy, to jeopardize my entire future for a woman I've known for a short time and have been dating even less.

But I love her. As much as I don't want to sometimes, I do. Even when she drives me crazy, I do. I can see us down the line, five, ten years into the future. Time is all too fleeting. Can we make a long distance relationship work? Will she even want to?

I blow out a breath. There's a lot to think about. There's no easy answer. At least I have until Sunday…

fifty-seven

. . .

Mackenzie

OUR FOURTH SPEECH is supposed to be a special occasion speech. Most people have chosen best man or maid of honor speeches, and one particularly creative guy gave a eulogy for his dead cat. Mine is a generic valedictorian speech —I will never, ever be valedictorian of anything, so this was purely a creative exercise.

Wes is more withdrawn than usual. During class we normally hold hands or at least glance at each other in between speeches. He's staring straight ahead, focusing on the whiteboard at the front of the room. It's like he can't bring himself to look at me. Is he remembering last night? I know I am.

He rocked my world. I didn't think there was any way penetrative sex could hold up in real life to the magical, life-changing scenes I read about in my favorite romance novels. It did. It wasn't just the orgasms, although that certainly helped; it was the connection we shared, two souls fused together for an intangibly short period of time.

When my name is called, I stand up and give my speech. It's... okay. Not the worst one I've had in this class, and certainly not my best effort. I'm distracted by the guy in the last row, all the way on the end. What is going through his head? Why won't he look at me?

And then it's his turn.

Wes looks pale. Then again, he always looks pale when he has to speak in public. He clears his throat and looks down at his papers. Blowing out a breath, his eyes rise to meet mine.

"My speech is a goodbye speech," he says, and my pulse throbs in the sore space between my legs.

"I've been here for five long years. Through my time at Newton, I've seen many good people come and go. I've shared in the joys and triumphs of a winning football team, and I've slogged through the frustration of having two consecutive losing seasons. In my time here, I've met some decently average people, and I've met people who have become my family. Most of my family is dead. The guys I live with? They're my brothers. My friends? They're my sisters. They're my new family now, whether they know it or not, whether they like it or not."

He's not stuttering. From a pure public speaking standpoint, he's not bad. He's not saying "um" or "like" every other word like other people do. He might be sweating, but it's barely visible; it's only because I know him so well that I can tell he's uncomfortable.

"And I'm about to say goodbye to them. I'm about to embark on a self-imposed exile to the place I hate most in the world, a place where I will have to start over one more time. Except this time, I won't have a family of football players to fall back on. This time, I won't have friends to lean on. I'll be alone, on my own, in the worst place in the world."

My stomach turns. It sounds like he's already decided. It sounds like he's made up his mind.

"I don't make friends easily. As a general rule, I don't like people, and the ones I do tolerate I tend to keep at a distance. It's incredibly challenging for me to open up to people. But when I do, when I let someone in… I don't often let them go.

"And now it's time for me to let Newton go. We can't stay here forever. Eventually, we have to go out and face the real world, and with it, real life responsibilities. We don't have to go home, hopefully we aren't moving backwards, but at the same time, we can't stay here in limbo any longer. It's time to plant our feet firmly on the ground and meet our futures with our eyes wide open."

I don't like the way this sounds. I don't like any of this at all.

"So, goodbye, Newton. Goodbye, Massachusetts. I'm going to miss you. Most of all, I'm going to miss what could have been. Thank you."

There's scattered applause as he moves through the room to retake his seat. He's clearly making progress from a public speaking standpoint. He's a far cry from the guy who stuttered and broke off during his first speech. Granted, he chose to speak about the most challenging aspects of his life in front of the public, when he doesn't even share that with me... yeah, that might not have been the best idea on his part.

But it's what brought us together. We had our first kiss after that disastrous first speech. For that reason alone, it will always have a special place in my heart.

I turn to Wes, ready to give him a high five. He's not looking at me, though. He's looking down at his desk, his face crestfallen. I want to reach over, to offer a hug or an arm squeeze or some sort of physical comfort. He doesn't want it. He's drawn in on himself, his arms tucked close to his sides.

"You okay?" I murmur, still watching him.

Wes clears his throat a few times and nods.

"Do you want to talk about it?"

He shakes his head. He's still not quite looking at me.

I have no idea what happened between him and his sister at breakfast this morning. Maybe it didn't go well. Maybe they got into a fight. I don't know, because he's not fucking talking to me.

When class is over, he doesn't kiss me goodbye like he usually does. He doesn't offer to walk me to my next class, even though I know he doesn't have time. He doesn't so much as look at me.

"See you," he mutters, collecting his textbook and notebook under his arm.

My stomach twists. "See you."

———

Sarah and Wes are at the little blue house by the time I arrive, fresh from practice. They're sitting on the living room sofa and talking—well, she's talking, and he's listening, which isn't a far cry from usual. He hasn't even opened the book in his hands, giving her his full attention.

Now that I see them side by side, the resemblance is uncanny. He's bigger, nearly twice her size, but they both have blond hair and light green eyes. She has freckles, whereas he has a collection of small moles. Their features are similar. It's clear they're related.

He looks up as I close the door, his eyes dark. Heaving himself to his feet, he crosses the room and drops a light kiss to my cheek. "Hey."

"Hi."

"How was practice?"

Oh, so are we not going to talk about the speech he gave in class, the one where he basically decided he's leaving and announced as such to the entire class? We're not going to address the fact that he then ignored me throughout class and once it was over?

Yeah, that's not going to fly with me.

But now is not the time to start a fight, not with his sister here from out of town and staring at me, judging me. I want to make a good impression. I don't want her to think I'm some dramatic, demanding girlfriend who wants to be treated with basic respect and dignity.

Oh, wait. I do. Because if I'm not Wes's peer, his equal, I don't want to be dating him.

"Practice was fine," I say, and the tightness around my eyes seems to clue him in that he done fucked this up.

Miles clambers down the stairs and then stops, deer in headlights.

"Um, hi?"

"Hey. Have you met Wes's sister yet?" I clear my throat. "Sarah, this is my brother, Miles. He lives here in the house, and they were on the football team together."

Sarah raises her eyebrows and looks him over. "Nice to meet you."

"You, too," Miles says. He coughs. "I'm going to head over to the ASC for an early dinner. You'll be around later?"

He addresses this to me, not my boyfriend, like it's a given that I'll be sleeping in Wes's bed again tonight.

"That's the plan."

Wes glances at his sister. "Do you want to join us?"

"What?" My words echo my brother's.

"For dinner. We're going to Double Chins'," he says. "You're welcome to come with us."

"It'll be a real family dinner," Sarah adds.

Miles looks to me. This isn't my decision. It's the perfect time for him to decide if he's truly on board with us being together or if he wants to stand in our way.

"Chinese sounds good," Miles says. "Let me know when you're ready."

Wes turns to me. "You ready now?" I nod. "Now is good."

My brother huffs out a laugh. "Okay."

He crosses to the hooks behind the door, grabbing his coat. I haven't even taken my jacket off. Sarah has hers folded over the back of the couch. Wes zips up his hoodie and is ready to go.

The walk doesn't take long. We're shown to a table right away. We slide into the booth, Bradford siblings across from Cavanaugh siblings. It feels weird not sitting next to Wes, but it would be more weird to make Sarah and Miles sit side by side.

"How's Sam?" I ask my brother as we peruse the menu.

He lets out a slow breath. "She's good. Last away game of the season. Next week is senior night and then she starts playoffs."

"I haven't seen her in a while."

"Yeah, me either." He totally doesn't sound bitter, not at all, I think sarcastically.

"Everything okay with you two?"

"I think so? I mean, I hope so."

"After that dinner before spring break..."

Miles sighs. "No, we got that figured out. I just... next year is going to be tough. She doesn't want to go back to Mississippi, but she feels like she can't stay here, and she doesn't have a job yet, so..."

My stomach churns with anxiety on his behalf. "That sounds tough."

"Yeah. I'm not thrilled. I've been putting out applications and I might have an interview next week," he says. "But it's in Somerset, so I don't know that the commute would make sense."

"You're set on moving back home?" As far as I know, that's still the plan...

"Well, it's not like I have any income that will let me pay rent right now," he says. "I hope I can find something right away. I might stay at home to save money, I might move out ASAP. It all depends. So much is in flux right now."

I sigh. "Yeah. It really is."

Wes and Sarah are talking quietly to themselves. I can hear their voices, their words too quiet to be distinct. I'm a little perturbed by their excluding us—then again, my brother and

I were talking and not including them, so maybe they're just doing the same.

What the fuck happened between this morning and now? We had sex for the first time—me for the first time ever, him for the first time in five years. We should be over the moon and overjoyed to see each other. We should be—

Unless he didn't have a good time last night. He was skittish this morning, too. Just because he came doesn't mean he enjoyed it. His whole issue has been the emotional impact of sex, not the physical. Even now, he's closed in on himself. His hands are folded on top of the table, his eyes on his menu, even though I'm pretty sure he's already decided what he wants to eat.

I nudge him gently with my foot. "You okay?"

Wes raises his eyes to meet mine, his face contorted with pain. "I didn't get in," he blurts.

"What?" I don't understand.

"To BU," he says. "I didn't get in."

"So… what does that mean?"

He has one more application pending, to Newton. He only has a few more days to give Michigan his final answer. The clock is ticking. The time to make a decision is looming.

He sighs and runs his hand through his hair. "I don't know. I have a lot to think about."

"Anything I can help with?"

"No. I… I think I have to do this one on my own."

I reach for him, trying to offer some sort of physical comfort. Wes folds in on himself, tucking his arms close to his chest.

"It will all work out," Sarah says.

Maybe it's selfish of me, but I don't know how we would sustain a long distance relationship, especially for three years. We don't talk on the phone much, and we text even less. What I enjoy most is the quality time we spend together, even if we're occupied reading our own books.

I don't know how this works long distance.

While I appreciate that he wants to build a future with me, I don't know that I'm ready to think about marriage and babies and all that comes with it. Wes is an old soul. He's a forty something year old man trapped in a twenty-two year old body. He's thinking about the future, about settling down. I'm only nineteen. I might be an introvert, but I still want to go to frat parties (every once in a while… like once or twice a year) and get drunk and explore the world around me. I'm not ready to settle down.

If Wes goes to Michigan, I can't go with him. I have a life here. My athletic scholarship has me on the basketball team for three more seasons, which doesn't necessarily coincide with years on the calendar. As is common with football players, both Wes and Miles needed five years to graduate, both of them sitting out their freshman seasons to preserve that year of athletic eligibility, or, in Wes's case, due to injury. I don't know what I want to do for a career; I don't even know if I'm going to stick with my English major. It might take me more than four years to graduate. I don't know how long my life is going to be on hold waiting for him to move back or me to move there.

I know I should be supportive. I know I should be thinking about him. But I've got to think about myself, too. And I don't know that I want to spend my college years wrapped up in someone who is twelve hours away. I don't know that I want to devote my life to someone who can't communicate to me when something is wrong and can't ask for it when he needs some support.

I don't want to break up: I'm crazy about Wes. But realistically, when I put myself first… I don't know that I can sustain this relationship if he moves to Michigan.

This makes today's goodbye speech make so much more sense. He might be wrestling with this decision, or he might have made up his mind already. Either way, he's in a different headspace. He's not opening up.

And yeah, maybe he needs to ruminate. Maybe he needs to put himself first, the same way I need to. Maybe he has to worry about his future and what he wants.

But he claims he wants me to be part of that future. So why isn't he talking to me?

Sarah chatters through dinner, telling us about her law school classes and the wedding she's going to in New Hampshire this weekend, and the job interview she had today. I wasn't aware she was trying to move here. I thought she still had another year of school left.

I don't have much to contribute. Miles asks her about Seattle—there are a lot of jobs for math majors in the tech sector, and while I don't think he wants to move clear across the country, it doesn't hurt to get information. Sam is a health and fitness major, so she can find a job pretty much anywhere with a decent fitness scene.

Wes and I are both quiet, which is not abnormal for either of us. Clearly, he has a lot on his mind. Evidently, I have a lot to think about, too.

Do I want to spend a minimum of three years doing long distance? I thought I was prepared for this, I really did. Faced with the reality of it... I don't know that I can. Wes is reticent on a good day. He communicates, yeah, but he doesn't *talk*. And I don't want to be the one that has to force a conversation every day or however often we talk. I'm busy enough with basketball and a boyfriend; I don't know that I can sustain a long distance relationship. But I also don't know that I want to give up on what we have so soon. I don't know anything anymore.

fifty-eight

. . .

Wes

MACKENZIE IS QUIET DURING DINNER, which I can understand. I'm not feeling particularly sociable, either. It's a lot to soak in.

I applied to half a dozen schools. I got into three; out of all of them, Michigan had the best aid package and is the only contender left at this point... as well as Newton, which I'm still waiting to hear back from. Where I am now, I would still rather pick Newton over Michigan even if they gave me nothing. It's the program I want to be part of the most, even without all of the intangibles that sticking around for another few years would provide.

If I have to stay here, if I decide to stay here, I'm sure I can find an internship or a job. Even if it's not in my field, I can at least find something to keep me afloat while I look for something more permanent in the physical therapy realm.

While I'm not enamored with the city of Boston, I understand that Mackenzie is from here and respect that she wants to stay here long term. If I want to stay with her—if I want to be with her—I'll have to make some concessions, and one of those means sticking within a close radius of where her family lives.

And I don't hate it here. I just don't love it. Newton is a college town, and I don't know that I would want to stay close by without being part of the university, and I don't have a particular neighborhood within the greater Boston area that I know well enough to want to move to.

Barrett is sticking around; his parents are from northeast of the city, and his family's company is headquartered downtown. Plus Diana wants to stay near to her parents, just not too close—she doesn't want to move back to Amherst, and still stay within easy driving distance. Worst-case scenario, I can ask them to split a two-bedroom apartment with me in the neighborhood of their choice. Not that I particularly want to live with the amorous couple, but it's a fallback option.

Tucker and Mason are off to grad school. They're still waiting for all of their acceptances to come in before they make a decision. Their deal is they have to go to the same graduate program, and while they've both been accepted to two programs, they're trying to keep all their options open.

That's what I need to do, too. But for some reason, my brain keeps focusing on down the line instead of the here and now. Mackenzie makes me think about the future, about what could be.

After dinner, we walk Sarah back to the train station, where she'll catch a ride into the city proper and her hotel for the night. My sister gives me a tight hug.

"Keep your head on your shoulders, Wessy," she says quietly. "You'll make the right decision."

I wish I had her faith in me.

Mackenzie is quiet on the walk towards Athlete's Village. When we're halfway to the house, she clears her throat.

"I think I'm going to head back to my dorm," she says.

She hasn't slept in her dorm more than one night a week in the past three weeks, and she normally tries to do it only when Claire isn't there. Claire is home today; I saw her in the dining hall at lunchtime, when she sneered at me and tried to pretend I didn't exist.

I change course, heading to the freshmen dorms. "If that's what you think is best."

For the first time in as long as I can remember, she's not holding my hand: her hands are tucked into her jacket pockets, even though it's definitely not that cold out. Her brother, beside me, raises his eyebrows.

We walk about ten yards. "What are you doing?"

"Uh, walking you back to your dorm?"

"You don't have to do that," she says.

"Yeah, I kind of do," I tell her.

"You're not my keeper. You don't have to—"

Woah, woah, woah.

"Mackenzie," I say quietly. "I want to walk with you to your dorm. Do you not want me to?"

She squeezes her eyes shut and takes a deep breath. "I'm sorry. I'm just tense. It's been a long day."

"Yeah, I know."

Last night was hard enough. Add in the tumult of this morning, and then the emotional overload of my speech, and now this...

"Do you want to talk about it?"

She sighs. "I think I just need some space."

"Oh. Okay."

She frowns at my lack of reaction. "Okay?"

"Yeah, okay, you need some space. What am I supposed to say, no, I won't give you space to process?" I roll my eyes— totally the wrong move, I know that now. "I'm not trying to be a dick."

Mackenzie narrows her eyes. "This is about the blowjob. I told you—"

Beside me, Miles goes red and spins on his heel, turning away from us. He tucks his hands into his pockets and whistles loudly.

"I don't care about the blowjob," I tell her. She scoffs. "I care about you, and you need space, so I'm giving it to you."

"How benevolent of you," she says with a sneer.

I clench my hands into fists.

"This conversation isn't productive. If you don't want me to walk you back to your dorm, I won't, I'll just say goodnight."

She lifts her chin. "Maybe that's for the best."

I don't want to touch her, not when she's more prickly than a porcupine. I take a deep breath.

"Have a good night. Text me when you get back to your dorm."

"Yeah, okay," she says, completely noncommittal. She turns on her heel and strides away towards the freshman housing complex, practically running away from me.

"Shit," Miles says. "You fucked that up."

Yeah, I'm realizing that. I'm just not sure what I did. Get rejected from grad school? A not insignificant part of me wants my girlfriend to soothe my ruffled feelings over the rejection. I want to curl up in my bed with her in my arms and forget this day ever happened.

But last night made things awkward, and this morning was worse. Couple that with my news at dinner… yeah, I can see how she's overwhelmed. *I'm* overwhelmed. It's like there's an elephant sitting on my chest.

"So you have my baby sister giving you blowjobs now," Miles says as we head in the direction of our house.

I roll my eyes. "Do you really want to hear about our sex life?"

"Oh, so you have a sex life now?"

"Oral sex is still sex."

He makes a face.

"And no, I'm not about to go into the private details with you—or with anyone else. I respect her privacy enough to not disrespect her in that way."

"It's a little different when she's the one yelling about blowjobs in the street."

I sigh. "She said this morning that tonight she would give me a blowjob, before everything blew up."

He snorts. "Blew up."

"I'm not keeping score."

"What does that mean?"

"I don't count how often I go down on her versus how often she does the same to me. It's not a competition. I want her to feel good."

Miles frowns. "Maybe I don't want to have this conversation after all."

I roll my eyes. "Like you and Sam aren't physical with one another? We used to be able to talk about this."

"It's different when it's my baby sister."

"I respect her," I remind him. "I'm crazy about her. I would never purposefully hurt her. That's not who I am."

I leave out the fact that last night she gave me her first time, something I don't take for granted, and something he doesn't need to know.

"I can't help the fact that I might have to go away next year," I finally say.

It's not that I want to. At this point, I almost have to go. If I want the rest of my life to go according to plan, that means putting in the work now so I can get to where I want to be later. Grad school is part of that.

I have to put myself first. Mackenzie and I have only been dating for a short time. While I'm prepared to do long distance until we're both done with school, I'm not ready to put a pause on my future career before it starts.

At the end of the day, nothing in this world is guaranteed. If I don't do grad school now, when I have a very good offer from a very good school admitting me, I will only resent her later on for making me wait. If I get into Newton, I can still withdraw from Michigan, but if I give up completely and go the internship route, I know in the pit of my stomach I'm going to regret it.

Still, I don't want her to go to bed angry at me. I don't want her to be upset, period. But I can't control her emotions, and she's entitled to feel them. It's been a whirlwind of a day. I don't blame her for needing some time to process.

Good night, baby, I text her when I get back to my place. *I love you.*

I wait close to an hour. There's no response. When I wake up from a fitful night's sleep, I don't have any messages from her.

fifty-nine

. . .

Mackenzie

THE OTHER NIGHT, Wes and I had sex for the first time, and I was on top of the world. The next morning, things got a little weird, and then he basically announced to our class that he was moving away before he even bothered to tell me he didn't get into BU. Yes, there's still a chance he could get into Newton. I'm not holding my breath. Not because I don't think he can do it—absolutely I do.

It sounds like he's already made up his mind that going to Michigan is what's best for him. I just don't know that him moving twelve hours away is what's best for our relationship, and that makes me feel petulant and selfish. I'm not being a whiny brat for knowing what I'm capable of. I'm not being a demanding bitch for not being ready to think about babies and marriage right now. I'm not being an unsupportive girlfriend for wanting him to stay here.

We've been dating for a minute. It's not my place to request he stay here. He's my best friend, but now that he's my boyfriend, I'm not prepared to suddenly start mapping out the next five, ten, fifteen years of my life. I'm only nineteen. This time last year, I was still in high school. I want to live a little bit, explore the world around me. I'm not ready for the future. I'm barely ready for now.

He texted me when he got home. I didn't respond. I didn't know what to say. I still don't. Nothing feels right. I can't talk to him without talking to him about this, and I don't know how to address it.

I wake up at the crack of dawn, or seven-thirty in the morning. I don't have practice today; we hit the road tomorrow for our last away game of the season, so today we're going to meet up and watch film in the ASC. I want to swim, to aggressively propel myself through some water, but I know the swim team is still in practice.

My feet take me in the direction of the natatorium anyway. I get there right as practice is breaking up and people are getting out of the pool to head to the locker rooms. My new best friend Deisy is sitting on the starting block, bouncing her feet in the water.

"Hey. Basketball girl."

"Hey, swimmer," I tell her, and we both laugh. "How was practice?"

She sighs. "Fine. I survived. But I didn't swim well."

"Why not?"

"Okay, so I swam fine," she says. "It's just that everyone else swam faster than me."

I wince. I've had those days. I've had more of them than I would care to admit.

"I'm about to go violently hit some tennis balls and scream until I can't breathe anymore," I announce. "You want to come with?"

She blinks. "Uh, yes! Definitely. Let me throw on some clothes."

My phone buzzes in my pocket. Without pulling it out, I know it's Wes. Sure enough, when I check the screen, he's wished me a good morning. Do I want to have lunch with him?

Not really. I don't want to see his face right now, because if I do, I'm going to say something I'm going to regret. And he doesn't deserve my frustration for something he has almost no control over.

I knew this was part of the deal. I knew he was about to graduate, that this could all be temporary. He wasn't wrong for being hesitant over this very possibility when we first started.

Somewhere along the way, I fell for him, and now he's about to be yanked away from me. I can't think about three years from now, when I'll (hopefully) be graduating and we can close the distance. It might be even longer until we're able to be together again.

Deisy appears wearing workout clothes and running shoes, her bag slung over her shoulder.

"Ready?"

I nod and together we make our way towards the indoor tennis courts attached to the natatorium. The tennis teams practice in the afternoon, though with how nice the weather's been lately, they might be heading back outside.

Grabbing a bucket of balls and two racquets from the equipment lockers, we have our pick of courts—only one out of the eight is in use, all the way at the end.

She's already warm from swim practice. Quickly, I warm up and stretch my tired muscles. I'm holding the tension in between my shoulder blades. I might need to go for a stretching session and an appointment with the athletic department's physical therapists.

We volley back and forth for a few minutes. I'm not putting my all into it; I'm barely hitting the ball.

"So, do you want to talk about why you want to violently hit tennis balls and scream?" Deisy says dryly, returning the easy serve I lob her way.

"Not really."

She purses her lips. "I think you should talk about it."

If I say the words out loud, I'm the asshole. If I say it out loud, it makes it real. I take a deep breath.

"My boyfriend is almost definitely going to grad school out of state."

"Okay…"

"And I'm here for another three years."

She winces. "That's not ideal."

"We've only been dating for two and a half months."

Deisy passes the ball to me three times before she speaks. "Are you sure you want to do long distance?"

"I'm really not."

"Oh."

The ball sails past her. She fishes a new one out of the bucket.

"Yeah. Exactly. I'm not… I don't know."

"Do you want to stay with him?"

"Yes."

She catches the tennis ball with her racquet and turns to me. "Really?"

I sigh. "I don't know."

"So…"

I whack the ball as hard as I can. It sails past her again.

"I don't want to break up," I tell her.

"So don't. Do long distance."

"But I don't want to be stuck here while he's there."

She blows out a breath. "So what are you going to do?"

"I really don't know."

sixty

. . .

Wes

I KNOW she's busy with her last away game of the season. I know she has other things on her plate. But it's been four days since I've talked to Mackenzie, and I'm starting to get worried. No, I'm not starting; I'm already there. My medicated anxiety has ratcheted up five levels in the last few days. I get that she needs space. Does that space mean she can't talk to me? She can't respond to my texts?

What makes it worse is that everyone seems to know that she and I were... amorous the other night. It's not like she was particularly quiet. Amir clapped me on the back Monday night with a smirk. Greg grins every time he lays eyes on me. Barrett and Tucker look like they're hiding a secret. And Miles? Yeah, he's not as oblivious as we would like to pretend. He knows we fool around. It's only a matter of time before he knows exactly what happened.

Normally, I wouldn't care that the guys know what we got up to. Coming on the heels of whatever tension this is... yeah, that's not exactly fun.

While she's away, I make more of an effort than usual to spend time with the guys. Barrett and I go to breakfast on Wednesday at the diner, before we head to our classes. Tucker and I work out on Thursday afternoon. That night, I have dinner with my five roommates, a rare occasion when we're not joined by any of the guys' lovely girlfriends. Not that I mind spending time with them. I don't. But sometimes it's nice to just hang with the guys again.

Miles is texting all through Jeopardy!, which makes me a little annoyed. I know he's planning some sort of party for after Sam's last softball game. That must be what he's up to.

"Have you talked to Mack lately?" he asks.

"I don't want to talk about it."

Tucker snorts. "That means no."

"You two are still fighting?" Amir asks.

"We're not fighting. She needed space. I'm giving her space." I pick up my book and try to hide behind the pages.

Barrett laughs. "You're just like the rest of us."

"I never said I wasn't?"

"I've seen you pull lines out of books. You think you're so slick," he says.

I mean...

"Where's your romance novel now? How are you going to fix this?"

He's not taunting; he's genuinely asking.

I blow out a breath. I don't know. None of the books I've read have given me a roadmap that will work. I need to give her space. By encroaching on her, I would only be making things worse.

I'm leaving in a matter of months. Weeks, really. We should be spending all of our time wrapped up in each other, not... whatever this is.

Miles' phone rings with a video chat. I can't see the screen from this angle.

"Hey, Mack," he says, and my stomach sinks like a rock. "We were just talking about you."

"Don't do that," she laughs. "Nothing good will come of that."

"Say hi to everyone," he says, and then turns the phone around to pan across the room.

"Hey, guys," she says, giving us a cheerful wave.

"Do you want to talk to Wes?" Miles stands and walks across the room to where I'm sitting.

"Um, sure."

Is it just me or is that dread in her voice?

Taking the phone from her brother's hand, I smile at the camera with an enthusiasm that is entirely forced. "Hey, baby."

"Hi. Listen, I've got to go," she says.

"Oh, okay."

"I'll talk to you later."

"Sure."

She hangs up in a hurry.

"Damn," Greg says, raising his eyebrows. "What the hell did you do?"

I really wish I knew.

———

Sarah has been overly involved in my life ever since our parents died. She changed from being a big sister to an almost parental role, making sure I got to school on time and enrolled in my college classes and paid my health insurance and credit card bills regularly. It has always concerned her how quiet I was, how alone in the world I am, how few friends I had. It didn't bother me, at least not overly so, but I know it weighed on her.

I wasn't in the car. The accident wasn't my fault. But my PTSD doesn't care. I've been to a half a dozen shrinks in the last five years, trying to get over it. I don't know that there is any getting over it. My parents are dead. Losing them was traumatic. They were ripped from this earth with no warning. Some idiot kid ran a red light and my parents paid the price.

My sister didn't want to go away to law school, but the financial aid package at the University of Washington was too good to pass up. After I changed my commitment from Michigan to Newton, she started applying to transfer to schools in New England, too. I tried to tell her not to, that she needed to live her own life. In the end, money made the difference. She's graduating with close to no student debt, and that wouldn't have been the case if she had come out here for law school.

She has one more year until she graduates. She can take the bar exam in any state that she desires. If I'm in Michigan for two more years… well, I don't know that she'll join me there. She hated it back home, even before the accident. More than likely, she'll go where the wind takes her, find a job, and then when I graduate, I'll join her there. After all the sacrifices my sister has made in the last five years, I can move to the city of her choosing. We don't have to live together—I really don't want to live with her ever again—but we can be in the same zip code. Being in the same time zone, after all these years away from each other, might be nice.

With all the weirdness with Mackenzie the last few days… it's times like this I wish my dad were still around. Not that I ever talked to him about girls. He was utterly useless in that regard. Still, it's the comfort of having a parental figure around that I can lean on and ask for advice. Who am I going to ask, Mr. Cavanaugh? Hey, can you tell me what's up with your daughter? Yeah, I'm sure that's going to go over well.

I don't know how to have this conversation with Sarah. I've never talked to her about girls. Sometimes she would tease me when I started dating someone new, the very few times it happened. For the most part, she left me alone, and I didn't make fun of her boyfriends. A tentative truce.

Now, though… I need some advice. Clarity. Someone smarter than me to tell me what to do. I know Mackenzie and

I need to have a conversation. I'm not sure I'm going to like what she has to say.

I'm crazy about this girl. But she's still a girl, only nineteen. We're in completely different places in our lives. And there's nothing wrong with that. It is what it is.

This is my chance to look in the mirror and decide what I really want. Do I stay with the girl I've been dating for two months, the girl I want a future with? Or do I go to Michigan, friendless and alone? This time, I won't even have the cold comfort of a new football team to fall back on. I'll be starting over from scratch.

I don't see a way to go away to Michigan and still keep Mackenzie. Long distance isn't perfect. She'll find someone better, someone her age who is smarter and more articulate and more suited than a monosyllabic bookworm with no friends twelve hours away.

Michigan only gave me two more days to make a decision. The clock is running out. It's now or never.

sixty-one

. . .

Mackenzie

AFTER OUR VIDEO CALL, I don't talk to Wes for another two days. I don't know how to have this conversation. Finally, I text him on the bus ride home: *We need to talk.*

He's standing in the parking lot with a book in his hands, but he isn't reading it. His chin is lifted, his eyes tracking the movement of the bus.

"Shit, girl," Pia says. "What did you do to that boy?"

"What do you mean?"

"He already looks heartbroken, and you haven't even gotten off the bus yet."

My stomach sinks. That's the last thing I wanted.

When I step off the bus, he offers me a small smile, uncharacteristically timid. "Hey, Mackenzie."

He almost never says my full name. He always calls me babe or baby. I like the little pet names. It's a subtle way he tells me how much he cares for me.

"We should talk," I say, and he nods tightly.

He doesn't take my hand. Wes walks towards the bench in front of the building. It's hard to forget we're in a grubby parking lot with weeds and dirt and gravel.

"How was your trip?"

"It went well." I roomed with Pia, who snored both nights, and it kind of lulled me to sleep. It reminded me of Wes's snoring, crazy as that sounds. It wasn't nearly as comforting, though.

"I can't stand this awkwardness, this tension between us," he says.

"Okay."

"If you don't want to be with me, I need you to come right out and tell me," he says flatly. "Don't tiptoe around it. Because this in-between thing we've got going on, where you ignore me and don't talk to me, that's not working for me."

"Fine. Then maybe we shouldn't do this anymore," I snap.

He rears back, like I've physically slapped him. "Is that what you want?"

"I don't want to stick around pining for you when you aren't here," I tell him flatly. "The long distance thing? That's not going to work for me. Either we're together or we aren't."

"We can still be together and make long distance work. I'll come out to visit every free weekend, and—"

"Wes, you're going to be twelve hours away," I remind him. "You're not going to drive here every weekend. You'll be busy with grad school. You'll need to study. And I don't want to be the reason you live half a life, coming back here all the time when you should be living it up in Ann Arbor."

"I don't want to live it up. I want to be with you."

"Yeah, I want you to be with me, too. But I don't want to hold you back from doing the things you need to be doing."

"I could still get into Newton. I could still stay here."

I pin him with a look. "Do you really want to wait for an if and a maybe? It's only going to hurt more when you have to leave. I'd rather we rip off the band-aid now than wait three more months. We might have even less time together if you don't stay here for the summer."

He swallows hard. "I hadn't even thought about summer. I was planning on staying."

"Where? You can't stay in Athlete's Village. You'll have graduated. What, you're going to rent a hotel room for two and a half months?"

"I hadn't gotten that far," he admits. "I was so focused on getting into either Newton or BU and then finding an apartment off campus. I hadn't planned on moving to Michigan. I don't *want* to move to Michigan."

"But you're going."

He sighs. "Yeah. I have to. It's what's best for my career."

Although not necessarily what's best for him as a person.

"I don't want to hold you back," I tell him gently. "You should be present and in the moment, not thinking about some girl a handful of states away."

He frowns. "You're not some girl. You're more than that. Give yourself some credit."

I swallow back the emotions threatening to rise up and overtake me. "I don't want to do this, but I feel like we have to. And it's better to do it now, when we have time to learn how to function with one another again, than at the end of the semester."

"I don't want to lose you."

"I'm staying right here. I'm not going anywhere."

That's half the problem.

"We can still be—"

"Don't," he says sharply. "Don't say we can still be friends."

"Well, we can. We can make it work. You were my best friend before we started dating."

"I don't think I can go back to just being your friend," he says flatly. "I know what you look like naked. I know what you taste like. Friends don't. I can't spend time with you and not want to be with you. After everything we've gone through, I can't go backwards."

"So then…"

"Then it's done. It's over," he says. His voice cracks on the last word.

And then my heart decides to shatter into a million pieces.

————

I don't know what to do. I have this inexplicable urge to crawl into my bed and cry into my pillow. I don't *want* to break up, but it's something that we have to do. It's for the best, for both of us.

So why does it hurt so fucking much?

Claire's side of the dorm room is messy, clothes strewn about everywhere. She's even piled a few things onto my bed. I shove them to the floor and crawl into my bed, curling into a ball. Even though I've been sleeping here since August, it still doesn't feel like *my* bed. It's just a mattress and some blankets. Wes's bed? Yeah, that felt like home.

I don't know where we go from here. He's my best friend. Really, he's my only real friend here on campus. Yeah, I have Deisy now, but we have a much more surface level friendship. We work out together. I hope that one day we can be actual friends who hang out and confide in each other and do all the things friends do, but we're not there yet. I have the rest of the guys and Sam, Mason, and Diana, but they're only friends with me because of who my brother is. Dareesa? We haven't spent time together outside of practice in weeks. She's firmly in the teammate category, not friend tier. Nothing against her. She's great. She just hasn't put any effort in trying to be more, and I can't be the only one who tries.

My world feels so much smaller now. An hour ago, I had —well, I knew it was about to end, but I didn't know it would end in such a spectacular fashion. As much as I didn't want it to end, it's better to do it now than to drag it out another few months.

Do I tell my parents? Miles? I don't know how this works.

It's not like we're publicly together on social media—I don't have to do a relationship status change on my U.Me page. Will Wes tell his roommates, or will they figure it out when I stop coming around? It's not like I've been around much since the night we had sex, anyway.

Shit. Do they know we had sex?

I don't regret having sex with Wes. There is no better man that I would want my first time to be with. He cherished me and took care of me and made me feel so, so loved. It's exactly what I thought sex would always be like. It was perfect.

It's just the next morning where the wheels fell off. Sarah's surprise visit probably didn't help matters, either. And then the rejection from BU...

Yeah, looking back, I probably didn't handle that as gracefully as I could have. It took me by surprise. Then again, I'm sure it did him, too. BU was his second choice school. And with Newton still not getting back to him, he was pinning all of his hopes on going to the school only a few miles away....

If he were to go to BU, if he were to go to Newton... yeah, my response would have been different. I could handle a relationship that crossed city lines. What I can't survive is him being twelve hours away for two or more years. And then he'd graduate, and I'd still have at least one more year of school left, and...

I'm weak. Sue me, but I know what I can and can't handle, and the distance would drive me insane. Two or more years of that? Coupled with my intense travel schedule during basketball season, and not having any friends, most everyone I know graduating... yeah, it would not have been an ideal situation for me. I know myself well enough to know it wouldn't have been good.

It wasn't a platitude; I do still want to be Wes's friend. Maybe not right away, but down the line, yeah, I can see us staying in touch and—

No. No, I can't. Because all I see when I look at him is the perfect first boyfriend, the guy who introduced me to good books and relationships and sex. The guy who loved me so wholly, so intensely, that he nearly burned himself alive trying to keep me warm. The guy who had enough self-respect to stand up for himself and tell me what I was doing wasn't okay in his book.

So I'm going to spend a little bit of time feeling sorry for myself, mourning the friendship and relationship that I lost, and then I'll start the process of picking up the pieces and moving on. For right now, though, I'm going to mourn the loss of the brightest part of my day, the person who made me so incredibly happy I couldn't imagine doing this without him, a half life where he was twelve hours away and I missed him all the fucking time.

Because that wouldn't have been a way to live for two (or more) years. We both deserve the chance to be happy. Missing him all the time wouldn't have made me happy, and with my basketball schedule and lack of income, it would be highly doubtful that I'd be able to come visit him more than once a year. It would be unfair to pin all of the visits on him, and considering how poorly he communicates over the phone and via text...

It was better this way, to end it before we both got in too deep. Even though he says he loves me, we're still young enough that he can find someone new, someone more suited to him, someone on his level. Maybe he'll meet her in his graduate program. She could be in his classes or live in the apartment next door. She might even be a client. It would be like something right out of a romance novel. The broken-hearted guy gets a second chance at love and finally finds it with the perfect heroine.

Because that's not me. I'm not perfect, and I'm certainly not perfect for him. I'm weak. We were together for two and a half months, and the first third of that was in secret. I want to be with someone who I can be with for a long time, someone who respects what I can and cannot give him. I'm not looking for happy ever after, but happy for now.

For a few weeks, I really thought that guy was Wes. I thought we could make it work. The stress of traveling for basketball every ten days really rammed home how difficult the distance makes a relationship. Now change that to being semi-permanently twelve hours away, and both of us with tough academic workloads, and add in my travel schedule… It all seems so impossible, so incredibly insurmountable.

How do other people do it? How do they manage long distance for weeks or months at a time? Years? We had the luxury of knowing it was a finite amount of time. Two years, plus however long it takes me to graduate. I'm still a freshman. I might take a fifth year, I might change my major, I might not graduate on time. So much is up in the air for me. And then add his graduate program on top of that…

Really, all of our problems would have been solved if he were to stay in the city. BU is only a few miles away. I could see him once or twice a week, we could spend the weekends together, he would be only half an hour away in case of emergency. We could still arrange for dinners together and sleepovers and date nights once or twice a week. He would still be local.

I understand why he feels he has to go to Michigan. I get that it's the best thing for his career. But it's not the best thing for our relationship, and I can't ask him to sacrifice his entire future for someone he's been dating for two and a half months, no matter how he feels for me. At the end of the day, we both need to put ourselves first: he has to focus on his career, and I have to be honest with what I can and cannot handle. And long distance? That would break me. I'm not strong enough for that, and admitting it only proves how much stronger I would need to be.

sixty-two

Mackenzie

EVEN THOUGH IT'S only the middle of April, it feels like it's the end of the year. Basketball is almost done for the year —we have one more away game left to the season. Midterms have come and gone. All too soon, it's time for the final home softball game of the year: senior night.

My brother's been working on something special for Sam for the culmination of her softball career. He's been in communication with her parents, who have come up from Mississippi for the weekend. I don't think he's going to propose: they haven't been dating nearly long enough to be ready for marriage, and I know she's unsure about her plans for after graduation.

I haven't told Miles what happened. I'm pretty sure Wes did. The day after I got home, Miles texted me to meet him for breakfast, and when I found him in the dining hall, he pulled me into a tight hug. We had breakfast just the two of us, and he didn't mention my boyfriend—ex-boyfriend— once. He spoke casually about this weekend, about our parents finally getting a chance to meet Sam's parents, about the small party he's organizing with a few of the other soft-ball players' significant others. There are four seniors and one junior who is graduating a year early. It's also the first time he's meeting Sam's parents.

"Where's Wes?" my dad asks. "I haven't seen you two more than a foot apart in the past few months."

I swallow. I don't want to say the words.

Instead, I nod to the first row, where he's sitting with the rest of his roommates and their girlfriends. "He's over there."

"You're not sitting with him?"

"Not today," I say lightly.

Dad frowns.

"It's fine. Everything is fine," I insist.

Ashley rolls her eyes. "Clearly."

"But—"

"They broke up," Miles interjects. "They're not together anymore."

My pulse echoes dully in my ears. My heart starts beating a trillion beats too fast. I think I'm going to pass out. I think I'm going to puke. I think I'm going to—

Dad cracks his knuckles. "I'm going to bash his face in."

"Please, don't." I lay my hand on Dad's arm. "It was mutual. It was both of our decision."

"He said he loved you. He said to my face—"

I swallow again. "I know. It was the right decision for both of us. He's going to be moving to Michigan in a few short weeks. It was the right time. It's better for this to happen now than a few months down the line."

Mom sighs. "Oh, honey…" She pulls me into a hug.

Inhaling sharply, I let myself take comfort in the support my mother is offering. She liked Wes. She liked us together. She's always had a soft spot for the quiet bookaholic who wore his pain—and his heart—on his sleeve.

Nobody is at fault. He didn't cheat on me. He didn't abuse me. He didn't break my heart. It just… didn't work out. If anything, the timing is at fault. We only have a few more weeks in the same city, in the same college town.

I've seen him around—in the dining hall, in our public speaking class, in the hallway once, now in the front row—but I haven't talked to him, haven't run into him. I've been giving him his space. I sit by myself at meals and in the front row during class.

Before the start of the softball game, the five graduating students are presented with bouquets of flowers and framed pictures celebrating their years of accomplishments. The team is tight-knit and supportive of one another.

I wish the basketball team gelled even half as well as the softball team does. I wish the girls I play with were even half as supportive as the softball team.

Blowing out a breath, I adjust in my seat and focus my attention on the game in front of me. Every so often, my eyes drift in the direction of the front row, and I have to swallow and force my gaze ahead again.

My mom slides her arm around my shoulder. "It'll be okay, Mack."

I want to believe her. I want it to be true. It's just that right now everything feels so impossible.

So I pull a Wes, and I pull out my e-reader. I lose myself in the thrall of a good book while the world moves on around me. Miles splits his time between our family, his friends, and dropping in on Sam's parents and brother, who are at the end of the row in front of us. Mom and Ashley discuss the plans for the senior prom coming up in a few weeks. Dad cheers and hollers for every hit, the world's biggest cheerleader for every single sport. It all flows in one ear and out the other.

The game is a bloodbath. Sam and her team are winning 9-1 by the bottom of the third inning. The ladies are determined to send their seniors off with a bang, and they succeed—big time. They are statistically out of the playoffs, but that doesn't mean they don't put in the effort when it counts.

My parents ask about my classes and my upcoming final

exams. They talk about my cousins and our neighbors and everything under the sun—everything except for Wes.

After the game, we all head to McRory's pub, where the back room is reserved for the seniors' send-off party. Between team and staff, parents, friends, and significant others, there are close to a hundred people crammed into the room.

Ordinarily I would be by Wes's side, holding his hand as he struggles with the crowds and the chaos. That's not my job anymore.

So I sit at a table with my sister and my parents and let the party continue on around me. I make small talk with Sam's brother, who is about five or six years older than me, and two inches shorter than me. We have absolutely nothing in common—he was a football player, doesn't like to read, only watches action movies, and is more interested in getting laid tonight with any available coed than in getting to know his sister's longtime boyfriend's family.

There are speeches from the team's coach and awards presented to the seniors. One of the girls' dads gets up and makes a clearly drunken speech. Ash and I hang out at our table. She's uncharacteristically quiet.

Sam is in the center of the room, chatting with Tamar and her parents. My brother stands and brushes off his hands before he makes his way confidently to her. He taps her on the shoulder and she breaks off in the middle of her sentence, breaking into a smile.

"Hey, babe," she says, and he kisses her cheek. "What's up?"

Miles takes her hands in his and swallows. "Sam… baby…"

There are a few nervous titters in the crowd. Her mom giggles shrilly.

"This last year and a half has been so amazing, I still wake up and have to remind myself this isn't some vivid dream," he says, and she smiles slightly. "You make me so incredibly happy. You make me a stronger person, a better man. You make me want to keep learning and growing and improving. I doubt I would have survived the last year and a half without you, and I know I wouldn't have wanted to. You're the best thing that's happened to me in my entire life. I love you."

She swallows thickly, her eyes wide.

"Sam, I can't offer you forever," Miles says, and she lets out a nervous breath. "I won't make promises I can't keep. But what I can do is love you, and keep on loving you for as long as you let me. So if you want to move back to Mississippi after graduation, or any other city on this planet, I'll move there with you. Because I want to be with you, from now until forever, and I'm not going to let you pass me by. I'm in this, baby."

My eyes well with tears of happiness for them. Despite my better judgment, I let my gaze drift over to where the roommates are assembled. Tucker has his arm around Mason, who's beaming with happiness. Barrett has Diana in his arms, murmuring something into her ear. Amir and Greg stand shoulder to shoulder. And Wes...

My breath catches. He's staring right at me, his face creased with sorrow.

My heart stops beating. My lungs forget how to breathe. I'm rooted to the spot, pinned there by his gaze, hungry and longing and pained and regretful.

I didn't want to break up. I didn't want to end it. But it made the most sense. It was the right decision, for both of us. I wouldn't survive the long distance, and he deserves to be with someone who is capable of fighting for him.

He'll find someone better for him, some quirky bookworm who is smart and pretty and has a strong social network. Maybe he'll chat up the library sciences students, or he'll trawl around the bookstores looking for women. As much as he'll probably hate it, it'll be good for him to spread his wings a little bit. He needs to expand his social horizons.

I wonder what he's thinking. Does he wish it had worked out? I know I do. I would give my right arm for a way for him to stay in town *and* attend graduate school at the same time, a way for him to stay close and still achieve his dreams.

Today's the day. He had to either accept Michigan's offer or let someone else take his spot from the waiting list. I don't know that he's heard from Newton yet, and if it wasn't good news, I don't think I'd be on the list of people who would be privy to that information anymore.

I want the best for him, and sometimes that will be something that isn't the best for me. I want Wes to succeed, to triumph over life's hardships. As painful as this is, as insurmountable as it feels, I know losing our relationship will only make him stronger. Yeah, it might harden his heart. It might be harder for the next girl to break into his shell. But when she does, she will discover a precious gem worthy of being cherished. Worthy of more than I am capable of giving.

Because I'm pretty fucking sure I'm in love with the bastard. I've never been in love before. But this fluttery feeling in my chest, the jittery feeling in my veins, the heart palpitations and stomach swooping that happens whenever he's nearby… yeah, that's not ideal. I can hardly breathe, hardly think when he's around, and then he says something, and it's like a fog has lifted because I can be a functional human being again. I feel like the best possible version of myself when I'm with him, and at the same time, being around him makes me want to be better.

I spent two days crying into my pillow. Claire even walked in on the middle of one of my crying jags, took one look at my face, and turned right around and left, so maybe there's some hope in the world. Now that I've done my mourning, I'm ready to get on with my day. I'm still a little sad, a little down in my feelings, but I'm ready to move on. I can be happy for my brother and his girlfriend and still wish my own relationship had ended differently.

Excusing myself, I head to the bar. I can't drink alcohol—not legally, anyway—and I'm not about to try to get the pub into trouble. I order a sparkling water with a splash of cranberry juice and lean against the bar top.

"You okay, Mackie?"

Exhaling slowly, I turn to look at Greg, who's watching me with a frown.

"Oh, I'm great."

He laughs. "Yeah, let's pretend like I believe that."

I shrug. I don't have the energy to pretend I don't feel absolutely miserable.

"So I'm guessing you've heard."

"That you and whatshisface?" He winks. "Yeah, it's been made clear that we're not to ask you about it. So I'm just going to stand here and sip my drink, and if you want to bare your soul, I have two comforting shoulders for you to lean on."

"Thanks, Greg." I offer him a small smile and take the drink the bartender hands me.

"You going to the Delta party tonight?"

I hate parties. Hate them. They're always full of drunk people groping each other or trying to get high. The guys sit around playing video games and the girls are expected to dress in skimpy clothes and preen under their lackluster attention. It's hell.

Tonight, though…

I take a sip of my drink. "You're going to be there?"

"Yeah. Of course."

"I might have to go this time."

———

Greg meets me at my dorm room at nine o'clock. I'm not under any impression that this is a date. He's a nice guy, doing a nice thing by escorting me across campus to the Delta house. We are most assuredly not going to the party *together*, we're just two friends who are walking someplace at the same time.

"Hey, Mackie," he says when I open the door. His eyes go wide. "Shit, you look hot."

My cheeks heat. "Thanks, I think."

I'm wearing a short black skirt, made shorter by the optical illusion of my mile-long legs, and a shirt that displays far more cleavage than I've ever shown save for a bikini at the beach. The light sweater draped over my arm can't possibly cover me up from head to toe… which is kind of the point.

"You sure you want to go out? We can stay in. Watch a movie or something. You got any of those book things?"

I laugh. "I think I'm good on staying in for a while. It's time to go out."

He swallows loudly and sweeps his arm out in front of him. "M'lady."

"Look at you, being a gentleman."

"I try," he says, giving me a roguish wink. "Not very hard, that is."

I laugh again. He jabs the button for the elevator and then presses it again a few more times.

"Relax. It's okay."

He blows out a breath and mumbles something. It sounds distinctly like "I'm going to hell."

The elevator doors slide open and we come across Dareesa and Lauren, both wearing skinny jeans and tall heels.

"Hey, girl!" Dareesa says. Her eyes flick over to Greg and then back to me. "Hot date?"

I develop a suspicious coughing fit.

Greg laughs. "I'm gorgeous, I know, but I'm always happy to hear it confirmed from other people."

Dareesa blushes and Lauren grins.

"We're just friends," I reassure them. "He's my brother's roommate."

"Ouch," Greg says, sticking an arm in the elevator for me to pass through. "And here I thought we were going to get married and have ten million babies."

"Please. You? Get married?"

"You never know, I might do it one day," he says defensively.

Greg is headed straight to the NFL, where he's going to have even more droves of women pawing at him than already do. He's going to have no shortage of willing and wanting women ready to sleep with him.

"Well, I only hope I'm invited to your wedding," I tell him, and he winks at me.

"Baby, you'll be in the wedding party."

"You guys going out?" I ask my teammates, trying to keep the conversation going.

"We were going to go see if any of the parties on Greek Row will let us in," Lauren says.

Some of the fraternities will card and only allow those over twenty-one in. Others are exclusive to Greek Life students. Still more will let anyone in... until the building reaches capacity, and then they cut off the line.

"You come with us to Delta, I'll get you in," Greg says confidently.

Dareesa eyes him curiously. "Really?"

He's a popular junior and he's a football player, plus he's the son of a former NFL player, so yeah, Greg has some sway. He doesn't use his power for evil, though. He's a fun-loving guy who likes to kick back and have a good time. And, yeah, occasionally he sleeps around. That's not a crime.

"Yeah. Any friend of Mackie's is a friend of mine," he says.

The elevator chimes and slides open. He gestures for us to

head out before he follows us into the lobby. When we get to the front doors, he opens them for us, then tucks his hands into his leather jacket.

Dareesa and Lauren are quiet on the walk over to Greek Row. I'm not upset they're joining us. If anything, it almost feels like fate. This is what college is supposed to be like: going to parties with my friends and teammates, going out on a Saturday night and living my life. Not holing up in my brother's house with a book and sitting on the couch hoping one day the cute boy will notice me.

Well, he did notice me. He fell in love with me, and me with him.

I rest my hand on Greg's arm, and he turns to look at me.

"I need to drink tonight," I tell him, and he nods seriously. "Don't let me get trashed. I don't want… don't let me get wasted. I just need to relax and have a good time."

"Of course, Mackie," he says, his voice softening. "I've got your back."

As he predicted, Greg gets waved into the party with the three of us on his arm. He sets his arm around my shoulders and maneuvers me through the crowd until we reach the keg. He pours four beers and hands them off to each of us before he takes his.

"Now what?"

"Now we hang out," he says. "We can chill in here or in any of the rooms." A thought strikes him and he swallows. "Don't go into any of the bedrooms with any guys."

I pin him with a look. "Seriously?"

"Look, I don't care what happened with you and Wes. If you want to get it on with some guy, great, fine, you do you. Just don't do it here," he says. "Go back to the guy's place and hook up there. If you hook up with someone here, it'll be all over campus in two hours. You deserve better than to be the latest rumor in the gossip mill."

I swallow. "I don't… I'm not trying to…"

"I know. And I'm not trying to be a patronizing asshole," he says, a little defensively. "These parties are awful. If you disappear into a bedroom with some guy, everyone will be talking about it. I won't stop you if you want to hook up with someone."

My stomach twists. "I'm not ready…"

He exhales slowly. "So you and Wes… it's really over?"

I sigh. "Yeah. We're done."

"That's too bad," he says lightly, taking a drink of his beer. "You guys were good for one another."

"Yeah, I like to think so."

"I mean, I've been trying to get you to one of these parties all year," he says. "You've never come."

"Hanging out with him was the most fun way to spend a Saturday night," I explain. "He's the person I want to spend time with, no matter the time of day. He was my best friend."

"So what happened?"

There's a lump in my throat. "He's leaving. And I'm not ready for two or more years of long distance."

Greg winces. "Yeah, that's a little rough."

"It's not that I don't l-love him," I continue. "I do."

It's the first time I've said the words out loud. It feels impossible, and at the same time, so incredibly right.

He sighs. "Sometimes it's the ones we love the most that are capable of hurting us in innumerable ways," he says quietly.

"If he were staying here, if he didn't have to move to Michigan, I would try to make it work. I want to be with him." I run a hand through my hair. "But I also know what I can and can't tolerate, and I'm not okay with two years of twelve hours between us. It's too far. It's not fair to either of us."

He frowns. "I'm sorry, Mackie."

"Yeah," I say, taking a pull of my beer. "Me, too."

sixty-three

. . .

Wes

MACKENZIE IS AT A PARTY. She's at a party with Greg. My roommate. My teammate. My brother.

I don't normally scroll through social media on a lonely Saturday night. Imagine my surprise when I get a notification that my girlfriend—*ex*-girlfriend—is at a frat party and getting drunk and having a grand old time. Without me.

I have half a mind to go to the frat party right now and confront her. Them. What are they doing together? Is he trying to make a move on my girl? Just because we've broken up doesn't mean she's suddenly available. She's mine.

In nearly five years at college, I have never been to a frat party. From what I've seen of them in books and movies and, occasionally, through my friends' social media profiles, there's nothing there to interest me. I'm not the type of guy who hooks up and has casual sex. I don't drink. I don't smoke. The only thing I'm even vaguely interested in is playing video games, and I can do that at my house.

Greg has invited Mackenzie to parties half a dozen times. She's always declined. I wonder why she accepted this time. I wonder why they're there together. It's not that they can't be friends. They get along well enough. But they've never been friendly in the way she and I were before everything started between us, and he's never tried to encroach on anyone else's girl before.

Her teammates are in the pictures, too. I would think everything is cool except for the fact that Greg has his arm around Mackenzie and they're talking really close. That's not how a guy talks to a girl he doesn't care for.

I'm alone in the house. Miles and Sam, Tucker and Mason, and Barrett and Diana are all at the frat party. Amir and Jill are at a field hockey party. Greg is with Mackenzie. And I... I am alone. I'm always alone.

This is what the next two years will be like: alone on a Saturday night, alone on every night. No friends, because once I'm at Michigan, I won't have the brotherhood of teammates to fall back on. I'll be starting over, not from step one, but from step negative one: I'll have lost my community, my friends, my girlfriend, and everything else I hold near and dear. I won't have the security of spending five years in the same place, growing up and figuring out who I am. I won't be stepping into a locker room of compatriots, of equals, guys who will shed blood, sweat, and tears with me on the football field and in the weights room.

I'll be alone in a new state, in a new graduate program, in a new world. I won't be a football player and student athlete. I'll be a whole new person, a whole new me.

Maybe that's why I torture myself by opening up Newton's graduate portal. For weeks I've been hopelessly refreshing the portal, desperate for an answer. One way or another, I want to know.

The portal loads. I nearly drop my phone.

Holy. Shit.

I got in.

I got accepted.

Newton wants me.

What the fuck.

I need to—I need to—

I have nobody to tell. My sister, yeah. That's it. My roommates won't really care. Mackenzie doesn't give two shits anymore. I have—

I have nobody.

That's sobering. While I was moderately concerned five seconds ago, this only serves to remind me how little people care about what happens to me, how few people there are in the world that give a shit about me. Who am I going to tell? Who am I going to share my news with?

The only person I want to talk to is Mackenzie. She's the one I want to be sharing this with. Even setting aside our relationship, she was still the best friend I ever had. She gets me on a fundamental level that I've never experienced with anyone else. Not my parents. Not my sister. Not my buddies on the football team.

It's her. It's always been her.

From fighting over books to staying in on a Saturday night to holding her in my arms, she's the only person I want to do this with. I don't care if she doesn't want to be my girlfriend anymore.

I know I said we couldn't be friends. I don't know that I'm capable of it anymore.

With this simple acceptance notification, so much has changed. I don't have to move away anymore. I can—I can stay. I don't have to move twelve hours away. I don't have to go to a school I'm not crazy about in a state I hate and surrounded by nobody I know.

I can stay.

I can find a cheap apartment off campus. I can still hang out with my friends who are sticking around campus for another year or two. I don't have to give up my entire life. Sunday mornings can still be spent at the diner with Tricia and all the ladies who cluck over me like I'm theirs. Rainy afternoons in the library with James the librarian.

I don't have to leave.

Quickly I read through the details of the acceptance notice, then read it again to make sure it sticks. Newton is offering a similar financial aid package to the one Michigan was offering. Sure, cost of living is higher, so I will need a little more money for rent and daily expenses, but that's not a reason to turn down acceptance to the best physical therapy program on the East Coast. And in the long run, this is what will make me happiest: in my top choice program, the school I've already been at for the last five years and know that I like, with the professors who know me and accept me for who I am.

Mackenzie aside, my friends aside, this is still the program I want to do the most.

And if Mackenzie is here... yeah, maybe I was a little hasty. Maybe we can be friends.

I don't pretend to believe she would take me back. I drew a line in the sand, she couldn't meet it, and we split. It was for the best.

But now I don't have to go away. The long distance point is moot. For at least the next two years, we're going to be in the same city—in the same school. I'll only be a few minutes away instead of twelve hours. We don't have to torture ourselves.

I want her back: I want to be with her. I didn't want to break up. I just wanted her to stop playing childish games.

Then again, she's young. This is her first relationship. She doesn't know what is and isn't okay in romantic relationships, and if my enforcing a boundary is what teaches her...

My feelings for her haven't changed. I'm still utterly in love with her. I still want a future with her, to get married and have babies and be happy together. Not yet—definitely not yet. But five or ten years from now... she's the one I see by my side. It's her. It's always been her.

I tell myself I'm fine. I pretend I'm okay. There's always

that one person that fucks someone else up for good. Mackenzie is that person for me. She's the one that's getting away, the one that is perfect. If we're a jigsaw puzzle, she's a stubborn middle piece trying to connect to the sharp edges of a corner piece. I don't connect to other people, only to her.

Do I go to the frat party and try to get her back? That might work in romance novels, but life isn't fiction, and I know I need to earn her trust back. Just because I'm able to stay here doesn't mean she will take me back.

It's been three days without her, and every single minute has been agony. Being in the same room as her? Painful. Not being able to hug her or hold her hand? Torture. Knowing this distance between us is because of me? Excruciating.

At the softball party earlier this evening, I almost stalked across the room and punched out the guy talking to her. I'm pretty sure he was Sam's brother. I'm fairly certain there's nothing between them. Still, I was ready to beat him to a pulp just for talking to her.

That's not healthy. I can recognize that. I'm not a jealous type of guy. Self-defense classes aside, I'm not the type of guy who gets into fights. I'll stand up for what I believe in, for those physically weaker than I am, but I'm not an instigator. Even when we were together, I didn't feel this type of murderous rage at the idea of Mackenzie talking to other guys. But between this guy tonight and now Greg... I'm seeing red.

Does my staying in town change anything for her? If I stay —and I'm not staying because of her, I'm staying for me— does that mean she would want to be with me? Regardless of her decision, I'm sticking around town for at least the next two years. After I graduate, I can take an internship and hopefully land a good starting job. There are a lot of sports teams in town, and even more colleges and universities with strong athletics programs. There's got to be some sort of program for physical therapy students to get their hands dirty.

Eventually, the goal is to work with professional sports teams, in whatever capacity I can. I know I'll have to put the work in now to get to that point later. I'm not about to get a spot in the Patriots' staff right out of school. I'll have to work my way up the ladder, learning as I go. The learning will never stop.

Does one year of potential long distance make a difference? I can't guarantee that I will graduate and immediately find a job here. Hell, by the time she graduates, she might be ready to move on and tackle a brand new city rather than the one she's lived in all her life.

But if she makes that decision, I will happily move there with her. I want to be by her side, wherever that is. I'm not interested in a quick hookup or casual sex. Mackenzie makes me long for a future for us.

Does she like going to parties? I hate them, but for her, I'd show up. Even if all I do is sit in the corner and not socialize much, I won't stop her from drinking and having a good time as long as she doesn't make me drink. We can go out on more dates—dinner out and trips to the bookstore and picnics in the park in good weather, ice skating at the Common in the winter. Exploring the larger city around us.

It's going to be challenging, sure. She has to balance school and basketball, and this physical therapy program isn't exactly a walk in the park. But I have confidence that together we can survive it, together we can survive anything.

If only she wants to get back together.

sixty-four

. . .

Mackenzie

SINCE THE PARTY the other night, Dareesa has reached out to me twice over social media and Lauren once, asking if I want to go out for coffee or a run or an emergency donut trip. I'm pretty sure they told all the girls what happened, too, because Pia invites me to lunch on Monday—I have a study group, so I suggest dinner, and then I never hear back from her before practice, and she doesn't bring it up again.

After practice the team heads to the ASC en masse for a team dinner to celebrate Ericka's birthday. If I'm honest with myself, I've been skipping these team dinners these last few weeks as much as possible, spending time with Wes and the cadre of football players he lives with.

Well, now I have no excuses not to spend time with my teammates. I don't have a devastatingly handsome boyfriend to distract me at all hours of the day from how friendless and isolated I feel surrounded by my teammates. I'm not a naturally social person. During free time, I would much rather curl up with a good book than paint my nails or play board games or whatever else the girls do when we're all together on road trips. I don't know, because I'm not part of the "in" group.

We have one more road game left, and then our season is done. Mathematically, we're out of playoff contention. That's fine by me. Our team does relatively well, but not nearly well enough to pull off a decent playoff performance. It's almost a blessing in disguise.

Pia settles in at the table beside me, Dareesa on my other side and Lauren across from me. They've been hovering more than usual lately, joining me at the breakfast table when I'm sitting by myself or waving hi when we cross paths on campus. It's like they're afraid I'm going to snap because I got moderately drunk one night, danced my ass off with Greg and some frat guys, and went home to my empty bed by myself.

My back is to the football table, so I can't really turn around and scope out the situation. Is Wes there? He's probably reading. Greg has been more attentive than usual, texting me to check in every day. Miles is being more overbearing than usual, too, showing up at my dorm room this morning to walk me to class.

I'm just... overwhelmed. I need space. I need to process. I need—

I want Wes back, but if he's leaving, it's better for this to end now than three months from now. I need to get used to living with this hurt.

"How have you been holding up?" Pia asks me, twirling her spaghetti around her fork.

"In regards to...?"

She raises her eyebrows. "Didn't you dump the boyfriend?"

I blow out a breath. "It was mutual."

"Yeah, it sure looked mutual," she says, shaking her head.

"What's that supposed to mean?"

"He's staring at you," she says. She hikes a thumb over her shoulder. "He's been staring all night."

"No, he isn't. He's reading his book."

She looks over her shoulder. "No, he's not."

Um… what? Wes is never not reading. He uses his books like a crutch to avoid social situations. If I'm honest, so do I. It's why I have my e-reader tucked into my backpack right now.

I turn around. Sure enough, Wes is looking right at us, his head cocked. When we make eye contact, he flushes pink, but he doesn't look away. He holds my gaze, his green eyes serious.

"Yeah, he's totally not still in love with you," Dareesa chimes in.

"What are you talking about?"

"He might have agreed to the breakup, but clearly he didn't want to," Lauren adds. "The boy is straight up pining over you."

Instead of making me happy, this only serves to kill my previously cheerful mood. I push my plate away.

"Great."

Pia frowns. "Not great?"

I shrug. "I can't go back and undo it. He's leaving in a few weeks. Moving to Michigan. And I'm here… for three more years."

Lauren winces. "Yeah. Long distance isn't fun. My boyfriend and I broke up in October. He promised we could make it work, but six weeks in and we were both miserable. And he's only in New Jersey. Michigan is so much farther away."

"Yeah. So it was better to end it when we did. It's not that I don't still care for him. I do. I just…" I sigh. "He was my best friend. My only friend here, really."

"What do you mean?" Dareesa says, wrinkling her nose. "You don't have friends?"

"I have, like, no friends," I tell her bluntly. "I've made one friend all year."

Pia looks offended. "What are we? Chopped liver?"

"No. No, not at all," I assure her quickly. "But you guys are my teammates."

"So?"

"You have to spend time with me on travel weekends."

She blinks. "I don't understand."

"We don't hang out outside of team activities."

Pia laughs. "Yeah, because you don't want to hang out with us."

I stare at her. "What are you talking about?"

"You're the first person to leave team dinner," she reminds me. "When you're here, it's clear you're a million miles away. You're always hanging out with the football team or reading or with your boyfriend." She winces. "Sorry. Ex-boyfriend."

My brain struggles to process her accusations.

"I'm not a social person. I don't..."

"Yeah, that's clear," Dareesa cuts in. "You never want to hang out."

"I do. I totally would."

"Except when we text you, you never answer," Lauren says. "You never respond to the group chat."

"Wait a second." My brain hurts. "There's a group chat? Why didn't I know?"

Lauren and Dareesa look at one another.

"We added you to a group chat the first week of the year. Remember? We were all at that freshman move-in mixer and you gave me your number?" Dareesa says. "I added you to that, and then to the team chat once they added us."

"Um, I don't have any group chats from any of you," I tell her.

Dareesa pulls out her phone. She scrolls through it. "You mean your number isn't 617-555-3839?"

"No... my number is 3939, not 3839."

"Shit," Lauren says. "Some random stranger has been getting all of our drunk selfies, then."

I let out a shallow laugh. "So..."

"So you're not ignoring us," Dareesa says.

"That explains why you're so quiet in the team chat," Pia adds. "I thought you just didn't like us."

"I do, I promise. I thought it was weird you guys only send me pings through social media and didn't text me," I admit.

Dareesa types something on her phone, and then my phone buzzes in my pocket. I pull it out to see a new text message. *Hey, girl,* it says, and I breathe a quiet sigh of relief.

Hi, I type back, and when I hear her phone buzz, I know we're going to be okay.

"So back to this you have no friends thing…" Pia says.

"I thought you guys were just not interested," I admit. "I didn't want to push. I'm the new girl, I'm a freshman. We don't really have a lot in common. I wasn't trying to… I don't know."

Pia slings her arm around my shoulders. "You're stuck with us, babe. This team sticks together."

My heart warms. "You know, I think I'm going to be okay with that."

sixty-five

. . .

Wes

MY SISTER IS CAUTIOUSLY optimistic when I tell her the good news.

"Are you sure you're doing this for the right reasons?" Sarah asks.

"What do you mean?"

"Are you doing this for yourself, or for her?"

I blow out a breath and roll over in my bed. "Mackenzie has no bearing on this decision."

"She doesn't?"

"No. Newton has always been my top choice school," I tell her. "They're giving me a similar enough aid package to Michigan that a few dollars and cents don't matter. This has always been my goal. Whether she's here or not, whether or not we're together, I want to stay here."

"Okay. If you decide you want to try somewhere else…"

"I did. I applied to a half dozen schools," I remind her. "Newton is the best combination of academic program and financial aid, not to mention all the intangibles that I want in a school."

"And you can probably work out with the football team," she adds.

"Yeah. Coach has asked if I want to volunteer with the linebackers this summer. It wouldn't be paid, but it would be great for my résumé. And it gives me something to do over summer."

"Wessy! That's great!"

"I haven't decided if I'm going to take him up on it, but I'm thinking it over."

"Why wouldn't you?"

"I don't know if I want to stay involved with football. That stage in my life is over. I don't know that I want to go backwards. Just because it's part of my past doesn't mean it will be part of my future."

"It might be good for you. A nice transition between undergrad and graduate programs," she says. "And it gives you something to do this summer."

"I know. That's why I'm still considering it. I don't know how much I would be able to commit once the term starts, and I don't know that it would help for me to be there for summer practice if I can't be there during the actual season. I don't know. There's a lot to consider."

She clears her throat. "Any luck on the apartment search?"

"Tucker and I looked at a few places this afternoon. We have an appointment to see two more tomorrow."

The rental market is crazy here. Everyone moves in on September first, so I'll have to find a sublease for June, July, and August once I officially graduate and get kicked out of Athlete's Village. I'm about three weeks too late. There are so few vacancies for next fall, almost everything is snapped up already.

"And you're still set on living on your own?"

"I don't like people," I remind my sister, and she laughs.

"Yeah, I've noticed."

"I've survived five years of roommates. I need a break."

It's not that I don't like having the guys around. I do. But I also need some quiet time alone, something I've sorely missed after spending four years in a house with five room-mates and another year before that in the dorms.

Besides, Tucker and Mason are moving in together—they're both going to Newton's psychology program for grad-uate school, so they'll be sticking around for another two years. Barrett and Diana are moving across the city, to be closer to his job at his father's company, and for her to go to Northeastern for grad school. Miles? I have no clue what he's doing, and I don't think he knows, either. It all depends on Sam, and if she decides to go back to Mississippi or stay here in the area.

Amir and Greg are sticking around for another year. They both have another season of eligibility left. We'll still be able to hang out on campus or around town, working around their practice schedules. I won't be able to access the ASC or the dining hall—I'll have to learn to cook, or find other dining options. I'm almost looking forward to the opportunity to try out the other dining halls on campus.

Sunday mornings, I'll go to the diner and hang out with Tricia and all the ladies. Whenever I have the time, I'll drop by the library and visit with the library staff, who will undoubtedly have new book recommendations for me. I don't know how much time I'll have to read—this program is supposed to be difficult, which is a good thing, even if it cuts into my free time.

I'm taking the necessary steps to secure my future. I accepted Newton's offer and rescinded my acceptance to Michigan. I'm actively searching for an apartment. In two weeks, I'll be able to register for classes, and then it will be official.

We have three weeks until graduation. Final exams are looming upon us. Now that I've got my future relatively figured out, it's the time for me to turn my attention to Mackenzie. I want to make things right with her.

She's looked happier in the last few days than I've seen

her since... I can't remember. Since we were together. She's hanging out with Pia and with Dareesa and Lauren, and I've seen her on campus with Deisy, that swimmer she's befriended. She's created a little niche for herself. Finally she's making friends.

I wish her nothing but happiness. I just hope she can sustain that happiness while being with me.

None of the guys have followed through on their promise to beat me up for breaking up with her. I think I'm doing enough beating myself up, all on my own. I miss her. I wish we hadn't ended things. It was right. That doesn't mean I wanted it to end.

Miles has been giving me a wide berth since it happened. He's not ignoring me, but we don't sit down and chat. We haven't been having our Sunday evening dinner and movie nights the last few weeks. Greg is conveniently never alone in the same room as me... maybe because he knows I'm not happy that he dragged her to a party where she got drunk and danced with a number of different guys, according to the photos Lauren posted.

I realize that Mackenzie is her own person. I recognize that she has agency in her decisions. But I also know she doesn't really drink, and she doesn't exactly party. She's like me: she's a homebody, an introvert, and she keeps her friends close, and her books closer.

If she wants to go to parties, I'll go with her. I won't drink and I might not talk a lot, but we can dance, or do whatever people do at parties. I don't care if she drinks every once in a while, so long as she isn't getting drunk every night. I don't want to be around people who rely so heavily on alcohol. It's not part of my life, and I would prefer not to be around it.

Mostly I just miss her. I can admit that maybe I got ahead of myself a little, thinking about a future for us when I should have been more concerned with the present. There won't be a future for us if I fuck everything up now.

In romance novels, this is the point where the person who fucked up makes the big, grand gesture to prove how much they've changed. I don't want to ply her with platitudes, but yeah, I have changed… or rather, my circumstances have, and with it, so has my outlook on my future. I've always wanted to stay here, even when it didn't make sense. I was willing to make a long distance relationship work. I wanted—

What I wanted doesn't matter. What's important is how she feels. Does she want to get back together? I don't know that she does, and I don't know that it's my place to convince her we should be together. If that's not what she wants, a well-timed plea on my part won't do much.

She has to want it, but she has to put in the work, too. We both do. Both of us made mistakes in how we handled things, her in hiding away from me, and me in forcing her to abide by my timeline for "fixing" things. When I needed support, she clammed up and looked away, and I don't know that I can forgive and forget that so easily.

Can I rely on her? I'm not talking about the everyday back and forth of a relationship. When the shit gets real and hits the fan, will she be there? Can I depend on her to provide me with the kind of emotional support and stability I need in a partner? Because I'll be there for her: I think I've proven to her that I'll always be there for her if she wants me.

I have two failed relationships under my belt. Sure, they were in high school, but that doesn't mean they didn't teach me things. I've been through enough to know what I need in a partner, and how to be a partner to someone else. Mackenzie has never dated before. She's never been in a relationship. She's new to this. She's still learning.

I can be patient. I can wait for her to get on my level. Not forever—I'm not that much of a masochist. But if she needs a little bit of time? Yeah, I can make that happen. My timeline isn't set in stone. I have flexibility in this. If I want forever with her, I need to give her a chance to come around to the idea.

We're young, and she's even younger than I am. We have forever to have a forever. Right now, we need to worry about our right now.

———

It's not the best idea for me to go to the bookstore. For one, I'm easily distracted. On top of that, my wallet cannot afford for me to go to the bookstore any more than the bare minimum. If this is what it takes to get Mackenzie back? Yeah, I'll be there every damn day, from open to close.

One of her favorite authors released the newest book in their series yesterday. I know she prefers to have a physical copy than an electronic one for this particular author. She has all of her books displayed in her bedroom at home. I also know she doesn't like getting mail on campus—the mail room in the dorms is only open in the middle of the day, when she has class, and it can take her a few days to find the time to go down to retrieve her packages. So if I were to buy her the book and drop it off outside her dorm room... yeah, that wouldn't be the worst present to get her.

Of course, I'm not expecting to see her in the bookstore. It's early, so early that we're the only people in the shop that's usually bustling with people. She looks up as the door chimes and, when she sees me, she ducks out of sight. She's nearly six feet tall. It's hard for her to hide successfully.

I cross the bookstore to where she is, hanging out in the romance section.

"Mackenzie." My voice cracks on the second syllable and I flush pink.

"Oh. Hey," she says, turning around to face me. She bites her lip and my baser instincts react.

She's fresh-faced, the only makeup a little mascara and

tinted chapstick, her dark blonde hair in a long braid. She's wearing jeans, and a long-sleeved t-shirt with a light jacket, nothing special. She looks absolutely fucking gorgeous.

"Hi." I clear my throat. "How've you been?"

"Fine," she says with an ambivalent shrug.

She's lying. She's not a very good liar, and it shows on her face.

I want you. I love you. I need you.

"Did you come in to get the new Sophie Gluck book?"

She blinks. "Um…"

I'm not going to tell her my plan. That would be weird. Still…

"Can I buy it for you?"

"I have money," she says defensively, hunching her shoulders.

She might have pocket change, but she doesn't have any income. She still relies on an allowance from her parents. She has to save to buy books—and given the voracious way she consumes them, she can hardly afford to buy everything she reads. She relies heavily on the library.

"I know. I'd like to buy you the book," I tell her.

She frowns, suspicious. "Why?"

Because I still love you. Because I want to make you happy. Because I know you came here to buy this specific book, and I want to be the one who gets it for you, so every time you see it you think of me.

"Because maybe we can grab a cup of coffee. And by coffee, I mean a cup of hot chocolate and a pot of tea, but the conventional saying is coffee."

I'm babbling. Why am I babbling? Normally, when I'm nervous, it's like trawling through sludge to get the words out. I'm not nervous, though. Anxious? Yes.

"Now isn't a good time," she says. "I have class."

Yeah, in two hours. She's done with the basketball season, so she doesn't have daily practice anymore. It's the perfect chance for us to meet up, to get some of this tension dissolved.

"Maybe another time," I suggest lightly, and she winces. "If you really aren't interested, we don't have to…"

She sighs. "I just don't know what it would accomplish."

"What? We can't make awkward small talk for an hour? Isn't that what we're doing now?"

She raises her eyebrows. "You want more of this?"

Yes. A hundred times, yes.

I shrug. "I mean, I think we have some unresolved—"

"I'm really not interested," she says, talking over me. "You're the one who broke up with me."

My heart skips a beat. "Is that what you think happened?"

She blinks. "Yeah. I was there. I remember it."

"Because you're the one who ended things," I remind her. "You're the one who said you didn't want to do long distance. You—"

"Let's not do this," she says. She glances around. The bookstore is empty, the only other person here is a bored cashier who isn't paying us any attention. "I don't want to argue with you."

"Okay."

"I don't want to go to coffee with you, either," she says bluntly. "I don't think that's a good idea."

My stomach rolls. "If that's what you think is best."

"It is."

"Well, I'll see you around, I guess," I say with forced lightness.

"Yeah, sure," she says.

I turn to leave. I'm two feet from the door when her voice stops me.

"Aren't you going to buy your book?"

I shake my head. "I got what I came here for."

Bracing myself, I push the door open and a brisk wind hits

me like a slap in the face. It's a stark reminder of what I'm up against.

She thinks I was the one who wanted to end us. She's under the mistaken impression that this was all my idea, when all I wanted was an answer. And yeah, maybe I was a little hasty in saying we couldn't be friends. I didn't realize just how much I would miss her. There's a Mackenzie shaped hole in my life where she used to be.

It's not the one time we had sex, or the numerous times we fooled around and performed oral sex on one another. And it's not the kissing and the cuddling. It isn't even holding her hand as we walked through campus.

It's eating dinner together and then going back to my place together, and waking up in the morning tangled in one another. It's knowing I can call her at any time of day or night and knowing she would answer, knowing she would want to talk to me as much as I needed to talk to her. It's being able to rely on her for emotional support or help talking things out as I work through something, and being a sounding board when she needs a listening ear. It's—

I love her, with all of my heart, with all of my being. As much as I want her to be in my future, I want her to be in my present all that much more. If we have to be friends, fine, I can settle for being friends. But I want more.

It's with this on my mind that I hit the library. I've got a speech due in our public speaking class. I'm moderately less terrified when it comes to speaking in front of others. I'm not exactly sure what Mackenzie did that took away my fear. I still stutter. I still get the nervous sweats. I'll never exactly be good at this. But I can survive, and sometimes that's all I need.

The last three speeches, I've gotten through it because I was able to watch Mackenzie, focusing on her instead of the intensity of thirty something people staring at me. The first one… yeah, that was a train wreck. If I hadn't been allowed to do my make-up speech for "extra credit" (or pity credit), I wouldn't be passing this class. At this point, my third time taking this required course I need to pass in order to graduate in two and a half weeks, I'll take whatever credit I can get.

It never bothered me when people were watching me when I was on the football field, because they were watching the team and not me specifically. Here, when I'm the center of attention, everyone's focus on me... it's terrifying. My mind goes numb, and at the same time, my thoughts come way too fast for me to process. I start to sweat—it's not a little damp-ness, it's a full body drenching of sweat, like it's the fourth quarter in a championship game and we're down two scores.

And now... it's game day, all over again, except my stomach is in knots. I hope this works. I sit quietly through the speeches ahead of me, reading and rehearsing. I can do this. I am doing this.

Professor Blake calls my name, and I make my way to the front of the room. My notes are on the lectern in front of me. No matter how well I've memorized the material, no matter how well I know what I'm about to say, I can't stop the words from swimming on the page.

This is it. The big one. The one I've been waiting for.

Thirty something sets of eyes are pinned on me. I watch as Professor Blake shifts in her seat and shuffles her papers. We make eye contact, and she nods.

I clear my throat. "My speech is a persuasive speech, titled: Why Mackenzie Cavanaugh should give me a second chance."

sixty-six

. . .

Mackenzie

MY HEAD SNAPS UP. Um, what?

Wes is looking directly at me. "First of all, before we begin, I need to apologize. I tried to put a time limit on how long it would take you to come to terms with a pretty big decision, and I was wrong for forcing you to adhere to my timeline. Just because my mind was made up doesn't mean yours was immediately, and I should have respected that you needed time to process."

My stomach twists. Is he really going to air all of our dirty laundry for the entire class?

"Now, the reasons why I think you should give me a second chance: we were good together. I support you; I'm here for you. I've won over your family and your friends. I'm staying here for another two years. And most importantly, I love you."

My heart stops. He's staying?! What happened to Michigan? He had to give them his acceptance by Sunday. Three days later, why is this the first I'm hearing of this? I would think this would be headline news. Running into him this morning was weird enough. That it was the first time since the breakup is even more weird. Why didn't he mention it this morning?

"We made a good partnership. We were a cohesive team. We went through some pretty important events… most of them were punctuated by the speeches we have in this class, now that I think about it. We had our first kiss after our first speech, when I had my meltdown. I told you I went to the professor to explain what happened. What I didn't tell you is I ended up telling her exactly how I felt about you. Somehow, saying it out loud made it so much more real."

My stomach clenches. He told our professor how he felt? That's so wrong… and at the same time, so incredibly Wes. He can't say the words out loud, so he tells his professor. He can't talk to me face to face, so he writes and delivers a speech. It's a grand gesture if I've ever seen one, and I know he's read every book on this.

"I'm here for you, and I like to think I've proven it time and time again throughout the last few months. I celebrate your accomplishments and commiserate with you on the lows. Whether you need a shoulder to lean on or a listening ear, all of my body parts are yours for the taking."

There's a snicker elsewhere in the room, and he startles, his face going pink, like he's forgotten we're in a crowded classroom with thirty other people listening in on what should really be a very private conversation.

"Slowly but surely over the last few months, I've convinced your brother, your parents, and all of our friends just how deeply I care for you, so now it's time I convince you, too. I want to buy you books, and cheer you on at your basketball games, and walk through campus with your hand in mind. I want to stay in with you and watch Jeopardy! and Wheel of Fortune, and read on the couch, and I even want to go to parties with you. Yeah, I might not be interested in the party scene, but if you're there, that's where I want to be. In case it's not quite clear enough, I'm fucking crazy about you, Mackenzie Cavanaugh."

My heart skips a beat. He would go to a party with me? He hates parties. He hates socializing. It's the very last thing he wants to do. But he would do it—for me.

"I'm staying here. I was accepted into Newton's graduate program, and I'll be here for two more years, and I'll figure out what happens after that later. We've got two more years where we can be together without issue, before we have to start worrying about the future. Right now, my plan is to move into the city proper and find a job here, so you can finish school and we can start a life together here in Boston, where you grew up and where your family is."

He's sacrificing his opportunities to stay here, because he knows I want to stay here. He's a man with no home base. He could go anywhere in the world if he wanted. He has no need to go back to Michigan, at least not now, and if his sister is serious about moving to wherever he is...

"Because I'm not thinking about right now. I mean, I am, but I'm also thinking about a future, our future, where we build something together, just the two of us. I'm thinking about five, ten, fifteen years from now. The future doesn't scare me. I hope that we're happy and healthy, but if we're not, I know we'll have each other to lean on. I'll be there for you when the going gets tough, and I know you'll have my back. In sickness and in health, for richer or for poorer—"

My stomach swirls. I feel sick. I think I might throw up.

But still I can't force my eyes away from his.

Wes forces a laugh. "No, I'm not ready for marriage. We're too young, both of us. We're not ready for that. But I am ready for forever, and I'm ready for a forever with you. And I think that forever should start right now."

I swallow. My heart pounds at a thousand beats a minute. He wants to get back together. He wants to be together.

And I...

I never wanted to break up, but now that we have, I'm kind of liking this new single girl life. Or do I just like having friends? I honestly don't know. Dareesa and I have breakfast before class nearly every day—Lauren prefers to sleep in—and they've invited me up to their dorm for movie night. We've also spent two evenings at the basketball house with Pia and the girls. One night we went out to the movies. Deisy and I met for coffee the other day.

It's been a lot of socializing in the last eight days. I'm exhausted, and at the same time, I'm exhilarated. I have friends.

Even Claire has been less of a bitch than usual. She's been sleeping in her bed—alone, without fucking her boyfriend—and has been bringing her guy around less frequently. I don't know if they're on the outs or if she's finally respecting that I don't want them to bang while I'm in the same fucking room, but I'll take whatever I can get. Since I started spending every night sleeping in my own bed again, we've settled into a tentative truce. She doesn't throw her shit on my bed, she keeps her textbooks off my desk, and keeps the chaotic mess to her side of the room. She doesn't lock me out of the dorm anymore, either.

Progress!

I've put in my housing application for next year. If all goes according to plan, I'll be in a house with Dareesa, Lauren, Rebekah, Amber, and Pia. Jacki and Miri have been voted co-captains, and Jaz is sticking around campus for one more semester to finish up her degree, though she won't be living in a basketball house next fall.

Deisy and I are planning on taking an anthropology course together next fall. It fulfills a general education requirement for both of us, and it should be fun, taking a class with my new friend. Tucker promised me that anthropology is actually interesting—it's his minor, so maybe he's a little biased—and that the professor is engaging, so hopefully it will go well.

It feels a little bittersweet that I'm finally settling in and making friends now that the school year is nearly over. I lost the majority of my freshman year to insecurity and fear. I should have reached out to my teammates ages ago. I should have made friends all along. Not that the football players weren't my friends—they were. It's just that I was always extremely conscious of the fact that they were my brother's friends first, his teammates, his roommates. Their alliance is with him, not with me, and I don't begrudge him that.

Save for Greg and obviously my brother, none of the guys have reached out since the breakup. Mason texted asking if I wanted to get coffee, and Diana and Sam are still talking to me in the group chat. Jill hasn't said a word to me, and I don't know if I care about that. Though I never thought she and Wes were particularly close, I understand needing to pick sides.

In light of his friends' lack of communication, I'm not sure if it changes the way I feel about a relationship with Wes. I like him. I love him. I want him. But the reality of a relationship with him isn't perfect. He's anti-social and would rather hide in his books than talk to people. None of this is new information; I've known this since I met him when I was fifteen, admiring from afar, and he was a freshman, tall and thick and gorgeous, way out of my league even back then, even if it had been legal. When he needs to think, he goes silent, blocking out the entire world around him.

And I... don't know if I want to do that again.

I like him. I love him. I want him. But I don't know that I can be with him.

It's not that I'm interested in dating other guys. I'm not. But I don't know that I'm ready for forever with him. I'm nineteen. He was my first boyfriend. There's a pretty big jump from "first guy I had sex with" to "only guy I've ever slept with, ever." I'm not ready to attend a wedding with him, much less participate in one joining us together in holy matrimony.

We need to back up here.

So he wants to be with me. Great. Fine. That doesn't mean we hop right back into a relationship again. If we want this to work, we have to start slowly. Maybe we'll start by dating again. We can go out on an actual date and spend time with one another without books being involved, actually talking and learning about one another. I'm not about to give up my newfound friends and new social life because he wants to stay in every night and read. I'm not saying I never want to read or I want to go out every night—I don't, I still want to spend the majority of my time with him, wherever that is. But I want the freedom and flexibility of being able to go out whenever I want, whether he joins me or not.

He hasn't asked me to give anything up. He's just trying to get me to meet him halfway. Can I do that? I honestly I don't know.

His springing this all on me in the middle of class is globally unfair. He's making a mockery of our breakup by broadcasting the details of our relationship to our entire class—for a grade. I don't have a way to respond, at least not right now. I'm trapped here in this classroom. Fuck, I have to give my own speech in a few minutes. How the hell am I supposed to process this?

I don't know what he wanted me to say this morning at the bookstore. He wanted a conversation, and I blanked him. He sought me out. This is, like, the definition of a grand gesture. He's following the textbook example, and I...

The class is waiting for an answer. They all know he's talking about me: we used to sit beside each other every class, and now we aren't. It's not like they don't know my name. He's staring directly at me.

My heart beats a thousand times a minute. There's a lump

in my throat I can't clear. I like him. I love him. I want him. But am I ready to be in a relationship with him?

I look down.

Wes clears his throat and looks at his notes. "Thank you for your time."

sixty-seven

. . .

Wes

AFTER MY SPEECH, I retake my seat at the back of the room. My heart pounds. I can't believe I just did that. I can't believe—

Fuck. She wasn't receptive. She wasn't into it.

My hands start to shake, and I clench them into fists as I stare at my desk. There are still eyes on me, I can feel it, despite the next person standing at the front of the room ready to give her speech.

She doesn't want this.

Exhaling slowly, I rotate my shoulders and try to regroup. So she doesn't want to get back together. Okay. Fine. I can deal with this. I can—

A shadow falls over my desk. I look up. The classroom is emptying out. I don't know where the last forty-five minutes just went.

Mackenzie is standing beside my desk, her books clutched to her chest. "We should talk," she says. "It was everything I wanted to hear… two weeks ago."

Swallowing, I nod. "Do you have time to grab coffee?"

She winces. "I have plans with—someone. Later? Dinner?"

My heart skips a beat. "You want to have dinner with me?"

Hesitant, she nods, like she's not sure. "Yeah. We can grab something in the ASC, away from… everyone. Just the two of us. I've realized some things since we've been apart."

My stomach twists. "Y-yeah. That sounds…"

She offers a faint smile. "Great. Six-thirty?"

"I'll be there," I promise.

I don't know who she's meeting. It kills me that I don't know. At one point in the not so distant past, I knew everything about her. Is she meeting up with a guy? Has she found someone new in the week since we broke up? Maybe the reason she's not interested is because she met some guy at that frat party and now—

No. I can't catastrophize. It doesn't serve me to jump to the worst possible scenario. We're going to have dinner. We're going to talk. We're going to get to the bottom of this. For better or for worse, we're going to talk everything out.

The afternoon passes in the blink of an eye. Work on a paper. Read a few chapters in my current novel. Get a run in. Drop off my lease agreement and security deposit. Rub one out. All part of a day's work.

Before I'm ready for it, it's time to head to the ASC to meet Mackenzie. I debate bringing her flowers or a book to smooth things over. No. I made my grand gesture. If she's not interested, me bringing her presents isn't going to change her mind.

She's in the lobby talking quietly with Pia when I approach. She cuts off in the middle of her sentence and makes eye contact. She says something to her teammate and then she gets to her feet, meeting me in the middle of the lobby.

"Hey."

She offers a faint smile. "Hi."

I swallow my fears. "Shall we?"

Mackenzie nods. This shy, reserved version of her is a far cry from the exuberantly enthusiastic woman I knew only a week ago. Did our ending things destroy her fire?

No. This is just awkward. It's only natural that she's on edge; I am, too.

Silently we swipe our student ID cards and make our way through the food line. She picks turkey meatloaf and mashed potatoes. Comfort food. I opt for the grilled teriyaki chicken and some rice, filling the rest of my plate with salad. My roommates are sitting at our usual table, making no secret of their watching our every move. Instead of joining them, I head for a table for two at the complete opposite side of the room, where they'd have to crane their necks obviously to watch us, and there's absolutely no way they can overhear us. We deserve privacy for this conversation—however it will go.

Mackenzie slips into the chair opposite mine.

"So…"

"Yeah."

"You wanted to talk?" I pluck a cherry tomato out of my salad, popping it into my mouth.

She winces. "Your speech…"

My heart pounds. "Yeah?"

"It was a lot."

I let out a heavy breath. "Bad?"

"I… don't know."

Okay. That's better than an outright dismissal.

Her eyes dart up to mine, wide and insistent. "You're really staying?"

"I'm staying," I confirm. "I put in a deposit on an apartment this afternoon. Newton has always been my first choice, and now that they've accepted me, there isn't anywhere else I'd rather be."

"So us…"

I set my fork down and meet her eyes.

"I'd like for us to be together, yes. But no matter what

happens between us, I'm sticking around for a minimum of two years."

She lets out a breath. "You're staying. And it's not because of me?"

"I'm staying because of me," I say. "It's the best choice for me. I'm putting myself first. It just so happens that by doing so, I'll stay close by."

"And you still want…"

"I love you, Mackenzie."

She swallows. Her eyes flick up to mine and then away. Her teeth sink into her lower lip.

"I want to be with you. Now, five years from now, yes, I want to be with you."

"I… I don't know about five years from now," she says. "That's a lot."

"What about now?"

"I miss you," she admits, and my heart skips a beat. "If we're together—"

I don't miss the emphasis she puts on "if."

"If we get back together," she finally says, "it would have to be different."

"Different how?"

"I've made friends." She almost sounds defensive.

"That's great! I'm happy for you!"

I am, wholeheartedly. She needs friends. She needs to have a support network wider than me and her brother.

Mackenzie's smile dims. "Yeah, well… you said you would be interested in going to parties?"

"Interested? No, not really," I admit. Her face falls. "Would I do it anyway? Yes, as long as you're there."

She's confused.

"I'm not interested in drinking or doing drugs or playing video games or whatever people do at parties," I try to explain. "But you want to go, so if you want to be there, I'll be happy to stand by your side and hold your hair back when you puke, and whatever else goes along with a Friday or Saturday night out."

"I don't want to drink to excess," she explains, a little self-consciously. "I just want... I don't know."

"You want to hang out with your friends and have a good time," I tell her. "I'm here for that. Whether we're sitting on a couch and reading or out somewhere with a group of your friends, I just want to be with you."

She considers this.

"Besides, I'll probably have parties and mixers and things I have to go to, too," I point out. "From what I've been told, grad school is as much social as it is educational. So I'll expand my social network, and with it, my calendar."

"You want to...?"

I laugh, a little self-conscious myself now. "Well, no. Not really. But it's part of the deal, so I've got to do what I've got to do. I'm not starting from square one, but I am starting over. I won't have very many friends on campus next year." I swallow. "I hope you're one of them."

Mackenzie pauses. "I want to be," she says quietly. "I just don't know if I will be."

"What's holding you back?"

"You're so focused on your future. Our future. But I need to live my life a little first," she says. "I'm only nineteen."

"I know."

"I'm not ready for marriage or—"

"Neither am I," I assure her.

"But you know you want to be with me. And that terrifies me," she admits.

"If you don't want..."

"I think we should date first," she blurts, and then she winces. "I mean..."

"So you want to..."

"We should date," she says again. "I'm not interested in

seeing anyone else. I only want to date you. But I want us to date before we settle into a full-fledged relationship again."

My stomach twists.

"Okay. And what would that entail?"

"A lot of what we did before," she says. "But we will need to talk more. Get to know each other better."

"I'm on board with that."

"It's not the sex. That's not what I'm talking about," she says.

"So… what are you talking about?"

"You shut down."

"What?"

"The morning after. You shut down. You shut me out," she says. "That didn't feel good."

I try to think back to that morning. So much has happened since then. I remember talking with her, before my sister showed up. I remember trying to…

"Shit."

Mackenzie cracks a smile. "Yeah."

"I'm sorry, baby," I tell her sincerely. "I was trying to process. I can see now how that would have made you feel not great. I'm sorry. I'll do better."

She nods. "I'm not saying we can't have sex again," she says. "But we need to be able to trust each other, and if we don't—"

"I trust you," I assure her. "I do."

"But we have to be able to show it."

I wince. Yeah. I see her point.

"So we can take it slow, build back up to it," she says. "We'll sit down for meals together, without your roommates or my friends and without our books, and we'll… talk."

"I'm on board for that," I tell her quickly. "The reading… it started out as a coping mechanism. I don't need it as much anymore. It's become a crutch. I've done it for so long. I'll have to learn how to do it without it. I'm not saying I won't," I add. "Just that it might take practice."

"That's okay," Mackenzie says. "You're demonstrating that you care about me and my silly requests so—"

"They're not silly."

She frowns.

"A relationship is about give and take. You have a reasonable, rational request. It's within my power to grant it. So I will," I tell her. "If you asked me to do something out of line, I would let you know. This is something that I am capable of doing with a little bit of effort, so I'm going to put the effort in. It will make you happy, so it's important to me."

"Wes…"

"Making you happy is my number one goal," I tell her bluntly. "Whatever I have to do to prove it to you, I will. Your happiness means everything to me, Mackenzie."

She swallows and looks away. My heart rate kicks up another notch.

"I know I have feelings for you," she starts, and then stops.

There's a lump in my throat I can't clear.

"I think I might…" She sighs and meets my eyes again. "I think I might be in love with you, and that terrifies me," she blurts.

My heart skitters to a stop. She loves me?

She loves me.

"Why does it terrify you?" My voice cracks. I cough.

"You're my first boyfriend," she says. "I'm not saying I want to see anybody else. That's not even on my radar. But it's incredibly scary to think that you and I might…" She swallows. "We might be forever, and all I know is us. I have no other experience."

"Do you want more experience?"

"Sometimes. Not really," she admits. "I've read enough books to know I'm not missing out on anything you can't give me. But there's a part of me that's scared you're going to destroy my heart if I give it to you."

"You know I would never do it on purpose."

She sighs. "Yeah. It's the unforeseen that gets to me. We have two years together. Then you'll be done with grad school, and I'll still have another year left, and—"

"We don't have to worry about that right now," I tell her in as soothing a voice as I can. "Whatever happens between us happens. We can't control the future. What we can control is our present, and what I want presently is to be with you, in whatever way you'll allow."

Mackenzie nods, chewing on her lip.

"So we'll start by dating again. Slowly."

"You're okay with that?"

"I'm okay with whatever gets you back into my life," I admit. "If all you wanted was to be friends—"

"I don't," she says quickly. "I want to be more."

"Well, I'd find a way to make it work."

It's not what I want. But if my only other option is to not have her in my life at all? Yeah, I'll take whatever I can get.

"We'll build our way up to having sex again. Truth be told, I'm okay if we wait a while."

Her face falls. "It wasn't good for you?"

"It was. It was great," I reassure her. "But you're clearly not ready, and if we're going to start slow, there's no need for us to rush. I want to be with you." Reaching across the table, I take her hand, running my thumb over the back of her knuckles. "We'll get there eventually, or we won't, and that's okay, too. Being with you is more important to me than having sex. I can't promise that won't change. For now, what matters to me is having you in my life."

She swallows.

"I'm fucking crazy about you, Mackenzie," I tell her quietly. "You're my best friend, yeah, but it's so much more than that. I can't even put it into words. You're the most important person in my life."

Her eyes go wide. "What about Sarah?"

"Even more than my sister," I admit. "She's great, but our relationship is very different than the one I share with her. She's not my partner. You're in a league of your own, baby."

"So we're going to date again," she says. Her hand tightens on mine. "We're going to be back together, but we're both going to have the freedom to explore new friendships and hobbies and—"

"I'll give you the world," I promise her.

Mackenzie releases my hand, and I feel momentarily lost. Until she rounds the table and stands in front of me. She gestures for me to move back and then she plops herself down on my lap. Her arms wind around my neck.

She laughs. "Did we just negotiate our entire relationship like a business transaction again?"

"I think so, yeah." I grin at her. "Do you have any regrets?"

"When it comes to you? None."

sixty-eight

. . .

Mackenzie

LOWERING MY HEAD, I offer him a soft, chaste kiss. Wes sighs and wraps an arm around my waist, offering me stability, while his other hand slides into my hair. He kisses me and it's so sweet, so perfect, it brings tears to my eyes.

I am so fucking in love with this man. He's perfectly imperfect, and perfect for me. My heart skips a beat and my stomach aches like I've just done fifteen bajillion crunches. I might not be ready for forever. I might not be ready for five years from now. But what I am ready for is right now, and sometimes, that has to be enough. My heart is on the most volatile rollercoaster ride of its life, and I don't know how to deal with the intensity of the variation in emotions.

He pulls back and frowns. His thumb caresses under my eye, where there's a suspicious trail of moisture. "What's wrong?"

"Nothing's wrong."

"You're crying."

The words burst out of me: "I just love you."

It takes a second, and when it hits him—his whole face lights up.

"You do?"

I nod, hardly daring to believe it myself. "I do. So much."

"Mackenzie…"

"I thought I wasn't sure," I blurt out. "I thought I didn't know. But I think really I was just scared."

"Of me?" He looks sick. My stomach twists at the idea that he would ever think that was possible.

"Of my feelings for you," I clarify, and he lets out a heavy breath. "I've never felt this way before. I've read about it in books, but I wasn't prepared for the intensity of my feelings. It's… a lot."

"Yeah, it is," he says, his eyes serious. "And if you're not ready for it…"

I swallow. "Yeah. So. Couple that with you going away for two years…"

"But I'm not. I'm staying," he repeats.

"I know. Now, I know. Before… it felt so enormous, so impossible. I couldn't wrap my brain around it all."

"That was before. That's a different chapter in our story," he says. "We've turned the page and started the next chapter. Our story isn't over. It's just beginning."

There's a lump in my throat. "I don't think I can put into words how much I love that you just related the two of us to a book."

Wes grins. "I mean, I've met you before."

"So… what happens now?"

"Now you kiss me," he declares, and I'm happy enough to comply.

He tastes like hope and sweetness and adoration, and a little bit like love.

Cheers erupt from the other side of the dining hall, and I smile against Wes's lips. Without turning to look, I know it's the table of football players we call our friends. He lifts his arm, and I know he's flipping them off or making some otherwise vulgar hand gesture in their direction.

"Come home with me," he says.

"Tonight?"

"Any night you want to." His eyes search mine. "I sleep so much better when you're in the bed beside me."

"Even with the night terrors?"

"I would much rather you wake me up from your night terror than you wake up alone in your dorm because of one," Wes says softly. "I want to be there for you, even when it's not so fun. As long as you can put up with my sweating and the snoring…"

"I can. It's hard to sleep now without it in my ear," I admit. Claire makes a soft snuffling noise in her sleep, but it's not the same as his foghorn-like snoring. It's the lullaby I didn't know I needed.

"So it's a deal," he says. "As often as we can, without it impacting our schoolwork or our roommates."

"Have the guys said anything to you? About my being over there?"

He shakes his head. "Should they have?"

"No. It's not their place."

Ducking down, he presses a kiss to my cheek before he pauses. "You and Greg…"

"He took me to the frat party. It was…" I make a face. "It wasn't what I thought it would be."

"A date?"

I do a double take. "What?"

"When Greg took you… was that a date?" It looks like it's paining him to say the words.

"Not at all," I reassure him quickly. "He's like a brother to me. All the guys in the house are. You all have known Miles and me for so long, they're practically family."

"And I'm not?"

"Not in the slightest. I love you," I say, and when the world doesn't end, I laugh at ever thinking it might. "I'm in love with you, and I want to be with you, and I have absolutely zero interest in any other guy."

"Good." He kisses my forehead this time. "I feel the same about you, for the record."

Even though I was pretty sure, I have to admit it does feel nice to hear it repeated back to me.

Wes sighs. "Think it's time to face the music?"

I tilt my head, unsure what he means.

"We need to go over there and talk to them, before they all storm over here."

"If we have to."

He steals one more kiss, full of love and devotion and a little undercurrent of need, before he sighs again and releases me.

My dinner is still on my tray, barely touched. I pick up my tray and my backpack and follow Wes across the room to the table where my brother and the rest of his roommates are gathered. They aren't hiding the fact that they're watching us approach.

Miles looks smug. "Got some news to share?"

"Nothing at all," I say lightly.

Wes glances down at me, and I wink at him, pursing my lips to blow him a kiss. Laughing, he drops a kiss to my temple and sets his tray down at his usual seat at the end of the table before he pulls out the chair opposite for me.

"Thank you."

"Because it sure looked like something happened over there," Miles continues.

"I don't know what you're talking about," Wes says.

Sam frowns. "So all the kissing…"

"What kissing?"

"And you two talking to each other…" Diana adds. "You've been avoiding each other for the better part of a week."

Wes laughs. "If you say so."

Mason lets out a noise of frustration not dissimilar to a

baby dinosaur's squawk. "You two are the worst," she complains.

"We're back together," I finally confirm, and the table erupts into chatter as everyone tries to talk to us at once.

"Good," my brother says.

I raise my eyebrows. "You're happy about this?" That's a pretty sharp deviation from how he acted the first time he learned we were together. Maybe he's found some sort of personal growth after all.

"You guys are good for one another. You make each other happy," he explains. "That's the most important thing."

"What caused this abrupt change in your philosophy?"

Miles shrugs. "I've seen you together. Both of you are happier when you're together. All I've ever wanted was for you to be happy, Mack. If Wes is the guy who makes you happy, then I guess I have to get on board."

Wes smirks at me, pleased as punch. "I told you I'd win him over," he says, and it's my turn to laugh.

Because he's right: in his speech a few hours ago, he did proclaim he had won over all my friends and my family, and from their reactions now, it's clear he has. These are the people closest to me, the ones who want the best for me. It means a lot that they are equally as enthused about Wes and I getting back tighter as I am. If I had any doubts—which I don't—it would only serve to corroborate that I made the right decision.

I don't need a boyfriend to be happy. My life isn't magically better because I'm dating someone. It's because that person is Wes that I feel so content with this decision. It's because I'm dating my best friend that I know we can do this. We don't have to worry about the future. We don't have to worry about five or ten years from now. We can focus on the right now, on loving each other. We don't need to be concerned about forever. We have the present to enjoy first.

epilogue

. . .

Seven months later

"SORRY I'M LATE."

Wes looks up from his book and marks his page. "You're not late," he lies.

"I said I'd be here thirty-two minutes ago. I'm late," I say flatly. I kiss his cheek. "It's nice of you to pretend, though."

He laughs and grabs my wrist, pulling me down onto his level so he can kiss me properly.

"Missed you," he says, brushing some snow off my shoulder.

"Missed you more."

It's been a busy five days since I've seen him. Between midterms and my traveling for a preseason basketball game, I've been out of town for the better part of the week, and when I've been home, we've both been busy with school. Our bus got stuck in traffic on the way back to campus, otherwise I'd have been here at least ten minutes early, I'm so eager to see him.

It's hard balancing everything—school and sports and a relationship and time with my family. It helps that my brother is nearby; he and Sam have an apartment in Brighton about forty minutes away, so we can get together for dinner or a football game around Wes' and my school schedule and their work schedules. Ashley is a freshman this year, busy with the cheerleading squad, so even though we're both on campus now, I barely ever see her. My parents do a good job at supporting us both. They're here for every home football game and every home basketball game.

It also helps that now I'm with my friends instead of with the roommate from hell. I'm in a house with Dareesa, Lauren, Pia, and two other girls from the basketball team, and we get along so much better now that they have my actual phone number and don't think I'm ignoring all of their invitations. It doesn't hurt that I actually want to hang out with them. Now that we're in a house together, Dareesa and Lauren are still close, but there is room for both of them to make friends with other people... including me. Pia and I are tight friends, too, and I have Deisy now.

I've also made some friends in my major; a group of five of us started a romance book club, and get together every two weeks to talk about our books... and maybe drink a little, too. We have fun. Wes has expanded his social network, too, going to mixers and events for his graduate program, and even though I'm so much younger than all of them, I get along pretty well with his classmates. Enough to hang out with them at the pub or at a house party, at least.

My life is so completely different than it was this time last year, I still marvel at all the changes. Wes and I are in a good place now. At Tucker's suggestion, he's started up with therapy again, and this time it seems to be helping. He's finally able to work through some of the trauma around his parents' death. About two months ago, with his therapist's support, we started having sex again. It's completely different than it was last spring. We're good. I trust him, and he trusts me, and we're able to open up and rely on one another in a way we couldn't before.

I love him. With my whole heart and my whole being, I

am absolutely in love with this man, my best friend, the person who understands me better than anyone else in the whole world. I'm still not ready to think about our "future" past his graduation next year. He's planning on doing an internship this summer with the New England football team, thanks to Deisy's brother's help in connecting them, and the ultimate goal is to work with them full time after graduation.

As for me… well, I still don't know what kind of job I'll be able to get with a degree in English, but I like reading books and learning about literature, so at least for now, I'm sticking with it. If preseason is any indication, I'm going to be getting a lot more playing time this season, which will keep me busy. And exhausted. It's the good kind of exhaustion, though, that bone deep weariness of a job well done.

Tricia, our waitress, comes over and delivers our meals. I haven't ordered; Wes knows what I like, and even if he didn't tell her what I want, she does, too.

"You look good, Mackie," Tricia says. "More coffee?"

"Yes, please." I offer her a smile. "Sorry to keep you guys waiting."

She waves it away. "You're fine, honey."

"I wasn't waiting long," Wes lies.

I shoot him a look, but I don't call him on it.

"I'd wait forever for you," he says, and I swoon, because this one isn't a lie.

This has become our Sunday morning tradition. Every weekend that I'm home, we meet for breakfast at the diner. We'll meet people here at other times, dinner with Tucker and Mason, Greg, Amir, and Deisy, but Sunday mornings are just for the two of us.

We try to get together as a group as often as we can. Balancing all of our schedules is harder than I expected. We're all busy, and even without Wes and Tucker's football commitments and Mason's involvement with the track team, we've still got Greg and Amir actively playing football, Deisy with the swim team, and me with the basketball team, and that's before we factor in school, study groups, and other family commitments.

Greg and Amir still make sure to hang out with me even though they have new roommates and new friends now. I'm still welcome at the football table any time, even if Wes and Miles aren't there to give me an excuse to crash it. I don't have a reason to spend the night on their couch now, though.

Wes has really blossomed living alone. I don't think either of us realized how much he needed that time by himself and the control over his surroundings that he wasn't able to maintain in a house with five roommates. I'm invited to stay over as often as I want, which usually ends up being about two nights a week during the basketball season, and maybe an extra night in the offseason. As much as we both admit to sleeping better beside one another, I don't want to be the kind of person who abandons her friends because she has a boyfriend, and we both need some time to ourselves to rest and recharge.

I don't know what's going to happen to us. I don't know what our future holds. I can't be concerned about what happens to us after he's done with grad school or when I finish college or anything after that. All I really know is that I really like what's happening now. Sometimes, that has to be enough, and for me, for us, it is.

afterword

Thank you for reading *Fumble*. This book is my baby and I absolutely love it to pieces.

You know what would make it even better? A review! Reviews are more important than readers realize. If you liked this book, please leave me a review!

Wes and Mackenzie's extended epilogue can be read here.

Join my newsletter to stay in the loop! Lots of unfunny quips, unsuccessful attempts at wit, and general grouching about the writing process.

xoxo,

Allie

about the author

Allie is a queer and AuDHD writer with a hyper-fixation on inclusivity and representation. She loves the color purple, Michigan football, and the Boston Bruins. When she's not absorbed by a book, she likes to spend time with her nephews.

Born and raised in Southern California, she now calls South Carolina home. She is allergic to the cold, rain, snow, and mosquitos.

also by allie lasky

Want to see how it all started? Read THE GAME PLAN to meet sweet cinnamon roll football player Miles and the feisty sorority girl who stole his heart.

———

The story continues with PUMP FAKE, a fake dating romance featuring an enormously overbearing found family, a loud-mouthed football player and his gun-shy swimmer, and an exploration into kink.

———

Meet the Neurospicy Book Club in THE THOUGHT OF YOU: Falling for my Grumpy Roommate, where Johanna finds out she's autistic… because her happy-go-lucky new roomie (and reformed playboy ex-football player) has to tell her.